Born in Glasgow and now a dual UK/US citizen, **T.F. Muir** is the author of the DCI Andy Gilchrist series - the first of which, *Eye For An Eye*, won the Pitlochry Award for the best crime novel by an unpublished writer, and the second, *Hand For A Hand*, continues to garner great reviews.

He is now working on his next Gilchrist novel, another story suffused with dark alleyways, cobbled streets and all things gruesome.

THE
KILLING
MOOD

T. F. MUIR

CONSTABLE

CONSTABLE

First published in Great Britain in 2023 by Constable
This paperback edition published in 2024 by Constable

A CIP catalogue record for this book is available from the British Library.

ISBN: 978-1-40871-869-8

Typeset in Dante MT by Hewer Text UK Ltd, Edinburgh
Printed and bound in Great Britain by by Clays Ltd, Elcograf S.p.A.

Papers used by Constable are from well-managed
forests and other responsible sources.

Constable
An imprint of
Little, Brown Book Group
Carmelite House
50 Victoria Embankment
London EC4Y 0DZ

An Hachette UK Company
www.hachette.co.uk

www.littlebrown.co.uk

For Anna

AUTHOR'S NOTE

First and foremost, this book is a work of fiction. Those readers familiar with St Andrews and the East Neuk may notice that I have taken creative licence with respect to some local geography and history, and with the names of some police forces, which have now changed. Sadly, too, the North Street Police Station has been demolished and a block of flats constructed on the site, but its past proximity to the town centre with its many pubs and restaurants would have been too sorely missed by Gilchrist for me to abandon it. Any resemblance to real persons, living or dead, is unintentional and purely coincidental. Any and all mistakes are mine.

www.frankmuir.com

CHAPTER 1

8.15 p.m., Wednesday, Early December
Fisherman's Cottage, Crail, Fife, Scotland

Rain battered the windows with blasts as hard as hailstones. Outside, the back garden lay as dark as the deepest pit, black enough to force an involuntary shiver down the spine. A good night to stay in, put your feet up, pour yourself a solid half, and watch the telly. At least that's what Detective Chief Inspector Andy Gilchrist was looking forward to on the lead up to Christmas. Which was why he eyed his mobile phone on the dining-room table with hostile suspicion as it vibrated as if coming to life. A lifetime of answering calls had him reaching for it to squint at the screen – ID Jessie.

'Nice of you to phone and wish me goodnight,' he joked.

'Yeah, you wish.'

He fingered the curtain, peered into the black night at rain streaming down the glass in glimmering sheets, and with solemn resignation, said, 'I'm listening.'

'Sorry, Andy. Just in. Suspicious death. Supposed to look like suicide—'

'*Supposed* to? What does that mean?'

'Exactly that. At least, that's what I'm thinking.'

'You're at the scene?'

'Didn't want to disturb you, with all your Christmas shopping still to do. Have you started yet, by the way?'

'Of course not.'

'Right. Anyway, thought I could take care of it myself, but now I'm here, I think I need a second opinion.'

'Where's here?' he said, and listened to her rattle off an address that cast up an image of the outskirts of St Andrews, somewhere on the road to Strathkinness if his memory served him.

'You want me to have someone pick you up?' Jessie said.

'That's kind of you, but I think I can manage.'

'You haven't been drinking, is what I mean. It's absolutely bitter. Black ice and threatening snow. Wouldn't want to invalidate your insurance if anything happened.'

Not like Jessie to be so overprotective, he thought. He eyed his tumbler, its contents golden, two cubes of ice still visible. Who had once told him in a fit of disgusted pique that *whisky's a warm drink*? He couldn't remember. But over the years he'd learned to have a drink any way he liked – white wine with meat, red with chicken, whisky with ice, or like his son, Jack, vodka with anything. Not that any of it mattered, of course. For Gilchrist, the end result was the same – a mellowing of stress, a softening of character, unless that last one for the road tilted the odds, of course.

'I'll be with you in twenty,' he said, and ended the call.

He gulped a mouthful that emptied the glass, then walked to the hallway for his winter jacket and his scarf and car keys.

*　　*　　*

Jessie had been right. The roads were dreadful, sparkling with sheets of ice now the rain had ceased and changed into the tiniest of snowflakes that grew in size as he drove on. He marvelled at Scotland's ability to throw another of nature's elements his way, his car's headlights now little more than two weak beams that reflected flakes that fluttered onto his windscreen like fledglings' feathers. But he kept his speed steady, the sensible side of the limit, and followed the directions on his satnav.

He found the address, a semi-detached stone villa, curtained windows glowing a false welcome, front garden already blanketed in deepening snow. He parked half-on half-off the pavement, behind Jessie's car. No sign of the SOCO van, which told him that she really was in need of a second opinion. Obvious signs of murder, and the Scenes of Crime Officers would be one of the first to call and secure the area. Still, suspicious deaths necessitated forensic examination, so why the delay?

The front entrance was unlocked, and he entered without announcement.

Several doors lay off a darkened hallway brightened only by a single lamp that stood on an antique nest of tables next to an old-fashioned telephone, coiled lead twisted around the table's legs like ageing vine. A door at the far end lay open, from which he thought he caught the sound of whispered conversation. As he neared, he realised it was more sobbing than talking, and without a word he stood in the doorway.

A young woman was seated with her back to him, clearly in distress, facing Detective Sergeant Jessie Janes who caught his eye, shook her head, and signalled for him to enter the room behind him.

He did as instructed, turned, and entered what he took to be the front lounge, only to find it was smaller than expected, and seemed more storeroom than living room. Every shelf and flat surface overflowed with books, magazines, bound paperwork. Newspapers stood in three-foot-high piles, wrapped in string, and formed a pathway of sorts that led to the only furniture in the room, an oversized hand-carved wooden coffee table on which stood a closed laptop surrounded by handwritten notes. Facing the table was a solitary armchair in which sat the upright body of a man, eyes shut, as if he had simply closed the laptop, sat back, and gone to sleep.

Gilchrist slipped on a pair of latex gloves, and set about the task of providing Jessie with that requested second opinion. And as he studied the body, he came to see that she had been right to call him. Not that it was obvious that a murder had been committed. Rather, it was the little things that didn't quite seem to fit – the way the body was propped upright on the armchair, hands neatly placed on the chair's arms as if to prevent them from falling off, eyelids closed, as if pressed shut with care, open-neck linen shirt tucked into belted jeans, turtleneck undershirt, trainers – not slippers – on sock-covered feet spaced apart just so. And it struck him then, that without realising, he'd already determined it to be an unnatural death – everything was just too neat. But were these quantum leaps in logic, prompted by Jessie's concerns?

He took a step back, and looked at the laptop and the mess on the table.

Again, it was the little things that didn't quite add up. A space seemed to have been cleared around an A4 page to the left of the laptop, with the single word *SORRY* handprinted on it. Which looked like no suicide note he'd ever come across. A pen lay across the page, positioned so that it lay parallel to the edge, as if it had been placed there with care. Other than the laptop, paper and pen, the rest of the table seemed like discarded detritus, as if the contents of a file had been tipped onto it. None had fallen to the floor though, which could be the assigned storage area for piled newspapers.

He resisted the urge to open the laptop, and was taken by the sense that it appeared out of place with the rest of the room – twenty-first century meets nineteenth. A careful flick of gloved fingers through the papered mess confirmed no charger, no lead, no mouse, no dongle, which had him thinking that the laptop had been put there for show, and worrying that he was trying to force-fit a crime into the scene. Was that what he was doing?

Back to the body. He leaned closer.

The face belonged to a man in his late forties, early fifties, perhaps? A handsome face, he'd have to say, with short dark hair neatly trimmed, greying around the temples. Square chin recently shaved, skin soft to the touch with no signs of dryness. Closer still to confirm the fragrance of aftershave, perhaps moisturiser. Shirt fresh with an ironed seam down both arms. Cuffs buttoned. Fingernails neat, a tad overlong, he thought, but no signs of ever having been bitten. The hands, too, felt soft, as if they'd never experienced a single day's grafting.

His thoughts were interrupted by Jessie saying, 'Ian Howitt. Forty-one years old. Born and raised in York. Single. Never married. Part-time lecturer in psychology at the uni. St Andrews, that is. Took up the position after the summer break. So he's a newbie.'

'All this from . . .?' Gilchrist said.

5

Jessie nodded behind her. 'Hollie Greenwood-Moy,' she said. 'That's with a hyphen.'

Gilchrist glanced over her shoulder, at the open doorway to the room in which Hollie Greenwood hyphen Moy sat, presumably still sobbing. 'And how does Hollie know all this?'

'She's shagging him. Or he's shagging her. I can never work it out any more. Against all the rules, of course.'

'What rules?'

'She's one of his students.'

Gilchrist mouthed an Aahh.

'Denied it at first. Shagging him. But she called it in. Said she'd an appointment with him to discuss one of his lectures. But when she turned up, he didn't answer the door, so she let herself in, and hey presto. There he was. Sitting like a dummy.'

He looked down at Howitt. 'So how did she know he was dead?'

'Earth to Andy . . . Hello . . .?'

He cleared his throat. 'She didn't touch the body, is what I'm asking. Did she?'

Jessie frowned. 'Apparently not.'

'Apparently?'

'So she said.'

'Was the door locked?'

'What door?'

'The front door. Howitt didn't answer, so she let herself in, you said. Did she have a key? Or was it unlocked?'

Jessie grimaced for a moment, then said, 'Sorry, Andy. *Shit.*'

'Let's go and ask her, shall we?'

She nodded, and walked from the room, somewhat disheartened, he thought.

CHAPTER 2

As they entered the room opposite, Gilchrist was struck by the contrast. No expense seemed to have been spared in this room's furnishings. The air was redolent of flowers and polish, with an underlying scent of having been recently wallpapered. Table lamps brightened ornaments that glowed. Photographs shone. Cornicing ran around the ceiling, and not a crack or rain-stained patch in sight. Paintings that could be masterpieces, for all Gilchrist knew, splashed the walls in blues, reds, yellows, colours that reminded him of the last trip he'd taken to the Caribbean, many years ago now, it seemed. Bold yellow and blue curtains hung from ceiling to floor, in a fabric that was a match for the seating – three sofas and a single armchair – all of which surrounded a glass-covered table that looked as if it had been made from a carved antique travel case.

A young woman, a teenager if he had to guess, sat on the closest sofa, her feet curled beneath her, blonde hair tied in a long ponytail that dangled over one shoulder. The darkest of eyebrows told him her hair was dyed, and the quality of her clothing – fine woollen cardigan, silk collarless blouse, needle-corduroys – that she had money; or at least her family had.

'This is Detective Chief Inspector Gilchrist,' Jessie said to her. 'The boss.'

She looked up at Gilchrist with mascara-run eyes that glistened with tears.

He held out his warrant card, and offered a sad smile. 'Hollie?' he said.

She nodded, and sniffed into a tissue.

'Greenwood-Moy?'

Another nod.

He took the armchair, and leaned forward. 'Are you able to tell me what happened?'

'I'm sorry,' she said, in a soft English voice that hinted of elocution and expensive boarding schools. 'It's such a shock. I never would've . . .' She pressed the tissue to her nose again, squeezed her eyes shut, and shook her head.

He gave her some time to recover, then said, 'You never would've what?'

'Expected it,' she said. 'I never would've expected Ian to have died so young. He was so . . . so energetic, so . . . so full of life. That's what made him such a brilliant lecturer.'

'And can you tell me . . . how long have you known Ian?'

'Since the start of the term.'

'And you and he became . . .?'

Her gaze sliced in a nervous glance at Jessie, then she nodded, as if in defeat. 'We fell in love. As simple as that.'

'How old are you?'

She glared at him, as if angered by the question. 'True love is oblivious to age difference.'

'I'm sure it is,' he said. 'So how old are you?'

'Twenty,' she relented. 'Next January.'

8

'And you said you'd arranged to meet Mr Howitt . . . Ian . . . this evening?'

'Yes.'

'What time?'

'Seven-thirty.'

'So, tell me what happened. Take your time. Talk us through it. Don't miss out a thing.'

She sniffed again, dabbed the tissue at her nose. 'I rang the doorbell—'

'Did you walk here?' he interrupted. 'Get a taxi? Or . . .?'

'Sorry. I got a taxi.'

'Where do you live?'

She told him.

'Carry on,' he said, and focused on her eyes.

She ran her hand over her ponytail, then said, 'I'd ordered a taxi for seven-twenty. It arrived five minutes late. So I got to Ian's just after seven-thirty.'

Gilchrist glanced at Jessie, pleased to see she was scribbling in her notebook – she would look into the taxi firm's call logs, interview the driver. Had he seen anything out of the ordinary? Was tonight the first time he'd driven Hollie – or anyone else, for that matter – to this address?

'I rang the doorbell,' Hollie said. 'And when Ian didn't answer, I let myself in.'

'Was the door unlocked?'

'No.'

Gilchrist said nothing, let silence ask the question.

'I have a key. Ian gave it to me a month or so ago. He trusted me.'

Start of the term would be early September. A month or so ago would put giving her a key close to early November, maybe

9

sooner. Which was a bit quick to be granting someone open access to your home. At least, that's what Gilchrist thought. 'You let yourself in,' he said. 'Then what?'

'I knew right away that something was wrong.'

'Why was that?'

'The silence, I think. Anytime I'd been to Ian's, he always had music on. He loved his music. He was so intellectual in that respect.'

'What type of music?' he asked, just to keep the interview relaxed.

'Modern neoclassical.' She returned his gaze, as if expecting him to ask what modern neoclassical music was. Thankfully he didn't embarrass himself before she said, 'You know, Sebastian Plano, Misha Mishenko, Natasha Nightingale. All the well-known ones.'

He didn't have it in him to admit he'd never heard of them, and gave a vague nod as he cast his gaze around the room, searching for a music stack, or CD player, even a record player – wasn't vinyl back in fashion? – but couldn't find any. Maybe Howitt played music on his phone. That seemed to be the modern way. Back to Hollie.

'And when you didn't hear any music, what did you do?'

'I called out his name, of course.'

'Of course.' A pause. 'Then . . .?'

'I walked through to the kitchen, to see if he was there.'

Gilchrist felt his gaze being pulled to the hallway. Walking from the front door to the kitchen, which he guessed was at the rear of the house, you would have to pass this lounge, and the other . . . storeroom, for want of a better word. 'And did you enter the kitchen?'

'Yes.' She frowned as if puzzled. 'Why wouldn't I?'

'I take it that the door to the . . .' he struggled for the proper word, then said, '. . . the door across the hall, where Ian was found, was closed.'

'Oh, I see. Yes. It was.'

'And to this lounge?'

'No. It was open, but I could see he wasn't in here. He seldom is.'

He nodded. 'Go on.'

'When I couldn't find Ian in the kitchen, I went through to the bedroom.'

Gilchrist caught Jessie giving the tiniest of smirks at that.

'But he wasn't there either. Nor in the other bedroom. Nor the bathroom. I checked my mobile to see if I'd missed a message from him. But I hadn't. I tried calling him, but got his voicemail.' She pressed her hand to her mouth. 'That's when I went through to the front room and . . .' She closed her eyes and her body shivered as tears spilled down her cheeks.

Gilchrist glanced at Jessie, who rolled her eyes in disbelief. He waited for Hollie to recover, before saying, 'I need to ask you only a few more questions. Are you able to continue?'

She nodded, sniffed, brushed a finger under each eye. 'I'll try,' she whispered.

Another roll of Jessie's eyes had Gilchrist giving a slight shake of his head to prevent her from stepping in. She pursed her lips, and returned her attention to her notebook.

'When you called Ian from your mobile,' he said, 'where were you?'

'Back in the kitchen.'

'And when he didn't answer, did you hear his mobile ringing?'

'No,' she said, a tad puzzled.

11

'Does he ever switch his mobile off?'

'No.' Another puzzled frown. 'Why would he?'

'Have it set on vibrate?' he asked, ignoring her question.

'I don't think so.'

A quick glance at Jessie to pass on his unspoken instruction – we need to find that mobile – then, 'Let me back up a touch here. So, Hollie, once you'd exhausted all options, and you couldn't find Ian, and you didn't know where he was, and he wasn't answering his mobile, only then did you try the door to the room opposite. Is that correct?'

'Yes.'

He held her gaze. 'Why?'

'What do you mean?'

'Why leave that door to the last?'

'I'd never been in that room before.'

'Why not?'

'Ian never allowed it.'

'Didn't allow it, or you were never invited to enter?'

She frowned, as if confused, then shrugged. 'Never invited to enter, I suppose.'

'Why?'

'I don't know. I think he just didn't want me to see it.'

'Did you never think to ask why?'

'No.' She flicked her ponytail as if to say it was a silly question. 'I wasn't interested in being shown around his house. I was only interested in being with Ian.'

He gave a tight smile, pleased to see her defiance was helping to push aside her tears. 'So I'd like you to tell me what you did when you opened that door to the room. Step by step, Hollie, please. Take your time. This is important. Start off by standing in the hall.'

She nodded. 'I knocked on the door, and called out his name a couple of times.'

'What did you say?'

'Ian? Ian? Are you there? And when I heard nothing, I turned the handle and pushed the door open, just a little. It was dark. So I called out his name again. He didn't answer, so I opened the door wider, and switched on the light. That's when I . . .' She closed her eyes for a couple of beats. 'That's when I saw Ian sitting there. It was so unnatural. He was so still that I knew right away he was dead. So I switched off the light, pulled the door shut, and called the police.' She looked at him then, and jerked a quick smile. 'And here we are.'

Here we are indeed. So many flaws in her account that he wondered if he just plucked at one, then her whole story might come apart at the seams. But not now. Later.

He pushed himself to his feet, a sign that he had no more questions – for the moment, anyway. 'We'll need a written statement from you. And a sample of your DNA.'

'My DNA? Why?'

Jessie said, 'Standard protocol.'

'How long will that take?'

'Not long.' Jessie again. 'Forensics should be here any minute.'

Gilchrist said, 'And while you're waiting, you might as well make a start on that statement.'

Hollie nodded. Gone was the pained disbelief of moments earlier, and in its place recovered defiance. She wasn't being fully truthful, he knew. She was hiding something. But what, he couldn't tell. Not at that moment. But he'd make a point of getting it out of her, sooner, rather than later.

CHAPTER 3

By midnight, Howitt's body had been removed to the Bell Street Mortuary in Dundee, accompanied by Sam Kim, the youthful and somewhat over-enthusiastic forensic pathologist who'd been appointed as the intended temporary replacement for Rebecca Cooper. Although with Cooper having been out of sight and sound for four months now, temporary was looking to become more permanent. Gilchrist was still undecided as to whether he missed the cut and thrust of his and Cooper's relationship, or just relieved to interact with an energetic new face, and a mind as quick and sharp as his own.

He was seated in Howitt's kitchen, reading Hollie's statement, when Jessie burst in and said, 'Andy. You've got to see this.'

He followed her through to the front room in which Howitt's body had been found, surprised to see an opening in the far wall – not a door *per se*, but what looked like a false bookshelf that had been pulled open to reveal a cupboard of sorts. Or so he thought.

Colin, the lead SOCO, wearing full forensic attire, stood at the entrance. 'Couldn't figure out why this room seemed so out of proportion with the rest of the house,' he said, 'until I found this.' He stood back to let Gilchrist enter.

The first thought that hit him was that it was some kind of secret den, a place that a devious man might have in which to keep his real persona hidden from others. Some ten feet wide by twelve feet long, the room contained little more than a desk with drawers at one end, and a wall at the other, which was taken up with what looked like a projector screen rolled down from the ceiling. A magnifying mirror stood on the desk at one corner, and a few cables lay abandoned across the desk, their USB connections telling him that Howitt must have set up his laptop, or some other computer, in here. Maybe this was where he came to search the internet for porn in secret. But if he lived alone, what was the point of secrecy?

He opened one of the drawers, and frowned at the contents. 'What's this?' he said, lifting out what looked like someone's furry scalp.

'A wig,' Colin said. 'One of many. Check the drawers below.'

Gilchrist did, touching none of the contents, one drawer at a time, noting numerous mascaras, foundation compacts, blusher brushes, beauty accessories a woman might use to make herself more attractive, and came to understand the reason for the magnifying mirror. He closed the drawers, reached for a switch on the wall, and turned it. The room dimmed. A glance overhead confirmed two rows of spotlights inset into the ceiling. He brightened the room again, and looked first at Jessie, then Colin. 'What is this place?'

Colin gave a knowing smile, pressed a remote fob that Gilchrist hadn't noticed, and turned his attention to the back wall. Gilchrist frowned as the screen came alive to a blank wall, then shifted with an audible click to an image of the inside of a room with a window through which a still-life mountain scene formed a snow-covered backdrop.

'What is it?' he said. 'A photograph?'

'One of many.' Colin clicked the fob again.

The screen changed to another image, another room, this time of a patio window with a vibrant green backdrop and blue sea in the distance. A cloudless sky gave the impression that he was looking out of some Caribbean hotel window, a first-class hotel at that.

Another click, and the scene changed to a panorama of sun-parched walls and red-tiled rooftops, reminding Gilchrist of a photograph he'd once seen as a young boy, of a resort in Yugoslavia before the country was hacked to independent pieces by the Yugoslav wars. He walked to the desk, took a long look at the screen, then sat on the swivel chair with his back to it. 'So,' he said, 'if you're sitting here with your laptop on, and you're on FaceTime or Zoom or whatever other digital channel you choose, the person you're talking to sees you sitting in front of whatever background you want.' He swivelled the chair around so that he faced Colin and Jessie. 'Right?'

Colin nodded. 'And the image is positioned far enough back from the screen that the person you're talking to sees it slightly out of focus.'

'Meaning that you can't tell if it's real or not?'

'Precisely. And it's more likely to fool someone than the fake backgrounds you get on Zoom.' Colin clicked the fob again, and the sand-coloured expanse of a mesa and butte desert swamped the room, the image so clear, so close, that Gilchrist felt he could step through the wall into the American southwest.

Jessie said, 'The sneaky bastard. He chats up whoever he likes, wearing his wig of the day, pretending to be someone he's not.' She glanced at the screen. 'And some*where* he's not. See that? It doesn't have to be perfect. It just needs to be a scene that someone sees over his shoulder in the background.' Then she stared hard at Gilchrist, and a shadow of anger seemed to settle behind her eyes. 'Are you thinking what I'm thinking?'

He wasn't sure what Jessie was thinking, but his own thoughts shifted to the tearful Hollie Greenwood-Moy. Howitt had trusted her enough to give her a key to his home. But how well did she know him? Well enough to know about this secret den, even though she denied that? Well enough to know of his mysterious side, that darker persona of his that he preferred to keep hidden? Somehow the manner in which she'd expressed her grief told him she couldn't have known. But again, you never could tell. Or perhaps he should be asking how well did Howitt know Hollie? After all, they'd been having an affair for only a couple of months or so.

He faced Jessie, and said, 'What are you thinking?'

'That he uses this place to trick women. He gets them on FaceTime, pretends he's living the high-life. Swiss Alps here, Caribbean islands there, a drive in the desert over there.' She paused, as if out of breath, then said, 'He's a romance scammer. I'd put my savings on it, if I had any.'

Gilchrist tilted his head, not fully convinced. 'Keep going.'

'Think about it,' she said. 'You're stuck in a dingy flat in downtown Glasgow or wherever, and it's pissing outside for ten months of the year, and along comes a rich sugar daddy, offering sights like these and the promise of a good time in the sun. For half the folk in Glasgow, that would be a difficult thing to resist. Knickers to the wind, and all that.' She faced the back wall. 'Look at that. Jeez, I could strip off right now for a chance at that.'

Gilchrist grimaced, not sure of Jessie's line of thinking. But he had to agree there was something uniquely disturbing about the room. He shook his head as his rationale found fault with the present circumstances. 'But he didn't have to use this room to entrap Hollie, did he? She's one of his students. He wouldn't have to talk to her in some faked setting like these. She'd see right through it, would she not?'

'Hollie would, yeah, but I bet if he FaceTimed someone out of town, someone who wasn't one of his students, they'd fall for it.'

'How would he know who to phone? How would he get their number?'

'Duh, Andy. This is the age of social media where folk are posting intimate details of themselves all over the place. The internet's overloaded with dating sites. You can find any number of women just gagging to meet someone from an exotic part of the world, or some rich punter willing to take them on an all-expenses-paid trip to some sun-soaked beach on some paradise island.' She snorted. 'If I wasn't so cynical, I could fall for it myself.'

Gilchrist pushed the chair back, and stood. He wasn't sold on that theory, although he had to admit it sounded plausible, and was worth looking into. He would instruct the IT team to carry out a forensic examination of Howitt's laptop, see what they came up with. Maybe they would find something to strengthen Jessie's theory. Which was all good and well. But first, they would need to establish cause of death, which with the discovery of the secret den, had Howitt's death by suicide even less likely.

And Hollie Greenwood hyphen Moy was not telling the truth, the whole truth and nothing but the truth. She was hiding something, he was sure of that. He would have Jessie set up another interview with her in the morning.

CHAPTER 4

10.20 a.m., Thursday morning
North Street Police Office, St Andrews

Gilchrist pushed back from his desk, squeezed the bridge of his nose to try to clear the tiredness from his thoughts. He'd driven to the Office in early-morning winter darkness, rain-laden winds whipping in from the sea. Now, the skies shone a brilliant blue, as if the morning storm had never existed, which brought to mind Billy Connolly's joke about the weather in Scotland – *if you don't like it, wait twenty minutes*. For all anyone knew, it could be snowing again by midday.

A glance at his watch had him picking up the phone. Hollie Greenwood-Moy had been instructed by Jessie to be at the Office for ten o'clock for further questioning. But she hadn't turned up.

'Any news?' he said to Jessie.

'Not yet. And she's not answering her mobile. Want me to knock her up? She rents a place in Queen's Gardens. It's a five-minute walk.'

'Give her to half past. In the meantime, any luck with Howitt's mobile?'

'Not a squeak. Not showing up anywhere. No pings on any masts. Wherever it is, it's stone dead. I'm betting the SIM card's been destroyed. Which makes this a defo for murder.'

'How about his laptop?'

'Haven't heard back from the techies yet—'

'Well chase them up, for crying out,' he said, louder than intended. 'Then get hold of Hollie, and drag her down here by her ears if you have to. And get onto the taxi firm to check her story. If she thinks she's having a laugh, she's got another think coming, damn it.' He waited for Jessie to leave his office, then took a couple of deep breaths. The beginning of any murder investigation was always critical, those early hours of discovery being the most important. Not always the case, but the longer the investigation stalled, the more difficult it became, and he was now eager to start that ball rolling, find something to focus on.

Just then, his desk computer beeped.

He returned to his seat, clicked the mouse; an email from Sam Kim with the subject heading – *Draft PM Report*. Well, at least that was a start, and good to see that she gave his instructions top priority. He scanned through the email for a quick preview, eager to see cause of death. And there it was – *suspected drug overdose*. He read on, and felt a frown crease his head when he read *twin burn marks on the upper torso, beneath the nape of the neck, consistent with having been tasered*. So, Howitt had been overpowered by taser, the burn marks to the back of the neck suggesting he'd been taken by surprise.

Gilchrist gave that some thought, then printed the report and read through it, taking more care this time. The cause of death

21

was as he'd expected, he supposed, but how had the drugs been administered – orally, or otherwise? They'd found no evidence of Howitt's having taken pills – no empty bottles – and with no track marks on his arms, Gilchrist was intrigued as to how the murder had been committed.

He found what he was looking for, confirmation of an injection site in the upper right biceps, which told him that Ian Howitt, forty-one-year-old newbie psychology lecturer at St Andrews University, had not committed suicide, but been murdered. At that moment, his phone rang, and he reached for it.

'Are you busy, sir?'

He smiled at Detective Constable Mhairi McBride's question. If he was in his office, he would no doubt be busy, and particularly at the start of a murder investigation. But Mhairi always afforded him the deference his position commanded. 'I'm listening,' he said.

'I think you need to see this, sir. Jackie's found something that I'm sure will impact the investigation, sir.'

Jackie Canning, researcher extraordinaire, had become Gilchrist's indispensable asset in any investigation, and a critical member of his team. Intrigued as to what she'd found, he said, 'I'm on my way, Mhairi.'

He found Jackie at her computer, crutches propped against the wall in the corner, Mhairi by her side, both focused on some image on the screen. A printer churned out pages with electronic regularity. Mhairi stepped back to let him stand beside Jackie and have an uninhibited view of the screen.

He frowned as he leaned closer. 'What're we looking at?'

Jackie, whose stutter was so bad she'd more or less given up speaking, clicked the mouse. The screen flickered as she backed through the website, to land at what he took to be the homepage.

A photograph of a beautiful young woman with dark eyes, large and round, which reminded him of his daughter, Maureen, smiled back at him. Hair glistened. Teeth sparkled. The image faded for a moment, to be replaced by that of a young man, every bit as fresh and lively as the woman. Love heart symbols headed short menus.

'A dating website?'

Jackie said, 'Uh-huh,' and clicked the mouse. The screen shifted to a collage of small photographs, all of which, he noticed, were headshots of men. The cursor shifted to one of the images, and with another click a face filled the screen.

'That's Howitt,' Gilchrist said, except that it wasn't the same Howitt who now lay on Sam Kim's post-mortem table, but a younger, fresher, more vibrant-looking Howitt, whose features had been air-brushed to take years and weight off him, give him a set of the whitest teeth. Another click, and a short bio of a man purporting to be Spencer Ames, popped up below the photo – no mention of Ian Howitt or of being a psychology lecturer at St Andrews University, but rather of Spencer Ames, a venture capitalist specialising in forward-thinking technology startups and emerging computer companies. Back to the headshot, and Gilchrist thought he recognised the background as the Caribbean setting in Howitt's secret room which, now he thought about it, could instead be somewhere on the Californian coast.

The screen shifted again to show a short statement – *Spence is looking for a long-term relationship with a financially independent woman in her late-thirties, early-forties. Must like long walks, candlelight dining, fine wine, and theater.* Gilchrist noticed the American

23

spelling and realised that in today's digital social media world, physical distance was no barrier. Any man could find the woman of his dreams, with the simplest click of a computer mouse.

But digital contact could take a prospective lover only so far. There had to come a time when a face-to-face was inevitable. Then the game would be up; no rich and handsome venture capitalist with long walks to take, or pre-theatre candlelit dinners with fine wines by the bottle-load, but a mundane university lecturer on a basic salary. So, what was the point of all this? Why would Howitt go to the trouble of setting up a fake dating site account, which was bound to lead no farther than the computer screen? And if it was all falsified information, why post a photograph of himself, albeit airbrushed to within an inch? Maybe because he knew no meetings would ever take place? That might work. But still . . .

Gilchrist read through the short statement again, his eyes finally settling on the words *financially independent*, which told him what he needed to know about Howitt's intentions. 'Any thoughts?' he said to Mhairi, more to test his own theory than to seek her advice.

'Jackie's got a copy of one of Howitt's bank accounts,' she said.

'*One* of his bank accounts? How many does he have?'

'Four with RBS, sir, and two with HSBC. All in the name of Ian Howitt. He had another two with the Bank of Scotland, but he's closed these down.'

'Do you know why?'

'No, sir, but if you look at one of his HSBC accounts—' She reached for a small pile of stapled papers, and handed the top two pages to him. 'This one, sir. I've highlighted a number of significant deposits.'

Gilchrist eyed the highlighted numbers, and found himself whistling at the amounts. 'Thirty-five thousand,' he said. 'Then two days later, another fifteen thousand plus. The following week, another eighteen? And so it goes on.'

'Yes, sir. In the space of forty-five working days, a total of just under two hundred thousand pounds was deposited into that account.'

'And the bank didn't raise any concerns?'

'Not that we're aware of, sir, but I'll look into that.'

Gilchrist turned his attention back to the computer screen and the airbrushed image of Howitt. 'Well done, Jackie.'

'Uh-huh.' She smiled, and her head of rust-curly hair wobbled.

'So,' he said to her, 'did you find any bank accounts in the name of Spencer Ames?'

She opened her mouth, as if an idea had come to her, then shook her head. 'Nuh-uh.'

He peered at the screen, his mind thinking back to the secret room and the background images that appeared on the wall with the click of a fob. The panoramic mesa and buttes that placed Howitt in the southwestern states; the American spelling on the short statement; the Caribbean island or, now he thought about it, the Californian coast; the closing down of the Bank of Scotland accounts. He puzzled at the outcome of his own logic, a major leap in his deductive reasoning. It could be worth giving it a shot, a longshot at that. But the problem with longshots was that they were often man-hour intensive, which always caused bean-counters' hackles to rise.

He pulled himself upright, decision made. 'Find out what you can on this Ian Howitt,' he said to Mhairi. 'Where was he employed before St Andrews? How did he earn an income, and

25

how much? Who is he? Why is he here? Does he have any friends or family? And check those closed Bank of Scotland accounts. Did the HSBC deposits originate from them? And if so, where did these funds come from?'

'Yes, sir.'

He placed a hand on Jackie's shoulder, gave a gentle squeeze. 'I know you're busy, Jackie, but if you've got some time, do you think you could find out if Spencer Ames has any bank accounts in the USA?' She looked up at him, and he winked her a smile, then nodded to the screen. 'I think this profile is set up to target Americans.' And even as he said it, he thought it such a longshot that he almost took it back.

But Jackie's hair wobbled, and she said, 'Uh-huh,' while her fingers flickered over the keyboard like a jazz pianist, and the screen shifted to a waterfall of website links that flowed like a torrent of words before his eyes, too fast for him to read.

'Again, well done both of you.' He faced Mhairi. 'Let me know what you come up with as soon as you can,' he said, and left the room.

CHAPTER 5

Gilchrist stepped outside. The Office heating was often set too high for his liking, and it felt good breathing in ice-cold air. Two construction vehicles eased down North Street, and he pressed his mobile to his ear to drown out the noise. 'Where are you?' he asked Jessie.

'Trying to talk to that bitch, Hollie Greenwood bloody hyphen Moy.'

'Problems?'

'She's done a runner, Andy. Well, that's what I think, although her flatmate says she told her she was going to visit a friend.'

'Why would she do a runner?'

'Because she knows more than she's letting on?'

'And why doesn't she answer her mobile?'

'That's what I asked, but her flatmate said she does that sometimes, just goes into herself, disappears for a day or two, then reappears as if nothing's happened.'

'Does her flatmate know about Howitt?'

'Says she knew she was dating someone, staying out all night now and again, but never told her who he was or where she was staying. She kept that to herself.'

'Well, he was her lecturer after all. Not something she would want to spread.'

'Nor would he, for that matter.'

Gilchrist gritted his teeth. He wondered why Hollie would ignore a police request, and do a quote unquote runner instead, and said, 'Who's Hollie's friend?'

'Oh you're never going to believe this, but it's another bloody hyphen. I mean, what is it with these English plonkers? And what happens when two bloody hyphens marry each other? Do they become bloody hyphen bloody hyphen?' She chuckled at that, which pulled a smile to Gilchrist's face. 'There's got to be a joke in there somewhere,' she said. 'I'll run that past Robert. But I'm on my way to Hollie's friend's, a Mrs Catherine Smythe-Brown. With a bloody hyphen.'

'Where are you now?'

'In the car park at the back of the Office, just about to drive out to hyphen Brown's.'

'Perfect,' he said. 'I'll be with you in ten seconds. We'll take my car.'

The drive to Invereden Cottage, on the outskirts of Cupar, took twenty minutes. When Gilchrist pulled his BMW into the drive-way, Jessie cursed under her breath. 'They call this a cottage? Bloody hell, if this is a cottage, I wouldn't mind living in their garden shed.'

Gilchrist had to agree as he eyed the three-storey mansion. Windows on the roof suggested a snooker room had been constructed in the attic space. Everything about the place looked as if money had been thrown at it. Christmas was three weeks away, but the lawn still sported the tell-tale lines of having been mowed. Or maybe it had been scarified. Who knew? Certainly not Gilchrist, who drew to a halt behind a silver Jaguar XF, paintwork sparkling showroom-new, parked in front of the main entrance. A set of four concrete steps led up to a pillared entrance vestibule, flanked by two growling lions' heads.

Their shoes crunched on the gravel.

'Nice view,' Jessie said.

Off to the side, fields rose and fell like stilled ocean swell to a line of pine trees in the distance where a small herd of beatnik-haired Highland cattle grazed, horns like stripped antlers in the late-morning sun. Gilchrist pressed the doorbell. Chimes echoed from deep within, and a few minutes later a shadow manifested through the frosted glass panels.

'Here comes the butler,' Jessie said. 'Can you believe it?'

The door cracked open, and Gilchrist suppressed a smile as an elderly man in a suit, collar and tie, said, 'Yes?' the word drawn out to three syllables at least.

Jessie held her warrant card out. 'We're with Fife Constabulary. Is she in?'

'I'm presuming you mean Ms Greenwood-Moy?'

'Got it in one. Where is she?'

'She's upset, I'm afraid to say. She's not keeping well.'

'She'll be more upset if she doesn't present herself to us promptly.'

The man stilled for several seconds, as if deciding whether to comply with country gentleman manners, or slam the door in her face like the master of the house. Wisely, he chose the former, and with the tiniest of nods, said, 'Wait here, please,' and eased the door closed with a gentle click.

Gilchrist grimaced. 'You ever think of applying for a job in the diplomatic service?'

29

'Don't think I'd be any good at it.'

'Noted.'

Jessie peered through the frosted panels. 'Do you think he's expecting us to follow?'

'Shouldn't think so. Which is why he closed the door.'

She clasped her hands together and blew into them. He hadn't noticed the cold, but an icy wind seem to flow from the fields and fleece the air with frigid fingers. 'Tell you what,' she said. 'I'm not fooling about. He'd better come back with bloody hyphen Moy soon, or we're going in.'

'Patience is a virtue.'

'Aye, so they say.' She scrunched her eyes, peered through the panels again. 'I see some movement. Hang on. Here they come, I think.'

The door opened, and the elderly gentleman said, 'Hollie says she's happy to meet with you.'

'She doesn't have a say in the matter. Where is she?'

'She's in the drawing room,' he said, and stood to the side as Jessie swept past.

Gilchrist followed, aware of the click of the door closing and the soft footfall that followed him. He entered an expansive high-ceilinged room with ornate cornicing above all four walls, and what looked like a circle of plaster-cast roses on the ceiling from which hung a set of lights as large as a chandelier. The air carried a hint of cigar smoke that teased his senses and had him patting his pockets for a cigarette. Now, when had he last done that? He thought Hollie looked small and defeated, huddled on a sofa by the window, legs curled beneath her.

Jessie approached her like a Rottweiler to raw meat. 'Right you,' she said. 'What do you think you're playing at?'

'I'm not feeling well.'

'I don't give a monkey's how you're feeling.' She held out her thumb and forefinger and squeezed them together. 'You're this far away from being charged with obstructing a murder investigation.'

Hollie gasped, pressed her hand to her mouth. 'Murder?' she whispered. 'I thought . . . I thought . . . it was suicide.'

Gilchrist said, 'Why did you think that?'

'The note.'

'The one by his laptop?'

'Yes.'

'I thought you didn't enter the room.' He watched her eyes dance left and right, as if searching for some way out of a trap. 'That's what you wrote in your statement, did you not? After switching the light on, you closed the door and called the police. Your own words.'

'I'm sorry,' she whispered. 'I wasn't truthful.'

Jessie said, 'Anything else you've lied about?'

'Not really.'

'And what does *not really* mean?'

'There's no need to be so aggressive,' the elderly man said, frowning at Jessie, then shifting a worried look to Hollie. 'Perhaps I can get you another Panadol, dear.'

Hollie shook her head.

'Why don't the pair of you take a seat for now?' he said to Gilchrist. 'While I put the kettle on.'

Not that he was waiting for an answer, for he turned on his heels and left the room, rather sprightly for someone his age, Gilchrist thought. He held out his hand to Jessie, an indication that she should sit, then took the sofa closest to him.

'Whose house is this, Hollie?'

'Uncle Paul's.'

'And I take it he's your uncle?' he said, nodding after the parting figure.

'Yes.'

'Your father's brother, or your mother's?'

'Mummy's older brother.'

'And he married your Aunt Catherine?' he asked.

She didn't seem to notice that he knew the name of her aunt, and said, 'She passed away when I was young. I never met her. I've only ever known Uncle Paul.'

He caught Jessie twitching, eager to challenge Hollie on yet one more lie. 'Any cousins?' he asked, more to keep Jessie out of it, than anything else.

'In England, yes, but not up here. Uncle Paul lives alone, and has done for as long as I've known him.'

Niceties over, Gilchrist lowered his tone. 'You know, Hollie, you could've landed yourself in a lot of trouble by ignoring your meeting with Detective Sergeant Janes.'

Jessie tutted, and Gilchrist gave her a frown that said – I'll take it from here.

Hollie pursed her lips, and nodded. 'I'm sorry. I . . . I just can't believe it. And now you think Ian's been murdered? Who would do such a thing?' She closed her eyes, hands pressed to her mouth. Tears spilled down her cheeks.

Gilchrist leaned forward, waited until he felt she'd recovered, then said, 'That's what we're trying to find out, Hollie. And this is where you might be able to help us. Do you know of anyone who could've had a grudge against Ian?'

She sniffed, shook her head.

'Anyone at the university, perhaps?'

'No.' She sniffed, dabbed a hand at her eyes. 'I couldn't imagine anyone not liking Ian. He was so popular. And such a brilliant lecturer.'

'I don't mean to pry into your personal relationship with Ian, but did you and he ever go out together? Someone might have seen you, and been upset by Ian . . .' He struggled for the correct word. 'By Ian being seen with someone so much younger.'

'We didn't go out much. Not really. We'd sometimes have a coffee at the uni, just the two of us. But there was nothing unusual about a student meeting her lecturer. Or a group of us would meet up after a lecture, and Ian would sometimes join us.' She ran a hand under her nose, then glanced at the door as if to make sure Uncle Paul was out of earshot. 'Which is why we were so looking forward to Christmas. To have some time by ourselves, together.'

From the kitchen, Gilchrist heard the chink of fine china, and suspected he didn't have long before Uncle Paul came back. 'So you were going on holiday together? Just the two of you?' he said, and watched her nod. 'Anywhere nice?'

'Barbados for four nights. Between Christmas and New Year.'

An image of Howitt's secret room manifested in his mind's eye, with its glamorous backdrops to fool whomever he was speaking to on his laptop. But not Holly. She was here, in St Andrews. But the dating website with an airbrushed Howitt smiling his beguiling smile, assured Gilchrist that Howitt knew how to play the game. He felt he knew the answer, but needed Hollie to say it. 'Ian's Christmas present to you?' he tried.

'No. It's my present to him. He didn't want to accept it, of course,' she said, as if to prove a point. 'But I insisted.'

33

Jessie cleared her throat, and said, 'Must've cost you a few bob, then.'

'I don't know what it cost. Daddy paid for it.'

Well, there he had it. Maybe Howitt was a romance scammer after all. He turned his head at the sound of china cups chinking on a tray, and reclined in his seat as Uncle Paul returned to serve tea.

CHAPTER 6

On the drive back to the Office, Gilchrist and Jessie agreed that Hollie's lying was not compulsive, but perhaps more force of habit. When Jessie challenged her on why she told her flatmate she was staying with her friend, Catherine Smythe-Brown, an aunt who'd died when Hollie had been a child, she'd said, 'That's what I always tell people when I'm going to meet Uncle Paul. In case anyone has any funny ideas.'

Not the clearest of answers, Gilchrist thought, but an answer nonetheless. He left Jessie to get on with contacting the taxi firm, while he checked in with Mhairi for an update.

'I phoned the manager of the Bank of Scotland where Howitt had his accounts,' she said. 'But they deal with large sums of money flowing in and out of hundreds of accounts on a daily basis, so there was nothing unusual to trigger them about Howitt's accounts.'

'Two hundred thousand in a month and a half?' he said, struggling to keep his voice level, his frustration under control. 'And there's nothing unusual about it?'

'The branch is in Aberdeen, sir, and the accounts were set up as business accounts. A lot of oil money flows through the city, and with oil workers flying in and out from all over the world, they're used to dealing in different currencies, too.'

Gilchrist cursed under his breath. Howitt had been smart, setting up business accounts in a branch where high deposits and international currencies might be considered the norm. 'So did his income originate in the States?'

'Yes, sir. The manager was able to confirm that, but when I asked her for a printout of all monthly statements, she said she needed to have that request put in writing on the appropriate letterhead.'

He nodded. Mhairi had managed to extract as much information as she could on the phone, but could take it only so far.

'One other thing, sir. The accounts were closed earlier this year, and funds transferred to Howitt's existing HSBC and RBS accounts which he'd opened in Edinburgh. But the last deposit into one of his Bank of Scotland accounts was over three years ago.'

'Was every deposit into that account US dollar-funded, or did he have some other source of income?'

'I'm not sure, sir. If it was US dollar-funded, the currency exchange would have been carried out at the American end.'

'But the bank would have a record of which exchange facility that money came from, surely.'

'I think so, sir. Would you like me to chase that up?'

Gilchrist grimaced. In the end, it all came down to time and money, but nowadays, most definitely money. What difference would it make to his investigation if the funds were proven to have come from the States? What they now had was sufficient to convince him that Howitt was someone who used women, tricked them out of their hard-earned savings for his own financial needs. He needed to focus his full attention on finding Howitt's killer.

'No, Mhairi, let's stay in the present. Those bank accounts are in the past.' An idea sprung to mind then, which he thought might round it off for him. 'Get Jackie to find out when the Spencer Ames website was last used. If it coincides with the closing of the Bank of Scotland accounts, I think it'd be safe to say that Howitt decided to concentrate his efforts elsewhere.'

'I've already done that, sir, and the dates coincide.'

He returned Mhairi's gaze, pleased to see she worked off her own initiative.

'And another thing, sir, something that's troubled me.'

'I'm listening.'

'I think the Spencer Ames website was Howitt practising.'

'What do you mean?'

'If he is a romance scammer, then I think he was learning his tradecraft, sir. Jackie's confirmed that the website was set up over six years ago, and was active for four years before being abandoned.'

'Is that unusual?'

'Not really, sir. But I think if I was going to be a romance scammer, I wouldn't want to put my own photograph on the website, for obvious reasons.'

'So why do you think Howitt did that?'

'I think that's when he started this whole romance scamming thing. Maybe he didn't realise at the time that there was money to be made at it. Maybe he started out as a genuine single—'

'As a Silicon Valley entrepreneur? I don't think so.'

'Again, sir, maybe he started off innocently, then changed. Which I think explains the personal photograph, sir.'

Gilchrist nodded at the truth in Mhairi's words. Putting a photo of himself out there for everyone to see might have been a beginner's mistake. 'But if he's now learned his craft, as you say, why keep his photograph out there?'

'Maybe he couldn't delete it completely, sir. The internet has a way of keeping all sorts of stuff accessible forever, it seems. Once it's posted, it's often impossible to un-post it.'

He nodded. How often had he come across some interesting newsfeed or link only to find out that it's old news, and not just days, sometimes months, even years. 'Okay, Mhairi, tell Jackie to stop searching for US bank accounts in Spencer Ames's name, and focus on trying to uncover any other pseudonyms Howitt might have used. Meanwhile, I need you to focus on searching his background. Find out who he was, and what he did before he came to St Andrews. It might give us a clue as to some new ID he's used.'

'Will do, sir.'

Jessie rapped the door of the taxi firm's control centre, one of the rare few, as it turned out, which didn't have staff working from home. The office was little more than a wooden table and chair in a cramped room that crackled with the background interference of radio chatter. The only colour came from walls covered in posters showing wave-fringed beaches, palm-fronded gardens, smooth-as-silk infinity pools, and a hammock or two in which to drink ice-chilled beer over the whitest of sands.

'I spoke to you earlier,' Jessie said, holding out her warrant card.

The controller, a woman young enough to be Jessie's daughter, God forbid, with blonde hair that could do with conditioning or preferably a shearing, and a middle parting of black roots, lifted a tattooed hand with raised finger in a *with you in a second* gesture.

Thirty seconds later, she pulled her headset off.

'Pande-bloody-monium in here at times.' She handed Jessie a pile of paper. 'Here's the records you asked for.'

Jessie glanced at the copies of last night's order book, nothing more than handwritten scribbles that were barely decipherable, almost illegible. She scanned through them for the time she was looking for, found it, and said, 'Who's JC?'

'Jimmy Chalmers. The driver.'

'Is he around?'

'Won't be in until later this afternoon.'

'Got a number for him?'

'We're not allowed to give that out.'

'Don't fanny about. What is it?'

She held up her hand again while she answered another call, then passed it on to some driver in a crackling flurry of jokes and backchat which Jessie struggled to catch through the static. Call done, blondie opened a dog-eared diary of sorts, found the page she was looking for, then handed it to Jessie.

'You didn't get that from me, okay?'

Jessie took a note of the number, then walked outside. The skies had clouded over, and a wind that threatened to chill to the bone shimmered along the street. Jimmy must have been waiting for some work, for he answered the call on the first ring with, 'JC. Hey, what's new?' with just the tiniest of hints of an American accent.

Jessie introduced herself, and said, 'Need to ask you a few questions about a hire you picked up and dropped off last night.'

'Oh, yeah? Sure. Shoot, hen.'

'Queen's Gardens,' she said, then gave him the number. 'Ring a bell?'

'Yeah, sure. Two of them. Students they was.'

'Two of them?'

'Yeah.'

'At seven-twenty?'

'Yeah. Upper-class little madams. Right pissed off they was because I was a few minutes late.'

'So where did you drop the other one off?'

'Dropped them both off at the same address, towards Strathkinness. And I tell you what, when I was that age we never had no money for taxis. Had to walk. But nowadays? Nowadays the kids've got money to throw away. Of course it's all their parents' money. Cost a fortune up here, what with university fees, accommodation, and then they need the dosh to go out and blow it all at the—'

Jessie interrupted with, 'After you dropped them off, did you see where they went?'

'Yeah. They walked up the path like they was the best of mates.'

'To the same address?'

'Yeah.'

Jessie was still not convinced the taxi driver was talking about the same hire, and said, 'Do you remember the exact address?'

'Sure, hen.' He recited it to her.

No doubt about it. Howitt's home. 'Would you recognise them again?' she said.

'No chance, hen. Kids nowadays all look the same. Although, come to think about it, one of them had a tattoo on the back of her leg, which you couldn't help but notice, it being freezing and all. Skirt up to here. Should've been wearing something for the weather. But that's kids for you nowadays. Don't seem to feel the cold.'

'What kind of tattoo?'

'Wasn't really paying attention. Just kind of noticed it. That's all.'

'Was it big? Small? Or what?'

'Kind of not too big, not too small, I think.'

'Bloody hell, did it run from the back of her knee to her heel, or what?'

'No, about halfway, hen. That's all I can tell you.'

On an outside off-chance, Jessie said, 'They didn't mention any names, did they?'

'No. Although I did catch them talking about someone, a . . . hang on, hang on . . . it'll come to me.' A pause, then, 'Polly. That's it. Polly.'

'You mean Hollie?'

'No. Polly. Definitely Polly. I'd bet my wages on it.'

Jessie scribbled the name down before she forgot it, then said, 'Thanks. If you can think of anything else, get back to me on this number, okay?'

'Sure. Nae problem, hen.'

Jessie ended the call, and stared off along the street. What she was going to do to that Hollie Greenwood bloody hyphen Moy when she got her hands on her. She tapped at her mobile, and got through on the second ring.

'Andy,' she said. 'That lying wee bitch is up to her neck in it.'

41

CHAPTER 7

Interview Room Number 1 in the North Street Office was less of a formal setting than the rooms in the Detroit Road Police Station in Glenrothes. A small room with bland walls, four chairs around a low coffee table, and a window set high enough on one wall to prevent passers-by from looking in, it was perfect for interviewing all but the most serious offenders. Besides, it was closer to home, and easier to secure, and Gilchrist had set up an interview that evening for 7 p.m.

Despite Jessie's vehement insistence, Gilchrist had decided not to charge Hollie with perverting the course of justice, or obstructing a criminal investigation, but instead chose to tread softly, and have Hollie come in and be questioned under caution with her Uncle Paul who, it turned out, was a retired solicitor.

Introductions over, and the details of the recording device explained to Hollie and her uncle, Gilchrist opened with, 'Thanks for coming in this evening, Hollie. For the record, you have agreed to be interviewed under caution, and are free to leave anytime you like. Is that clear?'

Hollie nodded.

Jessie said, 'Speak for the record.'

'Yes,' she said.

Gilchrist placed a hand on the table and slid it close to Jessie, a silent signal that he would take it from here. 'So, Hollie,' he said, 'in your earlier statement, you said you arrived at Mr Howitt's by taxi, knocked on the door, and when Mr Howitt didn't answer, you let yourself in with a key he'd given you earlier. Then, after calling out his name and searching the house in vain, you eventually found him dead in a front room. Is that correct?'

'Yes.'

'Is there anything you would like to change in that statement?'

'No.'

Gilchrist eyed Hollie for a moment, then shifted his gaze to her Uncle Paul, hoping he could read from his eyes that he knew she was lying, that she was only digging a deeper hole for herself. He returned to Hollie. 'I'll ask you once again, Hollie. Are you sure?'

'Yes.'

He took a deep breath, held it for a moment, then let it out. 'You never mentioned that you shared the taxi with someone else.'

'You never asked.'

'Bloody hell,' Jessie snapped, and pushed her chair back. 'Are you for real?'

Gilchrist ignored her. 'That's quite an omission, Hollie. That you arrived at Mr Howitt's with someone else.'

'I didn't think it was important.'

Gilchrist held Hollie's fierce look. Gone was the distraught young woman of the night before, and in her place a defiant teenager who believed she'd done nothing wrong, and was here of her own free will and could leave anytime she liked.

As if on cue, she said, 'I think I'd like to leave now.'

'In your dreams,' Jessie said.

Hollie grimaced, and glanced at her uncle who sat with a frown across his forehead as deep as the Mariana Trench. 'I thought I was here by choice,' she said. 'You told me I could leave anytime I liked.'

Jessie chuckled. 'Not any more, Ms Greenwood-Moy.'

Hollie pushed back from the table, as if to stand.

'Step out that door,' Jessie said, 'and I'll arrest you on the spot.'

Gilchrist leaned towards Hollie's uncle. 'I suggest you spend a few minutes with your niece and explain to her the seriousness of her situation, and that if she continues in this manner I'll have no option but to arrest her and charge her with attempting to pervert the course of justice. Not to mention that she's fast becoming the prime suspect in an ongoing murder investigation.'

Not strictly correct, but sometimes you just have to push.

'Interview terminated at seven sixteen.' And with that, he stood and walked from the room, Jessie behind him.

Upstairs, in Gilchrist's office, Jessie said, 'I would've strung that lying wee bitch up by her nipples and slapped it out of her.'

'Metaphorically speaking, I hope.'

'Whatever.'

'I don't know,' he said. 'Somehow I feel sorry for her. She's been duped by an older man, fallen in love, then found him dead.' He didn't want to say that Hollie reminded him of his own daughter, Maureen, who at that age had been vulnerable and deeply hurt after having fallen for the wrong man. Instead, he said, 'Her uncle's representing her, so I'm confident he'll convince her to tell the truth.'

'Oh, aye, the truth the whole truth and nothing but the truth, the lying trollop.'

They spent the next several minutes discussing their interview strategy, until Gilchrist checked the time, and said, 'Shall we?'

When they entered the interview room, Gilchrist knew right away that the mood had changed. Hollie's face was flushed from crying, eyes reddened and glistening with tears, a tissue pressed hard to her nose. She looked defeated, frightened, and diminutive next to her uncle, who gave a firm nod to Gilchrist as he took his seat opposite.

Jessie settled next to him, switched on the recorder, and said, 'Interview commenced again at seven twenty-three, with the same four people present.'

Gilchrist waited until he caught Hollie's eye. 'Are you able to continue, Hollie?'

She sniffed, and nodded her head. Her uncle leaned close to her, whispered in her ear, then she looked at Gilchrist, and said, 'Yes, I am.'

To show her that he was at least one step ahead of her, and knew more than she'd told them earlier, Gilchrist said, 'Why don't you tell me who Polly is?'

'Polly?' Hollie frowned. 'Polly who?'

'The person you shared the taxi ride with.'

'I don't know anyone called Polly.'

Something slumped in his stomach. Had Jimmy Chalmers got it wrong, even though, according to Jessie, he would've bet his wages on it? 'The name, Polly, was mentioned in the taxi,' he said. 'So, who is she?'

Hollie frowned for a long moment, then her eyes widened as if an idea had come to her. 'You mean Débora. Débora Paulet. Not Polly, but Paul-*eh*, emphasis on the second syllable.' She spelled it out, letter by letter. 'She's French. But everyone calls her Debbie.'

Well, if he'd asked for a lesson on French pronunciation, he'd just had one. 'So you shared a taxi with Debbie Paulet,' he said, careful to place the emphasis correctly.

'No. Her sister, Galina.'

'Galina Paulet?'

'Yes. She's French, too.'

'Excuse me,' said Gilchrist, 'but I'm confused. If Galina Paulet was with you in the taxi, why did you mention her sister, Debbie?'

'Because that's why Galina was with me. In the taxi. She wanted to challenge Ian about what her sister, Debbie, had picked up on the internet.'

Gilchrist glanced at the recorder to make sure it was on – it was – and tried to still a sense of excitement that stirred in his gut. He could feel Jessie's tension next to him, like heat off rock. He put his hands on the table. 'So what had Debbie picked up on the internet?'

'I don't know. Galina wouldn't tell me.'

'Come on,' Jessie snapped. 'Don't give us any of that pish now.'

'I'm not lying.'

'Aye, sure you're not. You've lied from the moment we met you.'

'Not this time. I'm not lying now. Honest.' She glanced at her uncle, eyes pleading, then back to Gilchrist. 'I'm telling the truth. Galina just wanted to show Ian what her sister had given her. To see how he would react. That's all. But when we found out . . . when we found Ian . . . she just screamed and ran away.'

'Where is she now?'

'I don't know. I haven't spoken to her since.'

'Do you have a mobile number for her?'

She did.

CHAPTER 8

Gilchrist excused himself from the interview, and left Jessie to take it further forward. He returned to his office upstairs, and phoned the number Hollie had given him. When the call was answered, he said, 'Galina Paulet?'

'Who's this speaking, please?'

He caught a hint of a French accent, and said, 'DCI Gilchrist, St Andrews CID.'

The line filled with silence.

'Where are you, Galina?'

'At a friend's.'

'Which is where?'

She told him, an address in St Andrews, near the New Inn as best he could recall.

'I need you to come into the North Street Police Station for an interview.'

'What kind of interview?'

'You shared a taxi with Hollie last night.'

'I didn't do anything.'

'I know you didn't, but I need to talk to you, to corroborate Hollie's statement. Can you come to the Office this evening?'

'I can't. I'm babysitting.'

'Okay,' he said. 'Stay where you are. I'll be with you in ten minutes,' and ended the call before she could object.

When Galina Paulet answered the door, he could tell she'd been crying. She was carrying a small child, bottle to its mouth, rocking it back and forth. He put his warrant card away, and stepped inside.

She led him through to a back room where a log fire blazed, and the TV flickered in muted silence – some channel showing ice-skating. She was wearing a grey woollen sweater two sizes too large for her, with tattered wristbands, and a pair of black jogging pants that had seen better days. Her dark hair, not jet-black, but close, was tied back in a loose bundle.

He sat down, and waited until she'd made herself and the baby comfortable, before asking her the baby's name – Tania – who she was – her flatmate's sister's, who had gone out for dinner with her boyfriend, not her partner, and certainly not the baby's father. It struck him that earlier generations' relationships could never have been as complicated as today's.

Small talk over, and Galina still tense but doing her best to appear relaxed, Gilchrist placed his mobile on the table between them, confirmed she had no objection to his recording their meeting – which he would supplement with note-taking – and said, 'Before we start, can I ask if you have a tattoo on your leg?'

She frowned, then nodded. 'I have one on the back of my left calf. A mountain scene. Mont Blanc in the winter. Why do you ask?'

'It was commented on by a witness.'

'A witness? A witness to what?'

48

'Why don't you settle down, please, and let me ask the questions? That way I'll be out of your hair in no time at all.'

She gave a puzzled look, and ran her fingers through her hair.

He didn't ask her to pull up her jogging pants so he could confirm the tattoo – far too intimate a request to kick off with – but instead spent the next few minutes confirming what she and Hollie had done when they let themselves into Howitt's home. She corroborated Hollie's statement until Hollie opened the door to the spare room and switched on the light.

'I screamed,' she said. 'I could tell right away that Mr Howitt was dead.'

'How could you tell?'

'He looked dead, you know? He didn't move. Even when I screamed.'

Well, he supposed his question deserved a simple answer. 'Did you enter the room? Approach the body?'

'No.' She hung her head, and tears ran down her cheeks. 'I ran away.'

'And left Hollie?'

'Yes.'

'Did Hollie enter the room?'

'I don't know. I never saw. I just left and ran home.'

'Why didn't you call the police, report what you'd seen.'

'I was frightened.'

'Of what?'

She shrugged. 'I didn't know what the police would do to me. Put me in jail like they do to students in France. Or what, I don't know, I was just afraid, you know?'

Gilchrist nodded. A young woman in a foreign country, unfamiliar with the British legal system, might very well be afraid to involve herself with the police. But maybe he could use that to his advantage.

'In this country, Galina, every citizen is innocent until found guilty. But it's important that they tell the truth to the police. *Very* important. And if you lie to the police, you could find yourself in trouble. *Serious* trouble.' He held her gaze. 'Do you understand?'

She pursed her lips and nodded.

'So tell me, Galina, what were you going to show Mr Howitt?'

'A photograph.' With single-handed dexterity, baby in the other, she pulled a mobile phone from the pocket of her joggers, tapped the screen, then held it out to him. 'This one.'

He took it from her, and with thumb and forefinger enlarged the image. It took him a moment to see through the deep tan, blond hair and thick moustache before he realised it was Howitt staring at him, mouth open in the act of speaking. In the background, snow-capped mountains peaked in a bright blue sky, a tad out of focus so you couldn't tell if the scene was live or not. And if you imagined wraparound sunglasses and a ski helmet, he could be looking at any one of a thousand winter tourists or Swiss ski-instructors. He glanced at Galina, but her attention was on the baby. Back to the photo. He reduced the screen, slid it to the left, and another image came into view – same scene, same Howitt, only a moment later, or earlier. Again, to the left, but a different photo – Galina and several others in what looked like one of the local pubs. He searched for more images of Howitt, but couldn't find any.

'Only two?' he asked.

She nodded. 'They're screenshots from my sister's laptop.'

He looked at the image again, enlarged the screenshot, shifted the photo to the edge of the image, searching for anything that might confirm it wasn't Howitt sitting in a hotel room overlooking the Alps, or wherever else he was pretending to be. But after several seconds he had to confess it was as convincing as the real thing.

'Your sister, Debbie, yes? Why did she take these screenshots?'

'Because he was screwing her out of money. Pretending he was someone he wasn't. He said he wanted to treat her to a skiing holiday over Christmas, in the Almhof Schneider resort in Austria. It's one of the most expensive hotels. Fifteen hundred euros a night. Just two nights he'd said. He pretended that he lived there, in Austria, and was staying in a chalet that had been left to him when his parents died. Which is where he said he was when he FaceTimed Debbie . . .'.

Gilchrist glanced at the backdrop again. He'd never been to Austria, but supposed it could be the view from an Austrian chalet.

'She'd never met him, and only spoken to him online through some dating app. I don't know which one. They were booking the room together. And she was flying out to meet him. All expenses were going to be covered. No costs to Debbie.' She snorted. 'That's what she thought. I don't know all the details. I think Debbie's still too ashamed to tell me. But he stole fifteen thousand euros from her.'

'I'm sorry.' It was all Gilchrist could think of saying.

'I'm sorry, too,' she said. 'But not that he's dead. I don't think he was a nice man. Debbie was so upset, you know? She was so mad at him, she could . . .' She stopped, gave him a look of guilt, then looked down at the baby again.

'She was so mad at him,' he said, 'she could kill him?'

Galina looked up at him, tears in her eyes, but said nothing.

51

'Where's your sister now?'

'In Toulon, south of France.'

He frowned. What he'd just heard put Debbie Paulet in the picture as prime suspect. But not if she was in France. 'Are you sure she's in France?' he said.

'I FaceTimed her this morning to tell her that I never got a chance to . . . how do you say it? . . . to challenge him, that he was dead. So she's definitely at home. In France.'

It wasn't out of the question for her sister to have flown to Scotland, kill Howitt, then return to the south of France in time to take a call from her sister. But why send her sister the screenshots for the purpose of challenging Howitt, if she had already flown to Scotland and killed him? That made no sense. Still . . .

'I'll need to speak to Debbie,' he said.

'Of course. I'll send you her number.'

'I'm old school,' he said. 'I'll write it down.'

She took her mobile back, and with one hand tapped the screen, scrolled through it with her thumb, then read out a number beginning with 0033, which he recognised was the international dialling code for France.

'One last thing,' he said. 'How did your sister know to send you the screenshots? How did she know you knew Howitt?'

'We were talking a few weeks ago, and she was so upset about losing all that money. She showed me a picture of Franz, saying if she ever came across him again she would . . . she was . . . she was so mad.'

'Franz?'

'Franz Wimmer. That's the name he was using.'

Gilchrist jotted it down. If Howitt was scamming women out of thousands of euros, making them mad enough to kill him, then it seemed that Franz Wimmer was as good a place as any to start. He texted the name to Jackie – copied to Jessie and Mhairi – instructing them to jump onto that first thing in the morning, and find out what they could about him.

Rather than drive to his cottage in Crail, Gilchrist thought he would call in on Irene. He'd meant to phone earlier, but the case of the day always seemed to make time speed by. He called from his car, and she answered right away.

'Thought you'd run off and left me,' she said, and gave off that throaty chuckle of hers that always warmed his heart.

'I'm heading to yours for a chat right now, if that's all right.'

'Of course. I'll put the kettle on for a wee cup of tea.'

As he settled down for the short drive, he gave a grim smile of determination. Tea it would have to be. With Irene's chemotherapy under way, they'd agreed to ban alcohol of any kind from her home, rather than try to abstain while it was on full view. So he'd removed her personal stash to his home in Crail, with the promise to return it once she'd recovered, which he worried could be a bit of a longshot – not the returning of her alcohol, but her recovery.

For her cancer had come back, and after witnessing the final undignified days of a friend who'd gone through a brutal course of chemotherapy only to die in the end – a ribcaged skeleton of her former self, too weak to lift a hand, too sick to smile, skin as see-through as tissue paper – Irene had sworn that she would never resort to chemotherapy. But Gilchrist, in that quiet persistent way of his, had convinced her not to give up without a fight. She had so many more memories to create and share with her daughter, Joanne, and so much more to do with her life. Although he loved her too much to lose her so soon after they'd found each other, he didn't want to be the sole reason she fought on.

So he'd focused on her creative side.

'What about exhibiting your photographs?' he'd suggested. 'We could do it through Joanne. She'd love to help.' But even as he spoke, he could see the disinterest in her eyes. So two days later, he purchased a book of photographs by Ansel Adams. Not that Irene needed any advice when it came to shooting landscapes in black and white, rather he hoped it might reinvigorate her enthusiasm for photography in some way, and with it her love of life. 'I thought you'd like to browse through it,' he said. 'Cast your critical eye over some other photographer's work.'

And she had, marvelling at the way Adams captured the essence of the scene with the simplest adjustment of light, a frozen moment in time, caught by the snap of a shutter. He ran his idea through Joanne, who'd jumped at the offer, and together they came up with a theme for publishing her photographs.

With some trepidation, he had to say, he and Joanne confronted Irene over a Saturday dinner – a Thai curry from the local, one of her favourites – and ran their idea past her.

'You don't have to do anything, Mum, just choose which photos you like, and we'll set it up and contact the publishers for you.'

Irene glanced at Gilchrist, as if in doubt.

'The *royal* we,' he said with a chuckle. 'Joanne'll be doing all the contacting.'

At first, Irene resisted. But somehow, setting that goal – find a publisher – lifted her spirits, and with it her desire to live long enough to see it through. When Gilchrist pointed out that her portfolio was large enough to publish more than one book, she finally relented – chemotherapy it would be.

The first week had been awful. Sick to her core every day, all day long it seemed, she told the doctors she would need to come off the course, she'd seen what it could do. But the consultants offered a different chemo, which turned out to be less physically upsetting, and although she lost her hair and over ten kilos in weight, the vomiting stopped, and she began to recover some strength. But more importantly, her cancer was being kept in check . . . so far.

Gilchrist parked on South Street and found Irene in the kitchen, dressing gown on, silk scarf around her head to hide her baldness.

'Something smells nice,' he said, and gave her a peck on the cheek.

'Made you a tuna sandwich.'

'How do you know I haven't already eaten?'

'Well, have you?'

'Of course not.'

She chuckled. 'See? And sliced tomato and jalapeño peppers to give it a nip.' She laid the plate on the breakfast bar, and poured tea into two mugs. 'Joanne came around today,' she said, 'with a rejection from another publisher. She said I could indie-publish, rather than continue to receive rejections.'

'We haven't had responses from all of them yet, have we?'

'Still a few to go. But if they wanted to take me on, they would've come back by now, surely.'

He took a sip of tea, then said, 'It takes time,' and cringed at his hapless choice of words. Time was not something you discussed with a cancer patient. 'But maybe Joanne's right,' he tried. 'Indie-publishing could be the way to go.'

'She started explaining it to me, but I wasn't really taking it in.'

'No need for you to understand anything. You just choose the photos, and Joanne does everything else. No pressure. No hassle. Just the finished product.'

'You make it sound easy.'

'I'm sure it's not, but Joanne's more than competent to sort it all out. She's already talking about a launch in the spring. Something to look forward to.' She seemed saddened by his words, and he pushed his sandwich aside. 'You all right?'

'I don't know. I worry that the two of you are going to all this effort for something I might never see.'

He moved closer to her then, pulled her to him. 'Firstly, there's only one of us going to all this effort, and that's Joanne. Secondly, you're going to kick this illness into the long grass, so you don't have to worry about it being in vain.' He knew from her tired smile that she was putting a face on for him, and he pressed his lips to her scarf-covered head. 'We'll get through this,' he said, and felt her body give an involuntary shiver. 'I know we will.'

She freed herself from him, ran her hand under her eyes. 'It's just . . . I've just had a bad day today.' She jerked a quick smile. 'That's all.'

He could tell she was hiding something from him, but didn't want to press her. She would tell him in her own time, no matter what, good or bad. He just prayed, as he had done for so many nights, that she would recover.

But he didn't have the heart to tell her that he didn't believe in God.

CHAPTER 9

7.15 a.m., Friday morning

Gilchrist parked outside Jessie's home in Canongate, and kept the engine idling while she scurried down the driveway. A burst of cold air as the door opened then crunched shut as she slumped into the passenger seat.

She gave off a loud shiver. 'Bloody hell. I used to like the snow when I was a wee girl. Must've been off my rocker.'

'All kids love the snow.'

'Aye, right.'

'Besides, it's coming up for Christmas. Who knows, we might have a white one.'

'Tell you what. I'd swap any colour of Christmas for a day in the sun.'

He eased out of Canongate onto Largo Road. 'So, good morning to you, too.'

'Morning. First stop, Starbucks.' She scrunched her face, ran her tongue over her teeth. 'Had a leftover curry last night. Good at the time. But ended up having too much wine, and now my mouth tastes like the bottom of a parrot's cage.'

'Don't like the sounds of that.'

'You should try tasting it.'

'No thanks.'

He eased through the West Port roundabout, and accelerated down City Road. 'So, have you found anything on Howitt's laptop?'

'Might as well start off with the bad news. It's been wiped clean.'

'For fingerprints?'

'Very funny.' She shook her head. 'The hard drive's gone, zapped, kaput. According to the IT guys, it's been fried with an electric current, as in, hooked up to some power source and blown.'

Gilchrist grimaced. 'So, the killer makes his way into Howitt's, kills him, then props his body on a chair to make it look like . . . I don't know . . . a natural death? Then leaves the laptop lying face up on the table? Why? Why not remove it completely? Why not take it away and dump it somewhere?'

'Because it's just as easy to fry it?'

'But why? You're not answering the question.'

'Because I don't know the answer.'

Gilchrist tried another tack. 'Is the hard drive recoverable?'

'Who knows? They're going to give it a try, but I wouldn't hold my breath.' She ran her tongue over her teeth again. 'This'll do,' she said, as he pulled up to Starbucks on Market Street. 'The usual?'

'Sure. Take this.' He handed her a tenner. 'You bought the last two.'

'Try the last four.'

'Ouch.'

'Ouch indeed,' she said, and closed the passenger door with a tad more force than he thought necessary. He thought back to the laptop on the table, Howitt's body facing it, as if all he had to do was reach over and tap the screen to bring it to life. If the hard drive had been zapped with a surge of electricity, why was there no evidence of it being burned? Surely there would have been some signs – melted plastic at the edges, signs of blackening – but he'd seen none of that, at least nothing he could remember. And if Howitt's killer had wiped the laptop clean, he – or she – must have come prepared with some transportable power source at the ready. But why? Why go to the bother? And even so, the murder scene seemed too clean, too tidy, too . . . what was the word? Too . . . well planned? Too . . . premeditated? Which, if you thought about it, might put a different light on who they were looking for.

Or maybe it was all much simpler than that, and he was digging for clues that would lead them nowhere, going round in circles chasing their own tails. Still, he would have Jessie follow it up with the IT techies, and see what they could salvage.

The window rapped. He reached across the passenger seat and opened the door. Jessie slid in, coffee in each hand, a paper bag tenuously gripped in one of them.

'Here's yours,' she said. 'A fatty latte.'

He took it from her, pleased to feel it piping hot, while she removed a blueberry muffin from the bag, trying not to spill crumbs, but failing.

'Sorry,' she said, and bit into the muffin.

Between sips, he said, 'What I don't understand is, why buy a skinny latte then stuff your face with a muffin?'

'Less fattening.'

'Wouldn't it be lesser fattening if you just skipped the muffin completely?'

'Wouldn't it be a better idea if you just drove?'

He took another sip, then slipped into gear. Rather than sit his coffee in the holder in the central console, he held it in one hand, steering wheel in the other, and eased along Market Street.

Two minutes later, he parked facing the wall at the back of the Office. Jessie exited with a blast of cold air. 'Got to rush to the loo,' she said. He was about to open the driver's door, when his mobile rang – ID Mhairi.

'Got some information on Franz Wimmer, sir. Jackie did a reverse image search, and Howitt's face appears on a number of dating websites.'

'All as Franz Wimmer?'

'No sir. So far, we've found one other name—'

'Stephen Ames?' Gilchrist tried.

'No, sir, Hans Denz.'

'Dense? Like heavy dense?'

'No, sir. Denz. Like Mercedes Benz, with a D instead of a B.'

'Ah. Got it. Sorry. Carry on.'

'Franz Wimmer crops up more frequently in dating sites. Both have different bios, but the same image of Howitt, although he's disguised, sir.'

'I'm listening.'

'As Franz Wimmer, he's born in Scotland, of Austrian heritage.'

'Scotland?' Gilchrist interrupted. 'Which I suppose would explain the accent when he's on FaceTime.'

'Exactly, sir. Hans Denz, too, claims to have been born in Scotland, but of German heritage.'

'Of course. Keep going.'

'As Franz Wimmer, he's blond and passes himself off as a ski-instructor now living in Austria. As Hans Denz, he's also blond, but with shorter hair and a grey beard, and his bio says he's a retired hedge fund manager, now living in Albuquerque, New Mexico—'

'Let me guess,' Gilchrist cut in again. 'That profile would have mesas and buttes in the background.'

'Exactly, sir.'

Gilchrist grimaced. It was beginning to slot into place, but what *it* was, he couldn't say with any certainty. 'So Howitt pretends to be Scottish-born of foreign parentage, but no longer living in Scotland. In both IDs, he's wealthy enough not to work, particularly Denz, who as a retired hedge fund manager should allegedly have a pension that would choke a horse. So he's using fake wealth and a semi-exotic lifestyle and international heritage to lure women into his trap to be scammed.' He paused for a moment. 'Have you been able to track down any of the women yet?'

'I was coming to that, sir.'

Gilchrist pressed the phone to his ear. 'I'm listening.'

'Most of the women he appears to have corresponded with live overseas.'

'Who are you talking about? Wimmer or Denz?'

'Both of them, sir. Jackie's made up a list of seven women so far, and counting. One lives in Australia, two in America, one in France—'

'Would that be Debbie Paulet?' he said, emphasising the French accent.

'Yes, sir. Another lives in South Africa, and another in Sweden.'

She paused, and Gilchrist said, 'That's six. You said seven.'

'I did, sir, yes. The seventh one lived in Edinburgh, Scotland.'

'I'd say that's a bit too close to Howitt's home for comfort, isn't it? There's always the chance he could bump into her.' Then he realised with a start what Mhairi was trying to tell him. '*Lived?* As in no longer living?'

'Yes, sir.'

'What happened.'

'She committed suicide over a year ago. In July.'

The meaning of Mhairi's words sunk into his gut as the possibility hit home. 'Did she commit suicide after being scammed by Howitt?'

'It looks that way, sir, although we don't have all the details yet. But when her body was found in her home, and the police were called in to investigate a suspicious death, her sister apparently went ballistic, threatening to sue the police for this, that and the other.'

'Why would her sister threaten to sue the police?'

'Because she was a police officer herself. The woman who committed suicide, sir, not the sister, who claimed the police let her sister down.'

'I see.' It was all he could think to say.

'You may have heard of her, sir. DCI Kenzie Dorrance. Lothian and Borders.'

Dorrance sounded familiar, but he couldn't place her. 'So what happened in the end?'

'Nothing, as far as I know, sir. It seemed to settle down after a few months, and no one was sued.'

'Keep digging, Mhairi, and try to track down some of the other women. They might not be able to shed light on Howitt's murder, but they could be worth talking to.'

'Will do, sir.'

'Oh, and do you have a contact number for Dorrance's sister?'

'I do, sir, yes. I'll text that over to you.'

When Mhairi hung up, Gilchrist ran the name Kenzie Dorrance through his mind, but nothing came to him.

CHAPTER 10

It took Jessie until mid-morning before she managed to track down Debbie Paulet in the south of France, and another thirty-plus minutes to arrange a FaceTime call with her.

Gilchrist began by introducing himself and Jessie, holding their warrant cards up to the monitor, then confirming that their call was being recorded. He advised Debbie that she was not being treated as a suspect, and that she could end the call any time she liked.

'Do you understand?' he said.

'Yes. I understand perfectly.'

He thought he detected a hint of Geordie in her accent, and said, 'You speak excellent English.'

'My mother's English, and my father's French. Both Galina and me are bilingual.'

Well, he supposed that explained it. 'I met with your sister, Galina, last night.'

'I know. She told me to expect your call.'

Jessie said, 'Why didn't you contact us then? I've spent half the morning trying to track you down.'

'I'm sorry, I turned my mobile off. I just . . .' She stared at the screen, and Gilchrist caught the sparkle of tears. She ran a finger under each eye, then said, 'It's all so sudden. I can't believe he's dead. It's so . . .' She lowered her gaze and shook her head, and when she next looked up, anger shimmered across her face like rippling shadows. 'Now I'll never be able to confront him, and make him give me my money back.'

Which, when Gilchrist thought about it, was as good a reason as any for Debbie not to kill Howitt. Not until he'd paid her back, of course. He leaned closer to the monitor, intent on keeping Jessie out of the frame. 'Can you tell us what happened, Debbie? How long have you known . . .' He was going to say Howitt, but instead settled for, '. . . Franz Wimmer? How did he manage to convince you who he said he was? Take your time.'

Debbie nodded, and sniffed. 'I'd been going out with someone for three years. We were planning to marry, and then he . . .' She gushed out a breath of despair, then looked hard at the screen, as if some decision had been reached. 'He had an affair with my best friend. I found out about it. We had words. And I ended it.'

The way she spoke gave Gilchrist the impression that Debbie Paulet was a woman who suffered no fools. Which made it harder for him to understand why she'd let herself be scammed. 'How long ago was this?' he said.

'March the sixth. This year.'

Again, decisive. No fooling. 'And when were you first introduced to . . . Franz?'

'August seventeenth.'

So, he thought, less than four months for Howitt not only to gain Debbie's trust but to wheedle his way into her life with sufficient belief to convince her to part with her savings.

Somehow, he couldn't square that outcome with the confident woman he was talking to. 'I take it you and he never met face-to-face?'

'Only through FaceTime. As we're doing now.'

'Keep going, Debbie. Tell us what happened. In your own words.'

She took a deep breath, as if to ready herself, then said, 'He caught me at a time when I was at my most vulnerable. I was . . . I was hurting. I lost my lover, my soulmate, the man I was going to marry. And I lost my girlfriend that I grew up with.' She squeezed her eyes, as if fighting back tears, then gasped, 'I was lonely. I was looking for companionship. I was looking for a friend, not someone to fall in love with, just someone I could talk to, someone who would listen to me, understand how I was feeling, how much I'd been hurt, and maybe someone I could meet from time to time.' She paused to take a breath. 'I can't believe I fell for him. I can't believe I was taken in by all his . . . by all his *lies*. I just can't believe it.'

Gilchrist gave her time to recover, then pressed on. 'Are you able to tell us exactly what happened?'

'Yes.' A firm nod of her head. Back in control of her emotions. 'At first, it was only texting, communicating with messages through the dating website.'

'Which website?'

She told him, and he glanced at Jessie for confirmation – she nodded.

'But when I look back, I see my mistake. I was feeding him my feelings first. I was getting all my hurt off my chest.' Another shake of the head. 'My mistake.'

'In what way, Debbie?'

'Once he knew how I was feeling, and what caused me to feel that way, he simply mirrored me. He said he'd also been hurt at the end of a long relationship, that his fiancée had run off with his business partner, and that he'd had to shut the business down.'

'What type of business?'

'He was a ski-instructor.' She gave off a laugh that rang with bitterness and scorn. 'So he said. Of course, it was all lies.'

'Keep going.'

'Over a few weeks of messaging, we got to know each other a bit better, then he asked if he could FaceTime me?'

'When was this?'

'October twentieth.'

He jotted a note to remind him to ask her why she knew all these dates.

'When I first saw him, I thought he was quite handsome, although he looked older than I imagined. He explained that when he was growing up, he was more mature than the others, that he always seemed old for his age. I liked that. I liked that he was mature.'

Gilchrist pulled back from the monitor and let Jessie lean forward.

'Why didn't you meet him face-to-face?' she said.

A shake of the head. 'He said he would like to meet me, but his work got in the way, and he wasn't sure if he could take time off. He was needed at the resort. He thought he might be able to make a short trip to Paris, but then he said he had a family flying in from Monaco at short notice. Friends of the royal family. He said they'd booked him for their personal instructor for the entire week. All of it was lies. Which was when he suggested I fly out and meet him in his Austrian chalet.'

'Hang on,' Jessie said. 'Your sister said you were going to stay in some posh hotel.'

'Yes. The Almhof Schneider resort.'

'So what happened to the chalet?'

'That was my fault.'

'What d'you mean?'

She sighed. 'Another mistake. I don't know. I suppose my subconscious was telling me it was all happening too fast, my inner self warning me to be careful, that I didn't really know him that well.' She shook her head. 'I told him I didn't want to stay in his chalet. He'd told me it was quite secluded. So I told him I would meet him, but only in a hotel. I was thinking, safety in numbers. You know?'

'And he agreed?'

'Absolutely. Because I realised later, that's what he'd wanted all along.'

'So he could screw you out of money?'

Her eyes welled up again, and she ducked her head and vanished from the screen. When she returned, Gilchrist noted several tissues in her hand.

'Are you able to continue?' he said.

She nodded. 'I thought I was being careful. I'd heard about people being scammed before, so I asked him for proof of his identity, and that night he sent me a copy of his passport, to prove he was who he was.'

Out of sight of the monitor, Gilchrist raised his hand to prevent Jessie from jumping in. She'd caught it, too. They'd found no passports or other forms of ID in Howitt's home. It might be worth obtaining a copy of that faked passport. He eased into it with, 'Do you still have a copy of that passport?'

'Yes. I'll send it to you if you like.'

'Please.' A glance at Jessie, but she was scribbling into her notebook. Back to Debbie. 'We're listening.'

'It was all going well,' she said. 'Or so I thought. He said he'd booked two rooms for four nights in the Almhof Schneider resort, which he said was one of the most expensive in the area. I'd no idea where it was, so I googled it, and couldn't believe it. I'd been to a few nice places in my time, but this was on another level.'

'And how were you going to get there?' Jessie said.

'Fly. First class. The only way to travel, he said. He would buy the ticket.'

'He sent you a ticket?'

'No. He said he was going to, but first he needed to confirm the hotel booking. Just in case there were any last-minute problems. And that's when it all fell apart.'

Gilchrist held up his hand to Jessie. Silence seemed as good a question as any.

'Four weeks ago he said that he needed to pay for the room to secure it. The hotel is always full that time of year, and the rooms had to be paid in advance. He wanted to pay by debit card, but the banks had only recently changed their partner, whatever that meant, and he was waiting for a new card to come through. He said he'd tried to convince the hotel that he would pay once his card arrived in a few days, but they said it was company policy, that the room needed to be paid for now. He didn't have enough cash because he'd lent a friend of his twenty thousand euros for a down-payment on an apartment.'

'And you believed this?'

'Yes.'

'Even though you'd never met him face-to-face?'

She fell silent then, and Gilchrist waited thirty long seconds, before saying, 'Did you eventually pay for the hotel?'

'Yes. I did. He tried to persuade me to transfer the money into his account, but I didn't want to do that, and told him I would pay by credit card. He told me he would pay the credit card bill for me, or repay me in full once his new bank card arrived. He said, he'd transfer it straight into my bank account—'

'You didn't give him your bank details, did you?'

'No. He told me not to give out my account details to anyone, not even him. That way I could be scammed. But it was all said to gain my confidence, and he said he'd transfer the funds to me after we met.'

'So what happened?'

'He said he would phone me from the hotel, and I could read the credit card details to the hotel over the phone. That way I would be covered by the credit card company, and be repaid by him before I paid the bill.' Tears welled in her eyes, and she shook her head. 'But it turns out that he wasn't at the hotel when he said he was, and when I read out my card details, the dates, the name, the security number on the back, everything . . . he had what he needed to go on a spending spree.'

Gilchrist felt his heart slump. That old phrase *love is blind* sprang to mind. Debbie Paulet might not have been in love, but she'd clearly been looking for it. 'How much did you lose in the end?' he asked.

'By the time I realised I'd been conned, he'd run up bills of over fifteen thousand euros. I contacted the credit card company, of course, but because I had willingly given out my card details, they said I was liable for the bill.'

Well, there he had it. Howitt had been a romance scammer of the worst kind, someone who couldn't care less about the wellbeing of whomever they conned, only that they had to have a good credit score to rack up a bill. There was nothing he could do for Debbie, except to say how sorry he felt for her, and encourage her to try to put the incident behind her as best she could.

Despite his best efforts, he could see that his words were having little effect. Debbie had been traumatised by the loss of a significant amount of money, but she was young, with many years ahead of her to recoup her losses. It must surely be worse for older people to be scammed, where their life savings are dumped down the drain at the behest of some cruel-hearted scammer, with no chance or ability to recover the loss, or earn it back.

He looked at Jessie, but she just shook her head – she had nothing more to ask or to add. A final glance at Debbie before he ended the call, and a thought crossed his mind. He didn't think his question would get him anywhere, but he asked anyway.

'In all your text messages with the person you believed was Franz Wimmer,' he said, 'did he ever mention any other person, a friend, perhaps, or an associate?'

'No.'

If he'd been looking for a dead end, he'd just found it. 'One final question,' he said. 'You were particularly detailed about specific dates. Why is that?'

'I keep a diary, and I've only recently submitted a claim to my insurance, so the dates are fresh in my mind.' She let out a deep sigh. 'I'm not expecting to be compensated, but I can't simply let it go without doing something.'

'Of course not.'

He thanked her again, told her that someone in the IT department would contact her later in the day for a copy of all her text
messages to and from Franz, including a copy of that passport, in
the hope that they might cast up something she'd forgotten.

When the connection ended, he pushed to his feet and shook
his head.

Jessie gave a tight grimace. 'It's a pity that bastard Howitt's
dead,' she said. 'If he was alive I'd cut his balls off for him.'

Gilchrist said nothing as Jessie left the room, his thoughts drift-
ing back to the body seated at the table – so innocent-looking in
death, but so heartless while alive. He'd come across many an evil
person in his years as a police officer, but the cold-heartedness of
conning innocent people out of their savings seemed as cruel a
crime as any.

CHAPTER 11

By mid-afternoon, Gilchrist felt as if his investigation was floundering. Neither Jackie nor Mhairi had been able to come up with any incriminating evidence on Ian Howitt. By all accounts, he seemed to have led a perfectly normal life.

Born in York, forty-one years ago, the only child to Peter and Janice Howitt – both deceased; went to Scarcroft Primary and Millthorpe Secondary, then Harlow College, north of London, where he graduated with a diploma in physical education. Another year in college made him decide that PE was not for him, and a change of heart had him applying for jobs in the NHS, in the physiotherapy departments. Back to Yorkshire, where he spent four years at the Duchy Hospital, Harrogate, followed by thirteen years in a private clinic in Bishopthorpe. Another change of heart had him trying his hand at teaching, where he landed a job in the University of York's PE department, then shifted in a somewhat dubious sideways move to History; never married, never got engaged, never appeared in DVLA's records; no fines, no speeding tickets, perfect driving record, full no-claims discount. The same with the Inland Revenue; no income tax penalties, no late payments, all PAYE and not a complaint in sight. If they'd been looking for a perfect citizen, they need look no further than Ian Howitt.

So, what had happened? What had turned Howitt from the perfect citizen to a cold-hearted romance scammer? From what Gilchrist could gather, the answer appeared to be nothing. Looking into Howitt's past had seemed a promising way to start his investigation, but now he'd read the reports, none of it was bringing him any closer to discovering who had murdered Howitt.

He pushed himself back from his desk, and stood. His muscles felt stiff from having been seated at his desk for the best part of two hours. He stretched his limbs, walked to the window, looked down at the car park, already settling into the darkness of an early winter's evening. Lights framed the windows in the buildings at the back, those that fronted Market Street. With tired disinterest he noticed a pair of blinds being drawn in a top-floor flat, then he raised his gaze to a grey sky in disbelief as snowflakes fluttered down. He turned at the sound of someone entering his office.

'Can you believe it's snowing?' Jessie said. 'Forecast is three to six inches tonight. It'll probably grind the country to a halt. God knows what the place would be like if we had the snow they get in the States. New York's under three feet at the moment.'

Gilchrist nodded. He'd visited North Carolina one winter, many years ago, the month of January as best he could recall. He remembered the ground being covered in more ice than snow, and northerly winds so strong that horizontal icicles had formed on fences at the side of the road. 'What's that you're holding?' he said.

'Something you need to see.' She slapped what looked like pages of a computer printout onto his desk. 'Just in from DI Billy Robinson.'

Gilchrist searched his memory, then said, 'Doesn't ring a bell.'

'Not surprised. He's with Northumbria Police, Ashington.'

'Okay.' He picked up the printout, noted it was a Crime Scene Report, and started reading. 'Talk me through it,' he said.

'Got a call early afternoon from Freddie Hunter,' she said. 'One of Colin's team, a SOCO who moved up to Scotland from England, stupid bugger.'

Gilchrist noticed the victim's name – Clive Keepsake – and his home address in Bamburgh Drive, Pegswood. 'Where's Pegswood?'

'West of Ashington.'

'Which is where?'

'North of Newcastle.'

He almost stumbled at that. He'd detected a hint of a Geordie accent from Debbie Paulet. Did that mean anything? Or was it coincidental? 'And this Freddie Hunter,' he said, 'used to work out of the Northumbria Ashington Office?'

'No, he worked for a private firm who were contracted to do forensic evaluations and searches as overload relief to the police.'

'Why did he move to Scotland?'

'Fell in love with a woman, and the rest is history.'

'Ah, right.' He read on, noted the position of the victim. 'Keep going,' he said, 'I'm listening.'

'Anyway, Freddie calls and tells me that Colin's given him permission to speak to us directly. Straight from the horse's mouth, as it were. And Freddie says he hadn't wanted to say anything yesterday, until he checked back at his old office to confirm it. Which he did.'

Gilchrist cast his gaze over time of death and noted the date – 12 August – four months ago, then flipped over a page – Cause of Death: Drug overdose, administered by injection. Suspected taser attack. Alcohol limit 417 milligrams per 100 millilitres of blood. 'Bloody hell,' he said, 'it's identical to Howitt.'

'So Freddie checks his old records, and that's when he phoned me. Told him I needed to see a written report, something I can pass on upstairs. So he gave me Billy Robinson's number, and I called him.' She sighed as if in frustration, then said, 'Why don't you jump to when and where the victim was found?' She raised her eyebrows and smirked. 'Same scenario. Sitting there like he'd gone to sleep. Enough drugs and alcohol in his system to drop an elephant. No mobile phone, no flash drives, no nothing, just his laptop sitting on the table in front of him, and that'd been fried. Only this time, there's clear evidence of it being zapped.'

'And a note?'

'Same thing. One word. Sorry.'

He raked his fingers through his hair. They'd found two bodies. Could there be more? If you thought about it, why not? And if so, could they be searching for a serial killer? 'Did Northumbria get anywhere with their investigation?' he said.

'They had a number of suspects, but they all had solid alibis.'

'So they've nothing, is what you're saying?'

'Zip. Nada. Just like us.'

'Right, get Jackie and Mhairi to put out a request on the PNC for similar scenes of death; no signs of violence; taser attack; drug overdose, alcohol limit off the charts.' He paused for a moment. 'The one-word note,' he said, 'did you get a copy?'

'Not yet, but can do.'

'Go for it. And highlight that on the PNC request. It's what makes these killings unique.'

'What I don't understand,' Jessie said, 'is why leave a note at all? And why fry the laptops? I don't get it.'

Gilchrist didn't get it either, but for the sake of argument said, 'The one-word note's a calling card, I'm thinking. The killer wants us to link these murders. He wants us to know he's out there, on the loose, and that we're looking for a serial killer. Why?' He shook his head. 'I don't know. To gain a certain level of infamy, perhaps?'

'Get his name down in history, is what you're saying?'

'Only if we find him.'

'Well, Bible John got his name in history good and proper, and nobody found him.'

'Noted.'

'And why fry the laptops?'

Gilchrist shrugged, but offered his thoughts. 'To destroy what's on them? So far, we haven't found Howitt's flash drives, CDs, or anything else he might have used to back-up his files. Or his mobile phone.' He lowered his head and eyed Jessie as if over an imaginary pair of specs. 'Talking of which?'

'I'm on it, I'm on it,' Jessie said, and scurried from his office.

CHAPTER 12

'We're in luck,' Jessie said.

Gilchrist lifted his gaze from the screen, rubbed his eyes, and stretched his arms to relieve the tension in his shoulders. He was getting far too old for all these late-night shifts. A glance at the window told him the snow had stopped, the skies now cloud-free and sparkling with stars, a sure sign that his homeward journey would be like driving on an ice-rink.

'We won the lottery?' he joked.

'That'd be the day.' Jessie took a seat in front of his desk, and enticed him with a sheaf of printouts. 'We came up dry on the national PNC with the one-word note, but you know Jackie. She contacted Interpol, and wham-bam, she got a hit in Copenhagen.'

'Let me see?' He reached for the printout.

'I'm thinking,' Jessie said, 'maybe we should start an Office lottery. Get Jackie to pick the numbers every week. That way we're bound to win. What d'you think?'

But Gilchrist wasn't listening. He was reading the Crime Scene Report, which had been translated into English for him. He noted the date; September, three months ago; Milas Volker, male, fifty-two years old, divorced, three children, two grandchildren, found dead in his one-bedroom apartment in Sundbyvester – which he assumed was a district within the city limits of Copenhagen. Volker's body had been discovered after neighbours complained about the stench coming from his flat. The Politi – the Danish police – broke down the door to discover Volker's body, three weeks expired, bloated with the gases of decomposition and oozing purged fluids.

Gilchrist read on to confirm the similarities between Howitt's and Keepsake's deaths. A tidy hand-printed sketch showed the position of the body: upright in an armchair, hands and arms resting carefully either side, feet positioned squarely, hair freshly combed – now that was a new one – facing a coffee table with printed arrows by the legs suggesting that it had been moved to that position, and on which sat a desktop computer, not a laptop. A search of the flat failed to locate computer leads, mouse, back-up discs, flash drives, or accessories of any kind. And to round it off, the desktop had been fried to the extent that the casing showed distinct evidence of fire. A forensic examination confirmed the inside circuitry was melted and distorted, damaged beyond repair.

'There's no mention of a taser attack,' he said. 'Probably because the body was too decomposed,' he added, answering his own question. He placed the report with deliberate care onto his desk, squeezed his eyes shut for a moment while he pinched the bridge of his nose between thumb and forefinger.

'You all right, Andy?'

'Well . . . it's a sorry state of affairs when we announce that getting one of those . . .' he slapped the report with the back of his hand, '. . . is considered lucky.'

Jessie pursed her lips with a tight grimace. 'Sorry, Andy. Bad choice of words. Won't happen again.' She pulled the report to her. 'What I meant was, that it could be a break in the case for us. I'm going to follow up with the Copenhagen police tomorrow, and see how far they got with their investigation, or if they have any suspects.'

He nodded. 'Good. Do that.'

'I have to say, you don't look happy.'

He tried a quick smile of reassurance, but his lips didn't work the way they should. 'It's . . . it's not that, it's just . . . it upsets me to think that it's another body of some poor soul which confirms that we have yet one more psycho out there, killing people for his own . . . for his own . . .' He was going to say *pleasure*, but it somehow didn't sound right, and with a heavy sigh of defeat he settled for, 'Ah, fuck it.'

He pushed back from his desk and stood. 'What time is it anyway?'

'Just after ten,' Jessie confirmed. 'You look as if you could use a pint.'

A pint sounded about right, he thought. But the roads could be iced over. Still, it wouldn't be the first time he'd broken the law and driven while over the limit. He just made a point of driving with care. 'Have the gritters been out yet, do you know?'

'Can't say that I've noticed. But they're usually on the ball up here. Not like Glasgow, where they grit when it's raining, and go home when it's snowing.'

He rolled his head to ease the stiffness. 'Where's Jackie?'

'At her desk. Working away.'

'For crying out loud, tell her to go home.'

'Can do, but you know what she's like, she'll just continue from there. Mhairi had to head off, though, something to do with her sister's twelve-week scan.'

'Her sister's pregnant?'

'That's what twelve-week scan usually means, yes.'

'I didn't know about her sister.' He faced Jessie. 'There's nothing wrong, is there? I mean, there's nothing to worry about, right?'

'Everything's fine, Andy.'

He gave a tired nod again, then said, 'A quick one in the Central, then?'

'You talked me into it. Let me grab my jacket, and I'll meet you there.' She paused in the doorway. 'Want me to invite Jackie?'

'Of course. Yeah. Sorry. If she's up for it. That would be good. And email me a copy of that Copenhagen report when you get a chance.'

'Here,' she said, 'have this one. I'll print another one in the morning.'

When Jessie left, he leaned down to his computer, switched it off, pulled his jacket and scarf off the coat rack. On the way downstairs, he thought of giving Irene a call, but she'd been going to bed earlier than normal, part of her recovery process. So he pulled up his collar, and phoned Joanne, her daughter.

'I spoke to your mum earlier today,' he said. 'She seemed more tired than normal.'

'She's okay, Andy. I saw her tonight, and she was sorting through more photos, trying to collate them into the . . . dah-dah . . . the next book to be published.'

An image of Joanne clawing the air into imaginary inverted commas pulled a smile to his face. 'She's not overdoing it, is she?

I worry that our idea of publishing her collection was the wrong thing to do, given what she's going through.'

'Don't. It's keeping her active, and giving her something to take her mind off it.'

He gave an involuntary shiver at the thought of *it*, which covered everything from drip-fed chemo to losing hair, weight, and the spirit of life, and dying a slow painful death. It seemed to him that *it* could never consist of positive thoughts.

Joanne interrupted his thoughts. 'You're not still at the Office, are you?'

'Yeah, well, kind of busy at the moment.'

'You need to take more time for yourself.'

'You sound like Maureen.' He threw a chuckle down the line, but he knew Joanne was not only meaning take more time for himself, but to spend more time with her mother. 'It's a bit late to pop round and see her tonight,' he said. 'But I'll check in with her first thing in the morning.'

'She'd love that,' she said. 'I've never told you, Andy, but I really appreciate all you're doing for Mum. She's had it tough. When we lost Jamie, she took it hard. She blamed herself for his suicide. I thought for the longest time that she'd never get over it. But you've made such a difference. So thanks. Thanks for being there for her.'

'Joanne, that's . . . that's . . .'

'That's the truth,' she said. 'I'll try to catch up with you over the weekend.'

And with that, the line died.

He slipped his mobile into his pocket, and walked on, feet slipping in the snow.

He entered the bar by the College Street entrance. Friday night, and the place was heaving. Glasses clattered and chinked.

Stools shifted and creaked. People chatted in voices that roared through the start-of-the weekend din. In a corner, under a muted TV, six students were throwing back shooters as if the world were about to end at midnight. As a reminder that Christmas was nigh, a string of multi-coloured fairy lights flickered above the gantry.

He ordered an Eighty-Shilling, and was about to take that first sip when Jessie said, 'That looks good enough to eat.'

'Would you like one?'

'A pint? And ruin my diet? No thanks. White wine for me, if you don't mind. Pinot, if they've got it.'

'Large?'

'Of course. Is there any other measure worth considering?'

'A double large?' Which pulled a chuckle from Jessie's lips. He placed her order, then frowned as he glanced over her shoulder. 'Jackie couldn't make it?'

'Said she was too busy.'

'Did you not tell her to go home?'

'Of course.' She gave a defeated shrug. 'But other than drag her out of the place by her crutches, what could I do?'

Well, there was that, of course. Jackie now spent more time working from home, and came into the Office only when she needed access to the PNC or the ANPR or other police databases. Saying she was *too busy* to go home meant that Jackie was searching through the police computer systems.

'Cheers,' Jessie said, and chinked her glass to Gilchrist's pint. 'Up yours.'

He nodded, and took a welcoming mouthful. From the corner of his eye, he caught the late night news on the TV in the corner. The camera zoomed in on a solicitor outside the Old Bailey, client by her side, mouthing into a nest of microphones. A ticker tape ran across the bottom of the screen – Breaking News – and he recognised the client, a woman who'd been accused of murdering her husband after suffering years of domestic abuse. From what he could see, she'd been found Not Guilty, which in a strange way pleased him. Not that he could ever condone murder, but certain crimes – particularly those carried out by abused women for revenge – might be considered as being justified—

Jessie interrupted his thoughts with, 'You look serious.'

He turned from the TV. 'This serial killer we're trying to chase down,' he said.

'What about him?'

'Three men dead. All positioned in front of their computers, as if they've gone to sleep. She's trying to tell us something.'

'She?'

He nodded. '*She*. Hell hath no fury like a woman scorned.' He nodded to the TV in the corner. 'Or a woman abused.' He sipped his pint and let his thoughts simmer.

CHAPTER 13

6.15 a.m., Saturday

Gilchrist grunted awake to ringing in the distance, then realised he'd forgotten to delete his mobile's alarm from the day before. Problem was, it was being charged in the kitchen, and its incessant ringing – some modern jingle that his daughter, Maureen, had set up for him – went on and on and on.

'All right all right I'm coming,' he grumbled, and stumbled from his bedroom. He found his mobile, and switched it off with a 'Bloody hell.' He looked around him, trying to come to terms that he was upright, and wondering why he didn't feel too swift. A dazed wander into the lounge offered an answer: an empty tumbler squatted next to a half-full bottle of Aberlour 12. Surely never.

The Crime Scene Report from the Danish police lay scattered around his chair like an abandoned manuscript. He clumped the pages together, and laid them on the table. Next he picked up the tumbler, replaced the bottle to the drink's trolley, noting that his home stock needed replenished, then entered the kitchen.

Now he was up, he switched on the TV, filled the kettle, and opened the blinds.

Outside, dawn was a good couple of hours away, but it could have been the middle of the night for all he could see of his back garden. Stars sparkled in a clear sky like a meadow of diamonds. He thought he could make out the duller stud of Mars, but he'd never been one for having a deep knowledge of the night's constellations. He peered into the distant darkness and leaned closer to the window, the glass cold against his skin.

He remembered as a child loving midwinter mornings, Christmas only a few days away, the anticipation of a snowfall, the thrill of digging his old sledge out of his father's garden hut, runners rusted from a year of lying unused, creeping fingers of frost on the inside of the windows, delicate slivers of ice that he could melt with his breath. It seemed incredible now, with today's central heating systems, how his family and others in that generation had risen to freezing mornings, considered it the norm, and just got on with it.

His kettle clicked, and he popped two teabags into the teapot.

While he waited for the tea to infuse, he checked his mobile for messages. Only two texts, both from Mhairi, and nothing in from Jackie, which surprised him, but in another way pleased him. Perhaps she'd gone home last night and watched TV, instead of staying up all hours of the night doing research at his, and his team's, behest.

The first message confirmed that Mhairi had found addresses and contact numbers for two of the women Howitt contacted in the States, and also one in Australia, adding that she would try to contact them over the weekend. The second text was the contact number for DCI Kenzie Dorrance's sister – Alice Ralston – with an address in Edinburgh, and asking if he wanted her – Mhairi – to contact Alice, or would he prefer to do so himself?

He gave that some thought then, decision made, texted – You call AR – and poured himself a cup of tea.

Back in the lounge, he read the Politi report again, but after twenty minutes had to put it aside, frustrated that nothing new sprung out at him. He thought of phoning the Politi and talking to the Chief Investigating Officer, an Inspector Karlsen, then decided that Karlsen could likely tell him nothing more than what was already in the report. So he spent the next half-hour jotting down notes, trying to work out the best way forward for his investigation.

It seemed to him that they could spend hundreds of manhours chasing down women who'd been scammed by Howitt's alter-egos – Wimmer and Denz. But what would that tell him? That they'd been taken in and now felt stupid? That they couldn't believe they'd lost their savings? That they'd willingly handed over hundreds, if not thousands of pounds of their own money, to someone who'd stolen some other person's identity?

No, he thought. That would be far too labour intensive, for no great return. If he was going to contact anyone, it would surely make more sense for him to follow up with that one woman for whom the romance scam had been more than she could bear – DCI Kenzie Dorrance, who had committed suicide.

He texted Mhairi back – Change of plan. I'll call AR, thanks.

By 8.30, he was showered and shaved and on the road to St Andrews. The skies were clear, not a cloud in sight, the sun an orange orb that was doing what it could to warm the eastern horizon. That early, the sea dazzled with flashes of light that danced over the waves, low and lively, as if sprinkled here and there by the fingers of God, each for no more than a moment in time.

He parked in South Street, rang Irene's doorbell, and let himself in.

He found her in her dressing gown, in the kitchen, ambling around the breakfast bar, a mug of tea in her hand, which looked as if it were about to be spilled. She glanced at him as he approached, but he saw no pleasure in her eyes.

'Here,' he said, 'let me take that.' He removed the mug from her grip, and led her into the lounge where she slumped into her favourite seat, the soft armchair in front of the fire. He clicked the remote, and the fire came alive with fake flames that flickered like real ones.

'Are you all right?' he said.

'Tired,' she mumbled.

He gripped both of her hands in his, gave them a tight squeeze, and tried to get her to focus on his eyes. 'Can you tell me what day it is?' he said.

'Saturday, you daft bugger.' She smiled, a weak effort that showed some teeth. 'I'm tired, that's all. Been up most of the night. Couldn't sleep.' She looked around, as if surprised to find herself in her own home. 'Could sleep for Scotland right now, though.'

He let out a sigh of relief. 'You had me worried for a moment. Thought you were having a stroke, or an attack of something.'

'No, no, I'm fine. Here . . .' She leaned forward. 'Help me up.'

'You sure?'

'Of course I'm sure.'

He did as instructed, and let her lead him back into the kitchen where he pulled up a stool and helped her sit at the breakfast bar.

'Would you like me to make some breakfast for you?' she said.

'Already eaten,' he lied. 'How about you? Can I get you anything?'

'If you could make a fresh pot of tea, that would be lovely.'

He made sure she was seated okay, then set about making a brew. He'd been in her kitchen often enough to know where most things were kept, and five minutes later placed a mug of fresh tea beside her.

'Not having one for yourself?'

'I'm all tea-ed out.' Which had her squeezing her eyes in a subdued smile.

He watched and waited while she took a few mouthfuls, then satisfied that the worst of it was over – whatever *it* had been – he pulled up the stool beside her, and sat.

'Want to tell me what kept you up all night?' he said.

'Oh, nothing, just the usual.'

'The usual . . .?'

'Oh, I don't know. I worry about what's going to happen next.' As if on impulse, she reached up and removed her headscarf to reveal a bald head. 'Look at it. I can't remember what I used to look like with hair.'

'You looked just as beautiful.' He leaned forward, gave her a peck on the lips, and said, 'C'mere. Let me give you a hug.'

She leaned forward, and he put his arms around her, surprised by how light she felt, as if she'd lost all muscle weight and her bones had turned hollow. On the face of it, he always thought she looked healthy, despite her illness. The whites of her eyes were clear, her skin an even tone and glistening with false health. He'd need to have a talk to Joanne, maybe arrange for another meeting with her oncologist. His thoughts were interrupted by Irene shuffling on her stool, and pulling back from him.

'Promise me,' she said, as tears welled in her eyes, 'that if I die before my hair grows back, that you'll bury me in a wig.'

'I thought you wanted cremated,' he said, with such deadpan tone and face that it took her several seconds to see the funny side. He smiled when she smiled, and she leaned close to reach for another hug.

With his arms around her, she said, 'I'm sorry, Andy, I hope you don't mind what I'm about to ask you.'

'Anything,' he said.

She stared off for a long moment, and when she looked back, he could see the steel of resolution behind her eyes. 'I struggled this morning,' she said, her voice so quiet that he had to lean closer to catch her words. 'I almost fell when I tried to get out of bed. But I managed to catch hold of the bedside cabinet. Everything was swimming. The room was spinning. I had to lie back down until I recovered.'

'How do you feel now?'

'Better. But it gave me a fright. For a moment, it made me realise how ill I am, and how close to . . .' She lowered her head, and her voice was the softest whisper. '. . . How close to the end I might be.'

He said nothing. Instead, he hugged her, pulled her tight to him, kissed the top of her head, felt the shiver or her sobbing take hold of her. And he waited. He waited in aching and helpless silence until he felt the moment subside.

She sniffed, dabbed a hand at her nose, and shook her head. 'I don't want to die,' she whispered. 'But I don't want to live like this.'

What could he say? How could he answer that? Spout out all the faked niceties that she would get better, that the chemo was doing its job, that it would take time, and she would feel like this before she got well again? No, he couldn't say any of that. He couldn't lie to her like that. But what he found shocking, was the reality of her illness, as if he was seeing it for the first time, as if he was only now understanding just how ill she was. She always put a smile on it, always spoke positively, and always, *always* looked in far better health than she clearly was. All of a sudden, he felt as if he'd failed her, that he should be doing more for her, helping her where she was weak and he was strong. Even now, with his arms around her, he could feel her fragility, weigh her frailty, and sense her closeness . . . to the end, perhaps.

But he had no answer for her, so said, 'You wanted to ask me something.'

She sniffed, nodded her head. 'I hope you don't mind. But this morning made me realise that I need help. I need someone to be there for me when I can't . . . when I can't help myself. And I don't mean homecare, or anything like that. That's far too impersonal for me.' She sniffed, and he had a sense that the moment of asking was upon him. 'Would you mind very much,' she said, 'if I asked you to move in with me?'

'For a moment there,' he said, 'I thought you were about to ask if you could move in with *me*,' and followed it up with a forced laugh at his weak joke. 'Of course I'll move in with you. I'll move in today, *tonight*, I mean. I . . . eh . . .'

'You've got somewhere to go today, is that it?'

'Yes, I have, but it can wait.'

'No, it can't. Off you go. I know what you're like.'

'Don't try to get rid of me so soon.'

'Is this what it's going to be like from now on, you disagreeing with everything I say?' She chuckled to let him see she was only joking, and he smiled in response.

'Let's get you settled before I head off,' he said. 'Here.' He helped her to her feet, led her to her favourite armchair, and fluffed up some cushions.

'I could get used to this,' she said.

'Looks like you're going to have to.' He made sure the fire was set at medium, that she had a blanket over her legs. 'Fancy some toast and marmalade? Could you face that?'

'Just half a slice, please.'

'Certainly, ma'am.'

'What do you think Joanne will say?'

'About what?'

'About us living together.'

'I think she'll be happy for you.'

'She won't think it odd? At our age?'

'Of course not. And if she does, just tell her we're going to get married.'

Irene burst out laughing at that, which surprised him, he had to say. It might not have been the most romantic proposal, and surely had to be one of the most spontaneous, but he hadn't expected downright ridicule.

'Oh,' she said, looking into his eyes. 'You're serious.'

'Well, it crossed my mind that as we'll be living together, then it might be about time that we tied the knot, so to speak.'

She looked up at him, and shook her head. 'I don't . . . I don't know.'

'I'm sorry,' he said, 'for springing it on you in such a . . . such a *flippant* way.'

'No, it's not that, Andy. It's not that at all.' She reached for him, and he took hold of her hands and kneeled beside her. 'I care for you,' she said. 'I care for you a lot. And I love you very much.

But . . .' She shook her head, then looked at him with a fierce gaze. 'I've got cancer, Andy, and I'm dying. That's the truth of the matter. What kind of a marriage would that be?'

'A short one?'

She stilled for several seconds, as if stunned by that simple truth, and when he smiled at her and winked, she burst out laughing. He laughed, too, and pulled her to him, this woman who was dying, this woman whom he loved, this woman for whom he would do anything.

If only he could . . .

CHAPTER 14

By midday, Gilchrist had arranged to meet Alice Ralston in the Dome, in Edinburgh. He hadn't been to the city for over a year or so, as best he could remember, and had never set foot in the Dome, so was pleasantly surprised by its upmarket surroundings, although the price of a pint of Heverlee almost had his eyes watering.

He dialled Alice's number to let her know he'd arrived.

She picked up on the first ring. 'I'm in the Club Room,' she said, and hung up.

He had to be shown the way to the Club Room, and when he entered he made eye-contact with a well-dressed woman sitting at a table in the corner. He carried his pint over, aware of peculiar looks from other patrons – were you not allowed to bring your own pint? – and pulled up a chair opposite. Even though it was just after midday, other than four more couples they had the room to themselves.

'Detective Chief Inspector Gilchrist.' He held out his warrant card. 'Andy for short. Thanks for meeting with me.'

She didn't smile, or confirm her name, but slid a card across the table to him – *Alice Ralston Ltd, Bespoke Jeweller to the Rich and*

Famous – no business address, no website, just a mobile number, the same one he'd just rung.

'You mentioned my sister on the phone,' she said. 'Kenzie's been dead for a year and a half now, so how can I help you?'

'I'm sorry she died.'

'Sure you are.'

Not quite the response he'd expected, but he ignored it. 'You were sisters.'

'Correct.'

'Were you close?'

'Yes.'

'So you must have known she was depressed?'

'We all get depressed, Inspector. But depressed enough to kill ourselves? No. I didn't know Kenzie was that depressed.'

'Did you know she'd been involved in a romance scam?'

'Not at the time. I only found out later.'

'After she died?'

'Correct.'

'Did she never confide in you?'

'We spoke. We were close. We could reveal our intimate sides to each other, if that's what you mean by confide. I knew she was seeing someone, but I didn't know she was being scammed.' She lifted her glass flute, its contents lively and golden with a brown sugar lump on the bottom – classic champagne cocktail, if he were a betting man – and took a genteel sip. Then she set the flute down with such care that he thought she was afraid it might crack. She sat back, and stared at him. 'What do you really want to know?' she asked.

'I want to know how an experienced police officer could let herself be conned into a romance scam, then end up taking her life as a result.'

'Is that what you think?'

'Well, didn't she?'

'God, you people are pathetic.'

He wasn't sure if people referred to police officers like himself, or men in general, so he said, 'Why don't you tell me Kenzie's side of the story then?'

'I'd rather not. I'd rather just forget about it. It's in the past.'

He returned her hard gaze, and thought of just getting up and walking away. After all, he had contacts in Lothian and Borders to whom he could speak. But he was here now, and walking off seemed too much like admitting defeat. He took hold of his pint, and said, 'Your sister, Kenzie, was one of a number of women who were corresponding with Ian Howitt, believed to be a romance scammer living in St Andrews. A few days ago, Mr Howitt was found dead. We're treating his death as a murder enquiry.' He took a sip of beer to give his words time to filter through Alice's mind, but she stared at him in silence. 'What I'm keen to know,' he said, leaning forward, 'is why Kenzie would sign up to a dating site in the first place. By all accounts, she was happily married.'

Alice grimaced, and reached for her champagne cocktail.

'Wasn't she?' he pressed.

'No. Does that answer it for you?'

Far from it, he wanted to say. No, she wasn't married? Or no, she was married, but not happily? He thought she meant the latter, but said nothing while she took another delicate sip, and waited until she returned her flute to the table. 'Did her husband know she had registered with a dating site?'

'Her husband was a nasty bastard,' Alice snarled.

'Which is the reason for Kenzie not being happily married.'

'Was that a question?'

'No. But this is. Why are you so unwilling to open up?'

'Because I don't see what Kenzie's death has to do with . . . with *anything*.'

He couldn't help but frown. Hadn't she listened to a word he'd said? Her sister had once corresponded with Howitt, now deceased, and at the start of a murder investigation he had to look at every possible connection. He decided to ease back, change tack. 'You used the past tense when you spoke of Kenzie's husband. Is he dead?'

'No. But *she* is. Which makes past tense appropriate. Jesus *Christ*, are you for real?'

Very much, he wanted to say, but her arrogance had him viewing her in a different light. The question now wasn't, Why was she not cooperating? but, What was she hiding? He watched her make eye contact with one of the staff, then remove a credit card from her purse. A half-hearted sip of her cocktail didn't quite finish it, and she shifted in her seat to adjust her jacket.

'Before you go,' he said, 'do you know why Kenzie was in trouble?'

He'd thrown the question out there as a long shot, not expecting much in return, and certainly not the reaction he got. Alice stilled, as if time had stopped – one beat, two beats – then restarted with, 'Who told you?'

He'd no idea, but he smiled, and said, 'One guess?'

She held his gaze for a long moment, then said, 'That *bastard*.' Her lips could have been a white scar. Her gaze darted side to side, as if deciding – fight or flight.

He helped her out. 'We're on the same side here. So why not tell me your version?'

That seemed to work, for she shook her head at a member of the staff who'd appeared behind him carrying a tray on which sat a portable card reader. 'Another one of these,' she said, 'with a better measure of brandy,' then nodded to Gilchrist's pint. 'And whatever he's having.'

Normally, he would have declined – he was driving, after all – but he felt that doing so might snap whatever tenuous connection he'd accidentally made. 'Just the half-pint,' he said. 'Heverlee.' He waited until the waiter's footfall diminished before saying, 'Why don't you start at the beginning?'

She snorted, and said, 'We don't have time for that. So, I'll cut to the chase instead.'

He gave a non-committal smile, and shrugged in agreement.

'It was all that bastard Jeff's fault. Her first husband, Simon, was a nice guy, really decent, loved her to bits and took care of her. But he dropped dead from a heart attack at the age of thirty-nine. Out of the blue. No one saw it coming. When she started dating Jeff, I told her she should give it more time, that she was moving on too soon. She was still hurting, and missed Simon like mad. But she was on the rebound, and you know what that does to your head. Christ, Simon had been gone for less than a year when she told me she was thinking of marrying Jeff. I was dead against it. I told her that. I couldn't stand the man, and to this day never understood what she saw in him. She'd no kids with Simon, but that bastard Jeff had a bundle, two boys and a girl, all teenagers, and every bit as bad as he was. But she had history with Jeff, knew him from way back, and went ahead despite everything.'

She paused for a sip of her cocktail, then lips on the rim, seemed to change her mind and threw it back. Empty flute back on the table, she said, 'At first it all seemed to be going well, as it usually does when everything's fresh and new. Then it started. The abuse.'

'He hit her?'

'No no no, Jeff was way too smart for that. Mental abuse. Playing games with her mind. *Fucking* with her mind, more like.'

If Gilchrist had any doubts about Alice's feelings for Jeff, they were quashed there and then. If she licked her lips, he could imagine venom dripping from her tongue.

'And fucking around. Putting it about. Apparently as he'd always done, although give Kenzie her due, she never found out about any of that until . . . well . . . until later.'

'And where were you when all this was going on?' and quickly added, 'I mean, I'd assume, that with you and Kenzie being close, she might have shared her concerns with you.'

'Not at first, because she knew how I felt about Jeff. But later, when she began to see through that bastard, she would phone me up, sometimes late at night and bleed out her heart. It was awful, the way he abused her, even once telling her he'd arranged for a weekend away to get drunk and laid.'

'Why didn't she simply divorce him?'

'It wasn't as easy as that.'

'Why not?'

'Well, she worked with him. He was her boss. Chief Superintendent Dorrance. He was up there, lording it over all and sundry. Untouchable, so he thought. Even in this day and age. Unbelievable, if you think about it. He told her that if she ever tried to divorce him, he would make sure she'd lose her pension, and get eff all from him, as everything – the house, the investments, the lot, were in his children's names.'

Gilchrist shook his head at the unfairness of it all, the way some men believed they had the right not only to do whatever they pleased in their marriage, but to hold their wives ransom to their financial needs. 'When her first husband, Simon, died, did he not leave her anything?'

'He did. Insurance paid off the mortgage, and she owned her home, a nice wee semi in the outskirts of Livingstone. Not the most expensive place on the planet, but a tidy wee nest egg.'

Gilchrist felt a punchline coming. 'But . . .?'

'But she'd signed it over as collateral against their new house, which Jeff bought within two months of their wedding.'

'Didn't she take legal advice? Didn't someone advise her against that?'

'Yes to both questions. But Jeff convinced her that her money was secure. Even when he transferred the title into his children's names. To keep it safe against someone ever coming after him for money. He could go bankrupt, and no one could touch the house. Even Kenzie, as it turned out.'

Gilchrist sat back. He couldn't help but feel sorry for Kenzie, the way she'd been effectively financially stripped of everything she owned. Their drinks came up, and Alice slapped her credit card on the tray, a clear sign, he thought, that she would stay with him for only that drink, and no more.

He said nothing as she lifted the flute to her lips, swirled its contents under her nose, as if sampling the bouquet of a fine wine, then clasped the glass with both hands and rested her elbows on the table. She stared at him over the rim. 'That's when Kenzie got herself into trouble.' Her hard eyes seemed to soften with the pain of some difficult memory, then she said, 'I'll never forgive myself.'

CHAPTER 15

Gilchrist returned her gaze, and took a sip of his beer.

'Kenzie felt trapped,' Alice said at length. 'Trapped in a marriage she couldn't get out of. Trapped in a job she couldn't leave. But being financially trapped? I know that's what hurt the most. That's what turned the tide. Tragically, in the end.'

'You said you'll never forgive yourself.'

She nodded, pulled back from the table, took a mouthful of her cocktail. 'I told her to forget about her job, forget about her marriage. Find someone else and move on.' She tutted, shook her head. 'It was easy for me to say that. I've never married, and never will. I have a successful career, making more money than I know what to do with. I told Kenzie I'd set her up, make her a partner, we'd work well together. But she said she couldn't do that. She'd made her own mistakes, and needed to get out of them by herself. She was tough in that respect. I admired her for that. It's what made her such a good police officer.' She paused then, as if to catch her breath, but when she wiped a finger to the corner of each eye, Gilchrist realised she was crying.

She sniffed, took another sip, and said, 'That's when I suggested she should sign up to a dating site. Look for someone who's not only attractive, but financially independent, I told her. If you're going to jump out of the frying pan, you're not going to land in the fire, not if I have anything to do with it.' She shook her head, and whispered, 'My God, I let her down so badly.' She gulped another mouthful, as if to wash the memory from her system, then shook her head again. 'She was slow to take it up, but when she did, she found she enjoyed it. She changed for the better. She knew her marriage to that bastard Jeff was in name only. It was over. She could put up with his fucking on the side, as long as he kept away from her. And she kept herself squeaky clean at the Office, which worked both ways, because she could dob him in, if she really wanted to. But that wasn't Kenzie. So, in the end, it was a stand-off between the two of them. He led his life, and she led hers.'

He thought he knew the answer, but asked anyway. 'So what happened?'

'She phoned me up one night, all excited, saying she'd met this man online several weeks earlier, and that they'd hit it off. Was he handsome? I asked.' Which brought a bitter smile to her lips. 'Not terribly, she said, but who was she to complain? His wife had died over a year ago, so he'd said, and he wasn't looking for anything other than friendship, someone to talk to, share his feelings with. Which suited Kenzie well. She was still treading with care in the dating game, not sure about it, and even less sure about the internet, as she was never a computer geek. For the first time in years, I could feel her happiness. It was as if I'd got my sister back. I told her to be careful, not to give out any intimate information, and especially no bank details. She laughed at that. Of course I won't, she said. But just to be sure, I told her to keep me abreast of everything.' Another sip, but with a sharp glance at Gilchrist.

'*Everything*, I said to her. Leave nothing out. If you're ever going to meet him face-to-face, let me know, and I'll come along with you. I'd heard about scammers on these sites, so I wanted to make sure she wouldn't fall for it. But I'd also heard of true love being found on them, too. So I knew it wasn't all pie in the sky.'

Gilchrist returned his beer to the table. 'But in the end, it was.'

Alice nodded. 'In the end, yes. It was. And I didn't know anything about it until it was too late.' The champagne cocktail emptied in an angry gulp. She raised the flute above her head while she searched for one of the staff. A wiggle of the glass told Gilchrist that contact had been made. She glanced at him. 'Another one?'

He shook his head. 'I'm driving.'

She returned her glass to the table and stared at it in tearful silence.

Gilchrist said nothing, didn't even sip his beer, just waited until the waiter replaced Alice's cocktail with a new one. Another one of those, he thought, and she might not be able to stand, let alone speak. With a renewed sense of urgency, he said, 'Kenzie didn't keep you abreast of everything, did she?'

Alice shook her head. 'No. She was too embarrassed. I only found out later, when I was clearing her things from that bastard Jeff's house. They'd lived separate lives under the same roof. The house was big enough to do that. She'd moved into another bedroom, and lived her life as if she was a single woman. That's when I discovered the demand letters.'

Gilchrist shifted in his seat, fearful of what was coming.

'She'd taken out a forty-thousand-pound loan. For what, I don't know. On top of that, she'd also taken out two smaller loans with another bank for ten and twenty thousand each.'

'Seventy thousand in total?' he said, and made a mental note to have Mhairi look into these numbers for him.

'I don't know why she took out these loans. I checked with both banks, who at first wouldn't talk to me, data protection and all that, but I got a solicitor to light a Bunsen burner under the arses, and found out that her applications had stipulated *home improvements*. Home improvements, my arse. I'm convinced they had something to do with the man she'd been corresponding with on the dating site.'

'Did you not take your concerns to the police?' he said.

'Weren't interested. Couldn't prove a thing. No crime had been committed. How about fraud? I shouted at them. But with Kenzie being dead, they wouldn't budge.'

'What happened to the debts?'

'The banks had to write them off.' She smirked, shook her head. 'Kenzie had taken each loan out in her own name, to make sure that bastard Jeff knew nothing about them. So they couldn't even go after him.' She stared at her cocktail, twirling the flute between her fingers, eyes glistening. 'And the sad thing is,' she whispered, 'if she'd only come to me for help, I would've cleared the loans off for her.'

Gilchrist stared at her. She was well dressed, and clearly had money. But seventy thousand to pay off someone's loans? That put her in a different league. 'The man Kenzie hooked up with on that dating site,' he said, 'did she ever tell you his name?'

'Only his first name. Hans, she said. My lovely Hans, she called him.' She pursed her lips for a bitter moment, then said, 'He wouldn't be lovely if I ever got anywhere near him.'

'Did she tell you his surname?'

'Denz. Hans Denz.'

Well, there it was, the moment of proof. 'If it's any consolation,' he said, 'We believe Hans Denz was a falsified profile for the man we know as Ian Howitt, and whose death we're investigating as a murder.' He flashed a quick smile at her. 'So I have to ask – where were you last Tuesday evening?'

Alice stilled, as if her nervous system had been short-circuited, her gaze locked on his. Then she said, 'You've got to be joking.'

'You have to admit, you have motive.'

It took a few seconds for a slow smile to part her lips. 'I was in Dubai,' she said. 'For a week. Staying in the Burj Khalifa. Check it out.'

'We will.' He slid his chair back, and pushed to his feet.

'Not staying for another?' she said, with the tiniest hint of a slur.

He looked at his beer, the glass almost full, his meeting with Alice having dulled any desire to drink. He ignored her question. 'Are you intending to be out of the country any time soon?'

'Next Friday. I've meetings in Monaco.'

'I'll have someone contact you later today,' he said, 'to take a statement.'

'Do you want a sample of my DNA, too?' she said, and chuckled. The champagne cocktails seemed to be working.

'Do we need to?'

'My God.' She shook her head. 'You're so serious.'

'Murder's not something we take lightly.'

She shook her head, widened her smile. 'Well, Mr Inspector, normally I would say that I hope you catch whoever did it.' His smile deadpanned. 'But Hans Denz, or whoever the hell he was, had it coming.'

He gave a half-smile in return, nodded, then left the room.

CHAPTER 16

On his way to his car, Gilchrist phoned Mhairi, gave her Alice's contact information, and instructed her to take a statement from her – over the phone would be fine, preferably a face-to-face on Zoom or FaceTime. Next he phoned Jackie, and asked her to look into three payments to Hans Denz of ten, twenty and forty thousand each, and to establish where they came from. Also, if possible, print out a copy of any related texts – if these were available to be copied. They still hadn't found Howitt's mobile phone, or been able to recover anything of substance from his laptop, so he felt as if he was fumbling about in the dark.

He found a parking spot near the water in Leith. He'd been to his son Jack's gallery only once before, not long after he'd opened it with his then-girlfriend-of-the-week, Kristen. Much to his surprise, their studio gallery turned out to be a success and Jack's girlfriend-of-the-week became the mother of his child, a beautiful baby daughter. Despite his initial misgivings over Kristen – she had a criminal record, was only a few years older than Jack, but looked twenty years older due to earlier abuse of drugs – she surprised him by turning out to be a devoted mother and loving partner to his son. Gilchrist feared their relationship could never last, not that Jack and Kristen were destined to fall out with each other, rather Kristen's desire to return to her homeland, Sweden, and raise their daughter there, conflicted with Jack's strong – read *stubborn* – Scottish roots. For the last year or so, Jack had split his time between Sweden and Scotland, but Gilchrist suspected it was only a matter of time before the international commute became too much, and something had to give.

Ten minutes later, he turned into the dead-end street in which Jack's gallery was located. It had once been a derelict warehouse, but Jack surprised his father by remodelling and refurbishing it into a modern-day studio gallery that Gilchrist had to say was a tad too spartan for his sense of comfort. But that was the artistic mindset, so what could he say?

He opened the door to the place, and entered with a sense of trepidation. Brick and blockwork walls had been coated with a thick varnish that shone in the overhead downlights as if they were wet. Spotlights seemed to pin paintings of all colours, shapes and sizes to the walls, some framed, some just paint-covered canvases stapled at the edges. Old floorboards creaked as he walked across them to what looked like an oil painting of an opened mouth, with primary colours that swirled around a dark throat like the spinning walls of a raging technicoloured hurricane. He checked the price tag – £8,250 – and let out his breath in disbelief. Who would pay that sort of money for a painting like that?

He looked around him. The place was deserted. Was anyone in?

The next painting was just as dramatic and surreal, but priced a tad cheaper, and as he eased his way along the gallery wall, mentally adding up the prices, he realised that the stock on display had to be close to two hundred thousand. Of course, that was the gallery's asking price. How much money would actually exchange hands was a different matter. Round the corner and into another spacious area, this time with sculptures he thought he recognized as Jack's.

Steel reinforcing rods – the kind you might find on a construction site – twisted and curled their welded way from the floor into shapes that could be mistaken for skeletonised gargoyles, or prehistoric lizards, or . . . some invading alien. Although his first thoughts had been – who on earth would buy these? – he came to see the satisfying artistic beauty of each sculpture. You would need a house the size of a mansion in which to stand one of them, but a glance at the five-figure price tags made him realise that owners of homes that size had to be Jack's target market.

A metallic clatter from behind burst his thoughts and had him turning around to face a figure in jeans and boots fronted by a heavy-duty welding apron. A welder's helmet topped the figure. Its shielding visor opened like the jaws of some hungry robot.

'Andy?'

Gilchrist eased forward. 'Jack?'

A leather-gloved hand reached up to remove the helmet, and Gilchrist had an image of a knight in armour undressing. Then Jack slipped off a glove, raked his fingers through his hair, and shook his head.

'Looks like you're growing your hair long again,' Gilchrist said.

'You're always complaining about something,' Jack said, and smiled a white-toothed smile as he moved into Gilchrist's hug.

When they parted, Gilchrist was struck by how tall Jack appeared, and how fresh, too. It seemed as if his entire body gave off the aura of health, fitness, strength, and effervescent youth. He supposed growing older had that effect on you. You never realised how fit and healthy you once were, until you no longer had it.

'You look well,' he said. 'Welding must suit you.'

Jack gave out a hearty laugh, then said, 'Why are you here? Is everything okay?'

'Haven't seen you in ages, and the first thing you ask me is – what's up? What's wrong with? – Hi Dad, it's great to see you after all this time.'

Jack raked his fingers through his hair again, as if undecided how to respond. Then he smiled. 'I tell you what, if I reach fifty and look half as good as you do now, I'll be best pleased.'

'Sounds like you want me to buy you a pint or two.'

Jack chuckled as expected, and said, 'So, what brings you down here?'

'I could ask the same of you. I thought you were in Sweden.'

'Got back two days ago.' He tightened his mouth, then shook his head. 'It's difficult.'

'What is?'

'Just . . . you know . . . trying to make stuff work out. With Kristen and Linna.' He shook his head, looked off to the side, and said, 'I don't know.'

'Don't know what?'

'If it's going to work out or not.' His eyes pierced into Gilchrist's, clear and bold and alive with youthful energy, as if letting him know he wasn't up for being pushed around. But there were too many unknown variables in his comment for Gilchrist to offer advice. What's not going to work out? Jack's relationship with Kristen? The studio gallery? The international commute? Being a father? Being separated from Linna? Or what?

Instead, he gave a non-committal nod. 'Well, it's early days, I suppose,' and changed to a more upbeat mode with, 'So how are you enjoying being a father? How's Linna?'

Jack's whole being seemed to liven at just the sound of his daughter's name. He ripped off his other glove, slipped his hand into a pocket, and retrieved his mobile phone. 'Here,' he said, and turned the screen towards Gilchrist.

He leaned closer.

'We got her a baby's tricycle, one of these plastic ones with the big wheels and the stabilisers. She's too young for it, I know, but I couldn't resist buying it for her. She can't reach the pedals, or figure out how to work it, but she'll grow into it, I'm sure.' He chuckled, and Gilchrist chuckled along with him. Another short video showed Linna in a bath, naked as the day she was born – only three months ago – kicking water, while Kristen sponged her.

'She's beautiful,' Gilchrist said, and meant it. He remembered doing the same with Maureen and Jack, bathing them in a small tub, although the toys nowadays seemed to be more colourful and larger. He smiled and gave perfunctory mumbles of approval as Jack swiped through photo after photo. When it looked as if he'd been shown the most recent, Gilchrist said, 'So what might not work out?'

Jack grimaced, slipped his mobile into his jeans. 'As you said, it's early days. Just got stuff going on between us. Me and Kristen.'

'Like what?'

'Just . . . you know. Stuff.'

'Nothing serious, I hope.'

'Nothing that a couple of pints and a voddie or two can't sort out.' He clapped a hand on Gilchrist's shoulder. 'There's a nice wee pub just around the corner. Does a brilliant pint of Deuchars. You'll love it. Come on. I've got the first round covered.'

'Thought you were on the wagon,' Gilchrist said.

'Not when I'm on my own.'

The last thing Gilchrist needed was to spend a Saturday afternoon in a pub with his son. Not that he didn't want to socialise with Jack, but when Jack hit the pub that early on a Saturday, it was almost guaranteed to turn into a hell-bender. He shook his head. 'Can't,' he said. 'I've got an investigation that's just kicked off.'

'I've told you before, man, you've got to cut back on Office hours. You're way too old to be working your butt off. And all for what? Money?' He snorted, as he untied the leather apron. 'Money's eff all good to you when you're dead.'

'I hear you, Jack, but I'm driving, too.'

'Stay over at mine, then. I've got a spare bed.'

'Sorry,' he said. 'I promised Irene . . . that I'd eh . . . I'd *see* her tonight,' not wanting to mention anything about moving in. 'Besides, weren't you busy welding your next work of art until I got here?'

'I was just finishing up for the day. About to lock up.'

'On a weekend? Isn't that the time to sell some stock in your gallery?'

'It's not exactly heaving is it? Besides, it'll all still be here tomorrow.' He clapped his hands, rubbed them together. 'It's the weekend, after all.'

Gilchrist smiled at him, returned his gaze, and struggled to hide his disappointment. The last time he'd met Jack, he appeared to have escaped the mantles of a penniless artist and become a successful gallery owner, a woman by his side, baby daughter to take care of. He'd thought Jack's newfound responsibilities had matured him and formed him into the man he'd always hoped he would be.

But here was Jack again, his wayward son of old, ducking out of work, excited about hitting the bar early on a Saturday afternoon, looking forward to giving it laldie all the way to a midnight closing. God only knew how many vodka shooters he would end up downing.

'Well, enjoy yourself,' he said, 'and give Kristen my regards, and a kiss to Linna.'

He backed away, hand to his ear, thumb and pinkie out in the universal *give me a call* sign, eyes on Jack, waiting for his acknowledgement. And when Jack said, 'Will do, man,' he turned and strode from the gallery, heels thumping the wooden flooring as if to deter his son from persuading him to come back and join him for a session.

CHAPTER 17

Gilchrist had just driven over the new Forth Road Bridge, when he got a call from Jessie. He took it through his speaker system.

'You're not going to believe this,' she said, 'but forensics found a memory stick in Howitt's home.'

'Today?'

'Yesterday.'

'Why are we only hearing about it now?' he snapped.

'Because it was broken. Looks as if Howitt took a hammer to it and threw it away.'

'You've seen it?'

'Got it in my greasy little mitts, even as we speak.'

'Wait a minute. Back up. I thought you said Howitt threw it away.'

'That's what it looks like. Tried to toss it into the bin in that secret room of his, and missed. One of the SOCOs found it wedged at the back of the leg of his computer desk. It could've lain there for years. But as it turns out it's less than six months old.'

If Jessie knew it was less than six months old, then forensics must have been able to access it. 'So it's damaged,' he said, 'but not completely, right?'

'They told me you were good.' She chuckled. 'Our IT techies worked on it with their latest digital doo-dahs, and managed to recover some files. Ninety per cent of the files are gone for good, but they've printed out bits and pieces of what they could.'

Gilchrist didn't fail to catch the excitement in her voice. He tightened his grip on the steering wheel, eyed the road ahead, and held his breath. This could be the break he was looking for. 'And . . .?'

'And we've come across a couple of files I think you'll find interesting.'

'I'm listening.'

'One page of an Excel Spreadsheet titled *Profiles*, with a list of five names in the first column. Are you ready?'

'I'm all ears.'

'Tom Cleveden, Bruno Fisher, Mark Westerbrook. I've never heard of them either, so don't ask. But the last two are Hans Denz and Franz Wimmer.'

'You think maybe they're in some kind of chronological order? The first one, Tom Cleveden, being the earliest profile, followed by later ones, maybe. With the last one, Franz Wimmer, being the most recent?'

'That makes sense.'

'And what's in the other columns?'

'Simple descriptions; hair colour, facial hair, glasses, accent, backdrop. I'm thinking that each time Howitt sits down at his computer for his face-to-face Zoom call with whatever background he's got set up behind him, he needs to make sure everything matches the profile.'

'So it's some sort of checklist?'

'Could be. But the second-last column is headed Bio, and contains numbers one to five.'

'Only numbers?'

'Yes, but don't despair. I've got another partial printout from a corrupted file. It's headed Bio 5 slash Franz Wimmer – number and name match – followed by a history of Wimmer's life, literally from his birth through schooling through employment and marriage – he's even got details of his pretend wife and kids – then divorce, to present-day employment.'

'Have you checked any of that against Debbie Paulet's statement?'

'Hold your horses, Andy. I've only just got this. But we'll get onto that.'

Gilchrist pulled into the fast lane to overtake a group of slower moving cars. 'You said *second*-last column.'

Jessie chuckled, and he knew the best was yet to come. 'You never miss a trick. The last column is a list of women's names. Not a lot of names against each profile, but enough to confirm what we've come up with so far. There's three next to Wimmer, Debbie Paulet being one of them. The other two names we'll need to look into. But we've got Kenzie Dorrance and six others we know about against Denz's profile, so it seems as if we've got some kind of record of who he's been scamming.'

'What about the other profiles, Tom Cleveden, and the others? Have you got a list of names against them?'

'Not all of them. As I said, the files were corrupted, so I suppose we're lucky to have what we have. But I'll make another copy of what we've got so far, and I'll highlight all the names we know about and put it on your desk. How does that work?'

'Perfect. I'll pick them up on my way home.' He was about to end the call, when he said, 'Any luck with Howitt's mobile?'

'Best I can tell you, it's last location was St Andrews. We've got it pinging a mast near the Old Course Hotel. After that, zip, nada. I'd say the SIM card's been removed and destroyed.'

He nodded in silent agreement, then said, 'From Howitt's home to the Old Course Hotel, that's close to a mile or so, wouldn't you say?'

'Agreed, yeah.'

'So if his mobile pinged a mast at the Old Course Hotel, the SIM card couldn't have been destroyed at his home.'

A pause, then, 'Agreed.'

'Well, you've got to ask the question – why? Why not destroy it right away? Why wait until you're a mile away? I don't get it.'

'The killer panicked? Or forgot he had the mobile? Or was interrupted, and had to leave Howitt's in a rush? I don't know. Could be any number of reasons. Maybe he stayed over at the Old Course Hotel. It might be worthwhile checking their register.'

'No, don't. That'd be a waste of time. The mobile pinging near there, doesn't mean they checked into that hotel. Could've been driving past in either direction. Or been staying in some other hotel. Or any number of B&Bs for that matter.'

'Okay okay, it was only a suggestion. So what's your brilliant idea?'

Truth be told, he didn't have one, but he found the possibility of the killer having been disturbed interesting. Maybe they could narrow the time of death down a touch, put it into a narrower time frame. But in real terms, what would that achieve? They'd already spent half a week's worth of manhours reviewing CCTV footage and coming up with nothing. No, the best way forward would be to concentrate on this latest information – the damaged memory stick – dig into it, and see what else they might uncover. Howitt's killer had tried to limit the discovery of digital records by frying his laptop, removing his desktop, memory sticks, CDs, disks, and any other associated computer paraphernalia. Gilchrist's team had found nothing that could help them. Until now. The fact that this damaged memory stick had been wedged behind a table leg only strengthened his view that this could be a slip-up by the killer, and a chance for them to gain sight of some of Howitt's personal files.

'Right,' he said. 'Let's start by trying to locate everyone named on that last column on the spreadsheet, not just those against Wimmer and Denz, but the other profile names, too, and interview them. Find out if they've already been scammed, and if so, by how much.'

'We've already located a number of them from overseas,' Jessie said. 'Australia, USA, South Africa, Sweden, and France. I don't know how far Mhairi got with trying to call them. Not far, I'm thinking, as the shame of having been scammed might still be too raw.'

'I hear you, but we need to make a start.'

'We could cross-reference each of the women against dating websites, and get printouts of messages between Wimmer and everyone he tried to scam. We could also . . .'

As Gilchrist listened to Jessie throw suggestions at him, he came to see that with the current manpower, they would soon find themselves overwhelmed with the sheer volume of evidence. All they were doing was creating a mountain of paperwork – interview statements, text messages, written reports, cross-referencing this against that, reams and reams of printouts. And all for what? Even if he asked for more staff, they would never have the budget approved. It was too manhour intensive, and likely for very little gain. He had to come up with some other strategy.

He interrupted Jessie, and said, 'Let's get back to basics. What we need is a list of each and every scammed victim's name on that spreadsheet. Then I want you to prepare a list of questions, nothing too detailed at this stage, that we ask each of them, one by one. But first and foremost, let's make sure they're all right, and that no one else has ended their life. Once we make contact, we can always go back with more searching questions, and dig deeper into their relationship with Howitt or whoever he was pretending to be. We're not trying to solve a scamming con here, we're trying to find which one of them had reason to kill Howitt, or arrange to have Howitt killed.'

'Contract killing, you mean?'

'I'm not sure. I'm just throwing ideas out there. We need to keep it simple, and the simplest answer I think might come from the mouth of one of the scammed victims.'

'What about the other two scammers who've been murdered? Clive Keepsake, and Milas Volker? Do you want us to contact everyone they've scammed?'

'No, we don't know what the Northumbrian or the Copenhagen police have come up with in that respect. Again, let's keep it simple. We'll stick with what we know, and expand as necessary.' He let his thoughts shift for a moment as some boy racer in a souped-up Ford roared past him at the speed of light. As it zoomed off into the distance, oversized aerofoil on the boot, lowered chassis that looked as if it had collapsed, paintwork that could hurt your eyes, he was struck by how *different* it looked against the everyday car.

'You still there, Andy?'

'Just thinking,' he said, as his thoughts refocused. 'What we need to be looking for in this first go-round of contacts, is something that's *different*, something that jumps out at us as not being normal.'

'Like what?'

What could he tell her? That he'd seen a boy racer blow past him and it had given him an idea? That his sixth sense was telling him they had to focus on what wasn't normal? That if the truth be told, he really didn't know? He struggled to pull his thoughts together, but all he knew was, whoever had killed Howitt had to have been someone he'd scammed, someone who wanted revenge. He was sure of that. But revenge for what? Revenge for being fooled by romance? Revenge for being cheated out of money? Revenge for being persuaded to take out loans they could never repay? Kenzie Dorrance had been tricked into doing just that. But she hadn't sought revenge. Instead, she'd committed suicide—

'Earth to Andy? Hello . . .?'

'Sorry Jessie, I can't tell you what different will look like. But I'm sure we'll know it when we see it.'

'Oh, you're a great help,' she said, then added, 'I could use some assistance.'

'Get hold of Mhairi and Jackie. If that's not enough, get back to me.'

'It *is* the weekend.'

'It is indeed,' he said, and ended the call.

CHAPTER 18

Jessie listened to the line click, and whispered a curse. She'd been planning to do a bit of Christmas shopping for Robert; the usual six pairs of underpants and socks, two sticks of underarm deodorant, and some cheap but fragrant aftershave. If Christmas never existed, she often wondered if Robert would just wear the same pants and socks until they disintegrated. But maybe not. He could always wait until his birthday.

She walked through to her living room and sat on the sofa in front of the electric fire. In the corner, her Christmas tree sparkled and glittered with fairy lights that seemed to dance from one branch to the next and change colours from white to pink and back again. Robert had helped her put it up, a mother–son tradition that brought a smile to her face. She still remembered buying the tree, fifteen years ago, when Robert was just a wee boy, not even at school yet, one of those artificial trees that came in a box and which took hours to put up – well, it used to, as she was hopeless at anything mechanical, if you could call putting up a Christmas tree mechanical. At the time, she'd not been able to afford a real Christmas tree, and even though the artificial tree had served them well, after six years she thought it had to be about time she bought a real one. But a visit into town soon put paid to that idea – twenty pounds for a tree that was no taller than herself – no height at all, really. Not that she resented spending twenty pounds on a real tree for her wee boy. But what she did resent was wasting twenty pounds every year thereafter for a different tree. No, her artificial tree would do fine for the time being. And it was still doing fine, thank you very much.

She picked up the pages she'd printed from the email the IT technicians had sent her, and thought back to her phone call with Andy. He'd been right to try to trim the workload, and the direction he'd pointed her in was as good an approach as any. She jotted down the names of each of the victims against Wimmer and Denz, and one by one extended that list to include those victims of Howitt's other profiles, Cleveden, Fisher and Westerbrook. Even though the files had been corrupted and were incomplete in places, she managed to create a list of eighteen women whom Howitt had contacted over the last several years, as best she could tell. Fifteen lived overseas, and three lived in the UK.

Jessie was no IT expert. She needed someone who had access to specialist software to find social security numbers, tax records, home addresses, phone numbers, next of kin, and other pertinent information that might help in their upcoming interviews. She phoned Mhairi and Jackie, apologised for spoiling their weekend, and arranged to meet them in the Office. Christmas shopping would just have to wait for another day or so.

She had just switched on her wee Fiat 500's ignition when her mobile buzzed with an incoming text message – ID Fran. Shit. Fran had sent three earlier texts letting her know she would be in

St Andrews for a couple of days, and it would be good to meet up. Jessie had ignored each of them, and was about to do the same again, when her mobile rang. Without thinking, she took the call.

'DS Janes,' she said.

'If I didn't know any better I'd say you were ignoring me.'

'Jeez-oh, Fran, you've just texted me.'

'I know. And you never get back to me. Is there a reason, Jess?'

'I'm busy.'

'You're always busy.'

'Well, there you go. What can I tell you? And I'm busy now. Just about to head off to the Office.'

'It's Saturday.'

'And tomorrow's Sunday, and I'll be busy then, too.'

'I've booked into the Rusacks,' Fran said, as if Jessie hadn't spoken. 'For two nights. Back to Glasgow on Monday. Even though you're always busy, you still have to eat.' A pause, then, 'I've reserved a table in the One Under Bar. Why don't you let me treat you to dinner tonight? Just the two of us.'

'I was going to take Robert out tonight,' she lied.

Fran chuckled for a long moment, then said, 'I can read you like a book, Jess. I don't think you were planning to do anything of the sort tonight. Robert can fend for himself. Life's too short. You have to enjoy it. Dinner at the One Under. How does six for seven sound? I won't be offended if you can't make it, but it really would be lovely to see you again, Jess.'

Jessie pressed her mobile to her ear. Something in the tone of Fran's voice seemed to immobilise her. She felt that glowing warmth slide through her once more and send a tingling shiver the length of her spine. She'd managed to resist Fran's earlier attempts to persuade her to take a trip with her to Spain, to Fran's holiday home, a villa with swimming pool on the outskirts of Murcia. But now she felt as if she was fast running out of excuses.

'Look, Fran,' she said, struggling to put some resolve into her tone, 'I really am up to my ears in it, and I don't think I can make it tonight—'

'Don't think, Jess? Or don't want to?'

Jessie held onto her mobile for a long moment, then said, 'I don't . . . I don't . . .'

'That's okay. I know you, Jess. I used to be like you, too, until I made a promise to myself to be true to who I really am. So don't worry. The table's reserved. Come as you are, casual as you like. No pressure. No pushing. A bite to eat if you want. A drink, too. Or just a chat. It would be lovely to see you again. I hope you can make it, Jess. Bye, sweetheart.'

The line died.

Jessie held onto her mobile for several seconds, before throwing it into the passenger seat as if it were a burning stone. She tucked her arms around herself, as if to stifle a chill, but felt a glowing warmth swell and settle deep down inside her. She looked around, conscious that someone might be looking at her, wondering what she was doing just sitting behind the steering wheel, engine running, going nowhere. Fran's insistent whisper echoed in her mind like the relentless ticking of a clock. *I know you, Jess. It would be lovely to see you again. I hope you can make it. Bye, sweetheart. Bye, sweetheart.*

Bloody hell. She gripped the steering wheel, plunged her foot onto the clutch, and jabbed the shift-stick into gear. As she eased her Fiat out of Canongate, she couldn't help chastising herself. 'What the hell's the matter with you, Jessie? You've got a murder investigation to take care of. Howitt could've been the most despicable bastard who cheated and abused women, but we still need to find out who killed him. And that takes precedence over everything. Even Fran.'

Satisfied in her own mind that Fran was no longer of any consequence . . . at least for the time being, and definitely not for that night . . . she settled down for the short drive to the Office.

CHAPTER 19

In the fishing village of Crail, Gilchrist turned off High Street, and found a parking space in Castle Street. He strode towards his cottage in Rose Wynd, head down against a stiff northerly breeze that was cold enough to have blown in from the Arctic. He clicked his fob, and his BMW beeped behind him. He'd taken a call from Chief Superintendent Diane Smiley, egregiously nicknamed Smiler, although no one would dare say that in front of her, and any likelihood of his successfully seeking additional funding for his investigation were now non-existent. Budgets were tight, and becoming tighter, Smiler had said, and in the next breath announced that all overtime was forthwith disapproved. *Basic hours only. Got that, DCI Gilchrist?* He'd got it loud and clear, but didn't want to tell her that his interpretation of *forthwith* was from the start of the working week, rather the moment he ended the call. The start of the working week seemed much cleaner, to his mind. At least, that's what he would argue when the shit hit the inevitable fan at the end of the month.

Once indoors, he turned up the heating, an attempt to ward off a chill that seemed to haunt his bones. Was he coming down with something? A cup of hot tea did what it could, but in the end he settled for a piping hot shower, and a good lathering from top to toe.

Refreshed and warmed, he took a seat at his dining-room table, spread Jessie's printouts across the surface, and studied the names of the scammed women again. And as he read through them, comparing those scammed by Franz Wimmer against those scammed by Hans Denz, he wondered if dishonesty could perhaps work both ways. Why not? After all, Howitt had duped plenty of women by changing his name and appearance and the pull-down backdrop whenever he wanted. But being on a dating site provided each of the women a certain level of anonymity, too, if they wanted to hide behind it. And why wouldn't they? The simplest form of anonymity would be to change their name. So, were all the names on these printouts accurate? Or were any of them made up? His gut was telling him that most might be correct, but some had to be faked, surely. And if so, how could he establish which were which? He could have the IT guys look into them, then decided it might be better to find out what was needed before he spoke to his IT department.

He picked up his mobile, and called Dick, his go-to guy whenever he needed some computer-related assistance under the radar, so to speak.

'Long time,' Dick said. 'What can I do you for?'

'Just a question, if you've got time.'

'I'm all yours. Shoot.'

Gilchrist explained his thoughts to Dick, and told him what he was looking for – proof that every person on particular dating sites were who they said they were, and if they weren't who they said they were, how could he find out their real names?

'The simplest way would be to check their IP addresses, which would mean logging into each of their profiles—'

'You mean *hacking* into their personal computers?'

'Of course. Wouldn't be too hard. In layman's terms, once I have a name and the corresponding dating website, I can confirm their connection protocols. That would give me access to everything I need, more or less. But it might not be as easy as that.'

'Why not?'

'They could be using different computers. They could be using one at home for all their personal stuff, like banking, utilities, that sort of stuff. And another from their place of work for their dating websites. Or vice versa.'

Gilchrist didn't think anyone corresponding to someone on a dating website would do so on their work computer. But you never could tell. The length of time some people spent on their mobile phones, for example, begged the question as to how they ever had time to eat, let alone work. So it wasn't beyond the realms of possibility. He said nothing while Dick went on to explain that once he had a name, he'd need to do some more digging – hack into their bank accounts, utility services, maybe even their Department for Work and Pensions records, or income tax records, to confirm identity. After a few more minutes explaining potential downfalls, Dick said, 'Does that answer your question for you?'

Although Gilchrist hadn't understood everything Dick told him, it was now clear that asking the IT department to do what he wanted would require warrants to be applied for – at least one per person – with no guarantee of their being granted. With today's data-protection sensitivities, the chances of their refusal was highly likely, even though they were being sought as part of an ongoing murder investigation. It didn't bear thinking about.

So Gilchrist did what he thought he had to do, told Dick he'd get back to him with a list of names and dating websites, then ended the call. No one in the Constabulary knew of his association with Dick, who'd helped him out in the past by providing information that could not otherwise have been obtained through the proper channels – and for proper, read legal. If it ever came out that Gilchrist had used such illegal means, not only would any such information be deemed inadmissible in court, but he would be fired, charged with a criminal offence, and likely lose his pension. Dick seldom asked for payment, which helped keep his illegal searches out of direct sunlight, and if you thought about it, also satisfied Smiler's instruction to cut costs.

Job done. Or was it?

The problem would arise, as it had in the past, of what to do with Dick's findings, especially if they led to a new line of enquiry. But as he'd often done, Gilchrist argued that lateral thinking played a major role, and in some instances he'd retroactively applied for the appropriate warrant. Which he could always do again, of course.

Back at his table in the dining room, he phoned Jessie for an update.

'Jeez, Andy, you're getting right pushy in your old age. I've got Mhairi and Jackie helping out, and I'll have something on your desk first thing Monday.'

The echo of Smiler's words reverberated in his mind, but he didn't want to mention that to Jessie, not at that moment anyway. Instead, he said, 'I need it before Monday, so why don't you give me what you've all come up with by the end of the evening?'

'I'll do what I can.'

When the line died, Gilchrist gave a rue smile. Jessie might complain about being pressed for an earlier response, but she was as keen as he was to find out who'd murdered Ian Howitt, and whether or not the deaths of Clive Keepsake and Milas Volker were related.

He walked into the hallway, pulled down the attic access ladder, and clambered up it. Several minutes later he placed his old suitcase on the bed with care, casting up in his mind the memory of the last time he'd gone on holiday. By himself, he thought, years ago, before he and Beth, an ex-girlfriend of his, had split up, or rather before Beth had dumped him, sold up her shop and headed off to Spain in search of a less inhibited affair. Being a detective could do that to you, have you focusing on work 24/7, with no time for anything else, and playing havoc with your private life, to the detriment of any relationship. Now here he was again, at some turning point in his private life. And not quite sure how to handle it.

Irene had asked him to move in with her, and on the spur of the moment, he'd agreed. But now he'd done so, he'd come to understand that the practicalities of living with her were not straightforward. If he moved into Irene's lock, stock and barrel, what was he supposed to do with his cottage? Lock it up for the winter? Rent it out on a short-term lease? He would never sell it. He thought he knew that much, at least. But would he end up having to do just that if he married Irene?

As he let those thoughts flicker through his mind, he came to see he was harbouring some doubts. He'd just thought *if* he married Irene, not *when*. Was his subconscious warning him not to jump into the deep end, but to take some time, suck it and see, wade towards the deep end one careful step at a time? He couldn't say, although his subconscious seemed to be telling him what to do as he packed underpants, socks and shirts into his suitcase as if he were about to head off for a long weekend.

He was interrupted by his mobile beeping with an incoming email – ID Jessie – and curt as it was – fyi starter – he was pleased when he opened the attachment to reveal a list of ten women's names, associated dating websites, dates of last outgoing messages, more or less evenly split between Franz Wimmer and Hans Denz – four to six, he counted. He forwarded the attachment to Dick, with a short message – Asap. Thanks, A – then returned to packing his suitcase.

CHAPTER 20

By six thirty-five, Jessie'd had enough. Her head was spinning, and her stomach was grumbling. Both Mhairi and Jackie had left the Office shortly after five, both promising to work some more on it on Sunday. She felt as if their efforts were paying off, as she'd been able to incorporate into her spreadsheet details of another twenty-six women whose names she'd received from the Northumbrian and Copenhagen Offices. All in all, she thought, the product of a good day's work.

She sent the list off to Gilchrist with another curt message – 26 more – and picked up her coat from the back of her chair. Robert had texted her earlier to say he was with a friend – no mention of who that friend was – and that he would be home before midnight, as he had a big job they were working overtime on Sunday and the following week, trying to get ahead of schedule before the construction industry closed down for Christmas and New Year.

Outside, her breath gushed in puffs of steam in the ice-cold air. And as she settled behind the wheel, she was thankful that at least it wasn't snowing. She eased out of the car park, through the pend, and instead of turning right as she usually did to drive home – a quick right into Union Street, short squiggle right, left, right onto South Street, left past the West Port, then a doddle down the southbound A915 to her home in Canongate – she found herself inexplicably turning left onto North Street. It started to rain then, that fine drizzle that seemed to freeze the instant it landed on her windscreen. But a squirt of her wind-screen washer – well done Robert for topping up the reservoir with anti-freeze washer fluid – and the wipers did the rest.

By the time she turned into The Links, her car was still only heating up – the drive from the Office no more than a mile. She found a parking space twenty yards from The One Under, squeezed out of the driver's door, the eighteenth hole of the Old Course links close enough to tap with her foot, and pressed her key fob.

She took care walking down the steps to the bar, and was welcomed by a blast of warm air and a jostling atmosphere as she stepped inside. Saturday night always seemed to be busy in St Andrews, but she found Fran seated by herself at a table in an alcove. When Fran saw her, she smiled and stood, and welcomed her with a heavy peck on one cheek, and a hug that almost had Jessie catching her breath.

Fran beamed at her. 'You look wonderful, Jess. Working over-time must suit you. Here, take a seat.'

Jessie felt her face flush. Was she supposed to tell Fran she looked wonderful, too, and how lovely it was to see her again? Instead, she slipped off her coat, threw it into the alcove, and slumped into her seat. 'Overtime's knackering. That's all I can tell you about that.'

Fran sat opposite, and tilted a bottle of Amarone into a wine glass. 'I knew you would come, Jess,' and stopped pouring when the glass was half-filled. Then she topped up her own, returned the bottle to the table with care, and held her glass out to Jessie. 'Here's to health, wealth and happiness.'

Jessie chinked her glass against Fran's with, 'Especially wealth.'

Fran took a delicate sip while Jessie took a mouthful. 'Health's wealth,' Fran said.

'What's that mean?'

'That without your health, you've nothing. Doesn't matter how wealthy you are, it won't stop you from dying.'

'Aye, but if you're wealthy you can enjoy spending it until you pop your clogs, rather than working overtime.'

Fran smiled, raised her glass again. 'Touché,' and took another sip. Then she sat back and smiled, her gaze wandering over Jessie's face as if taking in every detail and consigning it to memory.

'What're you trying to do?' Jessie said. 'Embarrass me?' and hid behind another mouthful.

'I'm sorry, Jess, I don't mean to. But I can't help it. It's your eyes, they're lovely and dark and so clear. And your nose, too, so fine and delicate. You really are quite beautiful. Has no one ever told you that before?'

'Not when they're sober. And when they're drunk, they're too busy trying to poke the fireplace.'

Fran stifled a laugh. 'That's what I love about you. Your sense of humour. Smart and quick, and so self-deprecating.'

'If I knew what that meant, I might agree with you.' Jessie returned her glass to the table, fixing her eyes on it, not wanting to look up until she had it clear in her own mind what she wanted to say. When she felt as if she had, she looked at Fran. 'Listen, Fran, I know what you're trying to do, but I told you last time we met, that I bat for the other side. You know what I'm saying?'

'I know you did, Jess, and again I'm sorry if I'm making you feel uncomfortable.' She reached for Jessie's hand, and Jessie surprised herself by not pulling away. She held Jessie's gaze for a long moment, then released her grip and sat back. 'Why don't we order some food? I'm told they do great burgers and fries here. But have what you want, why don't you?' Then she looked around the bar area, as if searching for someone, and when her gaze returned to Jessie, she said, 'Is this place okay for you? Would you prefer we went someplace more upmarket? I'm sorry, I thought this was the kind of place you would like.'

'Cheap and cheerful, you mean?'

'There's nowhere cheap in St Andrews.'

'I'll give you that,' Jessie said, and chinked her glass to Fran's.

'So this is okay? You're ready to order?'

'This is perfect. Burger and fries it is. Why is it all the food you like is supposed to be bad for you?'

'If you enjoy it, then it's good for you. That's my philosophy.'

'I'll drink to that.'

Jessie sat back while Fran placed the order with the waitress. Another couple of sips of wine, and she felt her body relax, her mind begin to shed the stress of the last few days. The start of any murder investigation was always intense, and it was a proven fact that the first forty-eight hours were the most crucial. But there was only so much anyone could do in a given period of time – and today's efforts had been worthwhile. Which seemed to settle her, as if her subconscious was permitting her to sit back and enjoy herself – have a few glasses of wine, a nice burger and fries, then home to bed and sweet dreams and all that.

As the evening progressed, Jessie repeatedly checked her mobile. Not that she was expecting any calls or texts, rather it was a simple ploy to keep Fran on the back foot, let her think that she could be called away at any moment. But give Fran her due, she didn't press her in any way, or make her feel uncomfortable, just had an enquiring chat with her, asking about Robert, what he was doing, how he was keeping, were there any girlfriends on the go? – questions that any interested or concerned friend might ask.

And Jessie did a bit of asking of her own, to be told that Fran had two children, both in their mid-twenties, was divorced, kept in touch with her ex-husband with whom she had a warm and friendly relationship, after he got over the fact that he'd married a lesbian.

Jessie burst out laughing when Fran said that.

'You should've seen his face. He didn't know what to say. He went from anger, to disbelief, back to anger and everything in between before he just sat down and cried.'

'He cried?'

'Like a baby. I couldn't believe it. But he told me he was crying for all the memories we'd had, all the good times, and some bad, and that if he'd known years ago that I was gay he would've let me go to be myself. So many wasted years he said. Which hurt me, I had to say. But then he said, no, he'd loved our years together, and the time we had, but the wasted years were mine, being married to a man when all the time I should've been with a woman.'

'Wow. That's a bit deep.'

Fran reached for Jessie's hand, and gave it a squeeze. Then she pushed back her chair and stood. 'I'm going to head off, Jess. I'm tired. But it really was lovely to see you again.'

Jessie said nothing as Fran gathered her things together, then with a quick peck on the cheek, she turned and strode to the door. She gripped the handle and was about to push out, when she turned and gave Jessie the universal *phone me* sign with her hand to her ears.

And that was that.

Jessie sat back, surprised by Fran's sudden departure, trying to work out if she'd said something wrong, coughed up some wayward remark that had hit a nerve by accident, then concluded that she hadn't. Fran had paid the bill, and ten minutes later left. As simple as that.

And it surprised Jessie how saddened she felt by Fran's leaving. She'd enjoyed her company, revelled in the way her eyes held hers, loved how she spoke softly to her, her voice seldom more than a whisper that seemed to brush over her being with the sensual lightness of a feather, and without any covert pressure to be anything other than her dinner companion for the evening. Just thinking of Fran, recalling the echo of her voice, the gentlest of whispers, sent the tiniest of thrills through Jessie, a tingling sensation that delivered a glowing shiver to her core.

She gathered her purse and her jacket, thinking that maybe she would give Fran a call in the morning. Or maybe not. Maybe it would be best to let things lie the way they were, and not rock the lesbian boat, so to speak. She was a mother, for crying out loud, with a son that needed her. Well, so she kept saying to herself. Robert still lived with his mum, but every day seemed to bring him a step closer to becoming independent. And one day he would marry, have children of his own, and she, Jessie, would become a grandmother.

Somehow that simple thought brought her back to reality.

She had a murder investigation to solve, and a busy day ahead of her, probably a busy week, too. She felt her body give one more involuntary shiver as she slipped on her jacket, and with a final glance around the bar area, she strode towards the door.

CHAPTER 21

5.47 a.m., Sunday

Gilchrist opened his eyes to a dark room. He'd been dreaming of being in the Office, trying to find the source of a repeated beeping. And now, here it was, in real life. He reached for his mobile on the bedside table – ID Dick – text message, not a phone call.

He glanced at it – call asap – and slid his feet to the floor, careful not to make a sound. Irene was still fast asleep. The medication she was on had her sleeping twelve hours a day, every day. All her life, Irene had been an early riser, and now complained that sleeping this much was causing her to miss too many hours of her waking time. Despite Gilchrist trying to convince her it was her body's way of recovering, she continued to resist by trying to stay awake late at night, and setting the alarm for seven each morning.

Downstairs in the kitchen, Gilchrist phoned Dick.

'Didn't mean to wake you up,' Dick said with a chuckle.

'I've been cursed with excellent hearing. Call asap you said. So what've you found?'

'Oh, you're going to love this. That second set you sent me, with twenty-six more names? That's a beauty.'

Gilchrist pressed his mobile hard to his ear, realised he was holding his breath, then said, 'I'm listening.'

'I won't go into the details of how I went about it, Andy, but once I got my teeth into it, I couldn't put it down.'

'You've been working on it all night?'

'Never notice the time these days, particularly when I'm into something. So, here's what I've uncovered so far—'

'So far?' Gilchrist interrupted. 'You think there's more?'

'Can't say right now, but I thought it best to get back to you and bring you up to speed with what I've got. That first list you sent appeared to be legit on a first looksee. Everyone seemed to be who they said they were. I was able to cross reference IP addresses with email and bank accounts. On the first go-around everything seemed fine. All except for one. Anna Wilson. I couldn't find her existence beyond what she had on the dating website.'

'And was this Anna Wilson on Howitt's list?'

'Howitt? No. Franz Wimmer.'

Of course. One of Howitt's aliases. 'And you think she's using a false name?'

'Most definitely, which isn't uncommon on dating sites. Who wants to present their true self as someone who's looking for a date? Many join it to find a partner for sex. Which is an even better reason for not wanting to give out your real name. So I wasn't troubled by that, even though this Anna Wilson had gone to the bother of not just using a false name, but trying to bury herself deep.'

Anna Wilson. Gilchrist jotted the name down.

'Then you sent me that second batch, and that's when things became interesting. Again, most seemed genuine enough, until I came across Petra Sunberg.'

'Is that Swedish?'

'Swedish, Finnish, Norwegian, who knows. It's Nordic anyway.'

'Keep going,' Gilchrist said, eager to hear what Dick had to say.

'So after I did a bit more digging, I find out that this Petra Sunberg has the same IP address as Anna Wilson.'

'It's the same person using different names?'

'Precisely.'

'And who's list was she on?'

'Hang on, let me see. Here it is. Milas Volker. But that's not all.'

Gilchrist held his breath, scribbled Petra's name next to Anna Wilson's.

'Next thing, I come across another name that's not ticking all the boxes, and when I try to cross-reference her details, lo and behold . . .'

'The same IP address?'

'Spot on. This time it's a Jennifer Downsview.'

'How'd you spell that?' Gilchrist jotted it down, then said, 'And whose list did she appear on?'

'Looks like Clive Keepsake's.'

'Anyone else?' he asked, as if he hadn't already hit the jackpot.

'That's all of them. Three in total.'

'Bloody hell,' Gilchrist gasped.

'Well, me being me,' Dick said, 'with the bit between my teeth, I just had to find out the real name of the person pretending to be Anna *et al.*'

'Any luck?'

'Yep.'

Gilchrist closed his eyes. This could be it. They'd come up with three murder victims – Howitt, Keepsake and Volker – and now they had three false profiles, but significantly, one false profile against each scammer. Was this the person who killed all three? Or was it simple coincidence? But if you didn't believe in coincidence, where did that put you?

About to learn the name of your prime suspect, came the answer.

'Ellice Ibbotson,' Dick said.

Gilchrist gripped his mobile tighter. 'Say again?'

Dick repeated the name, and Gilchrist wrote it down. He was about to ask Dick to send him everything he had on this Ellice Ibbotson, but if any of it was ever traced back, it would be end of career, maybe the beginning of a jail sentence. So he said, 'What else can you tell me about this Ibbotson?'

'Some basics. She's English. Thirty-six. Divorced. Ex-military. You're not going to believe this, but she served five years with Libya's Revolutionary Nuns as one of Gaddafi's bodyguards.'

'Nuns?'

'Don't let the name fool you. These women were highly trained in martial arts and firearms. Not to be messed with. Their mission was to protect Gaddafi at all costs, even with their lives if need be. The press used to call them the Amazonians. Her father's English, her mother's Libyan, so I'm guessing that's how she was able to join up. And that's about as far as I've got. Her driving licence is clean, as are her tax records.'

'You have an address for her?'

'Yes and no.'

'What does that mean?'

'The address on her driving licence doesn't exist. Well it does, but it's an abandoned building. And she's only got a PO Box on her tax records. So it's of no use to you.'

He could always get a warrant to open that PO Box, or put a hold on all mail, or even have someone on standby at the Post Office ready to make an arrest as soon as Ibbotson picked up her mail. But he was getting ahead of himself. He couldn't have Dick's illegal work backfire and come back to haunt him. 'Can you work back from the PO Box, and get an address from that?'

'Sometimes it's not as simple as that, but I'll see what I can do.'

'That's great, Dick. Listen, can you hold onto what you've got? I'll need to figure out what to do with this, bearing in mind it's all under the radar, so to speak.'

'Got it. I'll print out what I've got so far, and if you ever need it, just let me know.'

'Before you do, can I ask you one last thing?'

'Sure. Shoot.'

'Can you find out what car Ibbotson drives?'

'Already got that. A red Volkswagen Golf GTI,' he said, and read off the registration number.

Gilchrist thanked Dick, and ended the call, keen to read through his notes, and cross-reference the three false names against the lists from the Northumbrian Police and the Politi. Anna Wilson was indeed on Ian Howitt's list, Jennifer Downsview on Northumbrian Police's list, and the icing on the cake, as far as Gilchrist was concerned, Petra Sunberg on the Politi's list. Was it all beginning to come together now?

Ellice Ibbotson was now the prime suspect in a triple murder investigation.

But what to do with this information? That was his next problem.

He now had a name he couldn't use, and a car he'd have to pretend he knew nothing about. What he had to do was have Jackie carry out further research that would have her – and effectively his Office – uncover Ibbotson and the connection to the three murders.

But how to start that off, he had no idea.

CHAPTER 22

Gilchrist spent the next hour working on a strategy to maximise Dick's findings. He went through Jessie's printouts, cross-referenced the names against those he'd jotted down from Dick's phone call. He googled Libya's Revolutionary Nuns to confirm that they were indeed an elite all-female group devoted to protecting Gaddafi. He researched other dating websites for the name Ellice Ibbotson, but came up dry, as expected. His efforts came to a halt when he heard Irene's alarm go off, and he returned to the bedroom upstairs.

He sat next to her on the bed, took hold of her hand. Despite the thermostat being set higher than he was used to, her fingers felt cold. He rubbed them. 'How do you feel?'

Without opening her eyes, she smiled. 'It's lovely to hear a man's voice first thing in the morning.'

He leaned down and kissed her cheek. 'How does breakfast in bed sound?'

She looked at him then. 'That's almost an offer I can't refuse, but I'd rather get up first, if that's okay.'

'Why don't you have another forty winks, and I'll put the kettle on.'

She nodded and closed her eyes. He pulled the duvet up to her chin, then left the bedroom.

In the kitchen, he filled the kettle, and set the breakfast bar. Neither he nor Irene were big eaters first thing in the morning, but his call with Dick had sparked him wide awake, and hunger now gnawed at his stomach. He was slicing and dicing fresh fruit when he heard the thump of feet hitting the bedroom floor overhead. He set the knife aside, washed his hands, then walked upstairs to give assistance, if needed. But when he entered the bedroom Irene was closing the en-suite bathroom door.

Five minutes later, when she entered the kitchen, dressing gown wrapped around her, headscarf over her head, slippered feet shuffling over the wooden flooring, he gave her a gentle hug, and helped her onto her seat at the breakfast bar.

'Fresh toast always smells wonderful first thing in the morning,' she said, reaching for a glass of orange juice, and taking a sip. 'Oh, I meant to tell you last night, but it completely slipped my mind. Joanne spoke to Maureen yesterday.'

Gilchrist spread marmalade over his buttered toast. 'Ah, so how is she?'

'That's what I wanted to tell you, although I don't want you to worry, because you know what young women are like, but Joanne thought she didn't sound happy.'

He bit into his toast, and mumbled, 'In what way?'

'She didn't say, just that she thought she was maybe hiding something from her.'

'Hiding?'

'That's what she said.'

He didn't like the sound of that. Maureen could be the devil to get through to at times, and he'd found from hard-earned experience that the best way to deal with her was to ignore her, let her work through whatever mood she was in at her own pace. He saw an opportunity, and took it. 'I told you I visited Jack yesterday, so I was thinking it might be nice to visit Mo as well,' he lied. 'Make a weekend out of it, if you like. Would you be up for a quick trip to Glasgow today?'

'I'll pass, if you don't mind, but that's what I told Joanne, that you hadn't seen Mo in quite some time, and that I should perhaps encourage you to visit her. What do you think?'

'I think you're rather wise.' He peeled a banana, sliced it in two, placed one half on Irene's side plate, and spread the other on a second slice of toast. 'If I leave right away, I could be back in St Andrews in time for afternoon tea.' He bit into his toast, and waited for Irene's response. But when she said nothing, he looked at her, and saw she was smiling at him.

He raised an inquisitive eyebrow.

'If I didn't know you better,' she said, 'I'd say you're trying to find some excuse to get on with a bit of work.'

'Well, I have to confess that I was thinking I could call into the Office as well.'

She shook her head, but he saw no sadness in her face, just tired resignation, as if she realised this was the way it was and how it would always be. He thought it best to say nothing more, and together they shared breakfast in silence, the TV on with the sound down low.

As he was clearing the dishes, filling up the dishwasher, Irene seated in her favourite chair in front of the fire, he couldn't rid himself of the feeling that he was letting her down. She'd asked him to move in, be there for her, and at the first opportunity on the first morning he was going to head off to work. But what else could he do? He had information on a prime suspect that he had to find some way to share, with no clear idea how to do it. Perhaps the drive to Glasgow would invigorate his thoughts. And for all he knew, any delay in pressing on with his investigation might result in another murder being committed.

He really had no option but to get on with it.

On the seventy-plus miles drive to Glasgow, he phoned Jessie. 'I need you to chase up something for me.'

'And good morning to you, too,' she said.

He ignored her quip. 'Get onto Glenrothes HQ and get them to check CCTV footage for any record of a red Volkswagen Golf GTI near Howitt's on the night of his murder, or on the road to the Old Course Hotel. Remember his mobile pinged that mast? It might be worth running the registration number through ANPR for that night, too.' He recited the number. 'But it's a simple job to put on false plates or alter the number with tape, so I wouldn't hold my breath for that result.'

'Any hint as to why you want me to do this?'

'If you're ever asked, say it's just a hunch. But you need to keep it low-profile. *Dead* low. You got that?'

'Sounds to me like you've been waving that magic wand of yours again.'

Jessie knew of his involvement with Dick, and knew how much trouble he would be in if he were ever found out, and probably herself, too, by association, although he did what he could to keep her on the periphery. And the Automatic Number Plate Recognition System was computerised technology that read vehicle number plates using character recognition. If pressed, they would have to come up with some justifiable reason for requesting a search for Ibbotson's number. Still, he could worry about that later. In the meantime, he felt he had to shake the trees and see what fell out.

'Let's just keep it at a hunch for the time being,' he said. 'And get back to me if you come up with anything. As soon as.' He ended the call before she could question him further.

He had just crossed the Clackmannanshire Bridge onto the M876 when his mobile rang – ID Dick. He took the call on speaker.

'I think Ibbotson's definitely who you're after,' Dick said. 'Because it's looking like she might have gone to ground. Can't find a live address for her anywhere. But old Dickie-boy won't be beaten.'

Gilchrist eyed the road ahead. Ibbotson going to ground just added to his belief that she was his prime suspect, someone with military experience, and knowledgeable about how to stay out of sight of the law. 'I'm listening,' he said.

'That red Golf GTI I told you about earlier? It was previously registered to a limited company in Glasgow that's one of those internet businesses that doesn't need to rent office space. So, I'm looking at the transfer documents, and I'm thinking that ownership has just changed hands, you know, from private to business, keeping it under the taxman's radar, and when you add two and two together, it makes me think that the business address is the home address.' A pause, then, 'Maybe I'm way off, Andy, but I thought I'd run it past you.'

'Glasgow, you said?'

'Yes.'

'It just so happens that I'm on my way there right now. You got that address handy?'

Dick had.

CHAPTER 23

From the Kingston Bridge, the dark waters of the River Clyde could be mud sliding its way to the sea. Despite recent modernisation of the Clydeside, it seemed to Gilchrist that no amount of landscaping or lighting or riverside walkways or bridges or glass facades on high-rise buildings could shift the industrial atmosphere for which Glasgow had once been renowned. The council was doing its best, but to Gilchrist's mind, it just didn't quite cut it.

Across the bridge on the south side, he pulled off the M80 onto the slip road for the M77, and joined a plug of vehicles that drifted along at a steady fifty miles an hour. He'd set the address Dick had given him into his satnav, and followed the instructions as he took the exit for Pollokshaws and Barrhead. Five minutes later, he turned into Glentyan Place.

He drove slowly, noting the house numbers until he found the house he was looking for, a semi-detached wood-cladded bungalow that sat in a tidy row of homes, each with their own fenced gardens, and each well maintained. Ibbotson's address appeared empty, and there was no red Golf GTI or any other car parked outside. He drove on, and rounded a corner, where he drew to a halt.

The air felt thick and damp, and warmer, too, nothing like the bitter freshness of the chilling east coast. He walked back along the way he'd come, keeping to the pavement on the opposite side of the street. A flicker of a curtain at a window to his side had him opening the front gate and ringing the bell.

The door cracked open, and an elderly woman with blue-rinsed hair and a glitter-covered sweater stood swaying in front of him. Either he'd interrupted a party, or she'd put too much brandy in the Christmas cake.

He held up his warrant card. 'Sorry to trouble you,' he said, 'but you wouldn't happen to know when the lady who lives in that house . . .' He nodded to the address across the street and two down, and gave the number, '. . . might be back home?'

'Naw, sorry, son. I don't see much of her maself. She's in an oot, but ah widnae know whit she does. We aw keep tae oorsels aroon here.'

He nodded. 'She drives a red car, doesn't she?'

'Aye, and far too fast, too.'

He was about to leave, when he said, 'She lives by herself, doesn't she?'

'Never seen her wae no one, son. But as ah say, we aw keep tae oorsels.'

He thanked her, then walked on past Ibbotson's house. Nothing seemed out of the ordinary, just a normal home in a normal estate on the outskirts of Glasgow. A fine drizzle started then, and he returned to his car for shelter. But five minutes later, he had a sense of being watched by neighbours suspicious of a parked car, so fired the ignition and drove off.

He thought of parking up the street and waiting for Ibbotson to return home, but she could have gone out for the day, even flown off for a holiday over the festive period, and if he thought about it, what could he do if he saw her anyway? Arrest her? If he did, how could he explain his method of investigation? No. Best to wait until he heard back from Jessie. And if he had Jackie back her own research into Ibbotson's background, then he might be able to cover his tracks with Dick. He swung his car around, and drove past Ibbotson's again, taking his time, driving as slow as he dared. His view through the windows was restricted by blinds. The slab path lay clear of weeds, the lawn small and tidy and cut short, the wooden cladding clear of . . . which was when he saw it, a CCTV camera half-hidden by the fascia, not set to cover the front door or the side entrance, but instead pointing straight at him. He gave a silent curse, and accelerated away.

He worked his way back onto the M77, troubled that he might have been caught on camera. But what would the feedback show? A BMW easing past her home, not stopping, but driving slowly? Nothing to worry about, surely. But a solitary man walking past her home in one direction, then back again, to be followed by a car driving past slowly? That was where he must surely be noticed. Would that be enough of a warning to alert someone trained in an elite military group, a former bodyguard of Gaddafi no less? He gave another whispered curse, and drove on.

He waited until he joined the M8 again and about to cross the Kingston Bridge before he phoned Mo.

She answered with a surprisingly chirpy, 'Hi, Dad. How are you?'

'Keeping well,' he said, then exchanged a few pleasantries. 'I'm in Glasgow at the moment, and thought I could pop in and see you.'

Silence filled the line for so long that he thought he'd lost the connection. Then she came back with, 'Can't, Dad. I'm busy today. Got stuff on.'

'With work?'

'No. Just stuff. You know.'

He could tell from the tone of her voice, and the staccato manner in which she spoke, that she was not being truthful. 'So how's the new job going?' he asked.

'Okay.'

'Working you to the bone, the way they do in Fife?'

'Yeah.'

'Have you come across Dainty yet?'

Another long pause, followed by, 'Sorry, Dad. Got to go. Speak later. Bye.'

The line died.

He gripped the steering wheel tight, and tried to make sense of the call. He was deep in thought when he glimpsed the overhead sign to the City Centre out of the corner of his eye. On impulse, he swerved across two lanes to the blaring tune of angry horns. He'd never been to Maureen's new flat in town. She'd always found some excuse – she was out; she was busy; she had friends round; it wasn't convenient – but now he was down in Glasgow, he thought it was time he paid her a fatherly visit.

He navigated his stop–start way through Glasgow's rain-sodden maze of one-way streets, bus lanes, and traffic lights that were nowhere near synchronised, and managed to find a parking spot by George Square – it was Sunday, after all. Four minutes later, he stood outside Maureen's. Her flat was on the third floor to the rear of the building, he knew that much, but had no idea what the main door security code was. So he waited.

It didn't take long.

A couple, hand in hand, oblivious to all around them including the fact that the crotch on the guy's jeans was at his knees, strolled past. Or maybe staggered would be a better word. It took them three attempts to punch in the correct code, and when they fell inside, Gilchrist took hold of the handle, and followed them.

He ignored the lift, and skipped up the stairs, two at a time. By the time he reached the third floor, he was breathing hard, heart thudding in his chest. He really needed to return to jogging the West Sands again, make some effort to get back into shape before he lost it – whatever *it* was – forever. He was surprised to find himself standing on a balcony open to the elements, but sheltered by the floor above, with a view the length of St Vincent Street. As he took time to recover his breath, he eyed the city scene beneath him.

Glasgow on Sunday. When had he last seen that?

This was the city in which his late wife Gail had been born and raised, and where she'd lived and worked, and to where she'd eventually returned when their marriage broke down. He remembered one midsummer evening, one of those rare warm city nights, he and Gail strolling hand in hand through George Square, their love for each other still new and fresh. They'd been out for Sunday brunch, which ended up being a pub crawl, and seemed to be one of Gail's more popular ways to spend the weekend. He'd enjoyed it, too, at the time, but when he looked back on it all, their early relationship, their marriage, her moving to St Andrews, his overworked and under-earned career, the hours, days and weeks they seemed to spend apart, he'd come to understand that even back then the writing had been on the wall for everyone to see, himself included. But he'd been blinded, by love at first, then work later, until it was too late, and Gail had stormed from the marital home, Maureen and Jack in tow, to return to Glasgow to spend the remainder of her short life married to her lover, Harry.

As he looked down on the damp city streets, sadness seemed to swell through him and gather at his throat. So many memories. So many years passed. So much of life lost.

St Vincent Street glistened and shimmered.

He turned and walked back down the stairs.

CHAPTER 24

Gilchrist waited until he'd made his way back onto the M80 at Carntyne before he phoned Jessie.

'Your ears must be burning,' she said. 'I was about to call you.'

He knew from the sparkle in her tone that she'd found something. 'I'm listening.'

'Got a red Golf GTI passing the Old Course Hotel on Thursday evening at, here it is, five forty-three. Heading out of town on the road to Cupar. Registration number's close, but not exact, so we're thinking the E's been taped over to make an F, and one number's been blanked out completely. So I'd say we've got it.'

'Whose name's the car registered in?'

'Daleela Forrest.'

'What?'

'Daleela, with two e's. It's Arabic, I think. You sound surprised.'

'And Forrest, you said?'

'With two r's.'

Gilchrist grimaced, cursed under his breath. The name wasn't what he'd expected, but it was Arabic. Well, at least it sounded Arabic, which brought to mind Libya's Revolutionary Nuns.

Maybe, he thought, just maybe it made sense, tied it all together. On the positive side, it could open a side door to his investigation. 'Okay,' he said, dragging the word out as he tried to collect his thoughts. 'Get Jackie to find out what she can on this Daleela Forrest. I don't think that's her real name.'

'What makes you think that?'

'A hunch.'

'You and your hunches. We could be chasing up a blind alley, Andy. You do realise that, don't you?'

We could indeed, he thought, but there had to be a reason behind the name. Dick had told him the registration had been changed from Ellice Ibbotson to some company. But he hadn't given him the name of the company. He toyed with the idea of calling Dick, getting him to check it out a bit deeper, then decided against it. He had to keep Dick out of it now. He had to bring his investigation back within the constraints of the law.

'Let's wait to see what Jackie comes up with before we talk about blind alleys. In the meantime, I need you and Mhairi to start calling the names on the lists, try to find out who's been scammed, and who's not. Start with Howitt's list,' he said, which would work good and well he thought, until they came across the name Anna Wilson. That way he could bring his investigation back on track.

'Don't you want to have a look at this questionnaire you asked me to prepare?' Jessie said. 'In case it's not what you want.'

'No need to. I trust you.'

'Wow. Changed days.'

'Is that what you think?' he said.

'You've no idea what you can be like, Andy. One minute everything's hunky-dory, and the next you're looking for someone's backside to chew out. Not literally, of course.'

'Of course,' he said, while he searched his memory for the last time he'd had it out with Jessie. Not for a while, as best he could remember.

'You can be quite the taskmaster,' she continued, and he thought he caught a hint of mischief in her tone.

'Talking of which . . .' He paused for effect, then said, 'I need you to get back to me by close of business today with any anomalies you find in Howitt's list.'

'Didn't know Sunday was a day of business,' Jessie said, and killed the call.

Gilchrist gritted his teeth. Maybe he'd misread that hint of mischief. He eyed the road ahead, and drove on. He'd always thought he and Jessie made a good team; he the reasoning voice to her Glaswegian sarcasm – good cop bad cop, kind of thing. But a famous line from 'To a Louse', a poem by Robert Burns – *O wad some Power the giftie gie us / To see oursels as ithers see us* – echoed through his mind, words he might be wise to take cognisance of.

With heavy heart, he drove on.

It didn't take Jessie long to find an anomaly in Howitt's list. Anna Wilson happened to be the sixth person she'd tried to call, but Jackie had been unable to come up with a phone number that worked – a false profile if ever there was one. She couldn't even get past Go. So, she decided to follow up with Jackie on this Daleela Forrest with two e's and two r's, instead. But the problem with Jackie was her stutter, and if you tried to talk to her on the phone, it was hopeless, although Andy seemed to be the only person who could understand her, with this uncanny ability, it seemed, to predict what she was trying to say. So, she thought she'd try a bit of googling on her own.

But thirty minutes later, she was no further forward. She'd turned up medical centres, ferry routes, singers and woodland commissions. She tried three different search engines, but the best she could come up with were results for Daleela or Forrest, but not for both.

In desperation, she phoned Jackie. 'Any luck with Daleela Forrest?' she asked.

'Nuh-uh, uh-huh,' Jackie grunted.

'What does that mean?'

'Y . . . y . . . y . . .'

Then it struck Jessie. 'Yes and no?'

'Uh-huh.'

'So you've got good news and bad news.'

Jackie chuckled, a heartening sound devoid of any stutter or self-consciousness, then said, 'Uh-huh.'

'Would it be best if you emailed it to me?' Which seemed to be the sensible way forward.

'All . . . all . . . all . . .'

Jessie heard her mobile beep. 'Already on its way?' she said.

'Uh-huh.'

'Thanks, Jackie. I'll get back to you if I've any questions.'

She ended the call, and felt an odd sense of relief flow through her. Not that she didn't like Jackie. Rather, she found it stressful dealing with her. All of a sudden, she realised how inconsiderate she was. Her own son, Robert, was deaf, and had been from birth, yet she was able to communicate with him as easily as talking. She made a silent promise to herself to make more of an effort with Jackie, who was after all a critical member of their team, and someone they all relied upon to provide them with answers to any number of questions. And here she was again, working every hour under the sun – well, the rain – with no word of complaint.

She opened Jackie's email – fyi – and hesitated for a second before realising Jackie had forwarded three attachments. She opened the first one and saw that it was a company overview report registered with Companies House. She scanned the single page, and realised what Jackie's Yes and No answer meant. Daleela Forrest wasn't an individual, but the name of a private limited company that had been incorporated five years ago. She didn't recognise the correspondence address – some street in Glasgow – but saw that the Company Accounts and Confirmation Statement – whatever that was – were current through 24 February last year. Did that mean they weren't current through February this year? She didn't know the answer to that, but read on.

The Nature of the Business stated that it provided information technology consultancy activities, which she supposed could cover anything from fixing mobile phones to setting up top-secret computer systems, and everything in between. She opened the next attachment – Confirmation Statement – which turned out to be nothing more than a document that listed the Company Name, Company Number, and date of the Confirmation Statement, which was the same date in February as the Accounts. The last page was the Authorisation, which was nothing more than a cover-all statement that didn't provide the name of any individual.

The next attachment was an unaudited financial statement, which showed the value of the company's capital and reserves at just over one hundred thousand pounds at that date in February, which was an increase of twenty-odd thousand from the previous year. Not bad for fixing mobile phones, she thought.

The final page was a list of Company Officers, if it could even be called a list, which provided two names only: Daleela Ibbotson, Director, and Ellice Ibbotson, Secretary. More information on the Director confirmed date of birth – a quick calculation put her at thirty-six – nationality – British; country of residence, Scotland; the date of appointment as Director, which matched the date of incorporation of the company. Information about the Secretary provided date of appointment only, which matched that of the Director.

So, all in all, everything seemed in order.

Or was it?

Jessie scratched her head, and read through the attachments again. She was missing something, she felt sure of that. She could find no mention of Forrest, other than in the name of the company. She jotted down some notes, underlining a name here, a date there, which didn't really help, other than the fact that it showed she needed Jackie to do some more digging for her.

She tapped in a short text message to Jackie – Daleela? Husband? – thought of asking some more questions, then decided to leave it at that. Maybe Forrest was Daleela's married name. But even if it was, did it matter to the current investigation? She couldn't say. All she knew was that it was one of Andy's boxes that he would surely need ticked.

She sent the text to Jackie, and was about to get back to calling the other names on the lists, when she realised she hadn't heard from Mhairi, and thought it might be worth speaking to her, find out if she was having more success than she was.

CHAPTER 25

Gilchrist was easing his way along Auchtermuchty's tight Cupar Road, just where it narrowed past the junction with Back Dykes, fenced pavement on one side, building on the other, no room for error, particularly if there were vehicles travelling through town from the opposite direction, when his phone rang – ID Jessie.

'I thought my ears were burning again,' he said.

'Where are you?'

'Driving through Auchtermuchty. Why?'

'Got an address in Cupar that might be of interest.'

'I'm listening.'

'We've been going through these lists you asked us to, Mhairi and me, and we're getting nowhere. I'm thinking that it's a waste of time. But then Jackie phones back with an address for a Ritchie Forrest, that's with two r's. Turns out he was once married to Daleela Ibbotson.'

'Ibbotson?'

'Yeah, Daleela's the director of that company you asked me to look into – Daleela Forrest. And the company secretary is Ellice Ibbotson. So I'm thinking they're sisters. But this Daleela, who was married to Ritchie Forrest, now lives in Cupar.' Jessie proceeded to spell out what Jackie had come up with from Companies House, and how the accounts appear to be behind, and ended with, 'You got all that?'

'Just about.'

'So I'm trying to tick one of those boxes you're always going on about, by phoning up the number Jackie's found for Daleela, but it's disconnected. Nothing. Zip. Nada. So, I try the other number I've got, and call Ritchie Forrest, and it's got me suspicious.'

'What d'you mean?'

'It's just ringing out, not going to voicemail. No big deal, he's just not answering. But that sixth sense of yours might be rubbing off on me, and I'm thinking that I really need to talk to this guy. I can't get hold of his ex-wife, and now I can't get hold of him, and that red Golf GTI you asked me about belongs to Ellice Ibbotson, the Secretary of the company, and the accounts are behind, so . . .' She paused, as if to catch her breath, then said, 'What do you think?'

Gilchrist kept his eyes on the road ahead as he left the town limits and accelerated into the countryside. He really didn't know what to think of Jessie's convoluted phone call. It was clear she felt she was onto something, but what that something was he had no idea. It seemed such a slim line of enquiry that he was about to tell her just to forget about it. But on the other hand, there seemed to be too many coincidences just to discard it. Besides, Cupar was less than fifteen minutes along the road, on his way to St Andrews.

'What's that address?' he said.

*　　*　　*

161

As it turned out, the address was not in Cupar, but on the outskirts, a remote cottage that looked as if it had seen better days. The garden, too, could have done with being dug up or returfed. Weeds as long and brown as straw clung to protection from the wind behind a stone wall that bordered the road. Off to the side, nettles lined the base of an overgrown hedge.

Gilchrist pushed the garden gate, which opened with complaint against rusted hinges. Before trying the doorbell, he peered through one of the front windows, its glass grimy and cobwebbed, its wooden frame cracked with peeling paint and putty. The interior was too dark to make out anything, and he stepped back, eyed the roughcast wall, then the length of roof guttering from which weeds sprouted.

The entire property had an air of desolation about it, as if it hadn't been lived in for months, maybe longer. Even the wildlife seemed silenced. He tried the doorbell, but didn't hear the echo of a chime from within. He tried it again, then decided that it wasn't working. He could find no door knocker, but rapped the letterbox a few times, to no response.

Round the back, the cottage was just as desolate. Leaves had collected in windblown piles that hugged the corner fence in sodden lumps of red, copper, gold. Moss-covered stones added subdued colour. A face-pressed peek through kitchen window blinds left him none the wiser. It seemed as if no natural sunlight could enter the place.

He knuckled the back door, then stood back.

Twenty seconds later, he knuckled it again, and gave the door handle a frustrated twist. He caught the heavy click of an old-fashioned latch, and to his surprise the door eased ajar. He pushed it wider to his accompanying, 'Hello? Anyone? Hello?' and could tell from that first wave of tongue-coating stench of decomposition what he was about to find. Rather than step inside, he returned to his car for forensic gloves and face mask, then walked back to the kitchen door.

He found what was left of Ritchie Forrest – if indeed that's who he was – seated in an armchair in front of the television, face purple and bloated blue, sightless eyes bulging from their sockets, mouth peeled back as if in a mock scream to reveal a black tongue. Purge fluids had oozed from his nose and mouth to drip down his shirt, giving the impression of his having vomited over himself.

Gilchrist felt a chill shiver through him, and realised the house was cold. He checked the thermostat in the kitchen to confirm that it had been turned way down to 12. Just as well, he thought. If the thermostat had been turned up, the body's decomposition would have been further advanced. As it was, a close study of the body's swollen neck revealed a leather strap tightly knotted around it, which cut deep into the skin, telling him that Forrest hadn't been murdered by the same person who'd killed Howitt and the others. Despite the state of Forrest's body, he felt confident that Sam Kim, Fife's temporary forensic pathologist, could give him a better calculation of time of death.

He pulled himself away from the victim, and called it in. Sam Kim would be first on site, followed by the SOCOs. Then he called Jessie, told her what he'd found. He was about to tell her there was no need for her to visit the scene, when she told him she was already on her way, and would be with him in five minutes. Mobile back in his pocket, he tried to view the crime scene with professional dispassion, while he waited for Jessie and the forensic units to arrive.

It troubled him that they'd ultimately found the body through his investigation into Howitt's murder, but the MO was so different that he wondered if he'd accidentally stumbled on an unrelated killing. The positioning of the body in the armchair – arms and legs positioned just so – were similar to other crime scenes. But a leather strap around the neck, and a desk-top computer on the table in the corner were a first. Had the killer forgotten to remove it? Or was there some reason for leaving it for all to see?

He wandered around the rest of the cottage, opening drawers here, cupboards there, but found no other computers or digital accessories. Forrest's mobile phone was nowhere to be found, and a charge lead on the bedside table confirmed, at least to Gilchrist's way of thinking, that Forrest had once owned a mobile phone, maybe even an iPad or Kindle.

A rap at the back door announced Jessie's arrival.

He met her in the front lounge.

'Well that explains why he wasn't answering his phone,' she said.

'Looks like his mobile's missing.'

'No landline?'

'There is,' he said, and nodded to an old-fashioned phone set on a side table in the corner of the lounge. 'But the line's dead. We can check if it's disconnected.'

'Here,' she said. 'Jackie sent this.'

He unfolded a sheet of paper – a printout of a death certificate – and took a moment to read it. 'Daleela Ibbotson committed suicide two years ago?' he said. 'Was she living with him at the time?'

'According to Jackie, they were already divorced on the grounds of his adultery.' She glared at the body. 'They'd been married for only two years, during which time she reported a number of incidents of physical abuse. She'd started legal action against him when she killed herself.'

'But why commit suicide?'

'Money problems, I'd say. She was scammed. Turns out she was one of the names on Clive Keepsake's list. Her bank records show a number of large withdrawals over a period of four months leading up to her death.'

'Define large.'

'The smallest was three thousand, the largest twelve. She wasn't a wealthy woman. Anything she had left from her divorce, she lost in a romance scam.'

Gilchrist raked his fingers through his hair, struggling to understand the mindset of scammers who financially strip their victims without the slightest remorse. And once the money was gone, the victim was left devastated, pained, in disbelief at what they'd done, of how foolish they'd been to have fallen for the scam. And if you didn't have much money to begin with, it wouldn't take much to empty your coffers. Then what?

Commit suicide? That surely was one step too far.

'Oh, and you should see this,' Jessie said, holding out another folded sheet.

He opened it, then looked at her as the meaning of the birth certificate fired through his mind.

'That's right,' she said. 'Ellice Ibbotson was Daleela's *twin* sister.'

As Gilchrist struggled to work out the implications of that, Jessie's voice came at him as if from a distance.

'So Ellice has motive – revenge. If Daleela's husband hadn't been such a bastard, they would still be married, and she wouldn't

165

have been on a dating website and been scammed. And she also has the means, being ex-military. Revolutionary Nuns, my arse. She's a killer through and through.'

But it wasn't falling into place for Gilchrist. The timing seemed wrong. Too soon? Or too late? In his mental turmoil, he couldn't quite work it, although he had to agree when Jessie said, 'Which as far as I'm concerned, now makes Ellice Ibbotson our prime suspect.'

CHAPTER 26

Gilchrist said nothing while Chief Superintendent Diane Smiley adjusted her seat behind her desk and sat down with care, as if afraid to crease her laundered outfit. She lifted a stapled report from a pile of papers on her desk, and placed it in front of her. Her eyesight was eagle-sharp, so she had no need of spectacles, and he watched her gaze dance around the words on the page, before it stilled. Then she lifted her head and stared at him.

'Care to explain, DCI Gilchrist?'

'Ma'am?'

'Why you disregarded my clear instruction?'

'I'm not sure I understand, ma'am.'

'Don't play me for the fool, DCI Gilchrist. You're on remarkably thin ice, and getting thinner with every passing second. What was it about *overtime forthwith disapproved* you did *not* understand?'

He cast his mind back, struggling to recall when he'd last seen Smiler this angry. Her jaw ruminated as she ground her teeth, and he detected a tiny tremor in the tips of her fingers. Never, came the short answer. He realised that his earlier thoughts of trying to convince her that he'd understood *forthwith* to mean from the start of the working week, wasn't going to cut it. Time for a quick change in thinking.

'I didn't disregard your instruction, ma'am.'

'I beg your pardon?'

'No overtime will be submitted by myself or any of my staff for services provided over the weekend, or more correctly speaking, from the moment after your call.'

'And every one of your staff has agreed to this?'

'Yes, ma'am.' He hadn't intended to come up with such an out-and-out lie, but if he thought about it, he could always fluff up individuals' hours when the dust settled at the start of a new tax year, and a new budget had been assigned. Not perfect, but it would have to do for the time being.

'Well, I have to say, Andy, that's come as a surprise, and a welcome one at that. Do please tell your staff that I appreciate their effort above and beyond.'

'Yes, ma'am. I'll do that,' he said, even though he had a sense from the look in her eyes that she was being more than a tad disingenuous.

She pushed back from her desk, gave him what he took to be a knowing smirk, then said, 'Right, bring me up to speed with this latest body.'

Two hours later, Gilchrist gathered the key members of his team in Jackie's office, which was easier for Jackie to attend – crutches positioned at the side of her desk – and more convenient for Gilchrist if he needed her to research anything as it came to light.

He looked at Jessie first, then Mhairi, and said, 'Smiler's pulling out all the stops on this one. The discovery of Ritchie Forrest's body has turned this into a nationwide manhunt for Ellice Ibbotson.'

'By nationwide, do you mean Scotland, sir?'

'Yes, Mhairi, even though Daleela Ibbotson was scammed by Clive Keepsake, our key focus is on locating and arresting her sister, Ellice.'

Keepsake had been murdered in Ashington, Northumbria, and Daleela's name found on his profile on two dating websites. Gilchrist had raised with Smiler the possibility that Ellice had killed Keepsake because Daleela had committed suicide after being scammed by him. Ellice could also have murdered Ritchie Forrest because he was the reason Daleela had joined a dating website in the first place. Ending their marriage through his infidelity and abuse had given Daleela reason to search for another companion. Ellice had the motive, and being ex-military and part owner of a computer company, and assumed therefore to be computer savvy, she also had the means.

Tenuous connection didn't come close, but it had been sufficient to convince Smiler to seek approval from Chief Constable McVicar to expand his murder investigation. McVicar had agreed and approved not only funding, but the assistance of Strathclyde Police. Smiler had consequently withdrawn her ban on overtime.

So, all was good and well. Status quo restored.

What Gilchrist had to do now was find and arrest Ellice Ibbotson.

Warrants were issued, and a raid on her home by Strathclyde Police was scheduled for two o'clock that afternoon, which allowed time for Gilchrist to team up with DCI Pete Small, aka Dainty, in Glasgow. In the meantime, Gilchrist faced his team in the North Street Office, giving out last-minute instructions.

'I've asked that we don't have a police presence anywhere near her home, until we're ready to make the arrest. But her car's parked in her driveway, and Dainty insisted on having one of his team keep an eye on it, with instructions not to make an arrest if she leaves home, but just to follow her.' He nodded to Jackie. 'If she does leave her home, I want us to be one step ahead, and for you to keep an eye on her car via ANPR.'

'Num . . . num . . . num . . .'

'You're keying in the original number plate,' he said, and when she frowned, added, 'If the number plate's been changed, we'll be advised by Strathclyde. In the meantime, I want you to go with the plate we have on file until you're instructed otherwise.'

Jackie's rust-coloured Afro shivered as she nodded her agreement.

Next, he turned to Mhairi. 'You'll be point of contact for this Office. I need you to be in charge up here. Okay?'

'Yes, sir.'

'If anything turns up, let me know immediately.' He turned to Jessie. 'You ready?'

'As always.'

'Right,' he said. 'Let's get on with it.'

Gilchrist and Jessie arrived at Strathclyde Police HQ in Pitt Street, Glasgow, where Dainty welcomed them into his office. 'I'd offer you tea or coffee, but some fucker keeps raiding the kitchen. Beggars fucking belief.' He nodded to Jessie. 'Excuse my French.'

'Excused.'

'No reported movement in the property,' Dainty said. 'Car's still on the driveway, curtains still closed in the bedroom.' He glanced at his watch. 'Killing must be tiring work, the lazy bastard.'

Gilchrist didn't like the sound of that. 'When did she return home last night?'

'Don't have any record of that, but I'm assuming late.' Then he caught the serious look in Gilchrist's eye, and said, 'You think she might've been out doing another one?'

'It makes you wonder, doesn't it?'

Dainty grimaced. 'Don't know what the fucking world's coming to.' He pulled himself upright. 'Let's start the ball rolling. The sooner that demented bitch is taken out of circulation, the better.'

'Assuming she's guilty,' Jessie said.

'You got any better suspects?' Dainty said, then added, 'No, I didn't think so.'

The drive to Glentyan Place was done at speed but, at Gilchrist's insistence, with no blue lights. They parked outside Ibbotson's address – red Volkswagen Golf GTI now in the driveway – and Dainty followed his team of six, Gilchrist and Jessie behind him. The leader with the big key – the heavy duty double-handed log of metal that could impart a point load of three tonnes, sufficient to break down most domestic doors with one hit – almost jogged into position, keen to get on with the job of breaking the door down.

He stood poised, waiting for the nod.

Dainty pushed to the front. 'Let's be friendly,' he said, 'and try the doorbell.'

Thirty seconds later, with no response, he stepped back, and nodded to the lock.

One hit was all it took. The big key split the framework, burst the lock, and the door exploded open. Police officers in Kevlar jackets, helmets, visors, rushed into the house, heavy boots thudding the floor, hard voices shouting, '*Police, police, show yourself, clear left, clear right, police.*'

When the din died down to subdued shuffles and whispered curses from officers still fired up and disappointed not to have made an arrest, Dainty stepped into the bedroom, pulled the curtains wide, and eyed the scene. Emptied drawers hung open, wardrobe stood littered with hangers, bedspread lay ruffled where suitcases had been placed, and bed not slept in. He kicked a dresser drawer shut, and stomped back into the hallway.

'She's done a runner,' he said, and cursed under his breath as he returned to the front door. 'You couldn't make this up.' Then he shifted back into command mode. 'Someone somewhere must've seen something. I want door-to-doors on everyone in this street, starting with her across the road.'

Gilchrist followed Dainty's line of sight, in time to see a set of venetian blinds close with a flutter.

'She's got an accomplice,' Dainty shouted. 'Someone helped her move out last night. And they didn't go walking down the street. I want to know who that someone is. And I want to know make, model, number plate of every car, van, SUV, bus, lorry, horse and cart, on this fucking street. And I want it ten minutes ago. Got it?'

For a small man, Dainty could certainly hold his own, Gilchrist thought.

CHAPTER 27

No amount of shouting and commanding by a raging Dainty brought them any closer to finding Ibbotson. By five o'clock, with the day finished and dark as midnight, the street sparkling with ice, windows and house fronts glittering with fairy lights, Dainty dragged his hand down his face. He looked as if he'd aged three years in as many hours.

'You'd've thought some fucker would've noticed something.'

'Not if she did all her moving around in the night,' Jessie said.

Dainty glared at her for a second, then gave a frustrated nod of agreement. 'All we know is, she's got an associate, and whether that associate helps her in her grisly task of killing, who knows.'

Gilchrist said, 'Maybe she assists by driving only.'

'She? I'm thinking it's a *he*.'

'Why?'

'Someone strong enough to lug all the stuff away.'

'Maybe she didn't have a lot of stuff to lug away,' Jessie said. 'She'd only been living there for less than a year.'

'If she's anything like my wife,' Dainty growled, 'she could fill the fucking house in a weekend.' He grimaced, as if in pain, then said, 'I need to take a pish.'

Gilchrist watched Dainty stomp off. 'Penny for your thoughts,' he said to Jessie.

'Need more than a penny. Head's spinning with it all. I mean, I thought all we had to do was ring the doorbell and arrest her.'

Gilchrist had to agree. Ibbotson doing a midnight flit hadn't entered the equation. But now it had, he wondered if she'd left because he, Detective Chief Inspector Andrew James Gilchrist, had made a mistake. He'd been the one who'd visited her home yesterday. And it was he whom Ibbotson might have seen on her CCTV camera as he walked up and down the street, passing her house a couple of times, speaking to one of the neighbours, then driving off slowly. It didn't take too much of a quantum leap to realise that anyone with an ounce of military expertise would become suspicious in a heartbeat. But to up and leave?

That spoke of panic, or the sense at least that the noose was tightening, that a move needed to be made. But it also spoke of something else, something more worrying. Ibbotson could be decompensating, the strain on her mental health too much to sustain. She now knew that a connection had been made to all apparently random killings, and that soon she would likely be caught. But could that mean upping the ante, getting on with the job of racking up the numbers before her murder spree came to an arrested end?

'How about a penny for your thoughts?' Jessie said.

He grimaced, shook his head. 'I don't like it any more than you do. But if you ask the question – why move now? – I don't think we're going to like the answer.'

'Bloody hell, Andy, don't go all psychobabbly bullshitty on me.' She held his gaze for a long moment, then said, 'You don't think she killed last night again, do you?'

'Maybe that's the answer we're not going to like. Who knows? But what I do know is that we're looking for two people now instead of one. And likely killers.'

'Both women?'

'I think so.'

'I'm not so sure. I think I'm going to side with Dainty on that one. I'm thinking just one killer, and one to clean up, but guilty by association, I know, I know, no need to look at me like that.' She shrugged. 'So what now?'

'That's easy. We find them, of course. The hard bit is figuring out how to do it.' He smiled at the way Jessie rolled her eyes.

'Going by the door-to-doors,' she said, 'the old guy who lives across the street but one, what's his name – Iain McDonald? – might be worth talking to again. I don't understand why Dainty didn't rate him.'

'Because he came across as being confused, maybe?'

'How old is he?'

'Ninety-two, I think they said.'

'And still living by himself? Social services won't let you do that if you're going senile. So I'm betting he's still got it between the ears. For all we know he could be as sharp as a tack. Shall we?' she said, and led the way.

Iain McDonald took some time to answer the door. It opened with a sticky crack. He stood there in a threadbare dressing gown, pyjamaed legs, slippered feet, and white hair as wild as Einstein's in a force ten. At least he hadn't taken his teeth out, Jessie thought.

She held up her warrant card, and introduced Gilchrist and herself. 'We didn't get you out of bed, did we?'

'Naw, ah sleep mostly in the chair now, hen. Better for mah back.'

'Can you spend a few more minutes with us?'

'Aye, but you'll need to come inside. Ah'm no paying for heating up the street.'

Jessie stepped over the threshold, Gilchrist behind her, and waited while the elderly man closed the door. Then he shuffled along the hallway, into a dimly lit lounge. The TV was on mute. Closed captions shifted and changed on the screen in silence. The whole place was redolent of burnt toast and something more unpleasant, as if the waste bin hadn't been emptied in over a week, maybe longer.

'You spoke to a uniformed police officer earlier this afternoon,' Jessie said, 'but his report says that you were a bit confused on days and dates.'

'At mah age, hen, every day's the same. The only thing that changes is the shite they put on the telly. Just as weel ah'm no paying the licence fee no more.'

Jessie offered a friendly chuckle, then said, 'You said you saw a car last night. Were you awake?'

'Ah wouldnae have seen it if ah'd been sleeping, now would ah?'

'No, I meant – did the sound of the car wake you up, or were you already awake?'

'Already awake. Back gives me the yips. Huvnae had a good night's sleep in ages. But as they say, auld age disnae come alone.'

'I'm sorry to hear that, Iain. You don't mind if I call you Iain, do you?'

'That's mah name, and ah've been called a lot worse than that, hen.'

'Right,' Jessie said, adjusting her backside for more comfort. It felt as if the cushion's stuffing had been replaced with lumps of wood. 'The car you saw last night, are you able to tell us anything about it?'

'Like what?'

'Like what make and model it was.'

'Ah already telt that wee gnyaff what it was. Did he no write it doon?'

'He did, yes, but we're just following up.'

'Making sure ah've no lost mah marbles, you mean?'

Jessie smiled, as good a response as any.

'Vauxhall Corsa is what it was. Grey or blue paintwork. But ah couldnae say for sure. No at night anyways.'

She nodded, jotted it down, then looked back at him. She knew the answer, but thought it worth asking. 'Did you happen to get the number plate?'

'Naw, ah never wrote it doon is what you're asking. Cannae remember eff all these days. If mah heid wisnae screwed on, ah donno whit ah'd dae.'

'And what time did you say you saw this car?'

'Just efter three in the morning. Ah remember that.'

'Why do you remember that?'

''Cause ah take mah pills at three, and ah'd just taken them.'

Jessie glanced at Gilchrist. He shook his head. No need to know what he takes his pills for, just thankful that he remembered the time so clearly. 'Anything else about the car that you can think of?' she said.

'Oh, aye. It had a sunroof. Ah remember that cause mah son's always going on aboot wanting to put a sunroof on his Corsa.'

'So your son drives the same car?'

'Aye, but he keeps it in better condition than thon across the street.'

The way he said that had Jessie thinking that he'd maybe seen the Corsa before, and she asked him that.

'Naw. First time, hen.'

'But you remember it clearly?'

'Aye.'

'Your son keeps his in better condition, you said. So what was so bad about this car?'

'Had a dent in the rear offside wing. Brake lights and that were all working, so they must've been fixed.'

Gilchrist leaned forward. 'You didn't mention anything about there being a dent in the rear wing earlier.'

'That wee gnyaff in his police uniform never asked, so ah didnae mention nothing aboot it. Didnae think it was important, so ah did. Specially if he didnae ask.'

'Would you recognise the car again if you ever saw it?' Gilchrist asked.

'Ah think so, aye.'

Jessie raised an any-other-questions? eyebrow at Gilchrist, who pushed himself to his feet, and said, 'When you saw the car just after three o'clock this morning, was it five past three, ten past, or what?'

'Just efter three. No even five past.'

'And was the car arriving or leaving?'

'Leaving.'

'Did you notice how many people were in it?'

'Naw. It was too dark.'

Gilchrist nodded. 'You've been very helpful, Mr McDonald. If you think of anything else, please give me a call.' He placed his card on the table. 'We'll let ourselves out.'

By the time they reached the front door, Gilchrist had his mobile to his ear.

CHAPTER 28

Gilchrist got through to Mhairi on the first ring. 'I need you and Jackie to check the ANPR for a Vauxhall Corsa, blue or grey with a sunroof, leaving Glentyan Place in the early hours this morning, a minute or two just after three. It's uniquely identifiable by damage to the rear offside wing. We need to get its registration number as a matter of urgency.'

'How do you spell the street, sir?'

He told her, then ended the call as Dainty walked towards them.

'Get anything useful, Andy?'

Gilchrist brought him up to speed.

'For fuck's sake,' Dainty snarled. 'Surrounded by useless wankers who can't fucking think for themselves. And it's no use writing it down for them. Half of them can't fucking read.' Not a glowing report on Strathclyde Police, but Dainty was well known for egregious criticism, particularly when pissed off. 'I'll get our boys onto it, as well,' he continued. 'But the start they've got they could be halfway to fucking Timbuktu by now.'

It took Mhairi just over forty-five minutes to come back with a result – not Timbuktu, but Kilmarnock – by which time Gilchrist was driving through Glasgow, trying to make his way to Pitt Street HQ. He took her call on his car's speaker system.

'Jackie picked it up on the slip road to the M77, heading south,' she said. 'And she got a clear enough capture to read the number plate. She searched DVLA's records, and came up with an address for you, sir.' She read it out, some street he'd never heard of. 'It's in a housing estate off Hurlford Road, sir.' Another street he'd never heard of, while Jessie scribbled it down.

'Is it still parked at that address?'

'We can't tell, sir. Jackie tracked it as best she could, but in the housing estate there's limited CCTV access. But from the route it was taking, we'd say it was definitely heading there. We haven't seen it reappear on the ANPR system since.'

Jessie leaned forward to enter the address in the car's satnav system.

'Was she able to find the owner's name?' he asked Mhairi.

'Shifrah Ber,' she said, and spelled it out for him. 'And we can't find anything on her in the PNR, sir. Looks like she's clean.'

Years ago Gilchrist had been introduced to someone with that same first name, and suspected Shifrah Ber was most likely from Israel, or of Jewish heritage. 'Send what you've got to Strathclyde Police, attention DCI Pete Small,' he said. 'We'll give him a head's up from here. And get Jackie to continue digging. This Shifrah Ber must have some history.'

'Will do, sir.'

Gilchrist told Jessie to pass on the address to Dainty, as he pulled down a side street in search of a way back. But he was unfamiliar with Glasgow's one-way systems, and ended up doing a U-turn on West Nile Street to the accompaniment of blaring horns. Jessie couldn't connect with Dainty, and left a detailed message, and a request to call back pronto.

They were on the slip road to the M77 south when Dainty called back.

'Got the address confirmed at this end, too,' Dainty said. 'Looks like they've not moved. Where are you?'

'Just joined the M77, heading south.'

'Right. You should get there in about thirty minutes, depending on traffic. I'll have the Kilmarnock Office cover the address until then. I'll gather the troops and meet you there. If anything turns up, keep me posted.'

The line disconnected.

Gilchrist was ten miles outside Kilmarnock when a DI Blackman called. She told him that DCI Small had instructed her to contact him with the latest update.

'We have the address under surveillance,' she said, 'and confirm that a blue Vauxhall Corsa is parked in the driveway. Lights are on in the house, but other than that, no activity, sir. DCI Small faxed a copy of the arrest warrant. Would you like us to go ahead and make the arrest, sir?'

'No,' Gilchrist said. He couldn't say if the women were armed or not, but knew that at least one of them had military training.

'How far away are you, sir?'

'We should be with you in fifteen minutes. DCI Small will be with us shortly.' He didn't know where Dainty was, but the last thing he wanted was a DI to try to arrest a pair of women on the run. He had no idea who Shifrah Ber was, but if she was indeed Israeli, then she was more than likely ex-military, as Israel was one of only a few countries in the world which had a mandatory military service requirement for women, who would be conscripted to the Israeli Defense Force. No, there could be no rash decisions taken here. He had to be certain of who they were dealing with first. To make sure there could be no misunderstanding, he said, 'I want you to stand down until DCI Small arrives.'

'Yes, sir.'

Which didn't take long, as it turned out. Only five minutes after Gilchrist arrived, and another four minutes for Dainty to have everyone set in place and ready to go. The team with the big key looked as if they couldn't wait to tear down the house, let alone the door, given half a chance.

With all teams in place, Dainty gave the instruction to proceed.

Without a word, one team slid like a Kevlar-vested conga line down the side of the house into the back garden, while a second team readied themselves at the front door. In the street, two armed police officers viewed the scene through sniper rifle lenses. It seemed to Gilchrist that Dainty was taking no chances. Not even a warning rap at the front door.

All of a sudden, voices roared as doors front and back simultaneously blasted apart, and armed units rumbled into the premises. Gilchrist held his breath, worried that firearms might be used. But one minute later, with the shouting subdued, it was all over.

Gilchrist stepped over the front threshold. The frame was half-hanging off the wall, and the door had been hit with such force that the inside handle had embedded itself in the plaster wall. In the front lounge, two police officers were on their knees, cuffing a prostate woman on the floor, shouting out her rights. It seemed surreal to be standing in a room while armed and suited-up officers shuffled about, looking somewhat disappointed, as if they'd not had an opportunity to destroy anything other than the doors.

From the corner of his eye, he caught Dainty skipping up the stairs, and followed him. In the upper hallway, armed officers strode in and out of the bedrooms still fired up with adrenaline, rifles at the ready. But when Dainty saw him, he shook his head.

'Looks like there's only one of them.'

'Which one?' Gilchrist asked.

'Don't know yet, but I'll soon fucking find out.' He pushed past Gilchrist and scurried downstairs, feet thudding on the stairs like a drum roll.

By the time Gilchrist returned to the living room, the woman was on her feet, hands cuffed behind her back, with Dainty facing her. Although Dainty was arguably the smallest officer in the Force, his lack of height never seemed to bother him. He stood at least six inches shorter than the woman, maybe more, and glared up at her.

'Name?' he said.

The woman smiled down at him. 'You know my name.'

'I just want to hear you say it,' Dainty said.

'Shifrah Ber.'

Dainty nodded. 'And where's your associate?'

'Associate?'

'Don't play buggerlugs with me.' Dainty stepped closer. If they'd been the same height, it would have been eye to eye, but he almost had to crane his neck. Even so, he growled, 'I won't be asking again.'

In a calm voice, Ber said, 'I'm sorry. I honestly don't know.'

Dainty's lips turned white for a moment, then he snarled, 'Take her away.'

CHAPTER 29

Gilchrist entered the interview room, Jessie behind him. Dainty had elected to watch proceedings on the monitor, on the basis that he would be best positioned to instruct teams into action as soon as she coughed up Ibbotson's whereabouts. On the other hand, Gilchrist knew that Dainty had an inability to maintain composure when being lied to, and suspected that was the real reason for stepping aside.

Gilchrist took his seat and slid his card across the table to Ber's solicitor, a scruffy man with straggly hair and thin goatee beard. A stained blue suit hadn't been laundered in months, and an off-white shirt with curled collar tips could do with being boned, or even binned. Without a word, a creased card was pushed to Gilchrist – A. K. Billings of AKB Legal Services – no address, only a mobile number.

Gilchrist glanced at the recording light, to make sure it was on, introduced himself and Jessie, and added, 'And Shifrah Ber and her solicitor, A. K. Billings.' He looked at the solicitor, and said, 'Are you happy to be introduced as A. K., or do you have a first name you prefer?'

'I've advised my client to make no comment to every question,' Billings said, as if Gilchrist hadn't spoken.

'Doing so doesn't necessarily help your client,' Gilchrist replied, 'and could be seen as a silent admission of guilt.'

'As I said, my client has been instructed to answer no comment.' Billings sat back, and fiddled with his mobile phone.

Jessie said, 'That needs to be switched off.'

Billings ignored her, and continued to tap his mobile.

'Unless you intend to shave that thing off your chin with that,' Jessie said, nodding to the mobile. 'Switch it off. Got it?'

Another couple of taps, and Billings laid his mobile face-up on the table.

'Right. Shall we start?' Jessie said.

'No comment,' said Ber.

Jessie said, 'That wasn't a question.'

'No comment.'

'Jeez.'

'No comment.'

Gilchrist shifted his chair and leaned forward, letting Jessie know that he would take it from here. 'Let me tell you where we are,' he said, and held up his hand for Ber to keep quiet and hear him out. 'At this moment, you're not a suspect.' Not strictly true, but he felt he had to make a start. 'We were issued a warrant to arrest Ellice Ibbotson who we understood was in your home this evening. That's why we broke in. To arrest Ellice, not you. But . . .' He paused for a moment, and caught the hint of a flicker in her eyes, as if she were calculating possibilities in what she was hearing. '. . . As you were there, you were arrested . . . for want of a better phrase . . . as collateral damage.' Billings continued to eye his mobile.

Gilchrist reclined in his chair again, placed both hands flat on the table. 'So, Shifrah, do you see our dilemma?' He raised his eyebrows and shrugged for effect. 'We don't know how you fit into Ellice's life, or even if you do. But what I can tell you is every time you answer with a "No comment", all you're doing is raising our suspicions that you do indeed have something to hide, and that you're maybe not as innocent as we think you are.'

Billings glanced up. 'I've instructed my client to make no comment.'

Gilchrist smiled at Ber, and with a sideways nod at Billings, said, 'Well, I suppose if you're guilty of some crime and have something to hide, then your solicitor's advice could be considered sound. But if you're innocent . . .' Another shrug. 'What can I say? You don't have to take poor advice from your solicitor. In fact . . .' he leaned closer to the table, 'you don't even have to keep your solicitor at all. You have every right to fire him.'

Billings tapped at his mobile, and smiled.

'So, shall we start again?' Gilchrist said.

'I would like a moment alone with my solicitor,' Ber said.

'Interview terminated at 17:46.' Gilchrist clicked off the recorder, and he and Jessie pushed back their chairs and left the room.

Dainty met them in the hallway. 'I've come up against that wee shite before,' he said. 'Alex Billings. Sneaky as fuck.'

'Is he any good?' Jessie said.

'Depends on what you mean by good. Most of the time, he tells his clients to say fuck all, then tries to get them off on some technicality.' He puffed out his cheeks. 'Obstructive wee bastard, and he doesn't come cheap.'

'Well he doesn't spend any of his fees on clothes,' Jessie said, 'Or soap. Did you get a whiff of his BO?' She glanced over Dainty's shoulder. 'Uh-oh, looks like we're back on.'

Gilchrist turned in time to see Billings push through a swing door and scurry down the corridor.

Back inside the interview room, he clicked on the recorder. 'Interview recommenced at 17:49.' He confirmed the names of the group again, and said, 'Miss Ber has agreed to continue the interview without the presence of her solicitor. Is that correct, Miss Ber?'

'It is, yes.'

Jessie made a point of sniffing the air. 'And fresher, too. Where on earth did you pick him up? The dump?'

'He was recommended.'

'By whom?'

'A friend.'

'Does your friend have a name?'

'Just a friend.'

'I see.' Jessie sat back to let Gilchrist continue.

'For the record,' he said, 'please state your name, date of birth, and home address.'

She did, confirming her home address as the house in which she'd been arrested.

'Are you currently employed?'

'Self-employed. I'm a computer software designer.'

Gilchrist could almost feel Jessie's tension. Their profiling of the killer pointed to someone with in-depth knowledge of computer technology. A software designer fitted the bill. He decided to play around the edges of the interview. 'So how does that work? Who hires computer software designers these days?'

'Any company that's dependent on its computer network, really. Banks, insurance companies, various government departments, those sort of businesses.'

'And what services do you provide?'

'I design data modelling processes, create algorithms and predictive models. With cybercrime becoming more of a concern for many businesses, my services are migrating more towards information security analysis, mostly developing proactive measures to stay ahead of the game, effectively to ensure that the company computer systems remain up and running.'

She sat back.

Jessie said, 'You lost me after self-employed.'

Gilchrist smiled. Time to step in from the edges. 'Have you ever provided services for dating websites?'

'No.' A shake of the head, without the slightest hint of concern. If he'd been hoping to catch her out with his blunt change of tack, he was disappointed.

'How do you know Ellice Ibbotson?'

'Through a friend of a friend, initially. Then we found we had a lot in common, and it grew from there.'

'What grew from there?'

'Our friendship.'

'Do you provide any computer services to her?'

'Don't need to. She's computer savvy.'

'Knows her way about the software side of things, is that what you mean?'

'No. She doesn't write software. She's more knowledgeable of hardware, how to use it, what to do with it. Most people don't use a fraction of what their mobile phones can do for them. Ellice gets the most out of her mobile.'

'Why did you collect her from her home in Glasgow?'

'She asked me to.'

'Did she say why?'

'No.'

'And you didn't think to ask?'

'Why would I?'

'Because she had a car of her own, a red Volkswagen.'

'She didn't want to drive it.'

'Why not?'

'Don't know.'

'Did you know she'd cleared out her house? She'd moved out?'

'No.'

Gilchrist sat back and eyed Ber. She'd answered every question without hesitation, which told him that she was either telling the truth, or was one hell of a liar. 'How many suitcases did she bring with her?'

'None. Just hand luggage. That's all.'

'Hand luggage? Like carry-on luggage, you mean?'

'Yes. A small canvas bag. On wheels.'

Jessie slumped back into her chair. 'I don't believe you.'

Gilchrist held up his hand again to keep Jessie out of it. 'Ellice called you to ask for a lift to Kilmarnock. You drove up to Glasgow, picked her up with her one small case, then you drove her all the way back to Kilmarnock. So where did you drop her off?'

'Hurlford Road.'

'At her home?'

'No. Just the side of the road.'

'Was she meeting anyone?'

'Not to my knowledge.'

'Did she call anyone on the drive to Kilmarnock?'

'No. We just chatted.'

'About what?'

'Nothing, really. Just catching up, you know. As friends do.'

Gilchrist spent the following twenty minutes questioning Ber, searching for some flaw in her story, but finding none, while his mind was working in the background, telling him he was missing something, they all were, and coming up with what he didn't want to hear – the reason Ellice had a small case, and was dropped off on Hurlford Road, was to catch a bus to Prestwick Airport. Bloody hell, for all anyone knew she could be halfway to the States by now, or anywhere in Europe.

Even so, it didn't make sense.

His mind cast up images of Ellice's bedroom – ruffled bedsheets, opened drawers, abandoned wardrobe. Her home had been emptied like a midnight flit. But if what Ber was telling them was true, then who had removed Ellice's belongings? And where had they been taken to?

He sat back, tired and frustrated at being led down the garden path. Because that's how he saw it now. It was as if Ber had known all along how to play them, and he had no evidence to justify holding her, let alone arresting her. Her record was squeaky clean, not even a speeding ticket, and she'd answered his questions with a calmness that more than hinted at honesty. He felt as if he had no option but to let her go.

'DI Janes will take your statement,' he said. 'Then you're free to leave. Interview over at . . .' he glanced at the recorder, '18:33.'

He pushed his seat back, and left the room.

CHAPTER 30

Gilchrist faced Dainty. 'Any thoughts?'

Dainty grimaced, shook his head. 'One fucking carry-on bag? I don't believe it. I've got a team checking out flights from Prestwick, as well as buses and taxis from Kilmarnock. We're going back over the door-to-doors to see if anyone mentioned a second car or a van clearing out her house.' He pressed his lips into a white line, then shook his head again. 'I don't get it. Why get picked up? Why not just drive to the airport, if that's where she went? Why leave her car in the driveway?'

'To make it look as if everything was normal?'

'But she must've known we were onto her. She must've known we were coming.' Another shake of the head. 'But how? How did she know that?'

Gilchrist didn't like the logical answer to that question – his presence on Ibbotson's street had tipped her off, or much worse, someone with inside knowledge. He could be way off track, could be stirring up unstoppable flames, so he kept his thoughts to himself. 'The only way to find out,' he said, 'is to keep looking.'

Dainty nodded to the monitor on his desk. 'We could hold her for twelve hours. Let her sit worrying for a while. Maybe that would change her mind about trying to make us look like a bunch of fucking wankers.'

Gilchrist eyed the screen. Jessie was talking to Ber, taking her statement, but the sound was muted, so he didn't know what they were saying. He thought back to the way Ber had behaved in the interview, how she'd answered his questions with a serene confidence that he seldom came across, as if . . . as if . . . as if she'd been trained in interview techniques. Was that possible? Ibbotson had military training. Could Ber have had that, too – skilled in the art of deception? He hadn't asked her if she'd served in the Israeli military, because she'd been born in Scotland – did that exclude her from Israel's mandatory conscription? He couldn't say, and instead felt guided by his subconscious to hold something back, not give away how deeply they'd looked into Ibbotson's background.

'I think we should let Ber go,' he said. 'Maybe keep an eye on her.'

'Surveillance, you mean? You know how much it costs to put a team on someone 24/7 nowadays? A fucking fortune.' Dainty shook his head. 'Sorry, Andy, I'd never get it approved. Not unless we have something on her.'

Gilchrist had anticipated Dainty's response, and nodded his agreement. 'Best I can offer,' he said, 'is we flag her number on the ANPR. We don't need someone to watch her 24/7, but at least we'll have a record of her movements.'

'Agreed. I'll set that up.' Dainty stretched his shoulders, glanced at his wristwatch. 'That's it. I'll need to make a showing.' He strode to the door, opened it, and stepped into the corridor,

Gilchrist by his side. 'The wife's been nipping at me for weeks to have the in-laws over. Thank fuck this turned up, or I'd've had to suffer her parents reminding me how much better off she'd've been marrying someone other than a copper. Never worked out if they're just a pair of dozy bastards, or suffering from dementia.' He chuckled, shook his head. 'It's not funny, Andy, I know, but for fuck's sake, there's only so much a man can take.' He shook Gilchrist's hand. 'Anything turns up, you'll be the first to know.' Then he stepped into another room.

Gilchrist returned to the interview room and opened the door. Jessie signalled that she was almost done, so he closed the door and went in search of a way outside.

Night had fallen, and the air felt chilled and thick with a wintry dampness. He always thought there was something about Glasgow that caused it to harbour a sense of the dark days of heavy industry for which the Clyde had been world-famous. Even on a clear day, when the skies were blue and the wind was mild, the city seemed as if it could never shed itself of its grimy past. He found a sheltered spot at the main entrance, and dialled Maureen's number.

'Hey, Dad, what's the matter?'

'Nothing's the matter. Thought I'd give you a call to see how you're doing. So . . . how are you doing?'

'Good you?'

He grimaced at what seemed to be the universal response of the younger generation these days, as if good-you was all one word, and answered everything. 'I'm fine,' he said. 'I'm in Glasgow at the moment, and was hoping we could meet up for a chat.'

'We're having a chat now.'

'Right. But I was thinking more of a face-to-face kind of chat.'

'Do you have FaceTime set up?'

'Eh . . . not sure.'

'You've got an iPhone, haven't you?'

'An old one, yes.'

'Well that'll have FaceTime on it. Want me to call you back?'

This wasn't going the way he wanted it to, but Maureen seemed to have an ability to think faster than he could, and now he felt as if she'd backed him into a corner. 'Sure,' he said. 'Then what do I do?'

'Accept the call, and that's it.'

The line disconnected.

Five seconds later, his mobile rang. He eyed it, and with some trepidation swiped his finger across the screen to accept the call. All of a sudden Maureen's face appeared, teeth and eyes sparkling with the freshness of youth. She moved in and out of the frame, as if she were trying to make it hard for him to see her.

'When did you start wearing glasses?' he said.

'Only when reading, or when I'm on FaceTime.' She laughed, and he gave an obligatory chuckle in response.

'Are you at home?'

'Yes, why?'

'You're wearing a polo-neck, so I thought you might be outside, or else turned off the heating.'

'You need to stop being a detective, Dad.'

'You got me,' he said, and gave another chuckle. 'You settling into the new job?'

'Yeah.'

'So how's it going? Any problems?'

'No. Should there be?'

'Just asking.' She disappeared from the screen again, and he caught a glimpse of her in a mirror on the opposite wall, a head-and-shoulders image that shivered and jumped with every movement of her hand – facing her, the figure of someone else, a man, most probably her boyfriend, with whom she'd moved in earlier. And in that fleeting glimpse, he thought he caught the anger of the moment.

Then Maureen was back. 'Got to go, Dad. Love you. Bye.'

'Love you, too,' he said, but the screen had already blanked.

He held onto his mobile, and stared off along Pitt Street. What had he just witnessed? Should he give Maureen a call back, make sure she was okay? Or had she just been in a rush and couldn't spare any time to talk to him? He thought back to the image on his mobile, the press of the man's body against hers. Had the man's superior height made that moment seem all the more aggressive than it was? Had he witnessed something innocent and was trying to reconfigure the incident into something else? He didn't know. But what he did know, now he thought about it, with his daughter's face clear in his mind and the way she'd avoided holding her mobile steady, that she'd been wearing glasses not for reading, but to hide the yellowing bruise under her left eye. And why wear a polo-neck indoors? Was that to cover up more bruising?

Just then, Jessie stepped out of the building, and strode towards him.

When she caught up with him, she frowned. 'You all right, Andy?'

'Just thinking.'

'Looks like it hurts.'

'You're ex-Strathclyde,' he said. 'Do you still keep in touch?'

'I stay well clear of some of them, as you know. But others, not as much as I should. But yes, I suppose I do keep in touch from time to time. Why?'

'Got something I'd like you to look into for me. On the QT.'

'Lips are sealed.'

He smiled for effect, but deep inside he felt an unhealthy rage burning.

CHAPTER 31

Back in St Andrews, Gilchrist dropped Jessie off at her home in Canongate with a promise to pick her up first thing in the morning – they had a busy day ahead of them. He'd called Irene, and she'd surprised him by saying she'd ordered in a curry for them, and not to worry about how long it took to get back, it would just be a case of a quick reheat in the microwave.

While Irene pressed on with setting up their evening meal, two hours later than both of them typically liked to eat, Gilchrist spread an Ordnance Survey map onto the dining-room table. The idea had come to him on the way back from Glasgow, as his mind had continued to replay his interview with Shifrah Ber over and over, as if it was locked on some continuous loop, until it spat out an answer. Well, answer might not be the correct word, but definitely another avenue in which to search.

It had been Ber's calm demeanour that had given her away – at least in Gilchrist's mind. He'd sat in on countless interviews, and seldom come across anyone so unfazed by the process, even though her home had been broken into and she'd been arrested face down on her living-room carpet – enough to send most arrestees to their solicitor to press charges. But not Ber. Ber was experienced in interrogation techniques, of that he'd been certain. He'd instructed Jackie to look deeper into Ber's past, and although he hadn't heard back from her yet, if he were a betting man he'd bet the lot on Shifrah Ber being ex-military. So, working on the premise that both Ber and Ibbotson had military training, and the fact that so far none of the door-to-door interview statements had turned up anything new – no second car or van or anyone else to clear the house – Gilchrist decided that Ber had been lying. She'd collected Ibbotson and a few more suitcases from Glasgow. And if you took that as a given, then it made sense that everything else she'd told them in her interview was also a lie.

She'd picked up Ibbotson, of that he was convinced. But she hadn't dropped her off on Hurlford Road with a single carry-on case. That was a story devised to send them off on the wrong path; searching Prestwick Airport flight departures, bus routes and taxi hires, that would tie up police forces on a red herring, while they – the pair of them, Ibbotson and Ber – planned their slippery exit. Of course, it could all be conjecture, but the more Gilchrist had thought about it, the more he'd become convinced that he and the rest of the team had been conned; Dainty included.

Which was why he was now studying an Ordnance Survey map of Ayrshire.

Fenwick Moor, that's what he was looking at. Or more precisely, the stretch of the M77 between Glasgow and Kilmarnock that passed mostly through land as open and sparse as any in the UK. Because, if his thinking was making sense at all, that's where they would have made the switch. He'd convinced himself that there had to have been at least one other person involved in Ibbotson's disappearance, some mystery person who'd collected Ibbotson when Ber dropped her and her suitcases off somewhere on the M77 as they drove through the moors – and not a CCTV camera in sight. It was simple if you thought about it, and brilliant, too, the sort of plan a group of ex-military personnel might come up with. And with thought, came a fleeting flush of worry. Just who, or what, was he up against?

He'd also now decided that it was pointless keeping surveillance on Ber. She would know that's what the police would probably do. So she would lie low, keep herself to herself, stay at home for days on end, not make any calls on her mobile in case it was tapped, and not drive her car, other than to the grocery store, just lead a simple, honest and ordinary life. At least until the dust settled around her. No, the answer to finding Ibbotson had to be on that stretch of M77. But as he ran his fingers along the route, he came to understand that he was trying to do the impossible. It seemed as if there were any number of places for a car to stop and discharge a passenger with luggage. It didn't have to be on the M77 either. Numerous exit roads led into quieter country where a switch could be made with no one in sight. And at night, in the middle of winter, out in the wilderness, it would be pitch dark—

'Are you ready for this?' Irene said.

'Oh, sorry, sure.'

'You look frazzled, Andy. Is everything okay?'

'Sure. Yeah. Just thinking.'

'And from the looks of it, you're coming up with nothing. Am I right?'

He gave a tired smile. 'Regrettably.'

'Here,' she said, 'give me a cuddle.'

She shuffled up to him, and he put his arms around her, once again troubled by her frailty, and feeling ashamed that he hadn't been paying more attention to her. He kissed her cheek, and said, 'Let me clear this up, then we can sit down and have a bite to eat and a wee chat. How does that sound?'

'I'm not taking you away from anything, am I?'

'Nothing that can't wait until the morning,' he said, folding up the Ordnance Survey map. But he knew when morning came, nothing would have changed. Ibbotson would be just as impossible to find then as she was now. And the investigation into Howitt's murder would be no further forward. And Smiler would be on at him again with concerns over the budget being expended with no tangible gain in the case. But he wouldn't be the only one struggling to fit the bill. Dainty was in for it, too. Which almost brought a smile to his face.

He forced his thoughts away from his investigation with its manhour and budgetary constraints and picked up the first CD to hand – Mannheim Steamroller; *Christmas in the Aire* – and slid it into Irene's Bose player. He clicked it onto shuffle repeat, then adjusted the volume to provide soft background music. Back at the table, he took care as he heaped curry onto their plates, while Irene spooned saffron rice sprinkled with crushed cardamom pods and cinnamon cloves.

'I bought a fresh jar of mango chutney,' she said. 'But could you open the top for me? I don't seem to have the strength in my hands to do that any more.'

He obliged, and popped the lid with ease, another insight into how weak she'd become. He helped her onto her seat, then took his own beside her. 'Wine?'

'I know I shouldn't, but just a small one, please.'

He poured a glass for himself, even though he preferred beer with curry. He dobbed some spiced onions onto his plate, cracked a poppadom, and said, 'Has Joanne spoken to Maureen recently?'

'Joanne called today, but didn't say anything, and I didn't ask. Why?'

'Nothing really. I was just wondering if she still didn't like Mo's boyfriend, or if anything's happened to change that.'

Irene took a sip of wine, as if to give some thought to her answer, then said, 'The last time she mentioned Maureen, she did say she thought Maureen was thinking of moving out, trying to find somewhere else. I didn't say anything about that to you, because Joanne said she was only reading between the lines, and I didn't want to worry you.' Another sip of wine, then, 'Why? Has something happened?'

'No. Nothing. We were following up on a lead in Glasgow today, and I gave her a call. She seemed . . .' He shook his head as he searched for the correct word. '*Elusive*, would be the best way to describe her. I don't think she wanted to meet me. Which I understand, of course. Living away from home, the last thing you need is your old man turning up out of the blue to check out the place.' He chuckled to show how unconcerned he was, but didn't think he pulled it off.

'Are you sure there's nothing wrong?' Irene said.

'No, everything's okay. Well, that is if you can say a father wondering why his only daughter doesn't want to see him . . . is okay . . . then, yes, everything's okay. That's all.' He tried to change the subject with, 'More wine?' But Irene shook her head, and frowned as she forked spiced onions onto a poppadom.

'Would you like me to speak to Joanne, and ask her if she's heard anything more?'

He wanted to tell Irene not to mention anything to Joanne at all, but it struck him that Maureen might confide in her. So he said, 'As long as she's subtle.'

Irene chuckled. 'Maureen won't even know she's being quizzed.'

Gilchrist didn't want to say he disagreed with her, and simply nodded.

CHAPTER 32

Tuesday

Tuesday morning came and went, with no significant advance in his investigation. Gilchrist had Mhairi and Jessie spend the entire morning assigned to Google Maps driving the virtual M77 across the moors, searching for places where Ber might have made a switch. He hadn't wanted to share his thoughts with anyone other than his own team, because not only was he asking them to search for the proverbial needle in a haystack, he wasn't sure it was even the right haystack they were searching through.

Despite Dainty's vehement complaints about the needless cost of surveillance, he'd relented and arranged for a two-man team to spend the night, and another in the morning, watching Ber's home. He also managed to secure a warrant to tap her phone. The two-man team was still there, and just as Gilchrist had predicted, no movement of any kind was reported – no calls in or out, no showings at any of the windows, no visitors, no driving to the shops for daily groceries. Mail was even intercepted and checked for sender addresses, but it all came to nothing. A big fat zero. Shifrah Ber could be curled up in bed reading a library's worth of books, for all they knew. And if not for the flickering of lights on and off in the middle of the night, the house could have been as good as abandoned.

'She's fucking at it,' Dainty had said. 'She's having a laugh. And as for Ibbotson? A fucking ghost is what she is. Diddly-squat so far. Does she even fucking exist?'

Gilchrist agreed that it appeared odd, but still didn't share his thoughts on there being a third individual, or that Ibbotson could have been dropped off by Ber anywhere on the M77 at night. For all he knew, he could be wrong on both counts. She might have had a car sitting there, waiting to be driven off, and not necessarily parked on the side of the M77, but in any number of side roads on the drive through the moors to Kilmarnock. Or she could have met someone just as easily, then been driven away. He might bet on the latter. But truth be told, he had no idea.

Tuesday evening, Gilchrist pulled Mhairi and Jessie into his office for an update.

'Getting nowhere, sir,' Mhairi said. 'I've marked up a map with locations where a switch might have been made, but I wouldn't want to bank on any of it. There are too many variables. I've confirmed a number of properties off the M77 that have CCTV, but I've only spoken to six of them by phone so far, and haven't pulled any of the tapes. That would take time, sir, and most likely for little or no return.'

'Agreed, Mhairi. I'm beginning to think we might need to score through that line of enquiry.' He thought Mhairi looked relieved, and why shouldn't she be, having been stuck at her computer all day working on some hare-brained idea of his?

He turned to Jessie.

She shook her head. 'Jackie calculated the approximate times it would take to drive from Glasgow to Kilmarnock at different average speeds, but they don't prove anything. If a switch was made, it might have lasted less than a minute, and trying to plug that into the equation is meaningless, and leads us nowhere. Sorry, Andy, but I think we're wasting our time.'

Gilchrist took a deep breath, then let it out. Wasting time seemed to have been the order of the day. 'Dainty's getting nowhere, too,' he said. 'Looks like Ber's holed up at home for the duration. And Ibbotson's disappeared off the face of the earth.' He rolled his head, flexed his shoulders. Ber was playing a game with them, of that he felt sure, and Ibbotson had given them all the slip, good and proper. Without mobile phone data, or what car she might be driving, his investigation was as good as dead. He pushed to his feet. 'Let's call it a day. Go home, get some sleep, and be ready to start afresh in the morning.'

Mhairi nodded, and returned to her office, while Jessie lingered behind.

'That thing on the QT you asked me to do for you?'

Gilchrist frowned for a moment. He'd been so busy he'd let it slip his mind. 'You find anything?'

'Afraid so.'

He knew from the tone of her voice and the tightness in her face that it wasn't good news. But he said, 'Let's have it, warts and all.'

'His name is Noah Hendry. But he sometimes goes by the name of Noah Hendry-Smith, or just Noah Smith.'

'He's not on the PNC,' Gilchrist said. 'Jackie checked.'

'She did. But only for Noah Hendry.' Jessie shook her head. 'If she'd searched for Noah Hendry-Smith, she would have found he has a record of violence against women. His first wife divorced him, citing irreconcilable differences, but apparently she was persuaded to accept that by his solicitor in exchange for an easy divorce. The real reason was physical and mental abuse, the stuff they used to call a *domestic*.'

'So he's not a nice guy at all,' Gilchrist said.

'There's more, Andy.'

Gilchrist gave a heavy sigh. What was it about Maureen that she seemed to attract, and be attracted to, the worst of men? Now he understood the reason for the polo-neck – to hide bruising around her neck. He knew that, as certain as he knew the sun would rise in the morning. As a teenager, Maureen always resisted covering her neck which, being long and slim in a way that highlighted the photogenic beauty of her jawline, was one of her finest features – like that of her mother, Gail. But as those thoughts flashed before him with the speed and intensity of a lightning strike, an image of a man's fingers tightening around his daughter's neck manifested in his mind.

'Steady on, Andy.'

'I'm fine,' he said. 'Let's have it.'

'That was his first wife. His second wife left him, citing physical and mental abuse, and is still in the middle of legal action, and also filed for a non-harassment order.' She hissed air through her teeth. 'You need a minimum of two acts of violence before you can file for that. So we know she's reported him at least twice to the police. I got Jackie to look into that for me, and it turns out he's a right nasty bastard.'

Gilchrist blew out a rush of breath. How the hell had Maureen fallen for this guy?

'After an argument, she locked him out of the matrimonial home. She refused to let him back in, so he chucked a rock at her through a window – as one does. Luckily it missed her, but the police were informed and it went on his record. Another time a visit to the doctor ended up with her being sent to hospital for an X-ray. Turned out she had three broken ribs. She was advised by a friend to seek legal advice, and hence the filing for the order.'

'Any children?'

'None, thank God.' She hesitated, then said, 'That's all there is on Noah Hendry-Smith. But as if that's not enough, Noah Smith's on the PNC for stalking. As a teenager, he stalked and harassed his ex-girlfriend so much that she reported him to the police. He was given repeated warnings, but no action was taken. Apparently it all ended when his girlfriend left home for university. So, no harm done . . . well, in one sense, if you get my meaning.' She offered a grim smile, then said, 'And that's all I've got for you.'

He nodded, gave her a tight smile in return. 'Thanks, Jessie.'

'Right. Well. Unless you've got anything else for me, I'm off.'

'That's it.'

'Great. See you in the morning.' At the doorway, she paused. 'Now don't do anything silly. All right?'

'I'm fine, Jessie. I'll see you in the morning.'

Alone again, he turned from his desk and stepped up to the window. Outside, the sky lay as black as an executioner's mask. A sea haar had drifted inland, the finest of mists that not only dulled the night air, but could seep into every corner of town and chill the bones of its residents to the marrow. Beyond the car park below, windows at the back of the flats on Market Street displayed fairy lights that flickered with an ethereal glow that seemed to sink into darkness as the haar thickened.

Jessie had done what he'd asked, the question now was – what to do about it?

Maureen could be an opinionated woman with a strong mind of her own. But why on earth had she ever moved in with Noah Hendry? And now she had, how could he as her father ever convince her to move out? He saw it now, the father–daughter confrontation, her refusal to believe him, her persistent denial, and how could he be so selfish not to consider her true feelings? She would deny the reality of what had happened, make herself believe that they'd only been arguing, that they'd fallen out and made up, as lovers do, that everything was fine, that they would work through their differences as a couple, that Noah was a good man, and that with a strong and loving woman by his side, he would change.

But Gilchrist knew there could be no changing. Just as leopards can't change their spots, Noah Hendry could never change. He was a bully and an abuser of women, and would be until the day he died. Gilchrist couldn't see how yet, but he had to find a way for Maureen to end the relationship by her own free will. He had to tread with care, keep himself out of the picture, because if Maureen ever found out that he was the reason for the demise of her relationship – whether the reasons were just or not, or the outcome good or bad – she could abandon him, tell him to fuck off and never speak to him again.

Softly softly?

Christ, it didn't even come close.

CHAPTER 33

Wednesday

It took until Wednesday afternoon for Gilchrist to come up with the idea for a new lead. Except that it wasn't really a lead *per se*, but one of his off-the-wall impossibilities that couldn't even be argued as having logic, if you gave it some serious thought. No more than a flashing question through his subconscious, a hare-brained reaction, an idea that had sprung from the depths of convoluted rationale.

It had come to him while reviewing bank account details of the murder victims. Each of them had accounts bloated with ill-gotten gains from their series of scams. Ian Howitt had in excess of three hundred thousand pounds spread across four different bank accounts, with an average monthly withdrawal of ten thousand pounds, and no trace as to how it was spent. Clive Keepsake had close to a million in two bank accounts and three investment portfolios, but seemed to have lived a miserly life despite his wealth. Milas Volker had just under two hundred thousand euros, which serviced four mortgage accounts for property in

Amsterdam, which in turn generated a tidy income of over ten thousand euros a month.

What struck Gilchrist about it all was the single common denominator – money. Lots of it. More than each of them could individually spend as normal everyday citizens. And it was working through each victim's finances which had turned his thoughts to the suspects' financial records. He instructed Jackie to print out copies of Ibbotson and Ber's personal bank details, which she did in short order, and he was surprised to find next to no incoming funds in either of their accounts. No monthly deposits that might indicate a salary from gainful employment. No income from pensions, support payments, stipends, or other personal or government credit schemes. Except for the occasional modest cash deposit of five hundred pounds, credited into their respective bank accounts on or around the middle of each month, both accounts were effectively stagnant.

Ibbotson's RBS account had been opened three years ago with a cash deposit of seven thousand five hundred pounds, and had remained at that with the balance fluctuating from the monthly five hundred pounds and subsequent ATM cash withdrawals. And Ber's account was almost identical; again opened three years ago – within two months of Ibbotson's – with an initial cash deposit of ten thousand pounds exactly. And just like Ibbotson's, Ber's account fluctuated with the same monthly five hundred pounds deposit and similar cash withdrawals.

That was when he called Mhairi and Jessie to his office.

He showed them what he'd uncovered. 'This tells me that Ibbotson and Ber are in it together. They've had the same monthly deposits and similar cash withdrawals for the last three years or so, which has me asking two questions.'

'Who's paying their monthly bills?' Mhairi said.

'Exactly, Mhairi. And . . .?'

Mhairi pursed her lips, while Jessie puffed her cheeks and shook her head.

He held their attention for several more seconds, then said, 'I'm guessing that three years ago is about the time they started their murder spree together.'

'Jeez,' Jessie hissed. 'But we've only got cases going back a year and a half to two years.'

'If I'm correct,' Gilchrist said, 'then there could be any number of murder victims that haven't yet been linked to this case.'

'So how do we go about confirming that, sir? I mean . . . where do we start?'

Not like Mhairi to be lost for ideas, but he said, 'We start at the beginning, and focus on the money. We need to find out where it's coming from, and who's funding them.' He nodded to Jessie. 'Tell Jackie to put a hold on searching for that drop-off point on the M77. We're just spinning our wheels and getting nowhere.'

'Will do.'

Then to Mhairi. 'Get hold of the FIU. Hanson's the man. He's sharp as a tack, but twice as nippy. Have him look into it as a matter of priority. And if he gives you any flack, pass him over to me.'

'I'm on it, sir.'

Alone again in his office, Gilchrist's thoughts shifted to Hanson and his Financial Investigation Unit. A high-flier who never minced words, Hanson had earned a notorious reputation for firing three new members of his staff within days of joining his team because they hadn't come up to his demanding expectations.

If anybody could find something out of nothing, Hanson could.

Outside, dark clouds covered the town, low enough to touch, it seemed. Not yet four o'clock, and night was already settling. Midwinter was a week or so away, after which just the thought of lighter nights and longer days was sufficient to cheer you up. As if to remind him that summer was still months ahead, drops of rain spotted the puddled car park below. Bare branches shifted in a stirring wind, and within a matter of minutes the skies opened and a deluge thundered. As he stood there, watching the rain batter against the window, his thoughts were interrupted by his mobile ringing.

He eyed the screen – ID Dainty – and took the call.

'Where are you?' Dainty said without introduction.

'North Street. Why?'

'Ibbotson wasn't heading to Prestwick Airport at all, Andy. That bitch has fucking turned up in Fisherton.'

'Where's that?'

'A wee village on the outskirts of Ayr. Being dropped off in Kilmarnock was to lead us up the garden path. I'm going to pull that Shifrah Ber back into Pitt Street and read her the fucking riot act.'

'Slow down, Dainty. What's happened?'

'Shit's happened. And it's a mess.'

Gilchrist felt something heavy slide over in his gut. It had to be bad for Dainty to be so emphatic and angry.

'How quickly can you get down here?' Dainty said.

'You got the address?' He had one arm in his jacket and was halfway along the hallway before Dainty rattled it off to him. 'I'm on my way,' he said, and ended the call.

He found Jessie in Jackie's office, the pair of them focused on

212

her monitor. She almost jumped when he rapped the door, louder than intended. 'We've got another one,' he said. 'Let's go.'

'In other words,' Jessie said as she grabbed her anorak, 'hold onto my knickers and drop everything else.'

But Gilchrist was already skipping down the stairs and failed to catch her quip.

He had the engine running and the heater on by the time Jessie bundled herself into the passenger seat. 'Enter this address into the satnav,' he said, and ran it off to her.

'Over a hundred miles,' she said. 'Closer to a hundred and twenty, depending on which way you go.'

'We're going the fastest way.'

'I thought that,' she said. 'Let's see. It's telling me that the best estimate is two and a half hours.' She slapped her hands on the dashboard as he negotiated a mini-roundabout then powered out of it, overtaking a slower car on the inside. 'Of course, if you keep this up, we could be there in two hours.'

'Get Dainty on the phone,' he said, as he depressed the accelerator and powered his car up to eighty, then ninety.

'Make that an hour and a half,' Jessie said.

CHAPTER 34

As it turned out, it took just under two hours for Gilchrist to pull in behind the SOCO transit van parked on the pavement outside a tidy detached home at the entrance to an older housing estate – by which time the forensics examination was well under way. The air almost hummed with police activity. Radios crackled, bodies bustled, and police dragonlights lit up the garden like a druid's party. Already a group of concerned neighbours had formed a small gathering that stood by the crime scene tape like fans eager for an autograph.

Gilchrist introduced himself and Jessie to the crime scene manager, signed in, and was donning his forensic outfit when he caught sight of Dainty stepping out of the front door.

Dainty came up to him, pulled off his mask, and gave off an exasperated sigh. 'I don't understand these mental fuckers,' he said. 'I really don't.' He turned his head to the side and spat a gob of phlegm onto the lawn. 'Sorry,' he said, and dabbed his lips. 'I'm getting too old for all this shite.' He glanced at Jessie. 'I think she got a fright,' he said.

'Who? Ibbotson?'

'Almost got caught, by the looks of it.'

'Different MO?'

'Same, but different.'

Gilchrist frowned. 'You sure it's Ibbotson?'

He grimaced for a moment, lips tight as a scar, then said, 'It's her all right.'

'With a different MO?' he tried.

'Same as Ritchie Forrest.'

'Strangled?'

Dainty nodded. 'But she's decompensating. They all are. If I didn't know any better I'd say the whole fucking criminal world's decompensating, for Chrissake.'

Gilchrist tightened his lips. Psychological decompensation. Not a phrase he liked to hear, a sign that the killer's mental capacity to withstand the horrors of what he or she was doing could no longer cope. Whereas a serial killer might take care over specific aspects of the murder scene – the positioning of the body, the removal of trophies for reliving that unique moment of death, the passing of life, even the timing of each killing – the mental pressure of that irrepressible need to murder had become too much for the mind to withstand. When that happened, caution was often thrown to the wind, and the killings became hurried and . . . for want of a better word . . . sometimes messy. But on the other side of that coin, it could provide an opportunity for a new lead.

'Do we know the victim's name?' he asked Dainty.

'John Brentford Cumming. Thirty-five. Divorced. No kids. Works in Costa Coffee in Ayr, as a barista. Part-time, so I've been told. Moved into this house in January this year. No mortgage.' Dainty took a deep breath, then let it out.

'Must've done all right with his divorce,' Jessie said. 'Screwed his wife out of her share by the sounds of it.'

Dainty grimaced. 'Took me all of twenty years to pay off my mortgage, which has me wondering how the fuck a coffee-pourer can afford a place like this. He's been screwing somebody all right,' he said. 'But not his wife.'

'So he's another scammer?' Gilchrist offered.

'Appears that way. Don't have all his bank details yet, but at a first looksee inside, I'd say he's an expert at it. You want to see the furniture, and some of the paintings on the walls. Not that I know much about art, but there's fewer paintings in the Kelvingrove Museum.' He nodded to the front door with the side of his head. 'Once you've had a look, give me your thoughts.' He held his gaze on Jessie for a moment, gave a grimace and a shake of the head, then turned and walked away.

Gilchrist took care to step on the aluminium plates placed by the SOCOs, which led to the door like a slabbed pathway. Jessie followed in silence. Together, they entered the living room, which flashed like lightning as the police photographer went about her gruesome task. The first thing that caught his eye was an over-turned chair, beside which lay the body of a man, dead eyes staring at the ceiling, mouth open, teeth bared in a rictus grimace, blue lips swollen and distorted. A dribble of blood painted one corner of the mouth as it trailed to the floor.

As if on cue, the photographer pushed to her feet and nodded – job done.

Gilchrist moved to the body, Jessie by his shoulder.

Once again he was struck by the impossible stillness of death, as if at any moment he expected to catch the tiniest flutter of an eyelash, the twitch of a finger, or the shiver of a final breath. He didn't have to kneel down to confirm the MO was different. This crime scene was nothing like the others. Where Howitt's death had been subdued and almost eerily staged – laptop, pens, papers set in precise position, nothing out of place; and Ritchie Forrest's for that matter – Cumming's work area was a mess.

A glass-topped desk with stainless steel legs stood wildly askew to the wall, as if it had been struck with force and moved from its normal position. A matching chair lay on its side, alongside a laptop and desktop paraphernalia – A4 pages, Post-its, stapler, table lamp, paper clips, glass containers, all scattered on the hardwood floor. The laptop's screen was intact, which gave some hope that the IT guys would recover what they could. Two plant pots had toppled off a shelf, and lay shattered by the body. Pieces of broken ceramic and clumps of potting soil spread in disarray across the floor. The body lay on top of the soil, which told him that the plants had first been knocked over in some struggle, with Cumming then being overpowered to the floor after the damage was done.

'Solved it yet?' This from a bespectacled man in forensic coveralls, who seemed to have crept up unnoticed to stand next to Jessie. 'Reid Jamieson's the name. That's Doctor. Police pathologist for Ayrshire. Won't shake hands, of course. Here. Have you seen this?' He kneeled on the floor, taking care not to touch any of the detritus.

Jessie kneeled beside him. 'He's been tasered?' she said.

'Correct. Twin pinpoint burn marks on the neck. So, I'm thinking he's been tasered first, then strangled. Look at the eyes. See these red spots?'

'Petty-whatsit,' Jessie said.

'Petechiae,' Jamieson said. 'No cuts or open wounds. But see this? The bruising on the neck?' He eased Cumming's head off the floor, ran a gloved hand over the back of it, then looked at his fingers. 'No blood. Nothing.'

Jessie leaned closer. 'Bruising at the back of the neck,' she said. 'I'm thinking a thin cord around the throat, twisted tighter at the back of the neck with a handle, or a piece of wood, or something. Like being garrotted?'

'Precisely. And it wouldn't take long. Be over in a matter of minutes, I'd say. Maybe less. Thirty to forty-five seconds. After that, you'd be beyond help.' He replaced Cumming's head to the floor with care.

Gilchrist had to agree with the cause of death. But as to the sequence of events, he wasn't sure what to think. The crime scene and MO were similar to others, with the exception of the physical altercation. Had Ibbotson been disturbed? Cumming had been tasered before being strangled. He felt certain. That's how a woman could overpower a man. But still, something about the whole scene didn't sit right with him.

'Whatever happened,' Jamieson said, 'the poor soul's fought like hell for his life. See here?' He had Cumming's hand in his own, and was inspecting it. 'Unless I'm mistaken, I'd say we've got some of the killer's DNA under his fingernails. See?' He pointed at the tips of the first and second fingers. 'He's put up a fight right enough. I'll have his hands bagged and his fingernails scraped clean.'

'I'm thinking we might've got ourselves a result,' Jessie said.

'Early days, my dear.'

'Early days or not, it's some punter's DNA, which is a result in my book.'

Gilchrist leaned down again and peered closer. Cumming's fingernails were longer than he thought typical of those of a man, and certainly too long for anyone who did manual work. And the skin on his hands bore no evidence of ever having lifted anything heavier than a pen. But the faintest hint of blood under the second fingernail suggested that Ibbotson, or whoever had attacked him, must have been injured in the attack, and been left with scratches or cuts deep enough to break the epidermis. He pulled himself upright, and said, 'Let me know as soon as you have it.'

Jamieson grunted, which Gilchrist took to be his agreement.

Gilchrist stepped away from the body, and looked around him. Just as Dainty had said, the walls seemed crammed with framed paintings – oils, watercolours, all originals as best he could tell – gave the impression that much money had been spent, and raised the question as to where that money came from. Was this how single men earned a living now? By scamming women out of their life savings? And having done so, had Cumming been found out, targeted, then murdered as revenge?

He noticed marks on the table's glass surface, and realised they were fingerprints. But whose? They couldn't be Ibbotson's, surely? She would've worn gloves. But another glance at the mess around the room told him they could be looking at another killer. Not Ibbotson, but some other member of the team? If they found a match on IDENT1 – the UK's national fingerprint database – they would indeed have a result. And with one of the murders having been committed in Amsterdam, if a search on IDENT1 was unsuccessful, he could request Interpol to carry out a similar search on AFIS, the Automatic Fingerprint Identification System stored in Europe.

Jessie came up to him, and said, 'Why is Dainty convinced it's Ibbotson?'

'She was dropped off in Kilmarnock, which isn't a hundred miles away.'

'That's hardly convincing.'

'I know. But it's too much of a coincidence, don't you think?' But what he was really thinking was that they were missing something. He let his gaze scan the living room again, over the leather sofas, the hand-carved coffee tables, lifting his eyes until they settled on the paintings on the walls. And as he had done in Jack's studio, found himself carrying out some mental arithmetic and reaching a sum in excess of half a million pounds. Which was when he saw it, high on the wall in the corner, a CCTV camera positioned to cover the entire room, probably a requirement of Cumming's insurance provider.

But the twin red lights told Gilchrist it was live and active.

'Got you,' he whispered.

CHAPTER 35

Gilchrist was surprised to learn that neither Dainty nor anyone else had picked up on the CCTV camera.

'I saw it all right,' Dainty explained. 'But I thought it was a motion detector monitor, you know, one of these things that sets off the alarm when someone breaks in. We've got them in every room in our house.' He shook his head. 'Shows you how much I know about all this IT shite.'

It took thirty minutes for one of the SOCOs to access Cumming's computer – which surprisingly wasn't password protected – and to access then transfer the Video Management System file onto a flash drive.

Ten minutes later, Dainty had it set up on a laptop in the kitchen.

'Right,' he said. 'Let's see what this bitch has been up to.'

Gilchrist and Jessie crowded Dainty's shoulder as they watched Cumming seated at his laptop, while a figure clad from head to toe in black entered the room through the kitchen behind him. Cumming appeared oblivious to the figure's presence, his focus on the monitor in front of him. He seemed animated; smiling, talking, leaning in close, then pulling back, and it took a few seconds for Gilchrist to understand what was happening.

'He's on FaceTime,' he said. 'Or Zoom.'

He leaned forward, and found himself holding his breath as the figure in black crept closer towards Cumming. Had the person on FaceTime witnessed the attack? Could the IT technicians trace who he was chatting to? Was he in the act of scamming someone, or was he having an everyday conversation with a friend? Not that it mattered, he supposed. But what did, was the possibility of having a living witness to his murder.

'Something's happened,' Jessie said.

Where the light from the monitor had brightened Cumming's face, there was now a shadowed darkness. Cumming sat back, fingers tapping the keyboard, muttering to himself in muted silence, clearly frustrated.

'He's lost the connection.' Jessie again.

'No,' Gilchrist said.

The figure in black moved into action.

'The connection's been terminated.'

'Christ,' Dainty whispered. 'This is it.'

It all happened with a speed that stunned them. The figure rushed at Cumming, right arm outstretched to his neck, only for Cumming to jump up in shock, knocking over his chair, stumbling against the wall, then facing his assailant in a vain attempt to defend himself.

'Stop it there,' Gilchrist said. 'Wind it back.'

Dainty obliged, and in silence they watched the attack again.

'She's tried to taser him,' Jessie said. 'See that? When she goes for his neck? But the taser didn't work.'

'I thought these things were foolproof.'

'Clearly not.'

'Keep going,' Gilchrist said.

On the monitor, Cumming's chair fell to the floor as he threw a punch, which was evaded with ease, telling Gilchrist that his assailant – Ibbotson or whoever, because they couldn't identify her for certain – had martial arts training, most likely military. Cumming tried to flee, but his computer desk hampered his escape and, arms flailing in self defence, swept plant pots off the shelf to the floor as his attacker thrust an arm at his neck again. That time, the taser worked. Cumming seemed to freeze on the spot then topple full-length to the floor with such force that the monitor appeared to shiver for an instant.

'Ah, fuck,' Dainty said.

They watched in muted disbelief as the killer kneeled on the floor, wrapped what had to be a cord around Cumming's neck, then twisted tight, hands working like a corkscrew to a bottle of wine. From the raising of Cumming's body off the floor, Gilchrist could tell that the killer was putting all her might into strangling him. 'She's garrotting him,' he said.

Then she relaxed.

It was over.

'How long did that take?' Jessie said. 'Once she'd got that cord round his neck and started tightening it, he never had a chance. Game over.'

No one said anything as the killer moved to the laptop, inserted what Gilchrist took to be a memory stick into one of the ports. A tablet of sorts appeared in her hand, or maybe it was a mobile, into which she tapped commands. Less than a minute later, she retrieved the memory stick, slipped it and the tablet into a pocket and left the scene.

'Did she just copy Cumming's files?' Jessie said.

'Looks like it.' Dainty clicked the mouse to try to pull up another screen, but the monitor turned black. 'Ah for fuck sake. I've lost it.'

Gilchrist had already confirmed CCTV cameras in other rooms, but not in every room – two bathrooms and the master bedroom remained private. They should be able to access other videos, and follow the killer's exit, and entrance.

'What makes you think it's Ibbotson?' he asked Dainty.

'I'd bet my life on it.'

Betting your life on someone you couldn't identify with 100 per cent certainty was not the path to success. Gilchrist needed more than just Dainty's hunch. 'You know we can't present this in court as is,' he said. 'We can't identify Cumming's assailant from that.'

'We'll have our IT guys look into it,' Dainty argued. 'Get them to zoom in on some images and work their digital magic, or whatever the fuck they do, until hey presto, there she'll be, a full frontal of Ibbotson in all her murderous glory. I'm convinced.'

'I'm not,' Gilchrist said.

But Dainty seemed undeterred. 'One of our IT guys is a genius at this stuff. She's magic, I'm telling you. If there's any way to ID her, she'll find it, believe me. And besides, we'll lift DNA from under Cumming's fingernails.'

Gilchrist couldn't recall Dainty ever being so single-minded in an investigation. He'd worked with him in the past, found him to be critical and exacting through the investigative process, almost to the point of being cynical of evidence, as if it were never suffi-cient to take to court, that something more irrefutable had to be found. Still, he had to admire the man's enthusiasm, and if this IT genius of his could refine an image that would ID Ibbotson, then so much the better. But for Gilchrist, IDENT1 or AFIS was the more promising approach.

Finding Ibbotson, and arresting her, was what they really needed.

He turned his attention to the monitor again. Dainty had managed to call up another video recording, this time in the kitchen, through which the killer was seen walking with purpose then slipping out the back door.

'We'll track her,' Dainty said. 'There's CCTV outside. And there's bound to be cameras on other houses.'

'We can do door-to-doors, too,' Jessie said.

'I'd like to know how she got here,' Dainty said. 'Out here, it had to be by car. How else would she get here? Bicycle? I think fucking not. So what was she driving?'

'Maybe she was driven. Maybe she had an associate.'

'Maybe. We've got Ber, so that tells me there might be more of them . . .'

As Gilchrist listened to Dainty and Jessie discussing how best to track Cumming's killer, he found himself thinking back to the attack and his memory settled on an image of the flash drive being removed. What was the significance of that? Cumming was dead, and could no longer scam anyone. They would have to confirm that he was indeed a scammer, which had to be the reason for his murder. But what could the attacker gain from copying his files? Bank details seemed the obvious. Passwords another, if Cumming was naive enough to have them on file. But as he turned those thoughts over in his mind, he came to see the possibility of a more sinister reason behind stealing Cumming's files.

If Cumming was indeed a scammer – and it seemed likely that he was – then perhaps, like Howitt, he kept a list of those he scammed on a computer file. And if his scams had been as successful as the others – the mortgage-free home, the luxury furnishings, the oil paintings, the watercolours, which would suggest he had – then there could be any number of abused women listed on his files; women who would feel hurt, betrayed and angry, but perhaps most worrying of all, they would feel the burning need to seek revenge.

As Gilchrist struggled to work through the rationale of his convoluted thoughts, tried to make logical sense of them, he came to understand that Ibbotson hadn't copied Cumming's files to access his passwords or bank details. No, she'd done so to find the names of other abusees, women who'd been scammed and scarred, and for whom cold-blooded revenge could be the sweetest dish of all. Or if you worded it another way – she was recruiting.

'Surely never,' he whispered.

'You all right, Andy?'

He returned Jessie's worried gaze, and said, 'We need to find her.'

'That's what we're trying to do.'

'No. We need to find her. And *stop* her.' He eyed the monitor again, its screen frozen on Cumming's killer about to exit the kitchen. 'Before it's too late.'

CHAPTER 36

Thursday

It took until late Thursday afternoon before Gilchrist's team had a breakthrough, once again mostly thanks to Jackie Canning – researcher extraordinaire. Dainty and the Ayrshire Police had worked round the clock to locate a black Audi leaving a car park owned by a local business, adjacent to the primary school. Normally the premises were secured at night, but the owner had confirmed with door-to-doors that when he arrived at work that morning, he'd noticed the padlock was loose and unlocked – not cut through, or damaged in any way – but simply loose and unlocked. He'd explained that he thought one of his staff had been careless, which was denied when challenged. When asked why he hadn't reported it to the police or his insurance company, he'd replied, *What's the point? Nothing was stolen.*

An examination of his company's CCTV footage identified someone fiddling with the padlock at around eight o'clock the previous night, pulling the fenced gate open, then driving an Audi into the car park. The scene was carried out in reverse two hours later. Although the police were unable to identify the driver of the car, the footage was clear enough to read the registration plate number, which was then posted on the PNC with a note – *Approach with Caution. May be Armed.*

Once Jackie had the model, make and number, and against Gilchrist's instruction to abandon the impossible task he'd assigned her, she returned to her expansive research on the M77 and within three hours incredibly found a match.

Mhairi led Gilchrist through Jackie's findings.

'This is a captured image of the registration number plate behind Fisherton Primary School, sir, and here's another one of the same registration off the M77 yesterday afternoon.'

'Is that a garden centre?'

'Yes, sir. Jackie got a hit on the ANPR on the A726 to Newton Mearns.'

'So she, or they, or whoever, took the slip road to Newton Mearns?'

'Yes, sir.'

'Show me where the garden centre is on the map.'

Mhairi adjusted Jackie's monitor so Gilchrist had a clearer view, while Jackie zoomed in on the digital map and placed the cursor on the slip road.

'Thi . . . thi . . . thi . . .'

'This is where they left the M77,' he said to Jackie.

'Uh-huh.'

'Now show me the route she took and where it ended up.'

Jackie clicked the mouse, and a blue line highlighted the road. She moved the cursor and zoomed out, then back in, to give him the best view she could.

When he saw where she'd managed to track the car to, Gilchrist couldn't resist scratching his head in amazement. 'Why would you even think of looking there, Jackie?'

She giggled as her eyes held Mhairi's.

'She likes flowers, sir. She thought that if she was on that road, she would like to have stopped off at a garden centre, too.'

'That's it?'

'Yes, sir.'

Gilchrist looked down at Jackie, then leaned over and squeezed her shoulder. 'Well done, Jackie.'

Jackie beamed. 'And . . . and . . . and . . .'

'And there's more, sir.' Mhairi signalled for Jackie to continue. 'The car sits in the garden centre for seventeen minutes without the driver getting out. Then this happens . . .'

Jackie clicked the mouse, and another image popped up on the monitor, this time in the staccato fashion of a poor video replay, which eased forward in almost comical fashion to show someone exiting the passenger door, then walking through the car park trailing a small suitcase behind her – and he could tell from the way she walked and the manner of her attire, that the passenger was a woman. Then slipping into another car, a black Audi, same make, same model. The first Audi drove off, and ten minutes later, the reverse lights of the second Audi lit up, and the car eased from its spot and made its way from the car park without the slightest sense of urgency.

'That's as far as we've followed them, sir.'

Gilchrist blew out his breath. What had he just witnessed? This was all to do with Shifrah Ber's home, he was certain of it. The transfer of someone – Ellice Ibbotson, or someone else? – then the onward drive by the first Audi to Fisherton and the cold-blooded murder of John Brentford Cumming. Having seen the exchange of cars, he was at a loss to say whether Ibbotson was the driver of the first Audi, or the second, or even if she was in either car at all. It seemed to him that they were finding more questions than answers, and certainly more potential killers and Audis than he would have liked. He struggled to pull his thoughts together, and managed to say, 'Did you get the registration number of the second Audi?'

'We did, sir, yes, but it's not helping us.'

'Who's the car registered to?'

'We don't know, sir. That's the problem. The number plate's not showing up on DVLA's records.'

'For God's sake,' he said, louder than intended, then said, 'Sorry. I don't mean that as a criticism. But you have to admit it's frustrating.'

'Yes, sir.'

Frustrating was an understatement. Bloody maddening more like. But even so, what Jackie had discovered gave them one more lead, but where that lead would take them, he had no idea. He tried to keep his tone positive, and said, 'Again, well done. I want you to follow that second car on the ANPR. It has to have been parked somewhere overnight. It's unlikely they could suspect we're onto them.' That thought seemed to liven him up. 'And with a bit of luck, they might just let their guard down.'

Back in his office, he called Dainty.

'Your ears must've been burning,' Dainty said. 'Was just about to call you.'

Gilchrist pressed the phone to his ear. He couldn't tell from Dainty's tone whether he was about to impart good news or bad. 'I'm listening,' he said.

'DNA results are back. That skin sample from under

Cumming's fingernails?' A pause, which had Gilchrist turning to the window and staring outside. 'Nothing on IDENT1.'

'Ah, *shit*.'

'But Interpol's just got back five minutes ago with a match.'

'Is it Ibbotson?'

'They don't have a name to match. But here's the good part.'

'Christ, Dainty, just spit it out for crying out loud.'

'Cumming's killer is the same person who killed Milas Volker.'

'But they don't know who that is?'

'No. They don't.'

Well, that was that. Not quite a dead end. More like a brick wall.

Dainty cleared his throat, then said, 'They recovered a strand of hair from Volker's body, which didn't match his own. The logical assumption being that that strand came from his killer.'

Gilchrist wasn't so easily convinced. 'He didn't have a girl-friend, did he?' he said, fighting to keep desperation from his voice. 'It couldn't have been hers, could it?'

'According to his closest friends, Milas Volker was a racist.'

'I'm sorry?'

'The Politi interviewed Volker's friends and family who confirmed he was a racist, a bigot who hated all things black.'

Gilchrist frowned. 'You've lost me. What's that got to do with anything?'

'That strand of hair they found. It's not from a Caucasian woman. It's from an ethnic individual. Best bet, according to the Politi, is African.'

'But . . .'

'That's right, Andy. Ibbotson's white. And so's Shifrah Ber.'

'Which leaves us with . . .'

'A bog full of shite that's just got deeper.'

CHAPTER 37

Gilchrist made it to Irene's for seven in the evening.

'Looks like you've had a rough day,' she said.

'Do I look that bad?' he said, and slumped into the sofa in front of the fire.

'Tired?'

'Exhausted.' Then he pulled himself upright. 'I'm sorry. I'm being thoughtless.' He reached for her hand, and she took it and sat down beside him. He placed his arm around her shoulder, and eased her to him. 'How's your day been?' he said.

'Better. One of those days where I've had a bit more energy.'

'That's good to hear,' he said, and dreaded asking the next question.

But she beat him to it with, 'My next appointment's Monday, which I'm not looking forward to. It always seems to knock me for six.'

He pulled her to him. He'd been remiss in keeping abreast of her chemotherapy sessions. He didn't want to admit that he'd lost count, but a month or so ago, it seemed that she spent every day at the hospital. Now her treatment was coming to an end – the intensive part of it anyway – after which she would have some respite, fewer visits, no chemo, a chance perhaps to let her body recover from the relentless onslaught of drugs. Then it was onto the next course of treatment, a different chemical, less aggressive, and not as debilitating – at least that's what they were being told – but more encouragingly, fewer hospital visits, which would hopefully give Irene time to recover between sessions.

'You've almost completed your first course,' he tried.

'After Monday, only one more,' she said. 'I spoke to Gordon this afternoon. He seems pleased with the results.'

'That's good news,' he said, trying to sound upbeat. 'And once you've had some time to recover your strength, we'll make a point of going for walks along the beach. Not every day, of course, but every other day while you build up your strength.'

'That would be lovely.' She snuggled in, leaving him to his own thoughts.

Gordon Cunningham, Irene's consultant, said he was optimistic; her cancer wasn't shrinking *per se*, but not growing, although it was impossible to say with certainty where it had spread to. Only time would tell. But what did *optimistic* mean? Being a realist, Gilchrist knew that with cancer, you were never cured, only ever in remission, living with the constant dread that it could present itself at any time anywhere. If ever there was an illness that could haunt you to the core, cancer was it.

'Oh, Andy, I meant to tell you.' Irene pushed herself upright. 'Joanne called today. She was in Glasgow for some shopping, and she met up with Maureen. She had a chat with her, a heart-to-heart she said. She thought she looked tired, but Maureen said it was her new job, putting in too many hours, trying to make a bit of a name for herself.'

Gilchrist felt himself deflate. Mo was still in denial. The new job had nothing to do with the bruises on her face. But he said nothing, just returned Irene's concerned gaze.

'Then Joanne got onto the subject of boyfriends, the way girls do.' She chuckled at that. 'She said Maureen was evasive at first, but Joanne can be persistent when she puts her mind to it.'

'A bit like you?' he joked.

'Exactly. Then she said Maureen became tearful.'

'She cried?' He hadn't meant to sound surprised, but he really couldn't remember the last time he'd seen Mo shed a tear.

'More watery-eyed, I think she meant. That's when Joanne said she decided to tell it to her straight.'

Gilchrist found himself holding his breath. He didn't like the sound of that. If Mo felt she was being told what to do, then she would do the opposite, a trait of hers that he'd learned the hard way. Mo had to be coaxed and nursed and led towards taking action, something he'd somehow never been able to master—

'She told her what she thought about Noah. Straight as that. Said that she didn't trust him. Said she'd noticed a change in Maureen, that she wasn't herself any more, that she was being less open with her, that she suspected Noah was being coercive in their relationship, and how worried she was for Maureen's safety, and if there was anything she could do to help, all she had to do was ask.'

Gilchrist wasn't sure he was going to like the answer to his next question, but he said, 'And how did that go down?'

'Okay.'

Okay? Well that was a surprise. 'So what did she mean by that? Okay I agree? Okay I'll confront him? Okay I'll find a place of my own? Or okay what?'

'I think okay means it's a first step, Andy. I think it's an acknowl-edgement that she knows their relationship isn't healthy, and that she'll have to do something about it.'

He nodded. 'Maybe you're right. At least she now knows it's out there, so to speak, that others, namely Joanne, have noticed something's not right, and that she'll need to do something about it, maybe even confront him.' He wasn't sure he believed a word he'd said, but felt he needed to settle Irene's concerns. 'But thanks for talking to Joanne for me. And thank Joanne, too, will you? She's a good friend to have.'

Irene moved closer, snuggled in again, seemingly content at the outcome. 'You have to give Maureen some time, Andy. That's what women need, time to think things through at their own pace, let the reality settle in. She's not silly. In fact, quite the oppo-site. She'll come to terms with it, I'm sure. But in her own time. And when she does she'll realise it's not the relationship she's looking for, and will move on.'

'How was it left with Joanne?'

'Just like that. Open, I suppose. She's there to help Maureen if she ever needs it.'

He squeezed Irene's shoulder. 'That's good,' he said. 'Thanks again for your help. Should I send some flowers to Joanne?'

'Don't be silly, Andy. Joanne wasn't doing that as a favour. She was doing it as a friend to Maureen. She really does love her, you know.'

'I know. I'll send some flowers to you, then. How does that sound?'

She looked up at him, a smile on her face. 'You really are the kindest man. But you don't have to send me flowers, silly. I have all I need with you.'

He pressed his lips to the side of her head, let her snuggle close, feeling ashamed at having been so deceitful. He had no intention of letting Maureen come to terms with it all in her own time. Far too often, he'd seen the result of coercive relationships coming to an end, and never in favour of the abused. Acrimonious divorce or forced separation strengthened by a non-harassment order was often the best outcome, regrettably with children being treated as pawns to be played against one partner or the other. It was a no-win scenario, the true cost of which could never be measured by solicitors' fees.

But much more worrying for Gilchrist was the recognised fact of the criminal psyche; what often started out as domestic cases of mental or physical abuse often escalated over time to a more dangerous level – murder being the ultimate outcome.

He thought back to what Jessie had said about Noah Hendry-Smith's criminal record, and knew what he had to do. He would place a call first thing in the morning, and start the ball rolling. He didn't want Maureen to fall out with him, but in the end, that would be more agreeable than attending her funeral.

CHAPTER 38

Saturday

Two days later, just before midday, Dainty phoned Gilchrist.

'Izara Kikelomo,' he announced.

'Say that again.'

He did. 'That other Audi you passed to us? We found it last night in Shawlands. Parked up a side street where no one would notice it. We detained Ms Kikelomo this morning. Turns out she's an illegal immigrant from Benin. One of these mosquito-ridden hellholes in West Africa. Voodoo and all that shite. But I tell you, no amount of voodoo's going to get her out of this one. And she's coughed up some names, Andy. Said she knew about the killings, but wasn't involved in their murders.'

It took Gilchrist a few seconds to say, 'So who's murders are we talking about?'

'John Cumming, Milas Volker, and get this ... Michael Robbins.'

'Who's Michael Robbins?'

'An ex-pat who used to live in Spain. Used to, because he was murdered two months ago. Tasered, then strangled like Cumming.'

'Did the Spanish police investigate it?'

'Of course they did. But they got nowhere. I received an email about an hour ago from the CNP in Málaga. They attached a copy of the crime scene report, and toxicology results. No doubt about it, it's the same. Garrotted to fuck.'

'Did the CNP recover any DNA from the crime scene?'

'Yes, but not from one person. From three people.'

'And one of them could be the killer.'

'Maybe. But I wouldn't go holding your breath.' Dainty let out a frustrated sigh. 'I don't know what we're digging up, Andy, but it's some kind of network, and get this . . . Ms Kikelomo wants to strike a deal. Immunity and British residency in exchange for coughing up her contact, the leader of this network, so she says.'

'You don't believe her?'

'I'm having *difficulty* believing her. Put it that way.'

'If she's involved in any of the killings, she'll never get immunity. That'll never happen.'

'Haven't told her that, yet. We're just trying to work out what she can give us. She says she can't give us the names of anyone in this supposed network, because she says she doesn't know any names. Any real names anyway. That's how they communicate between themselves. First names only. All fake. She says she's only ever dealt with one woman, who calls herself Eve, the person who recruited her—'

'Could it be Ibbotson?'

'We don't think so.'

'Hold on,' Gilchrist said, as his sense of logic stumbled. 'If she doesn't know any names, and only deals with one person, why are you calling it a network?'

'Because she's been told she's part of a network. And she says she was a passenger in a car some time ago, when two others were picked up.'

'So, what's she saying? Four of them are the network?'

'Just part of the network.'

'For crying out loud.'

'Jesus Christ, Andy, don't take it out on me. I'm as much in the dark as you. She says she was told there are more in this network, and more are being recruited every month.'

Gilchrist thought back to Cumming's murder, and the copying of his files onto a flash drive. How many abused or scammed women were out there? And of those, how many might be prepared to join some organised network that arranges for them to kill for revenge? More than he cared to find out, came the answer.

'Okay,' he said. 'So why don't you think the person who recruits them is Ibbotson?'

'Because of her red hair.'

'The alleged leader of the network has red hair?'

'Yes.'

'Has no one ever heard of a wig?'

'No wig. She's sure about that. One hundred per cent.'

'Why?'

'Says she would know a wig if she saw it.'

'It's a bit thin, Dainty, I have to say.' A pause, then, 'Have you charged her?'

'Just detained her. Don't know how much of her shite to believe, to be honest. Which is why I want you down here, Andy.

I want you to interview her, then give me your opinion. We've got an interview strategy ironed out. We just need you to lead it, while we watch on screen.'

'When?'

'Soon as.'

Gilchrist was about to hang up, when a thought came to him. 'Was she able to give a detailed description of her point of contact?'

'She says she can, but she refused. Says if she gets a deal, she'll sketch her from memory.'

'She'll *what*?'

'Sketch her from memory.'

He grimaced as he worked through Dainty's words. 'And you believe her?' he said.

'Of course not. I asked her to prove she could sketch from memory, so she asked for a pencil and paper. I sent DS Smykala for that, and when she returned, Kikelomo told her to leave the room so she could sketch her.'

'And did she?'

'In twenty minutes flat.'

'Any good?'

'It's better than good, Andy, it's fucking amazing. It's so lifelike you'd swear it was going to wink at you. So I'm thinking, if we could get her to sketch this point of contact of hers, we could post the sketch on the PNC. We wouldn't want to go public with it right away, in case we give a heads-up and scare her off. We'll see what feedback we get first, and take it from there. But I'd like her to do that sketch, without promising any deal. And for you to let me know your thoughts on her.' A pause then, 'Fuck it. Here comes trouble. How soon can you get here?'

240

Gilchrist checked his watch. He'd planned to have a quiet night in with Irene, watch a movie or a mini-series. He could be in Glasgow by two o'clock. An hour in the interview and another with Dainty, and back in St Andrews for six.

'I'm on my way,' he said.

He found Jessie on her computer, eyes glued to the screen. He tapped the door, and she glanced up at him.

'You know what I'm thinking?' she said.

'What's that?'

'I'm thinking there could be any number of murdered scammers out there. Here,' she said, and shifted her monitor so Gilchrist could read it. 'Australia. There are twenty-three unsolved murders this year alone, which is just over ten per cent of the annual homicide rate. Scary when you think about it. But see here? Fifteen died from gunshot wounds, two from knife wounds, one by a hit-and-run, one by drowning, and finally, four by strangulation.' She clicked the mouse, and the screen shifted. 'Now of these four, one appears to have been done by hand – crushed hyoid bone and all that – where the other three have bruising around the neck, with deeper bruising at the back, suggesting garrotting. But the icing on the cake, is that these three were also tasered.'

'What?' Gilchrist leaned closer.

'See here. No doubt about it, Andy. First tasered, then garrotted.' She sat back and looked at him. 'You think they could have been killed by the same person? Or persons?'

What could he tell her? That some red-haired woman is suspected of recruiting a network of female killers? That their investigation had just expanded to include one more victim, Michael Robbins? That if Jessie's speculation was accurate, they could be looking at the widest murdering network since the founding of the Mafia – an exaggeration, of course, but bloody hell . . .

Defeated, he said, 'It's possible. But I don't know. What I do know is, you need to grab a jacket and come with me.'

'Where are we going?'

'To interview Izara Kikelomo.'

'Who?'

'Izara Kikelomo.'

'Should I know him?'

'Her.'

'Aye, right. With a name like that, I should've guessed it was a woman.'

CHAPTER 39

Gilchrist entered Interview Room 3 in Strathclyde HQ, Pitt Street, Jessie behind him, and took his seat at the table. Facing him sat a round-faced white-haired woman, wearing glasses that might have been fashionable ten years ago. She didn't look up when he sat, her attention focused on a notepad in front of her, until he passed over a business card. Again, without looking at him, she took it in exchange for one of her own – Miss Simona Fellet, Senior Advisor, Mullen Stevenson Law Offices. He noticed the address in Gourock, which intrigued him. At the mouth of the River Clyde, Gourock could conceivably provide a route to the UK for an illegal immigrant. Of course, how immigrants found themselves at the mouth of the Clyde was another matter. So, maybe not such a brilliant idea after all.

Seated next to Fellet, and to Gilchrist's right – opposite Jessie – sat an African woman he would put in her mid-forties, maybe late-thirties. She watched him with wide eyes that clung to him as if to miss nothing. He checked the recorder was on, then opened his folder. He introduced himself, as did Jessie – St Andrews CID

– who then nodded to Fellet who introduced herself with a strong accent – Polish if he were a betting man – and announced that she was representing Ms Izara Kikelomo.

Gilchrist eyed her client. 'Izara Kikelomo, you've been detained under Section 14 of the Criminal Procedure Scotland Act 1995 on suspicion of the murders of John Brentford Cumming, Milas Volker and Michael Robbins. You are not obliged to say anything, but anything you do say will be noted and tape recorded, and may be used in evidence.'

Kikelomo lowered her head, and stared at the table.

'Do you understand?'

She nodded.

'You need to speak for the record.'

'Yes.'

Gilchrist placed both hands on the table, and said, 'You were interviewed earlier. I've read the transcript in detail.' Not strictly correct, more of a quick scan for key points. 'Is there anything you want to add or change to that transcript?'

Without looking up, she said, 'No.'

'Okay,' he said. 'You said you knew about the murders of Cumming, Volker and Robbins, but that you were not involved directly in them. Is that correct?'

'Yes.'

'So what does *not involved directly* mean?'

'I knew about them. That they'd been killed. I knew that. But I didn't kill them.' Although her pronunciation was clear, her accent sounded like a slow-spoken mixture of Spanish and West African.

'You knew about them *before* they were killed?'

'No. Only after.'

'How did you hear about them?'

'From the person who killed them.'

'Can you tell me who that is?'

'I don't know her real name. I only know her as Eve.'

Confirmation the killer was a woman, just as he'd suspected.
'And Eve confessed to you that she'd killed them?' he said.

'Yes.'

'Did she tell you how she had killed them?'

'Yes.'

'What I don't understand, Izara, is why she would confess to
you. I don't get it.'

'She was training me. Showing me what to do, how it had to
be done.'

Gilchrist's mind flitted back to his and Dainty's earlier thoughts
on the killings being carried out by some kind of murderous
network. It looked like they might have hit the nail on the head.
'So this Eve, whoever she is, was going to have you commit
murder?'

'Yes.'

'And did you ever murder anyone?'

'No.'

'Was there any reason why you didn't?'

'I changed my mind.'

'So why didn't you report those murders to the police?'

'I was too frightened.'

'Frightened,' he said, more statement than question.
'Frightened of what?'

'Of her. Eve.'

'Why?'

'Because . . . because of who she is.'

'But didn't she recruit you to join her network? Wasn't that what you were trained to do? To commit murder? As directed by Eve?'

Kikelomo looked at him then, her eyes pleading. 'You have to understand that when I first met her, I was vulnerable. I was in pain. Mental pain. And angry. I wanted revenge for what had happened to me. I lost all of my life savings to someone who said he loved me, and wanted to meet me. But it was a scam. I can't explain to you how upset I was. All I wanted most of all was revenge. But once I saw what was being done, what Eve was doing, what she wanted me to do, I realised that is not how God wants us to behave. It was wrong. I saw then that I'd made a terrible mistake thinking that I wanted to be a member of her network. Now I want nothing to do with it. And with her.'

Gilchrist held her gaze, trying to see beyond her eyes. He wasn't sure he believed her. It sounded like a good enough story, but in all likelihood she was either a terrific liar, or a good actor.

'You said in your earlier interview that you want to strike a deal, yes?'

'Yes.'

'Immunity and British residency?'

'Yes.'

'In exchange for giving the police information on the murders?'

'Yes.' Her arms moved on the table, and for a moment he thought she was reaching out to him. 'I can give you what you want. I haven't done anything wrong. I haven't killed anyone. I thought I could, but now I realise I could never hurt anyone. Not for revenge. Not for money. Not for anything. You have to believe me.' She glanced at Fellet, but she sat by her side, stone-faced and tight-lipped. So much for legal advice.

Gilchrist lowered his head and eyed Kikelomo. Time to get tough. 'How long have you known Eve?'

'Five months.'

'Was that the first time you met her?'

'No. I met her only three months ago. Up until then, we corresponded by text.'

'And do you still have these texts?'

'No. Eve told me to destroy my mobile and all my computer records. Then she gave me a new mobile and a new number.'

Her mobile would have been removed from her home, and analysed by the IT techies. They could confirm dates and times. 'How did you get into the UK?' he said.

'Eve drove me. Through the Channel Tunnel.'

'And all the way up to Scotland?'

'Yes.'

'You have a passport?'

'Yes. An EU passport.'

'Have you left the UK since you arrived?'

'No.'

'Did you speak to Eve, or communicate with her, or someone purporting to be her, prior to five months ago?'

'No. Only Eve. That was the first time. Five months ago.'

Again, the IT team could confirm or otherwise. He paused for a moment to gather his thoughts. According to Dainty, Michael Robbins was murdered in Spain two months earlier. If Kikelomo met Eve three months ago, had she lied about being involved in his murder? And could she be lying about Cumming's murder? Had she been the figure dressed in black who'd so casually entered his home and killed him? She'd given saliva and hair samples for DNA analysis, but he hadn't received the results yet, which might be available to him in an hour or two. Even so, he felt he wasn't willing to wait that long.

'Can you roll up your sleeves, please?' he said to her.

She frowned, then with slow deliberation rolled her cuffs over her elbows.

'May I?' Gilchrist said, and took hold of her hands. He turned them over, inspected her skin, back and front, from fingertips to elbow – not a scratch – and felt a flush of anxiety shift through him for the first time. Cumming had skin under his fingernails. Where had that come from? Was he wrong about Kikelomo? Was she telling the truth?

He let go of her hands. 'You'll have to submit to a full forensic examination.'

Fellet spoke for the first time. 'My client is under no obligation to subject herself to such personal humiliation. She is not required to submit to any forensic examination. Unless you're going to charge her.' She held his eyes in an eagle-like stare. 'Well? Are you?'

He shifted his gaze to Kikelomo. 'Your solicitor is correct,' he said. 'You're under no obligation to agree to a forensic examination. But if you're telling the truth, then what harm can it do?'

Fellet said, 'For the record, I'm advising my client not to agree to this request.'

Kikelomo lowered her head, and pressed her hands to her mouth. She was silent for several seconds, as if deciding how best to respond. Then without looking up, said, 'I'm going to take the advice of my solicitor, and decline.'

Gilchrist said nothing. If the DNA analysis came back with a match, it wouldn't matter whether she agreed to a forensic examination or not. He leaned to Jessie, whispered in her ear, and Jessie shuffled from her seat and left the room. 'DS Janes leaving the interview room at . . .' he said, and recited the time.

Gilchrist spent the next ten minutes poking and prodding, searching for any flaw in her stance. But she stuck to her story of innocent bystander, and he was about to call for a break, when Jessie returned.

She introduced herself again for the recorder, then handed him a folder, which he opened and spent thirty seconds reading through. Then he closed it, and stared at Kikelomo. He now knew that her DNA results matched none of the samples collected at any of the crime scenes, and that she could not be charged with anything more serious than obstruction of a criminal investigation, a serious enough charge on its own, but not one that helped his investigation. Or was it?

He could never strike a deal with her for immunity from murder. But he might be able to do so for the much lesser charge of obstruction of an investigation. He leaned forward, and fixed his gaze on Kikelomo. 'I have evidence in this folder that will permit me to charge you with a criminal offence.' He wasn't going to tell her that the offence was not murder. 'But I'm willing to consider dropping all charges . . . provided . . .' He was aware of Fellet's eyes on him, and had an unsettling sense that she was about to call his bluff. 'Provided you cooperate with us fully in our ongoing investigation.'

Fellet said, 'And my client's request for permanent residency?'

'That's beyond our remit, and would have to be approved by the Home Office. But depending on how helpful your client is, well, we could certainly put in a strong word of recommendation.'

She eyed the folder. 'What's in that?'

For a moment he thought it might be best not to tell her, just keep her guessing, then said, 'Proof that your client is innocent of what she's being detained for.'

'So you can only charge her with obstruction of a criminal investigation.'

'Or not.' He paused for a long second to let the meaning of his words settle in. 'That's still a serious charge and carries the possibility of a custodial sentence, and the likelihood of your client's request for permanent residency being rejected.' He glanced at Kikelomo, and shrugged. Then he pushed to his feet. 'We'll leave you for a few minutes to discuss what you would like to do. Interview terminated at 14:47,' he said, and switched off the recorder.

In the hallway, Jessie said, 'I think she's jerking our chain. We should just charge the bitch and be done with it. That's what I'd do.'

'Let's give it a few more minutes and see what she comes up with. Meanwhile, I'm going to find a coffee. Want one?'

'Thought you'd never ask.'

By the time they returned to the interview room and reintroduced themselves, eight minutes had passed. Gilchrist took his seat, coffee in hand, and before he could say anything more, Kikelomo slid an A4 sheet of paper across the desk.

Jessie snatched it, and said, 'What's this?'

'Eve.'

'What about the others? The passengers in the car you said you'd picked up? Can you do sketches of them, too?'

'One only, I think. I didn't get a good look at the other one.'

'Sit with her face turned away, did she?' Jessie said, and slid the sketch to Gilchrist. 'I think she could get a job as a street artist in Central Station. What do you think?'

Gilchrist didn't know what to think. He frowned at the portrait, at the face that stared back at him, with eyes that could almost wink. He'd seen that face before. In fact he'd spent time with her while she downed champagne cocktails like lemonade, in between flying back and forth to Dubai wheeling and dealing in jewellery. She had more money than she knew what to do with. Now Gilchrist knew what she did with it. She funded a network of killers.

Kenzie Dorrance's wealthy sister.

Alice Ralston.

CHAPTER 40

6 a.m., Sunday
Outskirts of Edinburgh

The following morning, an arrest team gathered in Blackford Drive in muted silence outside a detached stone mansion, the latest home address of Alice Ralston. In the midwinter morning darkness, Dainty looked diminutive, agitated and cold, but eager to get on with the job of *handcuffing that murdering bitch, and putting her away for once and fucking all.*

Gilchrist blew into his hands.

'You think she's in?' Jessie said.

'She was seen returning home last night at 11:24, according to Lothian and Borders, and hasn't moved since.' He and Dainty had met with Chief Superintendent Mansfield late last night with the intention of arresting Ralston on the spot. But without an arrest warrant approved, ticked off, printed out and in his hands, Mansfield refused to budge.

So, Sunday morning it was.

Gilchrist had phoned Irene twice last night – at six-thirty to tell her he was running late and held up in Edinburgh, and then at eleven-thirty to tell her he was a member of an arrest team scheduled to make a formal arrest early Sunday morning, and that he wouldn't be home that evening. He and Jessie had booked rooms in the Holyrood Macdonald.

'Uh-oh,' Jessie said. 'A light's just gone on upstairs.'

Gilchrist faced the mansion. Sure enough, a set of bay windows on the second floor glowed from lights within. He walked over to Dainty, who'd also seen the lights go on, and said, 'We might not need the big key after all.'

'If that bitch doesn't open up right away, we'll be using that thing good and fucking proper.'

Gilchrist gritted his teeth. He'd never seen Dainty so tense before. Of course, he'd never been with him in the pre-dawn hours of a bitter winter's morning before. He supposed being chilled to the bone could do that to you – shorten your patience, and have you prepared to break down doors at the drop of a hat. He glanced at the mansion again, and with a sigh of relief noticed another light on downstairs.

'Looks like she's up and about,' he said to Dainty. 'You got the warrant?'

Dainty tapped his pocket in response, then signalled for the team to move.

It always surprised Gilchrist how quietly a group of men in Kevlar vests kitted out with firearms and lugging the big key could move. Like a silent dance line, they shuffled up the cobbled driveway and worked their way past an abandoned Porsche – in which Ralston had driven home the night before – to stand clustered at the front door.

Dainty rapped the door knocker. It broke the morning silence like a hammer hit. He pressed the doorbell, held it down for the count of ten. Then he rattled the door knocker again and stood back. The officer carrying the big key stepped in front of Dainty, and was about to swing it back, when an outside light came on.

'Hold it,' Dainty ordered, then rang the doorbell again.

From inside came the sound of keys turning, locks clicking, until the door pulled open with a heavy slap to reveal the tall figure of an elderly man with white thinning hair, standing there in dressing gown and pyjamas and slippered feet.

'Yes?' he said, as his eyes and mouth widened at the sight before him.

'Police,' Dainty said. 'We have an arrest warrant for Alice Ralston. Is she in?'

'She's in the back room,' he said, and stumbled back as Dainty brushed past him, followed by eight others.

Gilchrist was the last to enter, Jessie in front of him. He reached the end of the hall in time to hear Dainty in the back bedroom, voice loud and booming, detaining Alice Ralston for conspiracy to murder, then reading her rights. He thought the way Dainty and his team manhandled Ralston down the hallway, hands cuffed in front of her and wearing little more than a nightdress, was not how experienced police officers should behave.

Alice's bedroom was already being searched. He walked into the en-suite bathroom, unhooked a woollen dressing gown from the back of the door, and strode down the hallway. Outside, an easterly wind had risen, cold enough to slice through to the bone. Alice was being hustled down the driveway by Dainty, towards a car with its rear door already opened and its steaming exhaust clouding the air.

Gilchrist caught up with them as she was about to be bundled into the back. 'Hold on,' he shouted. 'Put this over her, for God's sake.' He thrust out the dressing gown. 'It's Arctic out here.'

Dainty scowled at Gilchrist as if surprised to see him standing there, then seemed to come to his senses. He took the dressing gown and threw it over Alice's shoulders, with little care. Then he put his hand on her head, pushed her inside, and clambered after her. The door closed with a dull thud, and the car sped off.

Gilchrist found Jessie in the front room talking to the elderly man who'd answered the door. He looked to be in his eighties, with skin that glowed with apparent good health, and a square jaw and aquiline features that somehow spoke of an aristocratic life. They were seated in opposing armchairs, Jessie with her notebook in hand. As Gilchrist entered, the man's gaze followed him all the way to the sofa into which he sank. Their eyes met for a brief moment, and he had the strangest feeling of having done something wrong, that the arrest they'd just carried out had been a mistake. The man's eyes shifted to the sound of something thudding to the floor at the back of the house.

'Go and check that out,' he said to Jessie. 'And tell them to be respectful.'

Without a word, Jessie slipped her notebook into her pocket and left the room.

Alone with the elderly man, Gilchrist held out his warrant card. 'Detective Chief Inspector Gilchrist with Fife Constabulary. And you are?'

'Aren't you out of your jurisdiction?' The voice was strong and commanding, as if used to giving orders – or taking no nonsense from someone as lowly as Gilchrist.

'I'm one of a multi-regional task force,' Gilchrist said, and held the man's gaze for a long moment, before letting his own drift around the room to take in the expensive furniture; walls lined with oversized mirrors and dull-looking paintings; family photographs in exquisite frames littered antique tables that shone with polish. One photograph in particular held his attention; a younger Alice, skin tanned, teeth gleaming, arms around a looka-like. Not quite twins, but close to identical in so many ways. Could she be her sister, Kenzie?

All this was taken in by Gilchrist in a matter of seconds.

He removed his notebook and faced the man again. 'Name?'

'Would you be good enough to tell me what the hell is going on? This is an utter outrage.'

'Your daughter, Alice . . . I take it she's your daughter . . .?' No response, other than a tightening of his jaw. 'Has been detained on suspicion of conspiracy to multiple murders.'

The man's eyes creased in puzzlement. 'Alice? Multiple murders . . .?' He paused then, and shook his head slowly, as if in apology. 'Alice wouldn't hurt a fly.'

'She's your daughter, then.' More statement than question.

'Yes. She is.'

'And your full name . . .?'

'Professor Sir Elliot Ralston.'

It took a few seconds for Gilchrist to recall why the name sounded so familiar: Elliot Ralston, as he'd been known in plain terms forty years ago, before being handed an honorary doctor-ate at some English university whose name he couldn't remem-ber, and long before his questionable knighthood, had been infa-mous as a ruthless industrialist who'd made millions, even billions, through petrochemical contracts in Saudi Arabia, long before the world ever worried about Saudi's human rights records. Global interest once hovered around Ralston over questions concerning his then-business partner, Miles Salcombe, a wealthy Englishman who disappeared without trace.

Salcombe, well-known for his womanising and drinking – despite Saudi's strict laws against both – drove his favourite Willys Jeep into the ad-Dahna Desert one November night, and was never seen or heard from again. His Jeep was found abandoned in the desert, more barren landscape than rolling sands, with no sign of Salcombe. Suspicion fell on Ralston who, because of the terms of their business agreement, would inherit the partnership in its entirety. But a rock-solid alibi – he'd been in the company of Sheikh Abdul bin Fareed al Saud, sixth cousin of the then ruler of Saudi Arabia, who assured the world – and the Mabahith, the feared Saudi Arabian police – of his innocence. Six weeks later, Ralston's company was awarded the largest petrochemical contract ever granted in the kingdom, and the rest, as they say, was history.

'I see from the look on your face that you recognise me,' Ralston said.

'Yes. I had no idea.'

'Few people do.' Ralston pushed to his feet. 'Unless you're going to arrest me, too, I suggest you call your riff-raff together and instruct them to leave immediately.'

Gilchrist stood, slipped his notebook into his pocket. At six foot one, he was taller than your average Scotsman, but he stood a good five inches short of Ralston's lean figure, despite the slightest of stoops due to his age. 'We have a search and arrest warrant,' he said, 'so we won't be able to do that. And I'm afraid I'm going to have to ask you to leave the premises while our search of the property is ongoing. Can I arrange a lift for you?'

Ralston smiled, a baring of long teeth that made his condescension seem all the more irritating. 'No need,' he said. 'Bentley's in the garage. I can drive myself home.'

'You don't live here?'

'No.' As he strode past, Gilchrist had the strangest sense of the man's malevolence. 'My solicitors will be in touch,' Ralston said.

'I look forward to it.' It was all he could think to come back with.

'They'll take great pleasure in wiping that smirk off your face.'

And with that, Ralston left the room.

CHAPTER 41

Gilchrist found Jessie in the back bedroom, supervising the removal of two laptops and a mobile phone. 'Could be a gold mine,' she said, slipping a mobile from the bedside table into a paper evidence bag. Her smile faded when she looked at him. 'What's wrong?'

He grimaced. 'Didn't like the way Dainty behaved. It wasn't like him to be so . . . so *aggressive* with her.'

'That's probably because of Pat.'

'Pat?'

'His daughter.'

'Ah, yes, of course.' He hadn't visited Dainty at home for years, and his daughter's name had slipped his memory for a moment. Now he had it, he remembered her. Small like Dainty, but where Dainty seemed unconcerned about his lack of height, Patricia had found it difficult to live with. Not much over five feet, if that, she seemed to go through life with an almost debilitating grudge. 'So what's Pat got to do with it?'

'I thought you knew.'

'Apparently not.'

'I was with Strathclyde when it happened. Six years ago, give or take, Pat put a downpayment on a new car, top of the range something-or-other. But the deal fell through, and she lost her deposit. Her boyfriend at the time, the one who'd put her onto the deal, and taken the downpayment from her, urged her to take legal action. Sue the bastards, he told her. He had a friend who was a great solicitor, and who'd get her money back, plus some. But he worked on a payment-upfront basis. So Pat being Pat – a bit dolly-dimple, I'd have to say – gave him more money to give to his solicitor friend. And that was the last she saw of him, or her cash. Over ten thousand I think she lost.'

Gilchrist let out a frustrated sigh. 'My God, she'd been scammed.'

'Dainty went ballistic, but he never found her boyfriend. False name, false everything. Probably left Glasgow to scam some other unlucky girl. Dainty sorted out Pat's finances for her, so she wasn't out of pocket, but he was an angry man for a long while.' She chuckled. 'Looks like he still is.' Then she nodded over Gilchrist's shoulder. 'What did laugh-a-minute have to say?'

'Alice is his daughter. And we'll be hearing from his solicitors, apparently.'

'Fatherly love. They never get it, do they?'

'Who?'

'Fathers. They think the sun shines out their daughter's arses. They never know the half of it. Maybe just as well, I suppose.' She turned to one of the officers, and shouted, '*Hey* you. You were told to handle stuff with care. Not boot it about the room.'

Gilchrist walked from the bedroom, lost for words. The truth of Jessie's words had hit home. They stung. But the truth often did. *Fathers never get it. They never know the half of it.* How true those words were. What was his own daughter doing at that very moment? How could he help her leave this flatmate, or partner, or whatever he was, without her knowing he'd been involved? Maybe the answer was to talk to her face-to-face, tell her some facts about who this man was. But as the rationale of that action worked through his brain, he came to see that he would need to be discreet, keep himself on the sidelines, or better still, out of the picture altogether.

He was about to step outside, when Ralston appeared at the bottom of the staircase, wearing red corduroy trousers and a matching heavy winter sweater. Christmas must be close right enough. As he brushed past, Gilchrist called out, 'We may have to ask you to come down to the local office to corroborate your daughter's statement.'

Ralston either never heard, or ignored the comment, for he clicked a key fob, and the garage door slid open to reveal the sleek lines of a Bentley Continental, its silver coachwork gleaming showroom-new in the garage light. Gilchrist stood on the threshold as the big car backed out of the garage, swung in front of him, clicked into Drive, then eased its way past the abandoned Porsche to cruise down the driveway with nothing more than a lazy purr from its six-litre engine. His mobile rang at that moment – ID Dainty – and he took the call.

'Duty officer's just logged her ladyship in,' Dainty said. 'She's a cool one, I'll give her that. Denies everything and anything, and tells me that the police are going to rue the day they ever broke into her home and arrested her. She was told she should call her solicitor, and she said she didn't need to. Said that Daddy would have called Silverman's already, and that the police had better start lawyering up.'

'Silverman's?'

'Silverman James, the most revered firm of solicitors in Edinburgh, if not the entire English-speaking world. Never lost a case, so they claim. Hard to believe, but rumour has it they're not averse to pressing the flesh with cash, sometimes gold. And big John Silverman's the worst. Struts about like a preening cock. Christ knows what his fucking hourly rate is, but I'd heard it's four figures, and I don't mean eleven pounds two and tuppence.'

Gilchrist had never come across John Silverman before, but had a vague recollection of his being involved in a case in Tayside, a number of years ago. From what he'd heard, the evidence was heavily weighted against the accused, but Silverman somehow managed to get his client a suspended sentence. He couldn't imagine that being considered a win, but in the unpredictable weighted scales of the legal system, maybe it did. And from what he'd seen and heard of Elliot Ralston, the man had a large enough bank balance to keep Silverman in gravy for the rest of his life. But more worrying, when he thought about it, Ralston's parting words – *they'll take great pleasure in wiping that smirk off your face* – sounded more of a threat than assurance of a legal victory.

'So next thing, I get a call from Silverman himself. On my own fucking mobile. I mean . . . what the fuck? How did he get that? I never give out my number.'

Gilchrist stared at the end of the driveway. The Bentley's exhaust trail had vanished in the stirring morning wind. Ralston must have phoned Silverman while he was pulling on his corduroys and sweater, which was proof he supposed that you didn't become a billionaire by sitting with your thumb up your butt. But even so . . .

'Would be good if you could sit in with me on the interview,' Dainty said.

'When's it set for?'

Dainty gave a half-hearted chuckle. 'I tried to set it for eight, but Silverman told me in that annoying fucking way of his, he couldn't make it until nine, and if anyone even so much as whispered to his client without him being present, he would sue them personally. That's what we're up against.'

Gilchrist glanced at his watch. Just after seven. Which gave him plenty of time. 'I'll see you there,' he said.

CHAPTER 42

Big John Silverman turned out to be not as tall as Dainty had led Gilchrist to believe. Size was relative, of course. But where Silverman was big was around his waist, which had to be on the upside of fifty inches, maybe more, although his made-to-measure three-piece suit did what it could to make him look slimmer. The interview room was redolent of aftershave, a spicy fragrance that reminded Gilchrist of an upmarket strip club he'd once been obliged to visit to make an arrest.

To Silverman's side sat Alice Ralston in a one-piece outfit she'd been given to wear while being detained. Her blonde hair – roots hinting of its natural red – was pulled back into a tight elasticated ponytail. It made her face look narrower, her nose more aquiline, her jaw square. She was her father's daughter, after all.

Dainty switched on the recorder, checked it was working, and was about to announce the introductions when Silverman said, 'One second.' He slipped his hand into his inside suit pocket and produced a phone-like device, which he placed with deliberation onto the middle of the table. Then he clicked it on. 'To make sure there's no hanky-panky.' Then he sat back, and pronounced, 'Proceed.'

Gilchrist could sense Dainty's unease. He could tell he wanted to object to Silverman making his own recording, but strictly speaking, there were no rules against him doing so. So Gilchrist leaned forward. 'If you're going to record this interview,' he said, 'we'll need you to make a copy for our records.' He smiled at Silverman. 'To make sure there is no, as you say, hanky-panky.'

Silverman eyed him as he would a fanged snake, unsure if it was going to strike or not. Then he tilted his head in a gentleman's acknowledgement. 'Of course.'

'Right,' Dainty said, and introduced himself and Gilchrist, followed by Alice then Silverman. 'Ms Alice Ralston has been advised why she is being detained,' Dainty said, 'and has been read her rights. But for the record, and for the avoidance of any doubt, I'm going to read Ms Ralston her rights again, witnessed by her solicitor.' He took his time, reading it out word perfect, as if in fear of Silverman giving him two marks out of ten. He asked Alice if she understood – Yes – then he opened his folder, took hold of a page and was about to speak when Silverman beat him to it.

'Before we start,' he said, in a voice that sounded more theatrical than legal, 'I would like your comments on this.' He reached down to a bag on the floor, which Gilchrist hadn't noticed, and pulled out a laptop. He placed it in front of him, opened it, and spent a few silent minutes working his way into whatever file he was searching for, then swung it around on the desk so that it faced Gilchrist and Dainty. He tapped the touchpad, and sat back. 'CCTV footage,' he said, 'of my client's arrest earlier this morning.'

Gilchrist hadn't paid any attention to CCTV cameras during Alice's arrest, but if you thought about it, the entire place – inside and out – must have had security cameras installed throughout. Eyes on the laptop, he watched Dainty hustle Alice down the driveway, hands cuffed. He pursed his lips when she seemed to stumble and Dainty jerked her upright with such force that she almost fell backwards. Another forceful jerk, and Alice was tugged tight to his side—

Silverman stopped the recording. 'Can you please read the time on that recording?'

Dainty sat there, tight-lipped. Gilchrist could feel the heat of his anger.

'Very well,' Silverman said. 'At that moment, it is precisely eleven minutes and five seconds past six o'clock in the morning. For your information, and for the record, according to the Edinburgh Met Office records, daylight was still an hour and a half away, give or take a minute or two. Also note that the temperature at six o'clock this morning was recorded at minus five degrees Celsius.' He enlarged the image on the screen so that Alice's body filled it. 'Can you please tell me what Ms Ralston is wearing on her feet?'

'Slippers,' Dainty hissed.

'And on her body?'

'That's what she was wearing when we found her. What do you expect me to do? Wait a couple of hours while she has a bath and puts on her make-up?'

'Again for the record, I can confirm that my client is wearing a silk nightdress.' He tapped the touchpad and the image reduced. 'My client advises me that when she retires to bed for the night, she sleeps only in a silk nightdress, no matter what time of year.' Another tap on the touchpad, and Alice's slender figure loomed large once again – all for theatrical effect, Gilchrist knew.

'So the woman you see here being frogmarched down her driveway in the middle of the night more or less naked in subzero temperatures after her house was broken into and to then be arrested under preposterous and falsified charges is in no fit state to be detained in a police cell and questioned.' And all said in a booming voice that bounced off the walls with no break for a breath, which Silverman now took. But he wasn't over yet. 'I demand that this woman, my client, be escorted to the hospital immediately, so that her health can be checked out, during which time I will be filing the most strenuous complaint to the Constabulary over the manner in which she, an innocent victim, and the daughter of one of this city's most revered citizens, has been treated. Your handling of my client, sir . . .' this aimed directly at Dainty, '. . . has been nothing short of an abomination. A shameful and utter abomination.'

Gilchrist had never seen Dainty so diminished. He knew he was seething, and that his natural means of defence was to come out spitting like a cornered cougar and swearing like a whipped sailor. But listening to a recording in which the interviewer effed and blinded was a big no-no. Gilchrist leaned forward. 'I would like to correct you on a few points, if I may?'

Silverman glowered at them. 'Correct me?'

'That's what I said, yes.'

'Well,' he said, 'I'll be interested to listen to this.'

'Firstly, your client was not arrested in the middle of the night, but more correctly, per your own assertion, an hour and a half before sunrise . . . give or take a minute or two.'

Silverman harrumphed.

'Secondly, your client was not frogmarched down the driveway—'

'Didn't you watch the recording?' he bellowed.

'I did, yes.'

'What on earth is that then, if it's not frogmarching?'

'I'll get to that in a minute. But if you care to look up the definition of frogmarching, you would see that it refers to hands being pinioned behind one's back. Your client's hands were handcuffed to the front, which to my way of thinking is a far more considerate way for an officer of the law to secure an arrest.'

Silverman tutted, but said nothing.

Gilchrist pressed on. 'So rather than use the term frogmarch, my preference would be to say more correctly that she was escorted—'

'Escorted?' Silverman's voiced boomed. 'Manhandled, would be more accurate.'

'With temperatures sub-zero, as you asserted, DCI Small was simply making sure that your client couldn't possibly slip on ice, which explains the tight grip.'

'Brute force, more like. I've already arranged for a doctor to examine my client's arms for any unnecessary bruising.'

Gilchrist held up his hand. 'I'm not finished.'

Silverman sighed, and shook his head. 'Continue.'

'Your client's house was not broken into, but entered by the front door, which was opened by your client's father, Professor Sir Elliot Ralston. Access was granted with no force whatsoever used.'

'A turn of phrase.' Silverman dismissed it with a wave of a pudgy hand. 'Continue.'

'Your use of the words preposterous and falsified are inappropriate at this stage of the interview process. Your client has not been charged, only detained, to give us the opportunity to question her over evidence we've recovered at several crime scenes.'

Silverman's jaws tightened, which suggested to Gilchrist that he might be unaware of what exactly Alice Ralston had got herself into.

'But for the record,' Gilchrist said, 'we'll leave as is, with a note of our objection.'

'Are you finished?'

'Not yet.'

'God in heaven,' Silverman grumbled.

'Your . . . *demand* . . . for your client to be taken to hospital is noted. However, your client is in no position to demand anything, *but . . .*' he added quickly, hand held up to prevent Silverman from objecting, 'I'm happy to consider it.'

Silverman seemed lost for words.

'We can arrange for one of our trained medical staff to check your client's health. Or you could have your doctor, the one you've already been in contact with, examine her here.'

'Hmmh.'

'Or we'd be happy to escort her to the hospital.'

'I can't allow that, my client turning up at a hospital in a police car.'

'Perhaps you'd like to escort her there yourself. In your own car.'

Silverman frowned at Gilchrist, as if knowing he was being tricked but couldn't figure out how. 'I thought you intended to detain her.'

'We can revisit that later. Once her doctor considers her well enough. After all, your client's wellbeing is of paramount concern.' He could sense Dainty's disagreement, which seemed to shimmer off him in electric waves. But thankfully, he didn't intervene.

Alice looked at Silverman. 'Am I free to leave?'

'It would appear so,' he said. 'For the time being.'

Gilchrist eyed Silverman. 'Should we have any concerns that your client might decide to flee the country?'

'Absolutely not. You have my word.'

Dainty snickered, which brought him a ship-sinking stare from Silverman.

'We've confiscated her mobile,' Gilchrist continued, 'and her personal computers in the meantime. But I'll need to insist that we have one of our own officers, in plain clothes, of course, attend the hospital with you. Just to make sure that there will be no . . . as you say . . . hanky-panky.' He smiled again, just to make his point.

For the first time that morning, Silverman appeared lost for words. Gilchrist could almost see the man's wheels turning – object to the police escort, and the hospital visit will almost certainly be refused. Drive her to the hospital himself, and she could use *his* phone on the way there. Decision made, Silverman pushed his chair back, switched off his recording device, slipped it and the laptop into the bag by the side of the table, then held out his hand to help Alice to her feet.

Dainty recorded the end of the interview, while Gilchrist said, 'We can have one of our officers collect some suitable clothes for your client, or you can collect them from her home on the way to the hospital. Whichever works best for you and your client.'

A glance at Alice, then Silverman said, 'We'll drive home first.'

'Good.' Gilchrist stood. 'I'll arrange for DS Janes to be her escort. She can sit in the front with you, or the back seat, again whichever you prefer.'

'I assumed DS Janes would drive her own car.'

Gilchrist stared hard into Silverman's eyes. 'Not a chance,' he said, letting him know he was nowhere close to the pushover he took him to be.

CHAPTER 43

Dainty cornered Gilchrist in the corridor. 'What the hell are you playing at, letting her go like that?'

'Getting you off the hook, is what I'm doing.' He turned his full glare on Dainty. 'For crying out loud, that footage of you huckling her into the car didn't look good. And it won't look any better in front of a disciplinary hearing.'

Dainty's lips pressed to a white line. Then he shook his head. 'Not my finest hour, I'm sure, but even so . . . I wouldn't have done what you did.'

'Let's just say it's a calculated gamble, a ploy to throw Silverman off course, if only for a short while. I'd like to think it took the wind out his sails.'

Dainty chuckled. 'He wasn't expecting it, that's for sure.'

'But it's not going to balance the books, because that footage of his didn't show us up in a good light.' Gilchrist paused for a moment, then said, 'I know what's eating you. I heard about Pat. I'm sorry. I never knew.'

Dainty shrugged. 'Maybe the best thing that happened was that I never found the bastard. Would've cut his balls off and shoved them down his throat, if I had. With the greatest of fucking pleasures.'

Gilchrist had no doubt that if Dainty ever had found Pat's ex, then having his balls cut off might have been the least of his worries. 'How's Pat doing, anyway?' he asked.

'She's okay. That's in the past now. She's met someone. A nice enough lad. Christ, I vetted the living shit out him before she got in deep. But it's working out. They bought a flat together in Kirkcaldy. Don't know if they'll marry or just keep living in sin. You know what the younger generation are like these days. The wife's not too happy about it, but what can you do?' He sniffed and shook his head, as if to emphasise his disagreement.

Time to get back on track. 'Moving forward,' Gilchrist said, 'you can't be front line with Alice Ralston. You know that, don't you? Silverman's got it in for you.'

Dainty grimaced. 'Fat bastard.'

'But we'll have Alice back in custody later today.'

'Don't be too sure, Andy. Silverman's as slick as they come. I'm betting he'll have the hospital keep her in overnight so he can fluff up his story of abuse. My client was so badly abused by the police that she was confined to hospital,' he mimicked. 'Christ, I can't stand that fucking creep.'

Gilchrist disagreed. 'There's nothing to be gained by that. Silverman's only delaying the inevitable. No, I think he'll want us to interview her, and when we charge her, he'll get her out on bail. That's when we have to watch ourselves. But in the meantime, be assured that Jessie'll make sure there's no hanky-panky.' Which brought a smile to Dainty's lips.

'I thought that fat bastard was going to have a heart attack,' he said. 'But you're right. Jessie won't stand for any of his nonsense.'

Gilchrist paused for few seconds, until he had Dainty's full attention. 'So, with you out of it, and Jessie and me on the front line, here's what I would ask you to do.'

Dainty listened in silence, and when Gilchrist was finished, said, 'Sure thing, Andy.'

He watched Dainty stride along the corridor in that little-man's big-stepping way of his. Then he glanced at his watch, and went to collect his car.

Sir Elliot Ralston's home was not what Gilchrist had expected. Where his daughter's had been mansion-sized with no expense spared on landscaping and furnishings, his appeared to be a simple terraced home in a quiet mews-like setting on the outskirts of Edinburgh. It had been Dainty's reaction to his own daughter's predicament that slotted the idea into Gilchrist's head. And the fact of how he, himself, felt about Maureen's situation, which consolidated his thoughts and spurred him into action.

The mews was deserted, not a car in sight, although recent tyre tracks that cut through the morning frost were evidence of a car being driven into the adjacent locked garage. Lights glowed from the upper windows, which somehow promised that the rest of the day would be dull and short. He rang the doorbell, and stood back.

Ten seconds later, he heard from within the rumble of feet trundling down the stairs. The door opened with a sharp click, and Ralston grimaced as if disgusted at the sight in front of him.

Gilchrist held his warrant card out. 'I need to ask you a few questions.'

'What about?'

'Do you want to invite me in, or would you rather we meet down at the station?'

With reluctance, Ralston stood back and scowled as he brushed past. 'Up the stairs to the right,' he said, and locked the door behind him.

When Ralston walked into the lounge, he had the courtesy to offer Gilchrist a chair by the window. He took one opposite, and said, 'I have a busy day ahead of me, so I hope you don't intend to take up much of my time.'

'That depends on you, on how forthcoming you are. Or how truthful.'

Ralston narrowed his eyes. 'I don't care for your attitude. Nor do I care to speak to you at all.'

'You can ask me to leave, if you'd prefer. But you and I are going to have a face-to-face chat, whether you don't particularly care to or not.'

'By God, Alice was right. You really are a nasty piece of shite.'

'If you say so,' he said, although he had to wonder why Alice would have said that about him, or when she'd had the opportunity. 'And now we've got the pleasantries out the way, can you tell me where you were last Wednesday night?'

'No.'

'Can't? Or won't?'

'Can't. Because I'd need to check my diary. Which I keep in my office.'

'Which is where?'

'George Street.'

Not that he thought it important where Ralston had been on the night of Cumming's murder. He wanted to hear how he responded, and if he'd been in Alice's company that day. 'We can

275

check that later.' He opened his notebook. 'We met with your solicitor, John Silverman, this morning. He's currently driving your daughter to the hospital.'

'Why? Has anything happened to her?'

'Not a thing. Just a check-up. Mr Silverman insisted.'

A smirk of sorts shifted across Ralston's face, but he made no comment.

'We should have your daughter back in custody later today.'

'I'm sure I'll hear from her.'

'I'm sure you won't.'

'I beg your pardon.'

'Not until we've finished questioning her. So it might be in her best interests for Mr Silverman to make sure her stay in hospital is not overly long. I'm sure he'll be in contact with you shortly, if he hasn't already.' He'd wanted to get that across to Ralston, the fact that his daughter would be out of reach for a day or two, and much longer if Silverman decided to play silly buggers with them.

No response, so he pressed one. 'Your daughter will then be detained in one of our custody suites for up to forty-eight hours, during which time we'll decide whether we have enough to pass her case over to the Procurator Fiscal's office. Depending on how she answers, of course.'

'And why are you telling me this, exactly?'

'To allay any concerns you might have over her silence in the short term.'

Ralston eyed him as he would a rotting carcass. 'You're taking great pleasure from this. I can tell. I can see it in your eyes.'

'Believe me when I say that I take no pleasure in this at all. I have a daughter of my own, and I'd like to think that I'm talking to you as one father to another.'

Ralston lowered his head as if to study Gilchrist with renewed interest.

Gilchrist said, 'I've never had personal experience of my daughter being arrested, so I don't know how you're feeling.'

Ralston pushed himself to his feet, and tried to stretch himself to his full height. But old age made the act look awkward. Then he looked at Gilchrist as if wanting to be rid of him from his home, but didn't know how best to do that. For a few seconds, the man looked torn, undecided, which must have been a first for someone renowned as a hard businessman and tough decision maker.

Gilchrist remained seated, and turned his attention to his notebook. He flipped over a couple of pages, then looked up. 'I'd like to ask you a few questions about Kenzie.'

'What the hell has Kenzie to do with anything?'

'I think Kenzie might have much to do with *every*thing.'

CHAPTER 44

With a face like thunder, Ralston strode past Gilchrist in those long loping strides of his, to stand at the window and stare down at the cobbled road below, as if calculating how long it would take Gilchrist to hit the ground if he tossed him out of the window.

Gilchrist watched in silence as Ralston muttered something beyond his hearing, hands behind his back, fingers twisting and squeezing as if intent on breaking a bone or two. Then he took a deep breath, and his entire being stilled. Without turning, he said, 'Kenzie was like her mother. Weak. No heart at all. And stupid. That was her. Weak and stupid. Both of them. God help us. Weak and stupid.'

Gilchrist waited for Ralston to continue, but he seemed to have said all he was going to on the matter of Kenzie. He knew the answer to his next question, but felt he had to ask it regardless. 'And you don't have any sons, only daughters? Kenzie and Alice?'

Ralston breathed in through his nostrils. 'Yes. No Sons. Only girls.'

'Two of them.' More statement than question.

'Only two. Thank God.'

'And was Kenzie the younger of the two?'

'I suspect you know the answer to that,' Ralston said, recovering his composure.

'For the record, please, so there's no later misunderstanding.'

'Yes. Kenzie was younger than Alice. By one year.'

'How close to each other were Kenzie and Alice growing up?'

'Inseparable. They could've been twins.'

'And as they got older?'

'They would speak to each other every day. Work got in the way. As it always does. Both driven by their own different passions; Alice in the jewellery business, while Kenzie . . .' he paused, took a deep breath, '. . . joined the bloody Police Force, of all things.' He hung his head, and shook it. 'What on earth did I ever do to deserve that?'

Gilchrist remained focused, and said, 'So Alice must've been upset when Kenzie took her own life.'

It took so long for Ralston to speak, that Gilchrist began to think he hadn't heard the question. But then he gave an involuntary shiver, and said, 'She was devastated. I've never seen her so broken. We both were, of course. Penny was gone by then. Her mother. Cancer. Five years earlier. I remember feeling so helpless, watching her get weaker by the day until her body could no longer cope. Blessing in the end.'

Gilchrist struggled to tune out his thoughts of Irene's cancer, how helpless he felt when there was nothing he could do to make her feel better. He said, 'And how did Kenzie and Alice cope with their mother's passing?'

'Took it hard.' He shook his head, and turned from the window. 'Look. What's any of this got to do with Alice being arrested?'

'*Detained*,' Gilchrist emphasised. 'Alice hasn't been charged yet. And who knows, maybe never will be.' He hoped he sounded positive as he told that lie. He felt certain they would uncover her connection to the spate of killings, but it was the depth of that connection that he was trying to work out at that moment. Time to cut closer to the bone.

'I've only a few more questions,' he said, 'then I'll be on my way.'

Ralston eyed him for a long moment, then returned to staring out the window, hands behind his back.

'What I don't understand,' Gilchrist said, 'is why Kenzie took her own life.'

'Because she was weak. I thought I'd made that clear.'

'No, I mean, with your wealth, and Alice's wealth, it would seem to me that all she had to do was ask for financial support, and it would be given. Wouldn't it?'

'Of course it would.' Another shake of the head. 'How she ever let herself be led by that deceitful husband of hers, I'll never understand. Conned her out of what was rightfully hers. How anyone can be that weak and stupid beggars belief. But that was Kenzie. Stupid. And weak. Her two most prominent characteristics. Stupidity. And weakness.' He let out a frustrated gush of breath, and shook his head. 'God in heaven, I don't know how she and Alice could be so different. I'll never understand it.'

'Coercive control,' Gilchrist said. 'It's more common than you think. Often a wife will do as her husband demands, simply to keep peace in the household. And over time, the manipulating husband will berate his wife, distance her from those she loves, have her doubt herself and her ability to do anything without his approval. It's mental abuse of the most insidious kind. Kenzie would have been hurting, with no clear idea how to deal with it.'

'Because she was stupid. That's why.'

Gilchrist stared at Ralston, astonished by the man's lack of compassion. Being the daughter of a man like that, a bullying tyrant, must have been hard for both girls growing up. 'You said Kenzie was more like her mother? Why do you think her mother was weak?'

'Because she was. She would never stand up for what was right. She'd buckle at the first hurdle. She'd done that all her life. Just given in. Utterly pathetic.'

'Maybe she felt she didn't have to be strong. After all, she had you. A successful businessman. A multi-millionaire, billionaire, whatever. What was there to be strong for?'

'For the children. And for me. I needed to have a strong woman by my side. Not some . . . some . . . *pathetic* excuse for a woman.'

He needed to edge closer. 'And when Kenzie was scammed by someone on the internet,' he said, 'how did you feel about that?'

'Vindicated.'

'Excuse me? Did you say . . . *vindicated*?'

'Yes.'

'How could you feel vindicated when your daughter had racked up bills of thousands of pounds that she had no hope of ever paying back?'

'Because what she'd done, how she'd let herself sink to the lowest of the low, how she'd let herself lose everything, *everything* for God's sake, was as I'd predicted. I told her she would end up in the gutter. And she did.'

'You *predicted* she would lose everything?'

'Yes.' He stared at Gilchrist as if struggling to work out how he couldn't understand the simplicity of what he was saying. 'Because she was weak. And because she was stupid.'

'And you told her that?'

'For years I'd been telling her that.'

'And Alice?'

'Oh.' He snorted. 'Alice is different. Nothing like her mother. Alice is a strong, *strong* individual.'

'Like you?'

Something in the tone of Gilchrist's voice must have sent a signal to the man's brain, for he turned and looked at him then, as if surprised to see him sitting there.

'Did you ever offer to settle Kenzie's bills for her?'

'Of course not. That would only aggravate her weakness.'

'Did she ever ask you to settle her debts?'

'No.'

'Did she ever ask Alice to settle her debts?'

'Not to my knowledge, no.'

'Did you ever worry that she might consider committing suicide as a way to get out of the financial trouble she was in?'

He hung his head again, and faced the window, and when he spoke, his voice was barely a whisper. 'I didn't think she was strong enough to do that.'

Gilchrist pushed himself to his feet. He'd heard enough. How any child could have been raised by that man and develop into an adult without mental trauma defied all sense of logic. Alice must be a strong individual indeed to have not only survived that, but to have created a successful career for herself trading high-end jewellery.

282

'Thank you for your time,' he said, and was dismissed with a wave of a hand. 'But before I go, I want to tell you that you've misunderstood Kenzie in the most hurtful way.'

Ralston turned from the window with such slow deliberation, it was like watching a theatrical performance. 'Hurtful?' he said at length.

'Your daughter, Kenzie, had chosen a career you didn't approve of. The bloody Police Force, as you so impolitely described it. Yet, when she found herself in dire financial straits, and abandoned by her husband, and with nowhere to turn to, rather than come to you or her sister and ask for help, she chose to take her own life. You said yourself that you would have settled her debts if she'd only asked. Yet you . . . with more money than you know what to do with . . . couldn't find it in your heart to make the simplest of gestures, and make her an offer.' He found himself returning Ralston's disbelieving look with a hatred he hoped could be read. He struggled to keep his voice level. 'The fact that Kenzie refused to seek help from you or her sister is not an indication of weakness or stupidity as you so rudely emphasise. It shows how strong she was. She chose to take her own life, rather than be seen to come begging to her father. Someone who'd put her down her entire life.' He slipped his notebook into his pocket. 'That to my mind, sir, is the ultimate show of strength.'

And with that, he turned and left the room.

CHAPTER 45

Outside in the bitter winter air, Gilchrist decided not to return to his car. Instead, he felt the need to walk off a burning sense of anger. He strode along colds streets bordered by stone buildings that reared like grey monoliths into a greyer sky. With no destination in mind, within fifteen minutes he found himself at a pub in Morningside. Despite the weather, several outside tables were taken, and he sat next to a couple who seemed more interested in smoking and checking their mobile phones, than with each other.

He closed his eyes and inhaled a lungful of second-hand smoke, revelling in the acrid taste it left in the back of his throat. How simple it would be to buy a packet of twenty and spend a few hours doing the lot in. He hadn't had a cigarette since the day his mother passed, and the irresistible pull had him stuffing his hands deep into his jacket pocket, standing, and setting off back the way he'd come. He'd almost arrived at his car by the time it took him to settle down. With Silverman responsible for escorting Alice to the hospital, and Dainty assigned to the sidelines, there seemed little to be gained by hanging around Edinburgh for the remainder of the day.

So he phoned Irene.

'How are you?' he said.

'A bit wabbit, if I'm being honest. I'm not long up.'

Not like Irene to sleep the morning away. She was normally an early riser, someone who preferred the rising sun to the setting – like himself.

'How was your night?' she asked him.

'Didn't get to bed until the back of eleven, then we were up early for a six o'clock arrest. Haven't had the best of mornings, but hey, it's Sunday and the weekend, and I could do with a break. When I get back, would you be up for a walk along the beach and a bite and a beer later?'

'You've talked me into it.'

He chuckled at her words, a simple joke of his batted back to him. He glanced at his watch – close to midday – and said, 'Barring disasters, I should be home before three. Does that work?'

'Perfect.'

He mwahed an exaggerated kiss down the line and ended the call.

Just the sound of her whispery voice lifted his spirits. It didn't seem right somehow, that abusive bastards like Ralston could bulldoze their way through life and reach old age in apparent good health, while individuals as gentle and caring and as loving a mother as Irene were hit with . . . he didn't want to even *think* the word cancer, or the phrase terminal illness . . . but . . . *fuck* it, that's what she had. And there was bugger all anyone could do about it. If ever there were a God, how could He be so unjust? How could He allow the likes of Ralston to bruise through life untouched, while Irene and other gentle souls went through hell?

285

He forced those thoughts to the back of his mind, and tried to recall his interview with Ralston, because that's what it had been, an interview, whether Ralston had thought so or not. Gilchrist had wanted to get a sense of how the man had felt after his daughter's suicide, if he harboured ill feelings against anyone for the loss of Kenzie's life, or blamed anyone other than Kenzie for her death. But the only moment in which Ralston had shown any compassion at all was when he'd admitted that he hadn't thought Kenzie had been strong enough to take her own life. It was as if, for just that split second, he'd understood how damaging his influence over his children had been. Other than that, it seemed to Gilchrist that Ralston had blamed Kenzie's suicide on her own weakness and stupidity, without recognising in any way that his own coldness and intolerance and downright hard-heartedness had contributed to her vulnerable mental state.

Gilchrist waited until he slipped onto the M90 before phoning Jessie. 'Where are you?' he said.

'Bruntsfield Clinic. It's private, overlooking some golf course. You want to see it. More nurses than patients. Even offered me tea and biscuits, or a glass of wine if I wanted. But I tell you, Andy, that fatty boom-boom Silverman's milking it. I swear he palmed a fifty to one of the doctors. Alice has a room to herself, and at the moment she's being checked out by a good-looking doctor and a couple of nurses.'

'Does the room have a phone?'

'What doesn't it have? I was going to ask you about that. Her phoning. Should I tell them to disconnect it?'

'No. Just remind Silverman that Alice is still under police observation, and as such not allowed to make any phone calls.'

'How are we going to monitor that? If we don't have someone in the room with her, she'll call whoever she likes.'

'Leave that with me,' he said.

It took Jessie a few seconds to say, 'Okay. Will do.'

He pulled into the outside lane, and powered up to eighty. He clicked Cruise Control and settled down for the journey home. 'What's the room number?' he said.

Jessie told him, and he assigned it to memory. 'If they keep her overnight,' she said, 'what do you want me to do?'

'Go home.'

'Sorry, Andy, you've lost me. I thought the point of me being here was to keep an eye on her.'

'It is. But if she's kept overnight for observation, she's not going anywhere. And I'll have Lothian and Borders have a uniform outside her room. Besides, Silverman's so sure of himself that he'll make Alice available for interview in the morning.'

'Bit risky, isn't it?'

'Yes and no. It's a calculated gamble, I'd say. In the meantime, stay put, and I'll call Lothian and Borders to arrange for someone to collect you from the clinic and take you back to St Andrews.'

Once Jessie hung up, Gilchrist called Dainty, brought him up to speed, then said, 'How did you get on?'

'Done and dusted, Andy. She'll see it first thing in the morning.'

Gilchrist thanked him, then phoned Dick.

'Long time no hear,' Dick said. 'What can I do you for this time?'

He'd thought long and hard about what he was about to ask Dick to do, because he wasn't sure how long John Silverman's reach was; perhaps long enough to have it confirmed that illegal phone tapping had been carried out against his client, that her privacy had been violated, that it was high time the police were brought to bear for their criminality? If so, and his actions were ever discovered, Gilchrist knew Silverman would show no mercy. Neither would his own bosses for that matter. Suspension would be the least he could expect, and likely much worse. But on the other hand – and this was what troubled him the most, that the police had to act within the law while working all hours trying to arrest those who broke the law – he was investigating multiple murders, and if it ever came to it, he would argue that sometimes you just have to take the gloves off, and fight dirt with dirt. At least that's how he tried to justify it to himself as he told Dick what he wanted him to do.

Call finished, he drove on, deep in the misery of his own undoing.

CHAPTER 46

Irene welcomed him with a pecked cheek and a tighter than normal hug.

When they parted, he thought he caught a tear in her eye. 'Everything okay?' he said.

'Just . . . you know . . . sometimes it gets to me, this worrying about what lies ahead.' She stretched her lips into a smile. 'But you don't need to hear me moaning. Come on. Let's get cracking before it gets dark.'

Ten minutes later, they walked arm in arm across South Street, and he smiled when he felt her pull him beyond the doors of the Criterion, as if she knew he'd like a pint first, then a walk along the beach second. 'It's too soon,' she said, and chuckled. 'We can stop in on the way back.'

They turned into Church Street, and Gilchrist said, 'How about the Central, then?'

'You're incorrigible.'

'Just thirsty.'

They crossed Market Street, Irene a tad wobbly on the cobblestones. As he opened the entrance to the Central Bar and stepped back to let her enter first, the place exploded with the raucous cheering of a goal being scored. On one of the TV sets, it looked like Spurs had taken the lead in some Premier League clash. The place was heaving, bustling with the last of the weekenders. 'Bit loud for a pair of old ones,' he said. 'Fancy somewhere quieter?'

Irene agreed, and together they strode down College Street, and turned left into North Street. For a moment, he had a sense that she felt he might have tricked her into his making a quick visit to the Office. But he chanced a skip across the road at a break in the traffic, and did what he could to blinker the Office windows from his peripheral vision. Even so, he noted lights on in the upper rooms, and struggled to resist the Siren-like pull of the building.

The Dunvegan Hotel was busy, too, crammed from wall to wall with golfers in Under Armour outfits, ruddy-faced caddies holding pints with chaffed-skin hands, and groups of Americans who always found some reason to play golf on the famous courses no matter what time of year – even the middle of a Scottish winter. But the golfing fraternity was far more subdued than any football gathering, and he and Irene squeezed onto two stools at the bar.

She placed her hand on his thigh, and gave a squeeze. 'This is you at your happiest, about to have a pint.'

'Is it that obvious?' She chuckled when he smiled, and he leaned into her and put his arm around her. 'What are you having?' he asked. 'A glass of wine?'

'Why not? You choose.'

'How about a light white, let's see . . .' He scanned the shelves, then said, 'How about a Pinot Grigio. And a gentleman's measure.'

'A large, you mean?'

'Is there any other measure?' He watched her cheer up at his silly words, and as her smile faded and her gaze shifted over his shoulder, he couldn't help but feel that she wasn't quite herself, that something was troubling her. All of a sudden he had a sense that he'd made a mistake enticing her to have a drink before their walk, and he caught the barman from the corner of his eye. 'We've not decided yet. Can you give us a minute?'

The barman nodded and stepped away.

'I thought you wanted a pint,' she said.

'I do, but maybe we should work up a thirst first. Would you rather do that? A hard walk along the beach? Before it gets dark?'

She glanced outside. 'I'm finding it rather cold,' she said, and gave a shiver. 'Colder than it looks. And I'm having second thoughts about walking along the beach, to be honest.'

He took hold of her hands. 'Is everything okay?'

She nodded. 'As good as can be, I suppose.'

'Well, keep your jacket and scarf on, and we can sit here for a while until you warm up. Or we can return home and sit by the fire.'

'The fire sounds nice. Do you mind?'

'Not at all.' He helped her off the stool, and led her through the bar crowd and back outside into the winter chill.

A northerly wind had picked up and swept along the pavement with renewed strength, it seemed. He realised how selfish he had been suggesting a walk along the West Sands on a cold winter's late afternoon with Irene so unwell. He gave a shiver of his own, slipped his arm around her, and headed up the gentle incline of North Street.

They took a different route back, turning into Greyfriars Garden onto Bell Street and left at South Street, bypassing the

291

Central Bar and crossing to the other side of the road when they neared the Criterion – just in case he had the sudden urge, or more likely Irene a change of heart.

Back indoors, she slumped onto the sofa in front of the fire, and he covered her legs with a throw blanket, trying to make her comfortable. He walked into the kitchen and filled the kettle, and fussed around the breakfast bar. A red light was blinking on her answering machine, and he chose to ignore it. Whoever the call was from would have to wait. He was about to open a chilled bottle of wine from the fridge, when he glanced at Irene and thought she still looked cold. So he removed a bottle of red from the rack at the end of the breakfast bar, and topped up two glasses with a gentleman's measure.

'There you go,' he said.

She took the glass from him, and chinked it against his with a 'Cheers.'

He sat down beside her. 'Anything you fancy watching on the telly?'

'You choose.'

He worked his way into a movie channel, and settled on a rerun of James Bond's *Die Another Day*. With Irene comfortable, he returned to the kitchen and prepared a small spread of cheese and biscuits, red and white grapes, and sliced apple. But by the time he carried the tray over, she was sound asleep. He muted the TV and sat next to her, grazing the cheese and fruit at his leisure.

He was on his second glass of red, when his mobile rang – ID Dick.

He took the call in the kitchen, out of Irene's earshot.

'Got two numbers for you,' Dick said. 'Two quick calls to mobile phones in the space of a couple of minutes, over an hour ago. Couldn't get a recording, so I don't know if they were made by your suspect, or a member of the medical staff. The first lasted a minute and a half, and the second less than a minute. So I'm thinking not medical staff, but your suspect passing on some message.'

Gilchrist agreed, asked for the numbers, jotted them down, then phoned Jessie, who answered on the first ring.

'You were right,' she said. 'Boom-boom Silverman insisted she stayed overnight for observation. According to the consultant, she won't be released until midday tomorrow at the earliest. Bit of overkill, if you ask me.'

'We've got to be careful with Silverman,' he said. 'Dainty's come across him before, and he's not to be messed with. So did Dainty sort you out with a lift?'

'Eventually. Once we got a replacement for me at the hospital. Some plod who looked as if he'd never been in a hospital before. I tell you, is it just me, or are they getting thicker?'

Gilchrist ignored the snipe. 'Where are you?'

'Passing through Cupar.'

'Okay. Listen. I've got a couple of mobile numbers I need you to check out when you're in the Office. Find out what masts they've pinged on the QT, and get back to me.'

Jessie paused for a moment, then said, 'Ah, right. Been waving that magic wand of yours again?'

'Silverman's an unknown quantity, Jessie. So let's tread with care. If these numbers turn out to be someone we know, then we'll need to come up with a story to fit.'

'Got it. I'll get Jackie onto it first thing.'

Gilchrist ended the call, and placed his mobile on the breakfast bar. He thought he had a fair idea who these mobile numbers belonged to, but wouldn't want to bet on it. And Dick hadn't said they were burners, so it was possible that Alice had slipped up.

And if she had?

That's when he'd have to face Silverman head on.

CHAPTER 47

Monday

By mid-morning, Jackie had printed out a map showing which masts both mobile phones had pinged, and when – all in Glasgow and the surrounding areas. Neither mobile was registered with a network provider, so they were likely burners. But both mobiles pinged the same mast in Newton Mearns around the same time – 21:23 and 21:30 – which gave Gilchrist the idea that the owners of each mobile had met at Alice's instruction.

With Newton Mearns being on the southernmost outskirts of Glasgow, effectively the last populated area before the emptiness of the Fenwick Moor, Gilchrist found himself warming to the idea that the mobiles had to belong to Ber and Ibbotson, a stretch of the imagination that would take some convincing. But the problem he now had was – what to do with this information? Which was the danger when you flew under the radar. Sooner or later someone was going to catch you out and shoot you down. He couldn't instruct his team to track these mobiles without first coming up with an irrefutable reason for doing so. And as he gave thought to that, the vaguest haze of an idea began to show itself . . .

His mobile rang – ID Mo – and he knew right away that she'd seen the PNC report on Noah that Dainty had placed on her desk. Oh well, it had to have been only a matter of time before she phoned. He took a deep breath, then answered it. 'This is a nice sur—'

'Did you have anything to do with this?' she snapped.

'With what?'

'I'm not stupid, Dad, so for God's sake don't speak to me like I am.'

Silence seemed as good a response as any.

'I don't want you interfering in my personal life. Which is what you've been doing. Haven't you?' A pause, then, 'Do you deny it?'

For a fleeting moment he almost did, then decided against it. 'I don't want any harm to come to you, Mo. And I thought you should have a better understanding of who you're . . .' He almost said *partner*. 'Of who you're living with. I mean, as a father, I think I have at least the right to—'

'You don't have the right to do anything of the sort,' she snapped. 'So stay out of it. I can look after myself, Dad. I don't need you or anyone else telling me who I can or can't have a relationship with.'

Any second now he feared she was going to end the call, the last thing he wanted. He needed to change tack, and do so fast. Apologising might take the heat from the moment, so he said, 'I'm sorry, Mo. You're right. I shouldn't have interfered. And I won't stick my head into your personal life again. I promise.' He held onto his mobile, dreading the sound of the call being ended.

But when it didn't come, he ventured, 'I care for you, Mo. You know I do. The last thing I want is for you to come to any harm.' No response. He pressed his mobile hard to his ear, thought he caught a whisper. Was someone with her? But a stifled sniff told him that she might be crying.

'I loved him, Dad.'

He noted the past tense, but kept quiet.

'At least I thought I did.'

He heard another sniff, and after a few seconds of silence thought he saw an opening. 'It's always difficult losing someone you love, or think you love, Mo.' He resisted the urge to mention the phrase coercive control. She didn't need to hear that from him now. Instead, he said, 'I'm here for you. If you ever need someone to talk to, just give me a ring. Any time. You know I'll do everything I can to help you. Okay?'

'Okay.' She sniffed again, then in a stronger voice said, 'Joanne called me. She told me about her mum. I'm sorry, Dad. I didn't know her cancer had returned.' He found himself lost for words, and before he could gather himself, she said, 'Got to go, Dad. Got another call.'

'Let's meet during the week. Have a chat about ... about things. Okay?'

'Sure, Dad. Bye.'

'Love you,' he said, and caught the burring of a dead line. He let out his breath, not sure if he was relieved or frustrated, and as he replayed their conversation he found himself trying to work out if he'd said the right thing or not. Mo could be the blue-touch paper to his lighted match, with a fiery temperament that reminded him of his late wife, Gail, and of how arguments could erupt from the most innocent of comments. Even so, Mo could

297

be the most loving and caring daughter any father could hope for. Enigmatic personality didn't come close.

He slipped his mobile into his pocket, and walked to the window. A blanket of clouds covered the town, low and dark with a purplish hue that portended heavy snow. The twenty-fifth was a week and a half away, so a white Christmas might be on the cards after all—

'You're not going to believe this.'

He turned to face Jessie, puzzled to see her face tight with anger. 'I'm listening.'

'She's gone.'

Even as he said, 'Who's gone?' he knew the answer.

'Alice Ralston.'

'Thought we had someone outside her room.'

'We did. But calling PC Plod brain-dead would be a compliment. Said he had to go to the bathroom, and the next time he checked on her room, she wasn't there.'

'Who'd you hear this from?'

'Dainty. Who heard it from Chief Superintendent Mansfield. He couldn't get through to you, so he called me.'

'When did Alice leave?'

'According to Dainty, she was caught on CCTV two hours ago, walking out the front door like a visitor without a care in the world. Casual as you like. Heading to the car park.'

'Two *hours* ago? Why are we just hearing about it now?'

'That's between you and Lothian and Borders.'

'Ah, for crying out loud. Anyone with her?'

'No.'

'But she must've been meeting someone. Silverman, maybe? Or her father?'

'Don't know that yet.'

'Has anyone tried phoning her?'

'She doesn't have a mobile. We took that from her, remember?'

'How about footage outside the hospital? There must be something.'

'Being looked at even as we speak. But haven't heard anything back yet.'

Gilchrist gritted his teeth. Bloody hell. This was serious. Or more correctly, this *could* be serious. Strictly speaking, Alice hadn't done a runner yet. But as he tried to rationalise his thoughts on that, he knew he was wrong. Why else would she slip out of sight? But she must have had someone to help her, surely. *Heading to the car park.* Had someone waited in the car park to drive her off? Who that someone was, he had his own thoughts on the matter, but didn't want to offer up a name. There seemed to be too many unknowns in his investigation, which now looked as if it was spinning out of control.

'I need you to chase up that footage of Alice outside the hospital. Jump on it right away. See where she went to. Did she get into a car and drive off? Or was she picked up? If so, by whom? Did she carry on walking? If so, where did she walk to? And get back to me soonest.'

'I'm on it,' Jessie said, and backed out of his room and strode along the corridor.

Alone again, Gilchrist stared out the window at the cold winter's day.

Enough was enough. He retrieved his mobile.

It was time to talk hard.

CHAPTER 48

Gilchrist's call was picked up on the second ring, as if Silverman had been waiting for it. Without introduction, he growled, 'Your client's missing.'

'By client, I assume you mean Ms Ralston,' Silverman said, in an unctuous tone that oozed with legal assurance.

'You know damn well who I'm talking about. Where is she?'

'I'm afraid I can't say.'

'Can't say, or don't know?'

'Don't know. And even if I did know, DCI Gilchrist, I'd be rather disinclined to share that information with you, after the manner in which she's been treated. Your Office hasn't heard the last of it, let me assure you.'

'You know how to contact her.' Statement, not a question.

'Once again, I'm afraid I can't say.'

'Well you'd better find a way to say it, and you'd better find it damn quick, because if you don't bring your client, Alice Ralston, to the Office this afternoon for her interview as arranged—'

'Are you threatening me?' Silverman's voice boomed with all the legal righteousness that a lifetime battling cases in court had taught him. 'I would remind you, DCI Gilchrist, that your Office elected to post a police officer outside my client's hospital room to ensure that she would *not* go missing. And I can assure you that I can't and most certainly *won't* be held responsible for the incompetence and failings of your Office. I can also assure you that I will do what I can to contact Ms Ralston, and if successful I will advise her that it is in her best interests to present herself at your Office as arranged. Failing which, you can damn well do what you like.'

Gilchrist whispered a curse as the line died. But he had no time to feel aggrieved by Silverman's attitude. He dialled another number, but his call was transferred to voicemail where Sir Elliot Ralston's clipped tones ordered him to leave a message.

He killed the call, and dialled the number again.

This time it was picked up, and a gruff voice said, 'Ralston speaking.'

Gilchrist tried a more friendly approach, and introduced himself before saying, 'I've been notified that your daughter has signed herself out of hospital . . .' Not strictly true, but sufficient for his purposes. 'And no one seems to be able to reach her.'

'What on earth do you want me to do about it?'

'Help me find her.'

'Why?'

The question seemed simple enough, the answer more tricky. But he forced his tone to stay level. 'To prevent Alice from getting herself deeper into trouble with the law.'

'You clearly don't know my daughter, Inspector. Because if you did, you wouldn't have asked for my help. Good day.'

The line died.

Shit, and *shit* again. Gilchrist stared at his mobile, as if willing Ralston to call him back. But after a few seconds, he gritted his teeth and returned his mobile to his pocket. So much for the hard talk – more pop than bang. The more he replayed both calls in his mind, the more it seemed to him that Silverman and Ralston had been expecting his call. But both of them had hung up as if . . . as if neither had wanted to prolong the call because they knew something he didn't know, and if you didn't speak, you couldn't have a slip of the tongue. Not that Silverman or Ralston, both experienced negotiators, would be expected to stumble over their words.

But still . . .

He turned from the window, and went to look for Jessie.

He found her in Jackie's office, both engrossed in something on the monitor.

'Any luck?' he interrupted.

'Depends on what you mean by luck,' Jessie said, and pushed herself upright.

'Don't like the sound of that.'

'And you won't like the sound of what's coming.'

'Christ, let's have it.'

'Here's what we've got so far. Alice was picked up by an Uber outside the hospital grounds and dropped off at HSBC Bank in Hanover Street. That's in Edinburgh. According to the bank manager, she asked for her lockbox, removed a couple of envelopes, then left. The manager said that she seemed to be in a hurry.'

'Did he know what was in the envelopes?'

'No.'

'Did he see where she went to after she left?'

'No.'

'So she's vanished?'

'Not exactly. Jackie's accessed HQ's CCTV system, and we have an image of her here.' She adjusted the monitor to give him a better angle. 'She crosses the road, walks up Hanover Street onto Queen Street, turns left, then . . .'

Jackie clicked the mouse, and the screen shifted to a view along Queen Street.

'Then she jumps into the back seat of some big car,' Jessie said.

'Looks like a Jaguar.'

'Whatever. And that's as far as we've got.'

'Who's driving the car?'

'Can't tell.'

'Can you zoom in?'

Jackie obliged, but the reflective sheen off the windscreen was too high.

'What time is this clocked at?' he said.

'An hour and a half ago.'

Gilchrist let out a frustrated gush. 'She's not wasting any time, is she?'

'That's because she's doing a runner.'

He gritted his teeth, and whispered a curse.

Jessie said, 'We've got a clear view of the registration number plate. But you're not going to like this, it's registered to SA Investment Trustees, a Saudi Arabian company based in London with one of its branches in Edinburgh.'

Of course, Gilchrist thought. The Middle Eastern connection. Sir Elliot Ralston would have some major contacts from his earlier association with the Saudi royal family. Not that the Saudis would know of Ralston's daughter's criminal goings-on. Rather, they would be on call – at the sharp end of a hot phone – to lend a helping hand whenever necessary—

303

'Jackie tracked it on the ANPR,' Jessie said, 'and got a hit on Western Terrace.'

'Where's that?'

'On the outer city limits, heading west.'

Even though the Automated Number Plate Recognition system could track a vehicle in real time, it couldn't tell you its destination. Gilchrist's knowledge of Edinburgh's road network was not great, but he'd visited the city often enough to make him think he knew the answer. Even so, he still had to ask the question. 'Where do you think she's heading?'

Jessie said, 'Best guess, Edinburgh Airport?'

He grimaced, tight-lipped, then said, 'She's leaving the country. Jessie, I want you to get hold of Mhairi, and the two of you to contact every major airline and find out what flight she's on.' He tapped Jackie's shoulder. 'And I need you to keep tracking that car, Jackie, and let me know the instant it arrives at the airport.'

'Uh-huh.'

Gilchrist had his mobile in his hand as he left the room, and had Dainty on the line by the time he reached his own office. 'Who's your contact at Edinburgh Airport?' he said.

'DCI McCullen. Why?'

'We think we've got Alice. And she's leaving the country.' He read out the make, model and registration number of the Saudi Arabian company car. 'Have your man arrest her before she has a chance to board a flight.'

'You bet,' Dainty said, and ended the call.

Gilchrist walked to the window again. Snow was floating earthbound in flakes as thick as feathers. Night was doing what it could to settle in. They were not too late to stop Alice in her tracks. And this time there would be no sympathetic shoulder for

Silverman to cry on. Gilchrist would personally read Alice her rights, then interview her until she coughed up what he now knew he wanted more than anything.

The name of the person who'd helped her escape.

And possibly the mastermind behind the entire murderous network. Which he found almost impossible to imagine was anyone other than Professor Sir Elliot Ralston.

Of that, he felt certain.

CHAPTER 49

'Sir?'

Gilchrist turned to face DC Mhairi McBride.

'Jackie got another ANPR sighting, sir. They didn't take the cut-off to the airport.'

'What?'

'She says they're on the M9 and now look as if they're heading for Glasgow.'

Jessie appeared behind Mhairi. 'Could be going to Stirling? But there's no airport there. So who knows.'

Gilchrist hissed a curse. 'Could she be heading for Glasgow Airport?' he said, and wondered if he'd got it wrong, that she wasn't flying anywhere, but being driven to some other destination, some secret place that only she and her father knew about. And it struck him that he'd included her father in that thought process. Which made sense, of course, with his Saudi contacts. Another question swelled into his mind – How many foreign nationals owned country estates in Scotland? Could she be heading to one of those, to lie low under the protection of some Saudi prince or some such person? Then the reality of the situation hit him. He needed to deal with what was in front of him, not worry about what might or might not happen. She was on the M9, and there was no time to lose.

'Get onto Glasgow Airport,' he said, 'and find out if she's booked on any flights out of there today.'

'We're on it, sir.'

Next, he phoned Dainty. 'You can stand your man down at Edinburgh Airport,' he said. 'Looks like she's heading your way on the M9.'

'You think she's flying from Glasgow?'

'That's what we're working on.'

Dainty gave that some thought, then said, 'Don't know if you're aware of this, Andy, but I've been told that several directors on the board of that Saudi company you mentioned are close to the royal family, and even have the ear of the king himself.'

'Meaning?'

'Meaning that we don't know what we're fucking dealing with here.' A pause, then, 'That car doesn't have diplomatic plates, does it?'

'No.'

'Well that's something. Looks like we've no option but to stop it pronto, and arrest the wee bitch, then batten down the hatches for whatever shite comes our way.'

'That's one way of putting it.'

'Any other way?'

'Let's not forget that she's now the prime suspect in a multiple murder investigation, which last time I looked takes precedence over having the ear of the king of Saudi, or any member of any royal family for that matter.'

Dainty chuckled, then said, 'Right, let me get on with this, and I'll get back to you as soon as we've got that bitch cuffed.'

The line died.

Gilchrist strode from his office and found Jessie seated at her desk, on the phone.

'Anything?' he asked.

She cupped her hand over the mouthpiece. 'Not booked on Emirates, BA, or KLM, which is as far as I've got. I've got Mhairi checking up on Prestwick Airport. She might be heading there instead.'

'Good move. Keep me posted.'

'How about at your end?' Jessie asked. 'Any luck?'

'Dainty's going to intercept them, and arrest her before she gets any farther.'

Jessie gave a thumbs-up sign as she returned her attention to her phone.

Gilchrist checked the time – 16:25 – then strode along the corridor.

Outside Smiler's office, he stopped, took a deep breath, then rapped the door.

'Enter.'

He opened the door, and stepped inside. CS Diane Smiley's office always surprised him, with its aromatic fragrance, gleaming work surfaces, and potted house plants that looked healthy enough for any arboretum.

'Ma'am?' he said, as he walked towards her, his tread softening as he stepped onto what he'd always assumed was a genuine Persian rug that fronted her desk.

'Take a seat, Andy.'

He pulled up one of two chairs, and again felt an odd sense of relief at her informality – always a good sign.

She placed her hands flat on her desk. 'You look worried.'

308

'More concerned, ma'am.'

'Okay,' she said, stringing the word out. 'Let's have it.'

'I need your permission to apply for a search warrant. For a property in Edinburgh.'

'A bit out of our jurisdiction isn't it?'

'Yes and no, ma'am.'

She leaned back in her chair, folded her arms and eyed him over imaginary specs. 'I'm not going to like this, am I, Andy?'

'Like is a relative term, ma'am.'

'Maybe so, Andy, but how is this request going to affect this Office? Or more to the point, how is it going to affect me?'

'We have a prime suspect for our ongoing investigation, ma'am, but she would appear to be in the act of fleeing the country.'

An eyebrow shifted upwards in mock incredulity. 'And you want a search warrant for the purpose of . . .?'

'Of searching the home of our prime suspect's father, ma'am.'

She leaned forward again, and rested her elbows on her desk. 'I'm not sure I follow.'

He wasn't sure he followed either, but he couldn't ignore his gut feeling on this one, and the irresistible pull of his sense of logic. 'I believe Alice Ralston, our prime suspect, is being assisted in her attempts to evade arrest by her father.'

Smiler's mouth opened in a silent Aahh, as the surname registered. She nodded for a moment, then said, 'Her father being . . .?'

'Professor Sir Elliot Ralston, ma'am.'

She frowned, sat back, and stared at her hands.

'It gets worse, ma'am.'

'I can't imagine how.'

'We have CCTV footage of Alice Ralston being driven off in a company car, a top-of-the-range Jaguar, we believe.' He held her

309

gaze for a long moment. 'The car isn't registered to any of Sir Elliot's companies, but to a Saudi Arabian company – SA Investment Trustees – with contacts to the Saudi royal family.'

'My goodness, Andy. Are you serious?'

'Absolutely, ma'am.'

'How quickly do you need this?'

'Strathclyde Police are in the process of intercepting the car on the M9, so it would be helpful if we could access Sir Elliot's home and phone records before he has the opportunity to . . . eh . . . to dispose of stuff, ma'am.'

'I see.' She paused for a moment, as if struggling with her thoughts, then said, 'And you're sure about the connection?'

Well, in for a penny . . . 'As sure as I've ever been,' he lied.

Decision reached, she stretched across her desk, and pulled her laptop to her. She opened it, and with the expertise of a skilled typist accessed Zoom, then angled it so Gilchrist had a clearer view. A digital ringing tone filled the room for several seconds before the face of the chief constable, Archie McVicar, appeared on the screen, deep-set eyes staring out from the monitor with a look as fierce as an eagle's.

'Diane,' his voice boomed. 'This is a surprise. A pleasant one, I hope.'

'I'm afraid not, sir. We have a situation that requires some high-level diplomacy and a bit of . . . ah . . . for want of a better word, sir . . . delicate string-pulling. I have DCI Gilchrist with me. He'll explain it to you, sir.'

Gilchrist swallowed the lump in his throat, leaned forward so that his face was in the smaller side-screen, then gave it his best shot.

CHAPTER 50

By the time Gilchrist returned to his office, he couldn't tell if his head was spinning from frustration or exhaustion. McVicar had grilled him in that cold-staring way of his, with concisely worded questions that not only cut to the bone, but sliced through the marrow. He felt as if his efforts to convince McVicar of Sir Elliot's involvement in his daughter's flight from justice – which could then lead onto the argument that Sir Elliot had to be complicit in his ongoing murder investigation – hadn't gone well. *You have no evidence, Andy, nothing to hang your hat on. We can't be seen to invade the private residence of one of this country's most respected citizens on a search warrant obtained on the basis of a whim, no matter how logical your rationale is. It's just not on, I'm afraid.*

When Dainty called, Gilchrist jumped at the opportunity to excuse himself from the Zoom meeting, and stepped out of the room.

'You're not going to fucking believe this, Andy. She's not in the car.'

It took a moment for Dainty's words to seep through the fog. 'What do you . . .? She's *what*? Are you saying she's *gone*?'

'I'm saying she's not in the car, Andy. If she ever was in the car in the first place, then they must've done a swap somewhere.'

'Jesus *Christ*.'

'Christ isn't going to help you with this one. And to make matters worse, some Arabic punter in the back seat, sitting there all high and mighty, read my guys the fucking riot act, and I mean *big*-time. Told our lot to expect a call from his ambassador. I didn't even know we had a Saudi ambassador in Scotland.' A heavy sigh, then, 'Anyway, that's who we're fucking dealing with here.'

'So where the hell is she? She got in that car. I saw it with my own eyes. We have her on CCTV, for crying out loud.' He almost cringed at the sound of his voice, which had risen in pitch in disbelief. What had just happened? A car swap in the middle of nowhere? No, not nowhere, but at any one of a thousand potential exchange spots on Edinburgh's roads, and no doubt at some spot devoid of cameras. Christ, it didn't bear thinking about. Meanwhile, as a vision of the hole he'd now dug for himself opened up in his mind, he wondered what he would say to McVicar and Smiler. The good news, he supposed, was that McVicar hadn't agreed with him and granted permission to issue a search warrant.

'There's no chance it's the wrong car, is there?' Gilchrist tried, clutching for straws. But he read out the registration number plate again, which was easy to remember – two letters and one number, a sign that the company had money, and lots of it.

'That's it, Andy, that's the car we stopped. I've checked it, too. Registered to SA Investment Trustees.' Dainty let out a grunt that could have been a cough or a curse, and said, 'She's given us the slip again, Andy. Could be heading anywhere. Manchester, Newcastle if she's gone south. Maybe Aberdeen if north. That's if she's flying out, of course. Who knows how many private planes and small airfields there are in the country. I've put out an All Ports on this, which is about the best we can do.'

Gilchrist didn't want to add to Dainty's disappointment. For all they knew, Alice might not be flying, sailing, or driving out of the country, but lying low in some Highland bolthole. The key to finding her was to locate and identify the exchange vehicle. But it seemed such a momentous task that he simply said. 'Shit.'

'Aye, and it's backing up on the fucking fan, ready to be let loose.'

Gilchrist gritted his teeth, then with grim resignation said, 'I'll have our team start looking for possible exchange spots, where the swap might have taken place. Who knows, we might find something useful.'

'I'll throw some bodies at it from this end, too.' Dainty whispered a curse, and said, 'You know that bastard Silverman'll be having a right fucking laugh. No doubt we haven't heard the last from him. He'll be lining up the charges like pints in a bar.'

Silverman was the least of Gilchrist's troubles. His worry was that he now had to face McVicar and Smiler and bring them up to speed – even though that speed might be a dead stop. 'Forget about Silverman,' he said. 'He's got some explaining of his own to do. Alice didn't just get out of bed and walk from hospital without help. She needed a phone to call an Uber. So someone's handed it to her, or called it in for her, and I intend to find out who.'

'Aye, good luck with that one. I've warned you about Silverman.'

Fuck Silverman, Gilchrist wanted to say. It seemed as if Dainty had the man branded into his brain. 'If you come up with anything,' he said, 'get back to me.'

'Likewise.'

The line died.

Gilchrist slipped his mobile into his pocket. For a moment, he thought of returning to his own office, ignoring Smiler and McVicar. He could tell them later. But experience had taught him that holding back bad news served no one. Least of all himself.

Best just to get on with it.

Back in Smiler's office, he took his seat.

Smiler lowered her head at him. 'You look worried, Andy.'

He glanced at her laptop, disappointed to see McVicar still there. He'd hoped she'd ended the Zoom call, that McVicar wouldn't be around to see him squirming. But he was out of luck. 'Yes, ma'am, I've just been advised by Strathclyde Police that when they attempted to make the arrest, our prime suspect, Ms Ralston, wasn't in the car.'

McVicar boomed, 'Repeat that, Andy, please.'

He did, then explained that he'd witnessed Alice get into the car in Hanover Street in Edinburgh – with CCTV footage as confirmation, if necessary – and that he suspected she'd made a swap somewhere on the outskirts of Edinburgh.

'Well I'll be buggered.'

Smiler raised an eyebrow, as if she'd never heard McVicar use foul language.

McVicar pressed on. 'We clearly can't consider a search warrant until we have Ms Ralston in custody.'

'Agreed,' Smiler said.

Gilchrist tried one last push. 'If she's hiding at her father's, it might be worth—'

'Don't push it, Andy. I need a great deal more than wishful thinking on this one. And if you didn't know that by now, it's high time you did.' All of which was spoken in a clipped sergeant-major's tone that seemed to cut through the air like a whip-snap.

'Yes, sir.' God, it was all he could think to say. If he'd been at school, he'd felt as if he'd just set himself up for six of the best. And maybe add on a hundred lines for the hell of it. 'Let me get back to you, sir.'

But McVicar's face turned to the side, as if his attention was elsewhere.

Then the screen died.

Smiler sat back with raised eyebrows and puffed-out cheeks. She exhaled, as if in exhausted relief. 'Well, Andy, there you have it.'

There he had it indeed. Not his brightest moment. Possibly his worst. His mind spun with confusion as he struggled to replay the sequence of events. The trouble with McVicar was that he would make a great poker player. In all the years Gilchrist had known the man, he'd never been able to read his thoughts. Those piercing eyes of his gave the impression he was looking straight into your soul. Or maybe it was how he spoke, in a voice that brooked no argument. Silent, Gilchrist looked around the room as if punch-drunk, wondering where he was, what had just happened. Then as his mind returned to him, he thought of running some fresh ideas past Smiler, maybe glean some insights of her own. Or better still, offer her some kind of explanation, maybe even an apology. But the truth be told, he felt so defeated that he simply pushed himself to his feet, said, 'Ma'am,' and left the room without another word.

CHAPTER 51

Tuesday

It took until three forty-five the following afternoon before Gilchrist had the break he was looking for. Despite Jackie's best efforts, she and the rest of the team had been unable to find any evidence of a car swap. Most likely place was on Corstorphine Road, on the western outskirts of Edinburgh, but that was only conjecture. For all he knew, Alice Ralston could be settling into life on a sheep farm in the Australian outback.

At first, Dainty's call had sounded like one more setback. *Another fucking kick in the goolies, Andy. That bird we interviewed, Kikelomo, the one who said she didn't want any part of Ralston and the rest of them, was found dead this morning. Not garrotted like the others. But shot in the back of the head, and another one to the face, which I was thinking is your coup-de-fucking-grâce.*

Gilchrist had cursed under his breath and pursed his lips. With Alice Ralston making a run for it, by killing Kikelomo were they now cleaning shop, making sure no one would be around to testify against her? Maybe this meant that Alice hadn't flown to distant lands, but was still in Scotland, sweeping up loose ends. In one way it made sense, but in another, it made no sense at all. Killing off everyone was no way to run any kind of network, murderous or not. The way to survive was to lay low, hunker down, and back each other to the absolute hilt and beyond. They must know his investigation was floundering, that without Alice they effectively had no case at all – circumstantial evidence could take you only so far, then you needed forensic proof, that unequivocal link to the victims. Failing that, it really was game over.

But after Dainty's first hit, came the punchline.

'They fucked up, Andy. Big time.'

'Excuse me?'

'Just after midday, I got another call.' A pause for theatrical effect, which was so unlike Dainty. But when Gilchrist didn't offer anything, Dainty said, 'They murdered the *wrong* person.'

Gilchrist frowned as he tried to work through the logic. If Kikelomo's murder had been a mistake, then who were they supposed to have killed? Shifrah Ber? Ellice Ibbotson? Someone else? And if so, who? Dainty's silence on the line told him he was willing him to work it out and come up with the answer. But it was no use.

'I'm sorry,' he said, 'you've lost me.'

'*Fariza* Kikelomo,' Dainty announced. 'That's who they killed.'

Fariza? But that wasn't her first name. He struggled to recall it, then it came to him – *Izara*. Izara Kikelomo. That's who she was. 'So, not Izara?'

'Not Izara. Her older sister, Fariza. Mistaken identity. The pair of them share a flat in Glasgow. And share a car, too. Seems like Fariza was about to do a bit of shopping when she was shot opening the car door. In the middle of the morning. In south Glasgow.

And no one saw a fucking thing.' Dainty grumbled, 'But what's new?'

Gilchrist pressed his mobile to his ear, his thoughts firing into overdrive. 'So where's Izara now? Have you spoken to her?'

'Turned herself in. Wants to tell us everything she knows in exchange for immunity from prosecution.'

'She's not insisting on British citizenship, then?'

'That's never going to happen. She knows that. But we could be prepared to drop all charges if she turns Queen's evidence. She says she can help us identify someone else.'

Gilchrist remembered the portrait she'd sketched of Alice Ralston, so lifelike it was as good as any photograph. 'I thought she hadn't seen anybody else,' he said.

'Only that first time she was picked up in the car.'

'So she was lying?'

'I prefer to say she was holding back.'

Gilchrist almost held his breath. 'Okay,' he said. 'What's she got? Is it good?'

'Oh,' Dainty said, and gave off a throaty chuckle, 'it's better than good. It's brilliant. And it's so fucking brilliant that that fat bastard Silverman's not got a hope in hell of getting his clients off of this one.'

Gilchrist felt a smile tug his lips. He'd need to speak to Izara, of course, make up his own mind as to how useful her information could be. But he knew Dainty well enough to know that what he was saying was accurate. Then he paused. '*Clients?*' he said. 'Plural?'

Dainty coughed out another chuckle. 'I was wondering when you were going to pick up on that. Yes, clients. Alice Ralston, and her father, Professor Sir Fucking Elliot Ralston, the murdering bastard.'

'Slow down, Dainty, you've lost me.'

'According to Ms Kike-lovely-lomo,' he said, drawing the name out as if reminiscing the best of moments, 'after she first met Alice, she was taken to meet someone who wanted to do a one-on-one interview with her. She says she didn't know her way around Scotland at the time, and was unfamiliar with the roads, but she'd seen enough pictures of Edinburgh Castle to recognise it the night she was driven there.'

'Did she remember the address?'

'She wasn't given the address. Just told that she was going to meet someone high-up, someone important, and that without that person's approval she wouldn't be permitted to join their group.'

'They didn't tell her who? Give her a name?'

'Of course not.' Another pause. 'But she didn't need a name.'

'Okay, I'm listening.'

'I'm looking at it now. A lovely portrait. Coloured crayon on paper. Amazing the way the light catches his eyes. Takes years off the man. But honestly, Izara's really talented. Unbelievable, in fact. She's got a natural gift, I'd say.'

Gilchrist knew Dainty was toying with him, but he fought off the urge to interrupt and instead let out an audible sigh, heavy and hard enough to let Dainty know he'd listened long enough.

'One guess,' Dainty said.

'I wouldn't want to risk ruining it.'

Dainty chuckled. 'Izara said she didn't know who he was. Said she'd never seen him before. Never heard of him before. But here I am, holding a lovely portrait of Professor Sir Elliot Ralston, in all his vain-fucking-glory.'

CHAPTER 52

Wednesday

Chief Constable McVicar was not known for his indecision, but when Gilchrist had shown him Kikelomo's sketch of Elliot Ralston, he was surprised by how decisive the man could be, and by how quickly he could muster support from the top. But what stunned him most of all was how guileful McVicar could be, slippery even, behind-your-back sneaky if you thought about it. Once Gilchrist, in the presence of Smiler, had brought McVicar up to speed with his investigation, the chief constable had surprised them both by insisting he meet with Kikelomo in person, and carry out his own interview.

As far as Gilchrist was aware, that was a first.

Gilchrist escorted McVicar to Strathclyde Police HQ in Pitt Street, Glasgow, where Izara Kikelomo was being detained. McVicar insisted that she be represented by a solicitor during his interview, and once everything was arranged, Gilchrist entered the interview room, followed by McVicar.

Gilchrist proceeded to go through the introductions, during which McVicar removed his cap and looked straight at Kikelomo with those eagle eyes of his. It struck Gilchrist that she seemed neither cowed nor fazed by his presence, but returned a straight-faced look that reminded Gilchrist of a child seeing some animal or insect close up for the first time. When he sat back to let McVicar take over, McVicar said, 'I have only a few questions to ask you, if I may.'

Kikelomo nodded.

McVicar slid the sketch of Sir Elliot across the desk to her. 'Did you sketch this from memory?' he asked.

'Yes, I did.'

'From only one meeting?'

'Yes.'

'And how long did that meeting last?'

'I don't know. Maybe ten minutes, I think? Maybe less?'

'Have you seen this gentleman since that meeting?'

'No.'

'Had you seen this gentleman before that meeting, either in person, or on the news?'

'No.'

'You'd never seen him at all, until you met with him? Is that what you're saying?'

'Yes.'

McVicar retrieved the sketch, and studied it as if struggling to think of something else to say. 'Extraordinary,' was all he could come up with. Then he pushed to his feet without a word, nodded to Kikelomo and her solicitor, and left the room.

Gilchrist noted the time and terminated the interview.

Outside, in the corridor, he faced McVicar. 'Sir?'

'How long were we in there?'

'No more than a few minutes, I'd say.'

'Perfect. I want you to have her sketch my portrait. In the meantime, I'm heading for a meeting. Call me once she's done.' And with that, McVicar strode along the corridor, the sound of his heels on the tiles clipping off the wall like a soldier's march.

Once Gilchrist provided the sketch pad and crayons, it took Kikelomo just under half an hour – twenty-three minutes, to be exact – to finish her sketch, and for her solicitor to hand it over to Gilchrist. 'She says she prefers oils,' her solicitor had said. But even so, Dainty had been correct – it really was amazing the way she managed to have the light capture the eyes, creating an image that was so life-like he almost expected McVicar's lips to part in a smile. He thought she'd got a couple of details not quite right – his face seemed a bit thinner than in real life, the shadows under his eyes more pronounced, his lips less full, pressed tight as if in annoyance, but even so, you were left in no doubt whose portrait it was.

He found McVicar in Detective Chief Superintendent McLay's office, on the third floor, seated next to Dainty and a woman in a dark blue business suit, whom he hadn't seen before. Without introduction, McVicar said, 'What've we got, Andy?' and pushed himself to his feet.

Without a word, Gilchrist handed him the sketch, and watched his look shift from a concentrated frown to eyebrow-raised disbelief. Then McVicar passed the sketch to DCS McLay who took less than two seconds to nod with a gritted grimace in a that'll-do-it smile.

'What did I tell you?' Dainty said. 'Un-fucking-believable.'

'Quite,' said McVicar, which caused Dainty to frown. 'Denise? What do you think?'

McLay handed the sketch to the woman seated next to Dainty. She held it up, her gaze dancing back and forth between the sketch and McVicar before finally settling on the sketch.

'Will it hold up in court?' McVicar said.

'I'd have to say undoubtedly.' She shook her head as if in wonder. 'You were with her less than five minutes, you said?'

Gilchrist said, 'If that.'

She looked at him, then held out her hand. 'Denise de Beck.' Her grip was dry and firm. 'I'm with the Procurator Fiscal's Office. I'll be leading the prosecution.'

'Pleased to meet you,' was all he could think to say. It seemed to him that he was the last person to be told what was happening.

De Beck turned to McVicar. 'I may need you to make an appearance in court, to let the jury compare the sketch to the real thing.' She flashed a quick smile of teeth and crinkled eyes, which vanished almost as soon as they appeared. Then she was all business again, and back at Gilchrist.

'I'll need to spend a day with you going over your investigation. How does tomorrow sound?'

'Sure,' he said, trying to recall what he'd already scheduled.

'I'll come to your Office,' she said. 'St Andrews, North Street, is it?'

'It is, yes, but . . .'

'But?'

'But we haven't any idea where Alice Ralston is.'

'We don't need Alice Ralston. Would be helpful, of course. But with Izara's written statement and this sketch, and her ability to recall the most minor of details, we'll charge and try Alice in absentia. Unless you find her first, of course.' Another crinkle of the eyes. 'From what I'm being told by DCI Small,' a glance at Dainty, as if to make sure he hadn't scuttled off, 'Sir Elliot is believed to be the money behind the operation. The kingpin if you like.' She paused for a moment, pulled her lips back to show some teeth. 'You looked perplexed, DCI Gilchrist.'

'Not perplexed. Just troubled by the speed of it all. I mean . . . we're still trying to pull our case together.'

'That's what we'll discuss in detail tomorrow. First thing. Eight o'clock okay?'

'Yes.'

Then to the others. 'In the meantime, we'll issue a search and arrest warrant for Sir Elliot, see what he has to say for himself. I've instructed a freeze on all his bank accounts, and we'll secure his computer and phone records.' Back to Gilchrist. 'As for Alice, keep searching, although I don't think you're going to find her anytime soon.'

Gilchrist frowned. 'Why do you say that?'

'I suspect she's fled the country in a private jet. Best guess the Emirates, maybe Saudi Arabia, although I can't see the Saudis' strict regs on alcohol going down well with her.'

'Why the Middle East?' he said. 'We know she was picked up in Edinburgh by a car owned by a Saudi company, but it's a bit of a quantum leap to conclude that the Saudis would give her refuge from British justice.'

She crinkled her eyes again. 'You wouldn't be expected to know, of course, but Sir Elliot's been on our radar for quite some time. We suspect he's been involved in assisting the purchase of numerous major properties with Saudi Arabian funds, money that's found its way to the British banking system by the back door. It's an extremely complex case and has been going on for more years than we're willing to admit, and we've got the devil of a job to prove it. In its simplest form, it's a rather clever scheme to avoid paying tax.' Another show of teeth. 'You look confused, DCI Gilchrist.'

'You suspect the money behind Ralston's network is funded by Saudi Arabia?'

'I didn't say that, and you certainly shouldn't promote that. We have to tread carefully around the Saudis. They're extremely well connected, if you get my meaning.'

He nodded as if he understood. But he could only just imagine what connections she was referring to. His head was spinning with it all. It seemed as if his murder investigation had opened another door through which the British legal system could search for justice. It didn't matter that the Ralstons' murderous network was about to be stripped of its operational funds, without its key participant – Alice – being arrested and charged, as long as Sir Elliot was brought to bear for some illegality – tax evasion, of all things. He supposed it could be similar to the ploy used by the FBI to put Al Capone behind bars – they didn't nail him for all the murders he'd committed, the protection rackets he ran, or any of the other illegal goings-on for which he was responsible. In the end, they nailed him for tax evasion.

Simple as, if you thought about it.

But even so, Gilchrist still felt he had an obligation to locate and arrest Alice Ralston, and to find sufficient evidence to build a case against Shifrah Ber and Ellice Ibbotson, not to mention initiating an investigation into the murder of Izara's sister, Fariza. He stood back and listened as Denise de Beck set out her case for putting Sir Elliot Ralston behind bars, and couldn't help but feel that he was somehow now superfluous to their needs.

CHAPTER 53

Three weeks later, Wednesday, early January

Despite Scotland being effectively closed for business over the Christmas and New Year periods, Gilchrist's investigation progressed with dogged persistence. CCTV footage showed the cold-blooded murder of Izara's sister, Fariza, in a Tesco car park in Shawlands, an established area in south Glasgow. Gilchrist watched the monitor with bated breath, as a balaclava-clad male approached Fariza from behind as she was fiddling with her car keys at the boot, and without hesitation raised a gun to the back of her head. She collapsed to the ground like a stringless marionette. One more shot, this time behind her ear, then the killer strolled away as if he hadn't a care in the world.

What struck Gilchrist about her murder was that no one seemed to notice anything for a further twenty-three seconds – he checked the timing on the screen. Shoppers went about their mundane routines, pushing shopping trolleys, criss-crossing the car park, until one elderly couple about to unload their trolley in a car parked opposite, noticed her body on the ground. One of them, the man, walked off – too old and stiff to run, by the looks of him – while the woman placed a call on her mobile.

It didn't take Dainty long through his network of snitches to arrest a suspect – two days to be exact – wee Hugo Morro, a low-life career criminal released under licence only three weeks earlier. Not yet thirty, and he'd spent more than half his life behind bars.

'Why'd you do it?' Dainty had asked.

'Needed the money.'

'What did you need the money for?'

'The wean, an' that.' He sniffed, shrugged. 'And other stuff, you know?'

Hugo had two young children to two different women. How he had time between prison stints to have had any kind of relationship Dainty could only guess at. 'Even so, Hugo,' he said, 'murder's a step up from dealing drugs and pimping birds.'

'Aye, well, if they gae'd you more on the dole, you widnae have to dae stuff on the side, know whit ah'm saying?'

'This could put you away for a while, Hugo. You'll be an old man by the time you come out this time.'

'Prison's no so bad. Three square meals. 'Sides, I fucking hate it on the ootside. Too much like hard work, an' that.' It took Dainty forty more minutes of coaxing and persuading, and making promises he knew he had no hope of keeping, before Hugo gave up his contact. 'You didnae get this from me, right?'

'Right.'

'Big Todd.'

'Big Todd who?'

'How the fuck would ah know?'

'You got a number for him?'

Surprisingly, Hugo did.

Todd Carluke was arrested that afternoon, and came clean within minutes. He didn't know who paid him, only knew that if he did as instructed money would make its way to him – nothing as covert as brown envelopes and chalked marks on walls, but by BACS transfer from an RBS account, which turned out to be the same account from which both Shifrah Ber and Ellice Ibbotson received their monthly stipends. It seemed that Alice Ralston, in her haste to close up shop, had become way too careless. Not that it mattered to Alice, of course, as she was believed to be holed up in a palatial mansion on the outskirts of Riyadh. Conversations at ambassadorial level had resulted in the Saudis denying everything and anything.

If ever Gilchrist had been looking for a dead end, there he had it.

But not so with Professor Sir Elliot Abernethy Ralston. Denise de Beck's case against him had grown arms and legs, and despite his daughter Alice being missing, sufficient links by way of bank transfers, phone records, eye witnesses, and of course Kikelomo's damning sketch, had big John Silverman stretched to the limits of his formidable legal expertise.

'You'll note,' Silverman boomed, 'that my client doesn't wear a beard.' He ran a thumb across the sketch. 'It makes him look like that Kentucky Fried Chicken gentleman, without the moustache.'

'Beards grow and can be shaved off,' Gilchrist said.

'You ever grown a beard, Elliot?' This to a somewhat subdued Elliot Ralston, who seemed to have accepted the fact that for once in his life he was in deep shit from which he couldn't buy his way out.

'Never,' he said. 'Always hated them.'

'See?' Silverman said, as if that was the irrefutable proof of the pudding. '*Never*.'

Gilchrist slid over a photograph, courtesy of Denise de Beck's surveillance on Sir Elliot, date stamped, and shot around the same time as Kikelomo had been introduced to Ralston two months earlier. He tapped the photograph. 'That looks like a beard to me.'

'Where did you get this?' Silverman objected.

'Doesn't matter.'

'This is a violation of my client's privacy. We'll be taking this further, I assure you of that. We can't have one of this country's most respected citizens being photographed behind his back at every step he takes. This is an outrage, sir. An utter outrage.'

'Finished?' Gilchrist said.

'Far from it.' He pulled the photograph to him, ripped it once, twice, and once more for theatrical effect.

'You do realise that you've just destroyed evidence, for which you'll be charged.'

'We'll see about that.'

'Yes, we will,' Gilchrist said. He smiled, and slid the pieces of photograph back to him. 'Luckily, we have plenty more photographs where that came from.' He removed another from his folder, and placed it face up towards Ralston. 'From the date, we can work out that you wore a beard for at least three weeks in the months of October and November last year.'

'If you say so.'

'The camera says so, which, as we all know, never lies.' He placed his hands flat on the table, and fixed Ralston with a cold stare. 'We have sufficient evidence to put you away for the rest of your life.' He shook his head. 'What I don't understand is, why?'

Silent, Ralston blinked at him.

'Why did you do it?' Gilchrist asked. 'Why did you fund your daughter's vengeful network? You have all the money in the world, all the trappings of a successful life. Why not just live it out in quiet luxury?'

Ralston's lips curled into a snarl that could be mistaken for a cruel smile. 'Do you know how many women's lives are destroyed each year through romance scamming?'

'Elliot,' Silverman said, placing a hand on Ralston's arm.

Ralston shrugged it off. 'Last year over fifty million was stolen from women looking for nothing more than some love in their lives. Fifty million pounds. That's more or less a million pounds every week. And what's this government doing about it?' He lowered his head, and eyed Gilchrist. 'You have a daughter,' he said. 'Maureen. And a son, too. Jack.'

Gilchrist struggled to keep his surprise hidden, but said nothing.

'Children are vulnerable. It's the duty of every parent to look after them until they can look after themselves.' He shook his head. 'I failed in that respect with Kenzie. I could do nothing for her when she was alive. But I knew I could do plenty for her . . . and others . . . after she'd died.' He sat back with folded arms. 'Besides, I don't have much time left. So my doctor advises me.'

Gilchrist had heard enough. 'So you financed your daughter, Alice, and encouraged her to murder anyone she suspected of being involved in romance scamming.'

Ralston shook his head. 'Not *suspected* of being involved. Irrefutably *proven* to have been involved. Besides, Alice didn't need encouraging. Quite the opposite. It was her idea. She'd met someone who's sister had also committed suicide after having been scammed, so she came to me and asked for assistance.'

Gilchrist struggled to keep his surprise hidden. Ellice Ibbotson's twin sister, Daleela, had killed herself. Had Alice met with Ellice, and then between them come up with the idea for murderous revenge? The timing seemed right. Ritchie Forrest's murder appeared to have been one of the first to have been committed. But he kept those thoughts to himself, and said, 'You mean Alice needed you to provide her with the names of Saudi Arabian contacts for her grand finale getaway. Her escape route if everything went to hell.'

Ralston smiled. 'Once Alice has her sights on something, she's obsessed, driven to see it through. I knew I couldn't change her mind, so rather than fight her, I chose to help her. As any good father would do.'

Gilchrist pushed his chair back and stood. He'd heard enough. 'Charge him,' he said to Dainty, then added, 'DCI Gilchrist leaving the interview at 16:44.'

CHAPTER 54

Ten days later, Saturday
The Fairmont Hotel, St Andrews

Gilchrist took hold of Irene's hand, and gave a squeeze. 'You all right?' he asked.

'Bit nervous, if I'm being honest.' She looked towards the entrance again, for the tenth time, he thought, and found himself glancing at his watch. They should have been with them ten minutes ago, but the drive up from Glasgow could find you tailing slow-moving vehicles on the country roads – at least, that's what he told himself.

'They're running late,' he offered. 'You know what the younger generation is like.' Which he thought was a touch ironic, because both he and Irene had found themselves in a rush of their own that morning, trying to check into the Fairmont Hotel – a two-night stay for the purpose of celebrating their engagement – before their lunch reservation. The short break seemed in perfect timing for the closing of his investigation, for which Gilchrist had filed his summary report only the other day.

Sir Elliot Ralston was effectively under house arrest, through some underhand deal worked out by his solicitor, John Silverman, whose reputation for never having lost a case seemed about to be shattered. Even so, Gilchrist had difficulty stifling the worry that big John could somehow find a way to have all charges against his client dropped. Ralston's daughter, Alice, was confirmed to be living in the outskirts of Riyadh, and with no extradition treaty between Saudi Arabia and the UK, looked as if she was prepared to spend the remainder of her life in the Middle East.

Ellice Ibbotson had been arrested trying to board a ferry to Amsterdam incognito, and charged with three counts of murder – Ritchie Forrest, Clive Keepsake and Ian Howitt. Milas Volker's and John Cumming's killer, whose DNA had been found at both scenes, remained elusive and free, at least for the time being. All the investigation teams knew was that she – her DNA confirmed she was female and of black ethnicity – had never submitted to a DNA test. A request through CODIS, the FBI's Combined DNA Index System, came up empty. A request to Interpol, to initiate DNA searches through other European countries' databases, had uncovered no one to date, although Gilchrist felt confident it was only a matter of time.

After a further six hours of intense interrogation, all of a sudden Kikelomo recalled Alice Ralston trying to persuade her to accompany her to Spain, even to the extent of having purchased a plane ticket for her, and all this around the time of Michael Robbins's murder. Jackie's research confirmed the ticket purchases, but only one return flight to Spain, made by Alice. Although Gilchrist believed that Kikelomo had not witnessed Michael Robbins being killed, his gut was telling him she'd been witness to at least one other murder, and that she was nowhere near as squeaky clean as she insisted. But her testimony was crucial to his case against Alice Ralston for the murder of Michael Robbins, since the Spanish CNP had found no new evidence, and with some reluctance, he'd agreed to go along with the immunity deal.

Shifrah Ber was found to have strong alibis for the dates of all murders, insisting that she only knew Ellice Ibbotson as a casual acquaintance. But Gilchrist remembered the cool manner with which she'd answered questions during her interviews, and suspected there was more to Ber than met the eye. During one of his gut instinct moments he'd contacted the head of the Australian Crime Commission – the ACC – and notified them of the possibility that three Australian murders by strangulation could be linked to Operation Eve, the task force name assigned to the investigation that had since taken on global proportions. As a long shot, he'd had Jackie forward the ACC a full profile of Shifrah Ber's DNA, and two days later the ACC came back with a hit on all three murders. An arrest warrant for Ber was secured, and a team assigned to make another early morning arrest. The big key was needed to gain access, but after the team burst into her home, they found it deserted. Despite appeals to all other UK police forces, Interpol and the FBI, Shifrah Ber might as well have been a ghost. Even so, Gilchrist again felt it was only a matter of time until she turned up.

Almost as an aside, Todd Carluke had been arrested and charged with conspiracy to murder Fariza Kikelomo, while Hugo Morro seemed content to have been let down by all of Dainty's promises, and been charged with Fariza's murder. Fariza's sister, Izara, had been granted immunity from prosecution, and had since moved to London, where she intended to promote and exhibit her portrait sketches.

Gilchrist was about to order another drink, when his mobile beeped. He glanced at the text message – ID Jessie – At reception. He frowned, then excused himself with, 'Back in a minute.'

As he strode into the reception area, Jessie gave him a fingertip wave, and removed a card-sized envelope from her jacket pocket. 'For you and Irene,' she said. 'A wee pressie for your engagement.'

He shook his head. 'I thought we'd managed to keep it quiet.'

'No chance. We're detectives. Finding out stuff is what we're supposed to be good at it. Right?' She chuckled, then added, 'None of us knew what to get you. But Jackie came up with the idea of tickets for a photographic exhibition in London. The Saatchi Gallery.'

'London?'

'The exhibition's on for three months. So you can work out dates that suit. There's also a voucher for an overnight stay in the Grand Royale Hotel. We all chipped in, but Jackie sorted it out for us; the hotel, the tickets. Said you'd both enjoy the walk through Hyde Park. Card and everything's been signed by us all.' She shrugged, as if realising she'd been blethering. 'Hope you like it.'

'You shouldn't have. It's . . . it's . . .'

'Better than a toaster?'

'It certainly is.' He chuckled, then said, 'Would you like to join us?'

'Can't, Andy. Got to head back. But before I do, I thought you'd like an update.'

He frowned at her teasing smile. 'I'm listening.'

'Sir Elliot's gone and done it,' she announced. 'Found dead at home. Left a suicide note of sorts, a printout of his latest medical report. Pancreatic cancer. Wasn't likely to make it through the year, let alone to court.'

'How did he . . .?'

'Bottle-load of pills, then tanked a bottle of The Macallan 12. Waste of a good whisky if you ask me. Already been in contact with whatsherface . . . de Beck. She's going to proceed with charging Alice in absentia. And Ibbotson, too.' She paused for a moment, then said, 'You look worried.'

Rather than feeling any level of emotion or shock at Sir Elliot's suicide, Gilchrist felt as if they'd now lost all opportunity to bring the case to complete closure. 'No. I'm fine. Just surprised. That's all.'

Jessie nodded. 'One less bastard to worry about. That's my take on it. Anyway, got to go. Love to Irene.' And with that she turned and strode from the hotel.

Back at the table, Gilchrist showed Jessie's envelope to Irene. 'That was Jessie,' he said. 'Here. It's a present from the Office.'

'That's so nice of them.' She was about to open it, when she glanced up and her eyes brightened. She raised her arm and gave a wave, as Gilchrist pushed to his feet and held out his hand. But Joanne ignored it, and went for the full hug instead.

'I'm so happy for you both,' she gushed into his ear, giving him a warm peck on the side of his face. Then she leaned down to her mother, and wrapped her arms around her, giggling and squealing with delight.

Mo was more subdued, a lighter hug and a peck on both cheeks, and a crinkle-eyed grin that told him she was pleased to see him. More importantly, he thought, she'd forgiven him for interfering in her personal life. With the help of Joanne, she'd located and moved into another flat in Glasgow, and to Gilchrist's surprise reported two acts of abuse by Noah to the police, effectively starting the legal process of applying for a non-harassment order.

'Lovely to see you, too, Maureen,' Irene said, as they gave each other a hug.

When they parted, Gilchrist said, 'What're you having?' and pulled out a chair for Joanne first, then another for Maureen. 'Champagne? Prosecco? Wine?' he asked, relieving them of their coats and scarves.

Joanne gave a shiver, not from the cold, he thought, but from the anticipation of the moment. She gave a wide-mouthed grin. 'We *are* supposed to be celebrating, aren't we?'

'We certainly are,' he said. 'Which I understand to mean champagne?'

'Please, thank you.'

'Mo?'

'Why not?'

'Champagne it is, then.' He chose to walk to the bar, rather than signal a waiter over, if only to give the girls – funny how he called them all girls – a private moment in which to be shown his engagement gift to Irene. He ordered a bottle of Veuve Clicquot Brut and another beer for himself – Heverlee. He wasn't sure if Joanne or Maureen knew the truth about his gift – if he could call it *his* gift to Irene – but the bangle had been made by a jeweller friend of hers, by melting down both their original wedding rings – plus a couple of Irene's rings she assured him she would never wear again – to create a one-off. It had been Irene's idea – *why not have something other than an engagement ring? I've enough rings to last me a lifetime.* So he'd acquiesced, although he still harboured a little guilt that the extra gold – all of it twenty-two carat – had come from Irene.

Back at his seat, Mo said, 'The ring's lovely, Dad. And so original. I'm happy for you both.' She looked around the room, then under her breath, said, 'Is Jack running late?'

'Couldn't make it.'

'Why am I not surprised?' She put a hand on his thigh, and gave a squeeze – a definite first – then retrieved her hand and smiled at Irene.

'I'm a lucky woman,' Irene said to her.

'I think so, too,' Joanne said, and gave Gilchrist her warmest smile.

'He has his downsides.' This from Maureen to Irene, as if to bring reality back to the moment. 'If you haven't already found them,' she added with a smile.

Irene seemed unfazed. 'At our age no one cares about downsides.'

'Well that's good to hear,' Gilchrist said, and was saved further embarrassment by the arrival of a waiter who took her time opening the bottle and topping up each of their flutes.

'Sir?' she asked, bottle poised over his glass.

'Of course,' he said, and eased his pint to the side.

They all raised their flutes, and spent an awkward few moments trying to chink each other's glasses without spilling any. Gilchrist didn't mind the occasional glass of champagne, but by choice preferred dry wine over bubbly any day of the week. The girls spent the next fifteen minutes chattering among themselves, with Gilchrist on the periphery, smiling and nodding and topping up their flutes when they looked as if they were about to run low. Mo, as usual, appeared to drink the quickest, and when he topped her glass with the last of the bottle, Joanne said, 'I think we should have a speech,' and grinned at him.

'I'd rather leave that until the big day,' he said.

Mo asked, 'Have you set a date yet?'

Gilchrist glanced at Irene, who obliged by helping him out. 'We're just going to take it week by week for the time being, but . . .' she leaned forward as if to conspire with the girls out of Gilchrist's earshot, '. . . we've just had the good news that I'm in remission again, and that I don't need to attend the hospital for a check-up for another three months.'

Joanne squealed, and clasped her hands to her mother's.

As Gilchrist watched Irene's eyes fill up, he said, 'I think that definitely calls for another bottle.'

Glasses chinked and girls chattered while he excused himself and retreated to the bar once again. He chanced a look back at the table, pleased to see Irene holding court while Joanne and Mo listened intently to what she was saying. It felt wonderful seeing Irene in high spirits and relatively good health, but more importantly he thought, at ease with herself and her condition. They had discussed marriage, but both agreed that rather than rush into it for the sake of being married before the inevitable happened – whatever that inevitable was – they should simply announce their engagement and live as man and wife.

After all, who needed wedding rings and a piece of paper these days?

Irene caught his gaze at that moment, and blew him a kiss. He pretended to catch it, then watched her giggle as she turned her attention to the others. He felt strangely satisfied that she'd agreed to their open-ended engagement. It was, after all, what they both needed – comfort in the knowledge that they would be there for each other, no matter how long or short a time they had together.

He ordered another bottle of champagne – *same again, please* – then walked back to their table. She caught his eye again as he approached, and together they exchanged smiles, which had him thinking of exchanging vows.

For better or for worse.

And he promised himself that he would think only of the better.

ACKNOWLEDGEMENTS

Writing is indeed a lonely affair, but this book could not have been published without considerable help and advice from the following: Howard Watson for professional copyediting to the nth-plus degree; Rebecca Sheppard, Editorial Manager; Sean Garrehy, Art Director; Brionee Fenlon, Marketing Manager; and John Fairweather, Senior Production Controller, for working hard behind the scenes at Little, Brown, to give this novel the best possible start in life. Thank you, as well, to Krystyna Green, Publishing Director at Constable, for placing her trust in me once more and for dishing out hard editorial love when needed. And finally, thank you to Anna, for putting up with me, believing in me and loving me all the way.